THE TIME ANOMALY

KATIE MITSUI

For my mother, who is my favorite librarian;
for Greg, who is my favorite storyteller;
and for the semi-colon,
which is my favorite mark of punctuation.

*"Life can only be understood backwards,
but it must be lived forwards."* – Søren Kierkegaard

PROLOGUE

For all intents and purposes, Johnathan Davidson may prove to be the most influential person that ever lived, and it was mostly by accident.

Looking at just the facts, he seems like a fairly average guy. He lives alone in a moderately priced downtown apartment in a small Midwestern city, had good grades and top percentile test scores in his school years but never rose particularly high in his professional life, and is pleasant enough to talk to but has no real close friends or family. He isn't the type that would have raised eyebrows in any way... at least not before the Event. You can examine his personal records, credit history, social media and all the things that modern humans leave their messy little fingerprints on, but none of those things would indicate that there is anything very special about him at all (which sounds rude, but still happens to be true).

We have to dig deeper for the answers, because on the surface it doesn't seem possible that without leaving a clear indication of how on earth he accomplished it, Johnathan Davidson apparently invented the only time machine that, thus far in the history of humanity, has been proven to actually work.

The trouble with his success is that when he made his fateful journey forward, he didn't go alone. Johnathan's machine somehow caused a snag, or ripple, in the fabric of time that dragged every person in an approximately 25-mile radius around him out of the present, each to reappear at a seemingly random point in time between his exit and reentry exactly 100 years in the future. In short, Johnathan unintentionally vanished an entire mid-sized city in an instant and scattered its residents forward into a future without any of the connections that anchored them to their pasts or present.

CHAPTER 1

The Time Event

Humans have always tended to romanticize time travel in works of fiction. The hero of the story is commonly portrayed as a stranger in a strange land, adapting to a new world in which he is either a remnant of the past or a herald of the future. Or when a group is lost in time, the challenge normally centers around them returning together (should they be so lucky as to return at all).

In reality, an entire community uprooted from time proved to be far more complex. The extremely staggered and unpredictable reentry dates of so many people in this case are what made the tactical applications so difficult. Unlike a single traveler, who likely could have slipped in and out relatively unnoticed, the world could hardly ignore hundreds of thousands of people vanishing all at once and then reemerging *anywhen* and *everywhere* for decades. If Johnathan had conducted his experiment in a rural area, fewer people would have been dragged forward in time with him; as it was, the entire city and outlying suburbs of Toledo, Ohio went with him – close to 300,000 people in total.

Note also that since the time incident took place in the early evening on a day with pleasant weather, there were thousands of people still commuting, or out in public places, rather than situated in their own homes as they might have been if it had been a dark and stormy night. This made it all the more difficult to predict where people might have disappeared *from* to know where to expect them to return to. It wouldn't help predict the *when*, but knowing the *where* would have made things slightly simpler to perhaps manage, if not contain. Experts generally agree that if the Time Event had happened in the dead of night when people were asleep in their own beds, it might have been a relatively simple matter of putting a motion detector in each house to sense people as they reappeared, and then merely playing the waiting game until everyone was accounted for.

Someone materializing in the same physical location where something else now takes up space creates a mashing of atoms that cannot coexist, and there have been many documented injuries and even fatalities of time travelers from Toledo who returned smack dab into the midst of wreckage, overgrown foliage, even the odd bird or animal with unfortunate timing... things that just hadn't been in that space when they left. The results of such occurrences are horrifying, and it was quickly decided that to minimize the danger to both travelers and rescuers alike, the "empty" city had to be preserved in just that condition while things were sorted out.

This meant that all research and rescue operations needed to be based outside the city limits. The logistics of having hundreds of people, both support services and experts, in an accessible, yet off-site location with easy access to the Toledo area took years to perfect and led to the creation of Lake City. This floating technological marvel off the Lake Erie shoreline became the base of operations for the researchers that were a separate branch from the search and rescue squads (run by the U.S. military as a special division) that serviced the area designated as the "Time Zone". The research and developmental tech that came from Lake City spurred many scientific and design breakthroughs as it was built and expanded over the decades, but those benefits were years down the road from the original Time Event and its chaotic aftermath.

In the early months and years after the ripple in time, the situation was most often compared to the bedlam of a natural disaster, or the confusion of a waking coma patient. But these are poor metaphors that ignore the uniquely solitary experience that each returning time traveler faced without a familiar support system of friends, neighbors, and even coworkers. Even as it became apparent that many people were coming back from time, there were no guarantees, and survivors of the Time Event were told to hope for the best ("to keep their spirits up"), but not to take for granted that anyone else they knew would be back any time soon.

Meanwhile, people who had reemerged found that the rest of the world had had years to adjust to the idea of a wormhole in time (or they might even have grown up knowing about it, if enough time had passed) and they, too, were expected to just accept this shocking situation. An elaborate counseling system and rehabilitation center was developed specifically to help travelers understand and accept their new reality, and the counselors were based in Lake City.

To further complicate matters, time travelers found that, upon their return, their ages were all out of whack based on how long they were in the time stream and when they came out of it compared to others they once knew. To try to keep track of people's relative ages, official paperwork began to list not only birthdates, but "reentry" dates, and "current adjusted age" which was a calculation dependent on personal time scale. These confusing new metrics opened the doorway to all sorts of fraud and identity theft, which became yet another frustration people reemerging from time had to contend with. It wasn't necessarily a rosy welcome to a new future.

It was also found that people returning from time were generally not equipped to go back to their old lives, jobs, or homes (the city and outlying suburbs remained off limits for safety purposes). People's degrees, technical accreditations and job skills may have become obsolete (more and more likely the longer they had been gone), so work study programs became an ongoing part of their rehabilitation. While working through such programs at Lake City, records were made accessible to search for

4

acquaintances who had returned and an automated alert system was instituted to flag the return of close friends and family.

As such, the reunion of people is at the heart of the aftermath of the Time Event. The more sensational stories quickly became the entertainment fodder of long-running television shows that milked the format of tell-alls and reenactments of time returns until the public at large either loved, hated, or loved to hate them. As years went by, the public became somewhat desensitized to the very real trauma and mental health issues most people experienced upon return, especially as other urgent world events took precedence. Through global upheavals, social shifts, wars and political tensions, the residents of Toledo were like a colony marooned on an island and released back into civilization one by one.

In short, the social, economic, scientific and psychological impact of Johnathan's little time experiment threw the entire country, in fact the world, into disarray for the next 100 years. This is the story of what happened, as we came to know it in the end.

CHAPTER 2

Johnathan Davidson – May 15th

Ok, well, today's the day I guess, because why the hell not. I'm never going to get any younger and my situation isn't going to improve on its own. I've chosen the timing to shoot for, exactly 100 years into the future. I'm assuming I'll only be moving in time and not space, though of course that's all just theory until we try it. Hopefully I won't come up on the other side of the world, or right here but in the middle of a brick wall or something, but this jump isn't so extreme that I expect to be at the bottom of a new ocean or in a new ice age. I'll find out... or not, if this kills me, I guess. In which case I won't know anyway so I suppose that's fine. And we're in an action-oriented, 'no guts, no glory' mindset here, remember?

Got to keep my inner monologue focused on the "journey" instead of going off on tangents. This... this is my walk-off-home-run-in-extra-innings-of-the-World-Series moment. Or maybe just a Hail Mary. Or whatever sports metaphor would be apropos here. Because as much as I'd like to fight it, they don't have anything that can help me at present, and the medical research needed to do something in the immediate future just isn't there yet. Gaining time has literally become my only hope. Luckily, I had already been working on the machine a long time before I was diagnosed.

It started off back in my college days, when I was studying physics and engineering, and was really into Einstein and H.G. Wells and the whole idea of time travel from an academic standpoint. It was honestly more of a hobby project than coursework though... but it started off in a real lab and had the basis of real science, and even the backing of an eccentric visiting professor who helped me get it off the ground. But school ended, and I switched into work mode, and put the half-finished thing in a box in my garage for a decade or so and forgot about it. It was only when I happened upon an artistic rendering of a time machine in an old graphic novel that actually seemed to have some realistic detail that my interest was sparked again. I literally saw it and thought, 'hey maybe I could make this happen' and started swiping miscellaneous parts from discarded projects at my work. This is the kind of thing dorky mechanical engineers like myself enjoy – why NOT try to build a real version of something from a fake schematic in a work of fiction? Basically, I am cosplaying at being a time traveler. Of course, the thing isn't going to actually work, but it's done now! So, I might as well give myself a "sendoff". I guess the past few months I just needed something to hope for... so I've been letting myself just pretend it will work while I finished building it. Why not? What harm can it do? The fine tuning and soldering and measuring were all very precise and orderly, and required concentration. I even got fancy and ran part of the software I wrote for it through an artificial intelligence program at work (off the clock, of course). I know that's kind of cheating, but it helped me get it done faster... I mean, as much as one can call it "done", seeing how it's all theoretical. Let's put it this way; it's a real machine with moving parts that uses electricity and stuff, it's not just an art sculpture. And building it has helped keep my mind off other things.

The macabre part of my psyche keeps returning to imagining the reactions of various fictional people (who love me very dearly of course) reacting to me breaking the news that I have a disease that's going to kill me, and that right soon. In reality, I didn't really have anyone to tell so it was just me and some doctors having awkward conversations and then referring me to other doctors. No one was there to be upset about it on my behalf, and I'm way too awkward to get upset in front of random medical people, so... just shove it down, down, down and save it for therapy someday. If I live to get it. At least they can stop taking all my blood and fluids and poking me with things now, because that part was getting really unpleasant. No more making excuses for needing time off from work for random appointments (my coworkers still don't know. I don't feel like getting sympathetic looks from people I can barely stand to share donuts with).

No more sitting in waiting rooms that smell like other dying people. No more second opinions to get; the conclusions are final.

So now I just do my work at the lab during the day on autopilot, and then stay up nights mapping out an imaginary life with an imaginary wife, just for that weird satisfaction of imagining the grief of someone who really cares what's going to happen to me and will miss me when I'm gone. How sick is that? I mean, I have an entire backstory crafted for her, and I do mean ENTIRE. Like, I spent weeks that I probably should have spent getting my affairs in order instead coming up with idealized but still realistic ways we could have met, all in my head. I've picked through all the options for things I would have said and done to make her fall in love with me; vacations we would have gone on; jokes I made that she would have liked; whole conversations we would have had about everyday things; the day I met her pretend family; and the day I asked her to marry me. I even have our wedding down to the gnat's ass of details and I mean like, flowers-and-first-dance-song-picked-out level of detail... with alternate side quest of a karaoke-style serenade at the reception that I could pull off because by coincidence she's the only woman alive under forty who considers Roy Orbison's "You Got It" to be the most romantic song in the world and by extreme coincidence this is one of the three songs I have the vocal range to sing. I'm disgustingly adorable in my own fantasies, apparently. No wonder she loves me so much. All that brain power to craft her just right so that she would feel real to me. So that way, when that final diagnosis came and she realized she'd have to live without me and cried, I could cry too and pretend I was crying for her and not crying for myself.

This is going to make me sound even more crazy than I already do since I've literally invented a frickin' time machine here (well, at least built something that resembles one), but I think my imagination is probably actually my biggest accomplishment in life. I have always lived my real life inside my head while my body does stuff in the here and now... and I've run a million scenarios in this noggin – run them to perfection. And yet I don't want to think about this particular plan to just skip ahead in time too much, just in case. Because as satisfying

8

as crafting a perfect fantasy is, once you've got it down pat the odds of it actually happening exactly that way drop to zero. And I've always found that once I have a daydream too perfect, I have to let it go because there's nowhere else to take it. So, the last thing I want to do now is to fantasize in too much detail about hitting this button and actually popping up in 100 years and finding out 'hey look! there's an over-the-counter pill that will cure me with one dose, available at any drugstore chain'. As soon as I think that out too much, it won't happen and I'll be the one that jinxed it.

If I had an actual psychiatrist and not just an imaginary one (the fake ones are cheaper, and they don't challenge me as much as the real ones would), they'd probably be scribbling notes now about what a sad sack I am to be prouder of my fantasy life and this machine (which is basically just one step up from a toy) than anything I've actually accomplished... and 'why is that, hmm, Johnathan?' They'd probably ask what kinds of scenarios I typically draw up in my head and how often, and I'd have to admit "every waking moment I'm not occupied with something else". I was like this for as long as I can remember, even as a child – a lot of people have imaginary friends but I never grew out of it. Sometimes I even have whole conversations in my head with people I actually know and then have to remind myself if that was real or not when I run into them. It's like I never stop practicing to have a real life.

My pretend shrink earns his pretend salary now and asks me why I didn't put as much energy into trying these things outside my own brain? Why not get out there and invent something useful and real that could make you a ton of money, or try to have a real "meet cute" with an actual existent someone instead of some figment of my imagination? And of course, I would avoid these questions because even in my own head I know I should have done that, I should have done that years ago... and it may be too late now. The answer of course is that I probably always thought of myself as too weird, or awkward, or ugly (or all of the above) to put myself out there socially, not that I'm actually any of those things. Not to brag, but I'm pretty superlatively average in terms of looks and

9

personality. I'm sure I could have found someone, but I just never really tried. So yeah, I took the easy path and just imagined myself a great life and didn't actually remember to get even a real good one. Pathetic, right? Even in my own head that's what this is. As for being a real inventor, well… people always told me how smart I was when I was a kid, and always seemed to be waiting on me to do something grand and exciting. And maybe I am some kind of misunderstood genius on the inside, but I just never felt the need to make myself the center of attention out in the real world. The truth is, I would rather not try than try and fail. I'm a coward and I know it. I know it.

I'd probably deflect my shrink at this point and say that at the very least I don't usually waste time thinking about things I can't change from the real past… I mean, I'm not actually crazy or anything. There's no value coming up with what I should have done to have the perfect comeback or the right combination of moves to successfully give Billy Powell his well-deserved comeuppance in the 3rd grade, right? It didn't happen; I did get an atomic wedgie; my lunch money was squandered 25-plus years ago; and that's that. However, running into that guy now as an adult, finding out he's still a bully and a jerk, and getting to verbally shellack him and put him in his place? That scenario I can daydream just fine.

But all in good time. If this here machine happens to actually work, and they can actually cure me in the future, I'll have all the time in the world to daydream, or try to meet a non-imaginary girl who loves Roy Orbison, or maybe just look up Billy Powell's final resting place and go spit on his grave. Whoa – too dark, Johnathan – take it back a step, man. Let's just focus on right now only and get ready to "go" just in case it does something after all! Wouldn't that be the best surprise I've had a while? So, let's document this momentous occasion for posterity. How, you ask, did I land on going forward exactly 100 years? Just because it's a nice round number, and people are superstitious that way, and I'm "people"? I mean… yes, that could be it.

No, there's sort of a method to my madness. If you're going to go into the future at all, what's the point of only going for a short test run first? What if it's a

10

one-time thing because the machine breaks or you can't recreate success because you just happened to stumble upon the exact right conditions combined with your actions just by chance? Then you are in the same situation but probably just lost your job for not showing up for a few weeks, no one would believe you weren't just on some sort of weird bender or spiritual journey, and all your house plants would need to be replaced. And you'd still be a dead man walking. No, go for broke or don't bother at all. What's that old proverb – "if you wish to drown, don't torture yourself with shallow water"?

Really, anything under fifty years is a bust. Science might get better but we're not talking about a sexy, high-profile disease I've got here so let's give it more time for someone to stumble onto something useful, get some funding, and make something out of it. One hundred years ought to do it. And it's better to go far enough out to start fresh, with any people I think of fondly safely gone and remembered and not old and dying on me as soon as I arrive. I've got enough problems of my own, which maybe sounds selfish. But the way I see it, if this machine doesn't work, fine. I can get sicker and sicker and die here and not that many people will even notice. If it does work and they still can't help me in the future; also, fine because literally no one would care then. And if it works and they can help me; swell. In all these scenarios I'm really the only one affected. I've just got to get far enough out to a time when they've had time for clinical trials and things because I don't want to be a guinea pig... but I don't want to go so far out that I'm like a cave man in comparison to modern society, or that everyone has left earth for the moon or something.

Speaking of one small step for man... I'm going to hide the book with my notes on how I built this lil' doodad because if I end up just electrocuting myself by accident, I don't want people to think I was actually insane thinking I really built a time machine. It's better that they think it's just some freak accident with a weird clock I was working on or whatever. I mean, I AM a mechanical engineer so it's plausible for people to think I'm just not a very good one. Besides, I was just making a lot of it up as I went along, on and off over the course of a decade,

11

with the bulk of it done at 2 a.m. on a college campus where beer may have been involved. I didn't exactly keep precise blueprints.

Hoo boy... it just occurred to me that when I hit this button, I might really electrocute myself and it really might be the last thing I ever do. But, more than likely, nothing will happen at all because this whole idea was ridiculous to begin with, and that's even worse because then I'll actually have to go and face reality instead of keeping up this last-ditch pretense that this is going to solve all my problems. It's one thing to talk in hypotheticals but am I really ready for either of those things to happen... right now-now? Alternatively, I could hang onto this thread and just sit around feeling sorry for myself for the next 'maybe a year if you're lucky'.

Fuck it. One hundred years seems like a good target so let's do this before I go another round in my head. Just ready, set, go. It's probably not even going to work.

CHAPTER 3

Trevor – 3 days after the Event.
Time populous
(the number still missing in time):
281,485

Trevor blinked and the sun was shining directly in his eyes, and he knew immediately that he was late for school. *God dog it* he cussed in his head. Mom must have taken DJ to pre-school early and he'd fallen back asleep while getting dressed or something, and of course Gary wouldn't have checked if he was up or not. Gary probably didn't even care if he skipped school, but he'd still whoop him if he was caught doing it. So up, up, super-fast get dressed, brush teeth, grab the backpack and a Pop Tart and he's running out the door.

Even if he was late, he'd take the long way because by this time of day the older kids would be smoking in the shortcut alley and he really didn't have time to get stopped and hassled when he was already late. School was only a few blocks away and he was a fast runner, he didn't need to take the shortcut. Maybe he wasn't even really that late.

Yesterday had been his tenth birthday, and he'd gotten the new-to-him video game he'd wanted so he must have stayed up too late playing it and overslept. He could have sworn it wasn't even late enough to go to bed, and now that he thought about it, did they even have his cake last night? He knew Mom had made it yesterday morning before she went to work, and he thought she and DJ had gone to pick up ice cream at the store after dinner. But he didn't remember eating either of those things. He must still be half asleep.

Trevor tried to wolf down his Pop Tart as he ran, but that was a mistake because then he had a mouthful of crumbs and nothing to drink, and he had to stop and cough for a moment because a tidbit of sharp frosting was tickling his throat. He tucked the other half of his hurried breakfast in his bag for later; maybe he could sneak it during class if the teacher wasn't looking.

He arrived panting at the front door of the school, and it was locked. He wasn't expecting that and almost fell over when he jerked the handle and it didn't budge. He went to the corner and peeked in the window of his homeroom and it was empty. Was it a Saturday? *God dog it, Trevor, did you come to school on a damn Saturday?* But his birthday hadn't been on a Friday, because Gary played poker on Friday nights with his friends and wouldn't have been there for his birthday dinner before he left for his shift. And he had been there with them, eating macaroni and cheese and complaining and teasing Trevor because only little kids like it with hot dogs cut up in it and ten years old is too old to be such a baby and making the whole family eat baby food. And then DJ crying because she was almost five and a half and *not* a baby and refusing to eat any more so Trevor ate hers too because he didn't care what Gary said and there was no point wasting his birthday dinner. The hot dogs and macaroni were all going into his stomach anyway, no matter how they were served. What was the big deal?

Why was no one at school on a weekday though? Maybe there had been a field trip today that he'd forgotten about? Or a fire drill and everyone was in the open field out back that they used for gym class? But they weren't. He walked around the whole building peeping in the windows and even knocked on the back door where the janitors' office was but no one answered. By this time, he had caught his breath and there was definitely no one at the school, so he turned to head home and that's when he noticed how quiet it was. Not *silent* quiet… there were some birds, and a dog barking somewhere but... quiet. Then it hit him; no traffic noise. In this neighborhood you could always hear the far-off hum of the highways, and motorcycles revving their engines, and buses lumbering by – but right now, there was nothing. He'd never heard it this quiet even in the dead of night, not once in his whole life, and it gave him the creeps. With a shock, he suddenly noticed the pileup at the intersection; not a car or two in a fender bender but at least ten cars scattered all over the road and two even in the front lawn of the church, almost to the steps.

He must have run right past the cars while trying to choke down his breakfast without even noticing because he was worrying about himself, but he was certain he hadn't heard a crash and an accident that big should have woken up the whole neighborhood. No one was even coming out to gawk yet. There were no sirens, and he didn't see any smoke or flames, so maybe the cars had just been parked like that? But they were all smashed up real good. He got a little chill up his spine, and almost simultaneously he had the horrifying thought that maybe all the people who had been driving those cars were dead inside of them. And he didn't have a cell phone (Mom said maybe next year) to call anyone whose job it was to go check. ("Where the hells' the damn cops when you actually need one," Gary would have said.) Trevor really didn't want to go check for dead bodies himself. But he also didn't want to go home and wonder about them either, so he took a deep breath and made himself walk up and look at the first car, and it was empty. They were all empty.

For a moment he was so relieved that he just sat down on the hood and forgot all about why no one was at school, and wondered who would crash their car and just leave it there, much less ten someones. When he had calmed down, he thought about it for a while and decided it had to be some kind of prank, maybe something the high school seniors were doing for the end of the school year. He thought to go into the church to see if they knew about the mess outside, but when he poked his head in, for

15

some reason the power was out and it was dark and creepy and kinda hot inside with the air conditioning off. Trevor didn't feel like exploring a hot, dark, abandoned church alone.

Instead, he went over to the little corner store, which had a sign right on it saying 'Open 24 hours' but no one was there either and the power was out there too. He couldn't imagine grouchy old Mr. G pulling a prank on his paying customers, so what the heck was going on? He checked the bathrooms and back office just in case, although it felt weird to go sneaking around where kids weren't normally allowed. He'd never been in an empty store before and it just felt *wrong*... and he didn't even *think* about taking anything off the shelves because if this *was* a prank that would be part of it, like that guy on TikTok who asks for help and if people aren't rude to him and give him a dollar, he gives them back a bunch of money for being nice people. His friend Jay always says those are fake because people see him recording and know it's a setup and if he wasn't filming them, they'd tell him to go away like any bum. But Trevor's a good boy, and he's not going to steal from Mr. G, just in case.

Maybe everyone had found somewhere to go, like the mall or something where the power wasn't out? He stopped by Jay's house (empty), and randomly yelled 'hello' a few times as he walked around the neighborhood, but no one answered. No one answered at Miss Harriet's, who was DJ's friend's aunt who babysat for them sometimes if Mom and Gary had to go to a wedding or a funeral or something that kids weren't invited to. Miss Harriet's big fat cat was sleeping on the front porch but no one else was home. He petted the cat for a while and then kept walking. There were still no cars passing by.

At home, it was hot without the air on, and Gary wasn't at the house, when he should have been home sleeping because he was on night shifts now and slept during the day. Weirder still, Gary's phone was there on the table, plugged in but with zero battery charge, and Gary never went anywhere without his phone. He tried the neighbors on either side but they didn't answer their doorbells, and they were both retired and never went out normally – they were *always* home. The whole thing didn't make sense. He went all up and down the street ringing doorbells but eventually gave it up and went back to his own house instead of heading to the next block.

By this time Trevor was starving and he felt like he'd walked about a million miles instead of just a few blocks around the neighborhood he'd lived in his whole life. With the power out he couldn't microwave anything and Mom always said the stove was ABSOLUTELY OFF LIMITS when she wasn't home, but on the counter sure enough his birthday cake was still there, uncut. They hadn't eaten it after all.

Cake as breakfast (more like lunch now) seemed naughty, but he'd had a rough morning and it was his cake anyway, so he cut himself a giant slice (*"happy birthday to me"*) and ate it while he thought about what to do next. Eventually he got down the old landline kitchen phone off the wall and called Mom at work, and it just went to the company's generic voicemail. He pulled out the school directory and called some of the kids in his grade that were his friends, and then even the ones he didn't like... but no one picked up at all. He thought a little more and then called Gary's work, and it also went to the company voicemail.

He didn't feel right calling 9-1-1 because Mom always said that was for emergencies only and really, *he* was fine. And maybe everyone else was fine too, if he could just find them. With the power out he couldn't watch TV, or play his new video game, and he didn't know any more people to call.

CHAPTER 4

The Wall Street Journal – 7 days after the Event. Time populous: 281,471

State of Emergency Declared in the Toledo Area

DETROIT, MICHIGAN USA – Lawmakers from neighboring states and a collection of experts from the national government gathered in Detroit for an emergency meeting on the mysterious disappearance of the entire population of their neighboring city across the lake. Until a probable cause can be determined, authorities still have roadblocks at all of the major highway entrances and at the Toledo, Ohio city limits, and public announcements about possible remaining danger in the area are being circulated to discourage good Samaritans, looters and thrill seekers alike from entering.

Surveillance videos from businesses, traffic cameras and private residences have not been officially released, but those leaked and shared through public forums appear to show an instantaneous disappearance of all humans throughout the city, seemingly at the same moment one week ago, Tuesday May 15th at exactly 6:32 PM CST. The people do not appear to move in any direction or be harmed in any way, but simply vanish into thin air from one moment to the next. Animals and plants do not appear to be affected. The landscape remains unaffected with no visible disturbances underfoot, negating early theories about sinkholes and earthquakes.

Machines, such as automobiles, motorcycles and airplanes that were in use at the time of the disappearances seem to have continued in their path of operation without their drivers to provide steerage, and many crashes and accidents have been documented from the air by emergency crews surveying the area. Although many small fires were initially reported at crash sites, none seem to have spread far or hindered surveillance by helicopter. Power in the area was knocked out due to a larger fire at the plant, and the electricity has been kept off while rescue teams are organizing to enter individual homes and businesses where appliances and machinery may have been left running and may create hazardous conditions for rescuers.

"The various sources of video footage have given us many angles and viewpoints to examine. So far, the images we are seeing do not appear to be doctored, but this has not yet been fully authenticated," Public Security Minister Rosa La Hoya stated at a press conference held this morning. Ms. La Hoya said authorities had no suspects in the incident and that the investigation was being treated as a scientific phenomenon rather than a criminal act of any kind.

The situation has been escalated to the federal level, and a state of emergency was declared in the area yesterday. "We're not going to hide anything and a full investigation will be conducted if any possible negligence in this tragedy is uncovered," the President of the United States declared in a press statement. "This will be treated like a natural disaster, with the full support of the national government to find our fellow citizens and bring them safely home."

A special task force led by the United States military is being assembled to address public safety concerns and mount a search expedition throughout the city to look for survivors. An extension of this team has already been dispatched to evacuate the zoo animals and scan for situations that could cause an unsafe condition for rescue crews. In addition, a team of experts with the Sadler Research Group from nearby Chicago have been contracted by the government to begin taking scientific readings of the disappearance sites and researching possible causes or influences.

Approximately 275,000 people normally reside in the Toledo area and all have effectively disappeared without exception and are being treated as missing persons. As word of the mystery spread throughout the world this past week, speculation and concerns are rising. Several foreign governments have demanded answers of the United States, questioning if the disappearances are the result of some type of military or scientific experiment gone wrong. Such accusations have been categorically denied.

"We want to know what happened," said Jeanette Hayes, a resident from nearby Ann Arbor, Michigan. "Where did everyone go? Are we in danger here too, and should we be evacuating? No one seems to be able to tell us anything at all." Bizarre theories ranging from alien abductions to spontaneous combustion are being traded all over the globe but so far, no official comments have been made to discredit any of them. Literally every theory, no matter how outlandish, seems to be on the table.

On the day of the event itself, initial reports of the mysterious vanishings were slow to trickle in, since by the nature of the phenomenon, they all came from people who were outside of Toledo itself when the disappearances occurred. People who had been mid-conversation with residents when they went missing, or who had been unable to reach friends and family that evening, initially assumed that they had been disconnected or that there was merely a problem with their phones or internet service. Air traffic controllers from other areas raised immediate alarms after not receiving confirming responses for active flights, and in fact there were several plane crashes confirmed later. The list of inbound and outgoing flights and the manifest lists of passengers are being included in missing persons tallies, but have yet to be publicly released while authorities confirm safe passage of other flights out of the area and account for passengers and crews.

People traveling by car towards the city immediately after the disappearances occurred also encountered multiple accidents that blocked the major roadways, but upon closer inspection, there was no human presence at the accident sites or in the crashed vehicles. Calls to Toledo emergency services went unanswered and raised suspicions that this was in fact a larger issue than anyone could have anticipated.

The National Guard has been called out to set up a series of temporary work centers every few miles outside the estimated affected zone. These sites will be a place for experts to gather, and for search and rescue efforts to be coordinated. We have heard unconfirmed reports that there is a plan is to get sweepers to move through the city systematically starting in the next 48 hours. Authorities say that additional volunteers may be requested once they have a working plan, but ask that people stay in their own towns until that plan is developed. Caution is being used until there is confirmation that none of the first wave of teams suffers any ill effects, and that there are no additional disappearances within the teams upon entering the city. This morning's press conference also addressed why the start of the search was delayed.

"This is a national disaster of an unprecedented nature and we cannot stress enough the possible dangers of entering the affected area," said Minister La Hoya. "We needed to set up emergency protocols on how to proceed with regular check-ins to monitor any problems, and how to report on suspicious activity. We are not even fully sure how far the danger zone extends, and are working to pinpoint where the city's inhabitants stopped being affected, or possibly identifying an epicenter for the phenomenon. It appears that at least twenty square miles of populated area were affected."

Further bulletins will be released as the situation unfolds and as events warrant. Anyone with information that may be useful to authorities is encouraged to contact the established national hotline.

CHAPTER 5

Journal of Raj Anil, intern – 19 days after the Event. Time populous: 281,452

June 3rd

I have decided to begin documentation of my personal observations and theories regarding the newly discovered time variance, since I am poised to begin a career intimately related to this singularity. At least, at the moment it is being treated as a singular event. God help us all if this becomes a thing of regularity.

I feel that I am on the cusp of a monumental journey, the full scope of which I cannot even begin to imagine. Time travel as a concept has captivated mankind for generations, and by great good fortune I find myself positioned to participate in what may prove to be the most significant scientific findings of the human race. Time travel!! I have never been so excited, and I pray that I will prove worthy of such a privilege to be part of this historic undertaking.

Clearly in the next few decades the discovery of time travel will see a disproportionate amount of scientific funding going towards this field of research, and though I am loathe to say it so bluntly when the driving force is so elegant in nature, I feel it is prudent in this case to "follow the money". I intend this journal to mostly contain records about theories, discoveries, and hypotheses published in the community at large, but I also feel that it is important for me to record my personal observations and reactions to what we know at given times in order to regularly check my own cognitive bias.

The timing (if I can be forgiven the pun) of this breakthrough works out perfectly for me. At the point of this entry, I have just wrapped up my final year of graduate school studying theoretical physics and I have been debating between pursuing a career in academia versus field work for some time. More importantly, before recent events came to light, I was already accepted for a research position with Sadler where I had intended to work while beginning my PhD track. I've confirmed with my sponsor there that I can pivot to join them in researching the time phenomenon, so that my work will be a combination of theoretical and practical at the site of the event itself. My dissertation will be influenced by first-hand experience working with this team.

Important dates to note:

May 15th – Tuesday 6:32:04 CST – the "Time Event" takes place

May 16th – Toledo is locked down at the borders and cited as 'a situation' in national media

May 17th – official reports confirm the disappearance of Toledo's residents causing widespread panic in neighboring areas

May 19th – worldwide media has socialized the leaked disappearance footage and experts begin weighing in on theories; everything from earthquakes to invisibility

May 20th – May 22nd – the U.S. Government officially declares Toledo under a state of emergency, and the Sadler group signs contracts with officials regarding data collection and analysis

May 23rd – May 28th – the National Guard begins sweeps and the first casualties and survivors are discovered. Social media platforms are going crazy with conspiracy theories; people in nearby towns are evacuating further away as a precaution

May 29th – officials share the theory of a time fluctuation and a summary of what they have learned from interviewing the first survivors found; the first sixteen survivors and the first eight casualties are officially identified (names withheld)

May 30th – 31st – word of the theory of time travel spreads worldwide, to widespread skepticism; rumors of a hoax on a massive scale and theories about the end of the world abound

June 1st – official authenticated video footage of a person "returning" is released, lending further support for the time fluctuation theory from experts, despite continued skepticism from many

June 2nd – further official confirmations from the scientific community lend further credence to the validity of time travel as the crux of the Event

June 3rd – I begin this journal as I travel by train from Boston to the Toledo area to join the Sadler team

I would like to document here more about both the early survivors and the casualties. My new supervisor sent me some background material to read on my ride down to meet with the team. This information is highly classified and I had to sign several non-disclosure agreements first, so I will not document any names in my private journal as a result.

To begin, let us examine the casualties, and I offer first a heartfelt prayer in their memory. May their unwitting sacrifice lead us to discoveries that can save others. The first casualty found was also the first to be verified through actual video footage. The victim, a 41-year-old man, was driving his car at 75 miles per hour on the highway when the Time Event occurred. When he disappeared into time, his unmanned vehicle continued its physical path of motion and crashed further down the road (along with many others). Eight days later, his reemergence was captured on a video feed at the automated tollbooth; he reappeared into thin air in the exact spot he had left. Without the surrounding air pressure of the vehicle around him, he was open to the elements and still moving at the speed of his vanished vehicle. He was projected onto the debris-strewn pavement at that speed, and killed almost instantly. They recovered his body by helicopter after seeing his location on that video feed. The autopsy has not been officially released yet but the reports I am now privy to indicate that aside from the damage done from that violent reentry, there is nothing unusual that was apparent in his physical makeup that showed any damage from the time journey itself. I'm not sure what indications they would expect time travel to display on the human body; perhaps some age markers if he had been gone longer? I expect that will be one of the many things we will be measuring and attempting to understand.

It was seeing this man reemerge on video out of apparently nowhere that sparked the theory of time travel, or at least made it rise to the top of the stack of unusual scenarios being theorized. Seven other bodies have been found so far (names withheld). Causes of death range from possible heart attack (pending autopsy reports), other traffic fatalities, exposure to gas build up, and most bizarrely, a window washer whose scaffolding platform reached the ground without him several days prior to his return. From these tragedies we have at least learned that each person's reappearance seems to happen in the exact same spot as they left. The fact that people have returned at all is a cause for sober celebration, though of course there are hundreds of thousands still unaccounted for. For those claiming this is a hoax, I don't know how they imagine this large-scale disappearance is being pulled off.

The survivors can tell us more. As of today, sixteen have been found, and there may be others yet to be discovered within the city limits. They all confirm that the last day they remember was May 15th and it was about 6:30 in the evening when they seemed to blink and everything "just changed". From their perspective, all other people instantly disappeared and suddenly there were remnants of car accidents all around them, and yet all traffic and ambient human noises had stopped. All of them have reported disorientation, but it is unclear if that is situational or an actual effect of the time anomaly they experienced. Otherwise, they seem physically unharmed. None seem to have any memory of the time between their departure and return, and we can confirm from independent verification of video feeds that they appear to be arriving in the exact place they left from, doing exactly what they were doing when they left. The going assumption is that they did not age during the time they were gone, but of course it is too soon to really verify if that is true or not.

Once I arrive in the Toledo area and get my training schedule, my first task is apparently going to be logging every detail of the interviews conducted with each survivor into a database so that we can begin to track any common metrics. Officials at Sadler are running on the hypothesis that more people will be returned to us, and hopefully as more data becomes available, we will be able to establish a pattern that will help us to project when and where more survivors will turn up. I will contribute more notes to this topic in my next entry. -RA-

CHAPTER 6

Trevor – 32 days after the Event.
Time populous: 281,399

He lost track at one point, but it's probably been a month now since he found himself on his own. Trevor's not exactly Mr. Social so being alone hasn't been so bad, but he does miss having people around a little. Certain people anyway. But Trevor's an optimist and he's sure they'll be back.

The first couple of days were the weirdest. He was so confused and exhausted that he slept like a rock that first night by himself, but when he woke up the next day with the stupid power STILL OUT, it was just too darn hot and stuffy to think about things too hard. Everything in the fridge smelled weird by now and the freezer was all drippy and gross, so he put down some old towels for the leaks and spent most of the morning going through the cupboards looking for stuff that he could eat cold or uncooked. He made himself a neat list in three columns in his school notebook.

Yums = Pop Tarts, Doritos, canned peaches and pears, spaghetti-Os, peanuts, peanut butter, an unopened jar of jelly, gummy vitamins, his cinnamon cereal, DJ's chocolate cereal (although she'd be mad if he touched it), three different kinds of crackers, half a bag of cheesy popcorn, Oreos, granola bars

Mehs = baked beans, cream of chicken soup (could be a yum if it were warmed up but definitely a meh when cold and gelatinous as it was), canned tuna, a bag of jelly beans leftover from Easter that were kind of hard but probably still edible, pickles, slightly stale bread

Yucks = gross fiber cereal, canned peas, canned green beans, canned beets, tomato soup, rice cakes, artichoke hearts, anchovies, Gary's protein shake mix, pickled jalapenos

The rest of the stuff in the cupboard wasn't food – it was just ingredients. But he had enough to last a few days, and the act of foraging had felt worthwhile, like he was accomplishing something. He feasted on peanut butter and jelly crackers and then put himself to work. He got out some garbage bags and threw away all the smelly stuff in the fridge and freezer and put it out by the curb (he wasn't sure when the next garbage day was but he didn't want to stink up the garage too), and then squirted some cleaning stuff on the floor where it had dripped smelly water and now the kitchen was clean. Mom would tell him "good job".

It occurred to Trevor that he'd never really been alone in the house for this long before, ever. If he was just a little bit younger, he might have been afraid. But ten years old is practically grown.

Looking back on it later in life, he often wondered why he didn't venture further in search of help, but at the time it made sense to him to just lay low in the neighborhood he knew best. It honestly didn't occur to him to just pick a direction and keep going until he reached civilization (meaning people). He had checked his local neighborhood fire station and police department on day two (no one was there), and he caved and called 9-1-1 on day three, but it was just some kind of recorded message playing so he hung up. In ten-year-old Trevor's mind, that exhausted the reach of authority figures, so the next plan of attack was all about survival until people came to him.

The first order of business had been food. Once he had cataloged what he found in his own house, he checked the houses of his nearby neighbors. In his mind that was "borrowing" and not "stealing" because when they came back Mom could get them new groceries, and a kid's gotta eat. (It would be many more days before he would venture back to the abandoned corner store, but that logic would eventually apply there too.) He also started putting out bowls with dry cat food the lady next door had; there were suddenly quite a few collared animals around the neighborhood that seemed to have ventured out open windows and doors, and they were definitely pets and not strays. He let a few out the door himself when searching for food; he couldn't bring them all home with him, but he could at least give them a chance to make a run for it.

Once he had his meals and snacks sorted out and documented neatly in a list in his notebook, the next order of business was turning the house into a kind of fort. Not that he was *scared*, but it felt too weird sleeping there alone in the quiet neighborhood with no power still and also it was hotter upstairs in the bedrooms at night now that summer was getting on. The living room became his new base of operations. The two couches pushed closer together with his and DJ's twin mattresses on top of the coffee table squished between made basically one giant bed in the center of the room. He brought down his favorite books, some colored pencils and an unused notebook for drawing, a deck of playing cards to play solitaire like grandpa had taught him when he was little, and his collection of action figures, which he lined up along the window sills to keep watch.

To make sure he wouldn't miss anyone coming home while he was sleeping, he tied a set of housekeys to the screen door handle of the back door and a jingly stuffed animal thing of DJ's to the screen door handle of the front door. At night they were also burglar alarms, so he could leave the doors open for the breeze. And best of all, out in the garage he found the camping lantern that Mom and Gary used when they would sit out in the back yard in the summer chatting with friends and drinking wine and beer. It had a battery, but it also had a solar powered feature so he could leave it to charge out on the porch all day and have a night light (for drawing) in the evenings. Overall, he was comfortable enough – and no homework, no bath time, no bed time. Not too shabby.

But he was also getting a little bored. No friends to hang out with, no baseball practice, not even an annoying sister to play board games with.

Within two weeks he had explored every unlocked house on the block, not trying to snoop into people's private stuff, but at least taking a look around and borrowing things. He started keeping a list of what he took so he could return them eventually, but mostly he was just poking around to kill time. He thought he heard a helicopter a few mornings really early and he definitely saw some airplane trails in the sky way off in the distance occasionally, so it was only a matter of time before someone figured out where he was and came to find him and tell him what was going on. He just needed to hang on a bit longer.

In a neighbor's garage he found a jumbo box of sidewalk chalk and started making a big "TREVOR LIVES HERE" sign outside the house one day for the helicopters, but then it started to drizzle and ruined it, and he didn't really feel like starting it again. Plus, he had already used up most of the chalk just writing his name the first time. At school once they had read a story about a kid stuck on a desert island who made an SOS sign out of rocks and coconuts on the beach, but that seemed like a lot of hard work to drag rocks and also, he couldn't remember what SOS actually stood for. Something that meant help. He tried going back to the school to see if he could get into the library to look for the book, because it was a fun story to read and he loved adventure stories more than anything, but he couldn't get any of the windows unstuck and he balked at actually breaking in. Instead, he took some flashlights and rode his bike down past the train tracks to the library on the other side of town one afternoon just to check if the doors were open. He knew how to get there because it was right by the old folks' home where grandpa had lived, and it was just one turn on his street and then straight down. He didn't even need a map. The library's front door was unlocked, and it turned out he didn't even need the flashlights because the library's youth department had lots of windows and some nice beanbag chairs too.

After that pleasant discovery of his own private library, the next few weeks seemed to fly by. When he woke up in the morning in his big sofa-bed-cocoon, as long as the weather was nice for biking, he would eat some breakfast, pack up some snacks in his backpack, leave some food for the stray cats, and then head down to the library. He had discovered a little alcove by the back entrance that already had a sunshade set up, so he had brought a few of the beanbags outside and made a relaxing nest for day reading. The water fountain still worked fine, so he started filling up his bottles there, and used their bathrooms too. They even had a supply closet full of useful items like toilet paper and Kleenex that he could raid. When it looked like it might rain, he brought a stack of books home with him, and just stayed in bed reading stories and eating snacks; exactly what Trevor would have called a perfect day.

The Birmingham neighborhood's public library branch had a lot more books than the school library did; he couldn't use the computers to look things up because there was still no power, but the shelves were organized by topics so it was easy to find things just by browsing up and down. He took a look at the grownups section but didn't find much that caught his attention besides a few recipe books that he thumbed through when he was feeling hungry and a delicious picture caught his eye. For the most part, he stayed in the youth and teen sections. The library even had comic books and graphic novels! He explored everything in the area, and he spent almost a whole day in the little kids' section just reading familiar things he knew Mom had read to him (and later to DJ) and found that *Frog and Toad*, *Captain Underpants*, *Where the Wild Things Are*, and all the Dr. Suess books were just as fun and funny as he remembered them. It cheered him up to read them and to remember the silly voices Mom used when she would read them aloud.

He spent most of his time perusing the books for his own age group and found that there were more adventure stories than he had ever imagined could exist, and one thing he picked up on right away was that adults were never part of the quests the characters went on. That made him feel a little better about being on his own – he wasn't alone or lonely; he was just in the early chapters of the story and about to have an adventure.

There was always something that happened right away early in the book to separate the children from their parents, because otherwise there would be no escapades, would there? Adults weren't going to try to explore a mysterious forest in a wardrobe, or make immediate friends with talking animals, or build a raft to sail down an unknown river, or explore a cave looking for pirate treasure. The grownups would simply do some lame grownup thing like call their insurance broker or whatever (Mom worked answering phones for an insurance broker and it sounded like the most boringest thing ever) and the book would be over.

With this backdrop of readily available fiction, and the innocent egocentricity of childhood, it's hardly surprising that subconsciously in Trevor's mind, the whole disastrous Time Event was nothing major to worry about, but was simply the mechanism for temporarily removing the adults from his life to set up the premise of his own adventures.

CHAPTER 7

Search and Rescue training notes [transcript] – 41 days after the Event. Time populous: 281,360

[Recorded at Site Two, June 27th]

Thank you all for your attention; this instructional is being recorded for your reference and for future training purposes. Please hold your questions during this session, and the section leaders in your breakout sessions this afternoon will address them.

Welcome to Site Two of the Toledo emergency site base camps. We are approximately 12 miles out from the northeast side of the city and our temporary base of operations is the Eagle's Landing Golf Course where we have set up provisional work facilities. Until further notice you will continue to be housed further east and shuttled in daily to this site.

My name is First Lieutenant Amanda Briggs, and I'm in command of Alpha Team Four. All of you have been assigned to be part of an Alpha, Beta, Delta, or Science Squad, and numbered one through ten in your paperwork and on your ID badges. Keep these with you at all times. All of you will be introduced to your individual section leaders when we break out from this introductory briefing. We've got volunteers from several military branches along with police and specialists of all types here, and we'll sort out the structure later. For the duration of this mission, you should consider the chain of command for these teams to supersede your normal roles in your various fields and command units, and we thank you in advance for your service.

The past weeks have been instructional to say the least, and as you have heard, the National Guard and our initial scouting teams have already identified 94 survivors, and 31 casualties. We have confirmed that at least 250,000 people – possibly as many as 300,000 – within the city limits and outlying suburbs disappeared at what appears to be the exact same moment. Only this small sample have been returned, and at apparently random intervals. So, we have a very long way to go before we can call this situation contained.

In the approximately six weeks since their disappearance, it has become apparent that the people of Toledo were propelled forward in time and that at least some of them have reentered into our present day. Whether you're a science fiction fan or not, that's the facts as we've been given them and what we're operating off of. Whatever your personal beliefs about the validity of time travel, let's table that discussion and focus on what we can do to help these survivors as they appear. I don't care if you think the whole thing is a hoax or just a load of BS, because whether we understand it or not, they're starting to pop up all over the place, and so far, the fatality rate is 25% and that is too high for anyone's comfort level.

Focusing only on what we can confirm, we do have people who have returned, who claim to have no memory of the time lapse, and they're coming back "in" exactly wherever it was they were on May 15th when they disappeared "out". With the confirmed casualties and the number of injuries on the ground, that means that there is still imminent danger to Toledo's residents, which is why the state of emergency is still in effect and will remain until further notice.

At this time, we cannot confirm or deny if this fluctuation in time is a singular event or if we can expect additional surges, so we should consider ourselves as working in a hostile environment as we undertake this mission. We will be venturing into the city looking for survivors, but we will try to keep our presence minimal to reduce risk to our teams.

Taking into account only what we can actually confirm so far, and upon the advice of experts, we have created an organized model for search and rescue that will now be outlined to this group. You'll all be working together, so regardless of which group you are a part of, listen up and understand your team's purview and how you intersect with the others.

First up are Alpha teams, which are made up of search and rescue personnel, mainly from our active military, paramedics, and first responders along with select K9 officers and handlers. These teams will move into the mapped areas and sweep for survivors, block by block. This will include targeted searches of all buildings and residences, floor by floor. No stone left unturned. Obviously, we're still learning about what time travel is all about here people, so we're well aware that searching a place once isn't enough because we could miss people who appear later after we've moved on to a different section. We'll be sweeping these same areas many times most likely, and we may find new survivors each time we do.

So… the different Alpha teams will move west and south in a planned grid, with later teams sweeping the same areas, and when we get to the end of the territory which we've been assigned to cover, we'll begin at the top once again, and again, and again as is necessary. We also need to sweep at different times of day and night since we don't have any guidance yet on when people's reappearances are likely to happen and it appears to be completely miscellaneous so far. The temporal continuum apparently doesn't work on a 9-to-5 schedule, so the various teams will also be divided in 6-hour increments for shift work so that we, as a unit, are on the clock at all hours.

Any survivors or casualties discovered by the Alpha teams should immediately be radioed in and recorded by exact satellite location. Survivors are to receive paramedic help in the field as needed and then extracted and moved back to our base here; casualties are to be documented and left for processing by our Beta teams. Alpha teams are reminded that survivors may be disoriented or panicked by their situation, and that makes them possibly a danger to themselves and to you, so your primary goal is to secure everyone's safety as you bring them in. Remember that this is going to be confusing for them, but they're not at fault, so they're not being 'detained' – we're there to help them.

Survivors may also have moved away from their initial reentry point looking for help, so upon contact, try to secure as much information as possible from them about where they came from with exact coordinates while it's fresh in their memory. Every detail that they tell us will be meticulously recorded, so we can refer to it later and see if we can learn anything from the patterns.

Next up are the Beta teams, which are to be comprised mainly of forensic experts and cleanup crews that regularly work with law enforcement. These teams are familiar with standard operating procedures for dealing with crime scenes because the principles for handling reentry fatalities will be similar. Though we hope to find Toledo's citizens alive and well, we have to prepare for the worst-case scenario. Anyone found alive will be escorted out of the danger zone by the Beta teams, and safe extraction is the primary mission.

Beta teams will thoroughly document any casualties that are found, similar to how a crime scene is treated, but in a minimum of time. It's important for us to keep the amount of people and equipment within the city limits as bare bones as possible since we cannot yet predict where more entries from time will happen. This is for both your safety and the safety of the city's residents – we want you moving in and out quickly, not lingering in the danger zone. Whatever you bring in, you take out, and do it fast and efficiently. Beta teams will work out of this site here for processing and extract via helicopter when called in by the Alpha teams. Site Two has four helicopters at our disposal and the pads are located on the second fairway immediately to the west of this building.

Delta teams have a more complex task; we've identified that a major roadblock, so to speak, is the amount of damage to vehicles (and property) that was caused by the time anomaly, because their drivers disappeared and the remains of the crashes are everywhere. Basically, every roadway is a mess. The Alphas will just have to contend with this wreckage while looking for survivors on their initial sweeps, but as soon as they have confirmed they have moved through an area and found it clear of people for the time being, the Deltas will come in and remove as much debris as they can, as well as any parked vehicles that might be in our way. This needs to be done as quickly as possible since it requires heavy duty equipment that takes up a lot of real estate, but clearing this immediately, street by street, should make future sweeps easier for the teams, and make reentry safer for the time travelers by far.

Deltas are certified to handle heavy machinery already, but we'll have additional on-site training back here at base for specialty equipment as needed. In addition to rubble, Delta teams will also clear out organic materials, perishables and animal remains from homes that could cause a spread of bacteria or disease. We've got some volunteers from the Humane Society on call to pick up any pets you find alive; and I know it's not our primary mission, but pick 'em up if you see 'em, folks. Call in any exotics you find though, and we'll bring in a specialty crew.

Science squads will be called in last of all, to take readings of the physical locations where any survivors or casualties are found. The priority here is for search and rescue but we do need to document as much as we can that may lead to unlocking the means by which people disappeared and/or returned. Although the Alpha, Beta, and Delta teams may disturb the environment as they work, all will have full body cameras for the science crews to refer back to if needed, documenting the scene exactly as it was found. We'll be setting up a more permanent location for data analysis outside of this emergency site location soon, but I do not yet have details to share.

Although debris and wreckage will be removed, all teams should strive not to move everyday objects out of place. You need to preserve the exact layout from the time of the event to prevent the injury or disorientation of returning travelers. I know that sounds odd so I'll say it again; *don't move things around.* Think of it like this; you're sitting in a chair when the Time Event happens and you disappear; one of us comes in and moves it six inches; a year later you reappear and fall on your ass, or you end up with a chair leg sticking right through your calf. You get what I mean?

I cannot stress enough that we have only found a few survivors and casualties out of hundreds of thousands in these first few weeks, so we do not yet know enough about the situation to assume a rate of return. It is possible that thousands of people could reappear all at once, right on top of you all while you're in the zone. So be on your toes and try to stay clear of high traffic areas like sidewalks in case pedestrians materialize; try to stay on the periphery as you move around on your sweeps, places where people would be less likely to be walking or standing. Hug the perimeters wherever possible; treat it like there are snipers on the rooftops and you're trying to keep out of the line of fire.

We also have flyers for you to put up in strategic locations with FAQs to help survivors until you can get to them, in case they return between your sweeps and don't know what to do with themselves. We're directing them not to try to travel far, especially if they have any injuries, but to get to the nearest police or fire station where we will leave emergency supplies and a way for them to call us for an immediate extraction.

Thank you all for your attention. I will now turn this over to Staff Sargent Willis to outline our territory maps. Please hold your questions on team makeup for the end of this briefing. Thank you.

Good morning, all. Willis here. Everyone should have received a hard copy map of the city with the respective territories marked by site. There is a QR code on the back that leads to the same information for your phones and tablets – please bookmark the page but be aware that cell service may be spotty in parts of the city due to damage to some of the transformers. We know at least one was completely destroyed by an aircraft crash, and there was some construction equipment at a site that caused some damage when it was left unmanned. This same information on the hard copy is what you're seeing up on the screen here; familiarize yourself with the details throughout your training period. We will be using exact coordinates to confirm the daily details of the sweep territories for each team at the start of your shifts each day, and your teams will all have satellite phones and air tags for us to track your movements.

For the squads reporting to Site Two, our territory will extend from the Harbor in the northern most point down through the neighborhoods of Birmingham, Oregon, and East Toledo, all on the east side of the Maumee River only. Major landmarks under our purview are the harbor itself, Mercy Health hospital, the water treatment plant, and the history museum. Note that the casino is not a part of our territory; that's under the purview of Site Three, whose teams will be working from the southeast in a similar pattern to ours.

As you can see, we're roughly dividing the city into four quadrants and are trying to move from the river outwards. As of yet, we don't have an epicenter or the limit of impact fully defined, so we are looking to start in the most populated areas where we theorize there should be more reappearances first, rather than beginning at the outskirts of the city and moving inward. This complicates things in the sense that we will need to move our teams in using the waterways each day, but we think that it's more likely we find survivors by using this methodology and will adjust as needed once we get going. Each team has its own transport vehicles that will depart from the jetties, here and here, on your maps.

Our Alpha teams will be staggered within the territory and should communicate with each other and the home base at all checkpoints to coordinate rescue of any survivors who flag them down remotely. Right now, parts of the city are still without power. We're leaving it off on purpose in some residential areas until we can do a thorough sweep to turn off stoves, ovens, space heaters, curling irons... anything that might have been left on and could cause a fire. We have already seen some effects of unmonitored appliances causing damage or a buildup of gas and carbon monoxide in unventilated areas. In other parts of the city, the power is out anyway due to damage in the aftermath of the Event, but we have a separate crew working on that. We intend to restore at least emergency power to the grid, and we have a skeleton crew at the water plant to keep up maintenance there. Landlines remain undamaged and the initial emergency broadcast message that was up for the first week has now been removed and we're back up and running. Calls are being relocated to external teams so if anyone calls 9-1-1 now, we should get directed straight to their location.

The intention is for you all to meet with your squads at the start of your shift for daily instructions, and at the end of your shift to recap your findings and confirm the territory covered. Expect that the amount of territory covered daily will vary greatly, depending on how many buildings are in the area (residential versus commercial sectors, areas with high rises, etc.) and how severe the wreckage needing to be cleared proves to be.

For sections of major roadways, it should be safest for the squads to stick to the shoulder areas, going in single file wherever possible to minimize your footprint. That being said, these highways and busy traffic areas may be the heaviest in terms of casualties or injuries for returning travelers if they were moving fast when the event occurred, and how much of a mess was left behind in the space. We assume these areas will need the most cleanup attention from the Delta teams and could potentially be the most disturbing in terms of dealing with any human remains. I know we're mostly military and you're all a bunch of tough mothers, but let's not pretend this is no big deal. We're all going to see some shit out there we wish we hadn't, so if you're having a hard time dealing with it, say so. I really mean that, and so does everyone up the chain – and don't forget, some of your team members are civilians... and we're all volunteers for this duty. You get me?

Public buildings and businesses that are found locked up for the night should theoretically have had few people in them at the time of the Event, therefore few people returning there. We ask that the Alpha teams note these as possibly unoccupied in the records. For private residences, a locked door is not an indicator of people's location at the time.

We have a limited number of motion detectors that we will ask the Alpha teams to place in particularly vulnerable areas such as emergency rooms and NICUs at the hospital, nurseries and daycares, assisted living homes, and other places where the people returning may be unable to seek help on their own steam. We're outsourcing the construction of more tech to help us there but it might be a few weeks before we actually get it.

This briefing will now adjourn; you will join your individual teams to get further instructions shortly and there will be some time for Q&A within your groups. Additional training will be given as needed, and as more information is gathered about the situation. Alpha squads will deploy first thing tomorrow. Thank you for your time. Dismissed.

CHAPTER 8

Journal of Raj Anil, intern – 87 days after the Event. Time populous: 280,963

August 10th

Despite my intentions to keep regular records of my personal observations, the last several weeks have been the busiest of my life and I have not had a moment's rest to tend to this journal. That being said, there is an exhilaration I feel being involved in this project even in a limited capacity. I almost cannot put it into words, but truly it has been a crash course in moving from theoretical to practical – in physics, and in life in general!

One of my colleagues expressed that our time with Sadler so far equates to what it means to learn to swim (or in our case, simply not drown) by being thrown into the deep end of the pool as opposed to watching a YouTube video about the breaststroke while safely on dry land. To my mind, this seems an apt metaphor. Although I have always taken great pride in my academic career and found it somewhat distressing how many people seem to have little appreciation for "book learning", I now have a newfound appreciation for the saying "experience is the best teacher".

Let me quickly recap my onboarding with the Sadler group; I arrived here in the Toledo area the evening of June 3rd and was assigned to the second of four emergency sites that had been erected outside the city limits as a base of operations. For the first week or so we were staying in a hotel about an hour further east and were shuttled into the work site daily, but they soon set up quarters for us on site to save time on commuting.

Our quarters at present are simple barracks, with showers, hygienic facilities, mess tents, and other common areas hastily but efficiently constructed to house the many volunteers and experts being brought in from all over the country (with some specialists from overseas also joining us in recent weeks). The whole setup is reminiscent of a military installment in a war zone, but without the impending threat of attack. At least, not human attack. There is still a prevailing unease that new time warps could occur all over the place, and many people have questioned if we should be staying so close to the abandoned city. I personally am less concerned with our proximity to the site of the Event; if time anomalies start to happen in other places, what's to stop them from happening anywhere? To me it seems pointless to worry about where something might happen when we have no way to predict or control it. And we have enough to worry about right now.

The Alpha, Beta, and Delta teams have ongoing activities within the city and launch at all hours of the day and night from the lakefront marinas here, moving west to the harbor area and down the Maumee River for their drop offs and extractions. Although some of us in the Science squads have daily briefings that we attend with these military teams, so far, our involvement with their work is very peripheral and we are also housed in a separate area so as not to get in the way of their complicated shift schedules. Our team is not working in organized shifts at all really; we're all working long hours into the night, but it's reminiscent of university life, so I actually feel very at home with the arrangements.

We stay here at Site Two, outside the city limits, but have access to the more permanent buildings that have been taken over to house the computer equipment needed to start recording data. The first few days, my counterparts and I were merely logging inputs from reports previously recorded, and that in itself was both fascinating (as the first recorded proof of time travel!!) and disappointing (as first-person narratives were mostly jumbles that largely stated they knew nothing). We soon found that there was redundancy in the process and we have since been reassigned to sit in on the sessions directly with survivors as they recount their stories. In this way, we are able to document more details at a fast rate, and ask for clarifications and more in-depth details directly. Standard procedure has become for at least two of us "clerics" to record data during a session to counteract any implicit bias or misinterpretation of comments made. And more and more survivors are found each day, so we find ourselves constantly stretched to our limits and are regularly working 14-to-16-hour days.

At present, at this site there are about 25 of us fulfilling the clerical duties; we all have backgrounds in the sciences, but we were also thoroughly interviewed to identify any multi-lingual skills or other work or studies that could have relevant impact. Before I arrived here, I expected my graduate degree in theoretical physics to be my most worthy characteristic, but since there are a number of renowned experts in the field all vying for placement with the team studying the quantum mechanics behind the time glitch itself, my qualifications are not quite up to par. Instead, my undergrad minor in psychology has been flagged as an adjacent skillset of note. It seems that the ability to coax every detail about the Time Event from the memories of the survivors is more useful to the team right now than my working knowledge of string theory (a fair point, since the professors and doctors whose works I studied are here in the flesh), so I will seek patience and be of use where I can.

In addition to our transcription duties, we are sifting through each survivor's (and casualty's) detailed medical history and personal information, up to and including their whereabouts that day, who else they were in immediate contact with (this at least gives us probable coordinates for other potential return sites), what they were doing, etc. All of that information is logged into the systems here, and they are talking about using AI to run hypotheticals based on this data to try and identify any commonalities that would help with predictions. So far, we are attempting to do this manually, and checking the equations of others, but nothing is definitive.

These first three months can almost be considered as a training course, with the expectation that with each reappearance of another test subject, we will add more data points and eventually build a working predictive model. The statistics being employed are actually quite complex, more so than if we were simply taking a population of 275,000 disappearances and calculating an average rate of return across different scales, which would be simple math.

Some variables can be verified by the travelers themselves. For example, if they can confirm that they were at their office at the time of the event and can confirm that four specific coworkers were in their immediate vicinity, we have the exact names and locations of those four people and the only variable is the time at which they will return. In theory, this means that there are four people whose whereabouts (but not "*whenabouts*" so to speak) are known, so if those people happened to live alone, we might also be able to confirm that their dwelling can be marked in some way as a site where we do not expect anyone to return (barring unknown house guests they may have had). But even knowing their precise return site, with time itself being such an open-ended variable, how do we place any kind of marker that would help our search and rescue teams to prepare for their return when it might be 500 years from now? Hypothetically, if a survivor can confirm that they were the only person in a specific place, such as a residential home, we can now document that no more returns should be expected at that location; but we also cannot completely dismiss it from our simulations because a returning relative or neighbor might come to that location when they reappear, looking for them. All of this is made more complicated because we mostly have to go by what is on public record since the people who could verify the details of others (like whether they live alone) are also in the wind.

In another scenario, a person might be able to confirm they were just boarding a crowded subway car with at least fifty other people. We can confirm the platform and station they were at, and we know this to be a high-traffic site for potential returns, yet the other fifty people's names are unknown so we cannot "check them off" in any organized way from our larger lists of the disappeared.

In short, we are always working with half of a calculation at best, and though we can mitigate the tactical problems by taking actions such as putting information about what to do upon return in highly trafficked areas, it's impractical to think we have the manpower to have people stationed in these locations or even monitoring them remotely by video; there might be no one returning there for years, or there might be ten arriving tomorrow. And of course, something that hangs over our heads is that our efforts to ease the experience for returning travelers isn't really helping us with the larger picture of deciphering the time incongruity itself, or predicting its path, which is what we ideally would like to do to get ahead of the situation. But how does one get ahead of time?? This is not entirely a hypothetical question in light of our current situation. All we can do for now is log massive amounts of data to be sifted and sorted to hopefully help us in the long run.

This type of work, which is largely data entry and analysis, is simultaneously satisfying and dull. Like any work done correctly and efficiently, there is pride to be taken in the work itself. It is said that the devil is in the details, and the smallest details now may be the key to unraveling the mysteries of time, so everything and anything must be recorded. The work itself, it must be said, is somewhat tedious.

Today's session by contrast was quite enlightening, and, I dare say, even entertaining. We were recording the details of one Trevor Martin, ten years old, and it became quickly apparent that although he was only this morning recovered at the history museum by Site Two Alpha Team Eight and brought here for processing, this enterprising young man was not a newly reappeared time traveler at all. In fact, as we delved deeper into his story, it is likely that he may have been one of the very first people to reemerge from the time stream, but has avoided detection for almost three full months.

Although he was thoroughly polite and respectful to all of us, he also had a wary demeanor about him and seemed loath to give up his hard-won independence, almost as if he had been captured rather than rescued, but at the same time was relieved to be so. Being a child, he had a bluntness in the way he described his activities over the past weeks, which he recounted at first with reluctance. As it became clear he would not be blamed by us for any misbehavior or for the situation at large, he relaxed somewhat and told us with pride about his resourcefulness in surviving on his own. When we explained to him that the working theory of the disappearance of the residents of the entire city, including his family, was time travel, he seemed only mildly surprised and accepted it much more readily than any adult survivors have so far.

I found it refreshing to speak to this young man in more ways than one. For starters, children are simply more resilient than most adults, and can accept change much more gracefully. Lacking a lifetime of skepticism, even a groundbreaking thing like time travel, which up until this point was firmly entrenched in the category of science fiction, seems more possible, plausible, maybe even expected through the eyes of a child. In fact, Trevor seemed almost to have come to the conclusion before we had finished our explanation, and merely commented that he had "read a book about something like that". Compared to some of the adults we have interviewed recently, he was certainly a cool customer.

I also found it fascinating to glimpse what a 10-year-old does with a complete lack of supervision. In truth it sounded like a true quest. From scrounging for food (he definitely hadn't been eating very healthily and is being treated for slight vitamin deficiencies by the staff here) to exploring all around his neighborhood, doing necessary chores and cleanup, and

47

keeping himself entertained, he seems to have accepted the challenge of survival wholeheartedly and has taken on responsibility far beyond his age. Although now there have been over 400 documented survivors (plus over 100 casualties), they were spread far and wide throughout the city and suburbs and didn't stay in one place for long, and Trevor had not encountered any of them. In fact, he had not seen or heard from another human since the Time Event, as everyone he personally knows is a local, and as of yet, not returned. In that respect, the information we gleaned from him is unlikely to be useful for our efforts, as he cannot confirm the locations of any others, either returned or still lost in time. But I did thoroughly enjoy participating in his interview. Who knows how long he might have lived under the radar before our search and rescue teams found him if he had remained in his own neighborhood? But as it happens, he actually found us.

It seems that after reading some interesting books about dinosaurs at the local library and lacking the power to Google more information, Trevor landed upon the idea of moving his headquarters into the natural history museum a few miles west of his home. I must say, it was impressive how organized he was (for a child his age) in his preparations. He had attached to his bike a small trailer of the kind used by parents to shuttle small children around at the park, and in it he had packed a camping tent, blankets, a lantern, food to last a week, spare clothing and toiletries, notebook and pens, a map of the city, and even a disposable camera (which I wouldn't have guessed children today would even know how to use in this digital age!). A five-mile bike ride is nothing to sneeze at, carting all his own supplies and navigating streets filled with crash debris and other damage, but he made it to the museum without incident and set himself and his tent up in the employee lounge near the dinosaur section. There he actually cleaned up the staff refrigerator before raiding the vending machines and procuring a T-Rex model from the gift shop to build for his entertainment. He was there two days before he spotted the Alpha team just arriving at their drop site and came out to the steps of the museum to greet them, like the king of the museum meeting honored guests.

To date, Trevor is one of some seventy minors who have been safely recovered, and one of the challenges of this facility has been to coordinate accommodations for their welfare. For all the survivors, of any age, this has been a challenge since they cannot return to their homes to collect personal belongings due to safety concerns – the city is strictly off limits once you have been escorted out of it. Hotels, vacant apartments, and temporary housing have been acquired in nearby large cities (mainly Detroit, Ann Arbor, Lansing, Cleveland, and Columbus) and donations of clothing and other necessities have poured in from all over the world. But for minors, the situation is more complex as so far none of their parents have reemerged from the past yet to claim them. Some have been sent to stay with close relatives that could be verified, but the majority have been parsed out with foster families throughout the Midwest.

Even with the cooperation of several states, the foster care system can only accommodate so many and will soon be stretched to the limit. Approximately 20% of the population of Toledo is under 18 according to the latest census data, and will therefore need some type of fostering (when and if they do return). It's also unclear what may happen if the rate of reappearances remains constant to these first three months – it is possible we will have survivors coming back for decades, so some of these children will have grown up by the time their parents come back, and that is a sobering thought. Imagine what it will be like for families pulled apart by this Time Event… say a parent with a toddler. If the child reemerges soon, but the parent does not, they could end up returning when their child is an old man – maybe three times their own age! – who has lived a long, full life, but as an orphan. Surely the parent will still mourn their "lost" child. They will be fundamentally strangers, likely with different forms of survivor's guilt and regret.

I have heard that the national government will be stepping in with emergency funding to begin construction of semi-permanent facilities to help with the overflow in the short term. In the meantime, just like the other time travelers, the children will spend a week or so in one of the four sites while we process and document, and then be sent on to await further developments.

The impact of all this is almost too much for me to bear, from an academic standpoint. I find myself going down rabbit holes each time I think of another aspect of life that will be affected if the disappeared do not return soon. My father has always said to me, "you cannot boil the ocean", and I repeat that phrase to myself often these days when I find my thoughts overwhelming me. But it is difficult to focus on single tasks while there are so many unknowns that my mind naturally wants to explore.

Speaking of my father, he sent me new glasses in the mail today. I simply have no time off from the project right now to go home to have my yearly eye appointment with him. He has used my latest prescription and they seem to be a tad weak, so perhaps he can send me a slightly stronger pair. I will Facetime with him and my mother tomorrow, but right now I am too exhausted for a long conversation and should head to bed. -RA-

CHAPTER 9

Wikipedia – 6 months, 5 days after the Event. Time populous: 280,338

From Wikipedia, the free encyclopedia

This article needs additional citations for verification. Please help improve this article by adding citations to reliable sources. Unsourced material may be challenged and removed.

For other uses, see Time Travel (disambiguation).

Toledo Time Event redirect here. For other uses, see Time Anomaly (disambiguation).

Introduction

Time travel as a concept describes movement between certain points in time, in parallel to movement between different points in space. Prior to the time anomaly that was confirmed to have occurred on May 15th of this year, time travel was still a widely recognized concept, but mostly in the realm of philosophy and science fiction.

Since the breach of the fabric of spacetime, scientists and officials have put forth various tutorials on the basics of relativity to help educate the public and demystify the concept. Their efforts have helped to distill panic about the effects of this temporal disruption, but they have so far been unable to explain how the Time Event was actually achieved.

History

Albert Einstein's theory of relativity says time and motion are relative to each other, and he postulated that time travel was theoretically possible through "time dilation", or how one's perception of time is different to another, depending on their motion or location. He pioneered the concept of spacetime, a mathematical model that combines the three dimensions of space and one dimension of time within a four-dimensional model.

Popular theories over the years regarding time travel use speed, gravity, light, warp drives and wormholes as theoretical ways to create a curvature of spacetime and link paths through the universe.

As far back as the early 20th century, physicists like Flamm, Einstein, and Rosen were postulating on the idea of 'white holes' (a theoretical reversal of a black hole) that could be used as "bridges" across spacetime, connecting two different points. These bridges became more commonly referred to as wormholes (shortcuts through spacetime), but have been completely hypothetical as technology was insufficient to even find (much less manipulate) them for experimentation to prove or disprove any theories. Later researchers described these bridges as likely spheroidal, with the possibility of adding stabilizing exotic matter to a wormhole to make it traversable, with opposing theories claiming that only backwards (past) or only forward (future) journeys are even possible.

Although some physicists have hypothesized that wormholes are actually common, but not at a size that would affect humans or anything that exists outside the quantum scale, there is incompatibility between general relativity and quantum mechanics that have so far deterred any successful attempts to prove this.

Prior to the events in Toledo, all arguments on the topic were considered purely academic, and the scientific community at large is putting new attention on this topic now. Additional articles and information will be added as they become available.

See also

1. Basic introduction to the mathematics of curved spacetime
2. Complex spacetime
3. Four-dimensionalism
4. Philosophy of space and time
5. Wormholes
6. Time geography
7. Toledo, Ohio USA

CHAPTER 10

Captain Holmes, Beta Team Six – 9 months, 12 days after the Event. Time populous: 279,708

23.4%. That was the casualty rate for people returning from the time stream after nine months of search and rescue efforts were officially launched. In Captain Holmes' opinion, that was a piss-poor statistic, and unacceptable under his watch.

He didn't care that he was just one of many people involved, or that they were all dealing with something entirely new. These were American lives, on American soil, and he was accountable. They were all of them accountable.

The Beta squad he led was one of the best, and he had no complaints as to how quickly and efficiently they transported survivors out of the Time Zone to safety. That portion of their bailiwick was stellar. And when it came to dealing with fatalities, their thoroughness in documenting the forensics or how they tracked and measured the remains was top notch as well. His team was conscientious, careful, and quick – all things the Beta teams needed to be in this volatile work zone – but at the end of the day, 23.4% just wasn't going to get it. They needed solutions, and they needed them yesterday (not a facetious statement in this new era of time traveling reality).

It had only been a few months, but already they'd seen more than any of them wanted to of strange deaths. Sure, the Alpha teams were on the front lines and had to make the initial discovery, but after making the call they could walk away from the situation and move on. The Betas were the ones who had to get their hands dirty, so to speak. They'd had everything from a horrific scene where a flock of pigeons had been flying right through a person's reentry zone (the Hitchcockesque result giving them all nightmares for weeks), two elevator shaft falls from unfortunate travelers returning into mid-air, to a crushing incident where a fire that broke out from an abandoned meal being cooked on a stovetop had weakened the entire structure of the building to the point that the reemerging person immediately triggered the collapse of an entire floor within the apartment complex. All this, alongside more "ordinary" situations such as cardiac arrests, insulin shock, and many injuries and fatalities resulting from phantom auto collisions, which were fast becoming an unfortunate norm.

Ignoring even the fact that if those casualty rates remained steady, they would eventually be looking at somewhere around 75,000 dead civilians (practically enough for a whole damn war) which would be psychologically damaging to the entire nation, but logistically the situation had opened up all sorts of issues they just weren't prepared to deal with. Sure, the people were returning at a staggered pace, not all at once, but that was a still a lot of bodies to contend with. Not to mention, there was basically no such thing as 'natural causes' here – everything was basically an accident that needed to be investigated, albeit in a condensed timeframe – and there were extra considerations outside the norm involving recording everything for analysis related to the Time Event. It didn't help that they didn't know exactly what they were looking for, so they had to look at *everything*.

On scene, they were a whirlwind of activity, everyone on the team working like they were about to miss the last helicopter out of Saigon. Their photographer Mack took hundreds of shots in a matter of minutes; every angle and perspective he could get. He had spent years as a crime scene technician and knew the drill. He and Lieutenant Foster worked in conjunction; Foster quickly laid down the number markers and picked them back up as they moved about – it was a high-speed ballet, CSI on speed, your favorite detective show on fast-forward, and an impressively efficient operation. Meanwhile their lab techs took forensic readings and worked to tag and bag as quickly as possible while maintaining the integrity of the scene. They had five others on the team that held canopies when weather dictated, moved equipment, documented locations, and performed the thousand and one other tasks that needed to be done before they could recover a body and retreat out of the hot zone.

One thing that was helpful was that the city coroner's office and morgue had been flagged as a relatively low-risk reentry zone since it hosted a small staff and most would've already left for the day when the Time Event occurred. The Betas were given permission to use that facility and its equipment on site within the Time Zone, and even better, it was tucked away in an area with easy access by helicopter so they could move in and out with relative ease, all without exposing their team to reentry danger. The Alpha and Delta squads had to come in daily from outside the perimeters, but the Beta teams had an actual base of operations with the necessary tools already in place.

Storing the human remains was another issue that needed a long-term solution; normally, deceased people had family around to make decisions about their remains even if they hadn't left instructions of their own. But here in Toledo, there were too many people still missing to keep track of who knew what, and even if there were relatives in other parts of the country, with the mystery of the wormhole still looming large, the determination was made not to release remains until more readings could be taken. Arrangements had been made to safely store the deceased offsite in other city morgues temporarily, while a large containment facility with cold storage could be permanently erected. No cremations, or anything else that would damage the remains, until more tests could be run to see if there were indeed any indicators of time travel that manifested in physical signs. It was a controversial call, and since no permissions had been specifically given, organ donors were first up on the list for these examinations.

Holmes wasn't a particularly morbid person, and truth be told, he'd rather be off with the Alpha squads, sweeping with the other soldiers, than running a Beta team that was basically an ambulance service half the time, and the other half dealing with the gruesome aftermath of a lot of death. But his age and health had deterred him from more active duty, and he could still be of use here, so he kept his mouth shut and did what was necessary.

Between alerts, he had begun keeping notes with suggestions for improvements in procedure – he could see a lot of changes that could be made to potentially improve those unfortunate fatality stats. Most revolved around prioritizing high traffic areas and looking for preventative measures to employ; his notebook was filled with scribbles like 'cushions on highways', 'fence off forested areas', 'bird deterrents - sonar??'. Right now, that doesn't seem like much, but his instincts are good ones, and in the next ops meeting he'll have a chance to get his say. Let the Alphas have the glory; the real work begins with the Betas.

CHAPTER 11

Special report from CNN – 1 year after the Event. Time populous: 278,580

One Year Later: the city of Toledo remains quarantined due to the time anomaly

WASHINGTON DC, USA – Across the country, a moment of silence was observed this morning in support of the citizens of Toledo on the one-year anniversary of the mysterious time fluctuation that has devastated the region. At the time of this publication, exactly 2,336 survivors have been recovered from the time stream, and 564 casualties have been confirmed. The majority of casualties have come from people reemerging into unsafe conditions such as at the speed of moving vehicles they had occupied (mainly automobiles and trains). There have also been several reports of severe shock leading to stroke or heart attack, and other medical conditions brought on by reentry stress (after some debate, suicides have been accounted for in these statistics as it has been determined that factors like depression and anxiety directly related to the Time Event should be included).

Although rescue teams continue to discover more people returning from the past, these reappearances are still erratically spaced, and unpredictable.

"Even after a year, we have not yet identified any determinate factors that would allow us to even imprecisely predict reentry times and locations," said Dr. Lansing of the Sadler Research Center. "Although we are thoroughly exploring the data to find connections, so far nothing of statistical significance has been proven, and the reemergences still appear to be completely random."

The Sadler group continues to coordinate the scientific data collection within the city itself, and the documentation of the first-person accounts from the survivors.

Government funding has also been approved to continue rescue efforts through the Alpha, Beta and Delta teams, which have been recognized as a temporary specialty branch within the U.S. military. Several foreign governments have pledged financial support for scientific research and equipment in exchange for the inclusion of their scientists in the Sadler project, which is working in conjunction with the military teams on site.

The International Council of the Sciences (ICS) and the World Science Federation (WSF) issued a joint statement this week that their significant fundraising efforts, largely from private donors, would be pledged to the study of the Time Event for (at minimum) the next five years. "The sheer fact that within only a few generations we have come from the theory of relativity as a concept to a concrete and realized occurrence is astounding," said Dr. Ivan Hathaway, Director of the WSF. "The study of this Time Event is something that will shape the fields of quantum mechanics, astrophysics and theoretical physics for decades, and we would be remiss if we did not put forth all of our resources towards this endeavor."

Although there are still many complex situations to navigate, the general consensus is that the coordinated efforts of the military, government, and scientific communities to aid in the rescue of returning Toledoans has been remarkably organized, drawing international praise.

Due to the ongoing unsafe conditions in the city caused by the sporadic reappearances of its citizens, the entire region is still closed off to the public and only authorized personnel are permitted into the area. Returning survivors have not been allowed back to their homes, but a program for relocating them to neighboring cities has been set up, and the generous donations of various charities have kept them supplied with necessities. Though many have returned to the workforce in their various fields by applying for positions in their new locations, special emergency funding from the U.S. government has also been granted to the survivors as a type of stimulus. Survivors also have been given special deferments on state and federal taxes.

Initial reactions

Immediately after the incident, when details were scarce, there was some fear in neighboring states as rumors spread that other cities were in danger. Fortunately, officials were quickly able to confirm that the impact was limited specifically to the Toledo area and that the edge of the Time Zone had been mapped. Although there is still worldwide interest and concern, coming in the wake of wars, a global pandemic, and years of climate crisis, even something as spectacular as time travel can be looked at as a localized phenomenon that the average global citizen considers from a more academic standpoint simply because they are not directly impacted.

While some stockpiling of supplies took place in the American Midwest by people convinced that they needed to prepare for an Armageddon-like event, the most immediate impact came from the trade routes that have been disturbed due to the closing of the city limits. Toledo's location in the middle of major train and trucking routes caused supply chain disruptions throughout the country and forced the rerouting of goods and services destined for Chicago, New York, and other major cities. Stock prices dipped temporarily due to materials shortages, and then rose in the next quarter as significant investments in tech companies surged as manufacturers and processing companies were asked to increase production of materials and equipment used by the scientists and rescue teams.

Internationally, a surge in demand for the raw materials, componentry, and engineered materials used for technological equipment used in the Toledo area by the search and rescue teams has boosted the economy in some regions. In order to speed production and minimize shipping delays, processing and manufacturing facilities in Mexico, Brazil, and other countries closer to the U.S. modified some facilities to shift their production to goods in high demand.

The survivors

Historically, Toledo has been known as "the Glass Capital of the World" due to its prominence in the glass industry, but since the Time Event it has been redubbed the "Wormhole" in common parlance. As a reminder, the names of all survivors and casualties are public information, and can be searched in the public parametric database. People with friends and family missing from the Toledo area can flag their names in the database and create alerts to be sent to their phones if anyone they have flagged reappears. All of the time survivors have been asked to make an extensive list of family, friends and coworkers, while company directories, school yearbooks, and other databases have been used to create a system for alerting them of anyone returning who is connected to them, even if remotely.

On this one-year anniversary of the Event, our reporting team met with a selection of survivors to give their perspectives on their experience and to highlight some examples of the impact they have felt.

* * *

Name: Jason Moore   **Age at the time of the Event:** 19

Reentry date: October 5th (143 days in the time stream)

"I was just finishing my sophomore year at the University of Toledo when the time shift happened. I was lifting at the gym so I didn't even realize what had happened until I finished my set and saw the whole place was deserted. I'm back in my own hometown now, and they arranged for me to transfer my credits and I'll finish up my schooling here. All my stuff that was in my dorm back at school I can't get to, but there's nothing I couldn't replace. I think I got really lucky by only missing a few months of my life, and it's not as hard for me because I didn't know many people in Toledo and can just go back to my regular life without it feeling too strange. I feel bad for people who have lost their whole family, and I hope they're working on a way to bring people back from time faster. It'll be a lot harder for people who are lost out there for years. For me it's been really just an inconvenience, and not a personal tragedy."

Jason is a student who was recovered at the University's gym, and suffered no injuries from reentry. He is originally from Tennessee and did not have other family members residing in Toledo. He was able to confirm the exact location of several classmates that were with him at the time of the Event, whose names and locations have been recorded.

* * *

Name: Tracy Butera   **Age at the time of the Event:** 31

Reentry date: March 7th (297 days in the time stream)

"Most of my family lives in Cleveland so I actually have somewhere to go until they let us go back home, and thank God this didn't happen right before the wedding or my parents and my whole family would have been in town too and disappeared with the rest of us. My fiancé, Robert, and most of his relatives and our friends disappeared along with us and none of them are back yet. I don't think I've really processed what happened yet – one minute everything was fine and then instantaneously everything is turned upside down and they tell me I've missed ten months of my life. It's like Covid times all over again, like a whole year just dropped off my radar. And Robert's been missing a whole year with everyone who cares about him missing the whole time too. Somehow that makes it seem worse to me, that no one was here to worry about him, so that's what I'm doing now. I'm not really sure what else I can do except keep praying that he comes back safe, and soon."

Tracy is a teacher, and was recovered in her car at the parking lot of the Lincoln Elementary School where she works. She reemerged into several inches of snow, which to her perspective appeared instantaneously. Being unprepared for the dramatic change in weather and finding her cell phone battery dead, she attempted to alert her coworkers by blowing her car's horn and was heard by an Alpha team in the area. Her wedding has been postponed while her fiancé is still lost in the time stream.

* * *

Name: Gerald Lockner   **Age at the time of the Event:** 58
Reentry date: July 25th (71 days in the time stream)

"I was hoping to retire this coming year, but I'm not sure what will be in the cards for me now. Elaine and I have lived here for 34 years, and all our memories are sunk into that house that I'm not even allowed to go back to now. I was just about to replace the roof too, and if squirrels get in there again in the fall while no one is there, they'll make a mess of the attic and rip up all the insulation. I hope they figure all this time nonsense out soon so I can get back home. And I hope I don't get too old before the grandkids get back, or I won't have the energy to wrangle 'em no more. They're a handful all right, Eddie's just turning five and starting T-ball and wants me to throw with him every minute. Charlotte's three, and just wants to be carried everywhere, and Elsie's still a baby but getting into that crawling phase. Who knows if they'll even be the right ages at the same time again, this whole thing is too confusing for me to keep straight. I'm not sure I even believe any of it, but that's what they tell me."

Gerald is an auto repair specialist at a privately owned body shop in the area. He was recovered at his local fire station after reappearing at his own home and finding his family and neighbors missing. He called 9-1-1 and his location was reported to search and rescue teams. His wife, Elaine, and other family members have not yet returned. One of his old acquaintances from high school was among the confirmed casualties last month, but otherwise none of his connections have come back.

* * *

Name: Sarah Judd   **Age at the time of the Event:** 28

Reentry date: December 24th (223 days in the time stream)

"This is the longest I've ever gone without talking to my twin sister in my whole life… and really, it's twice as long as I even know because to me it seems like five months, but really, it's been a year since we all disappeared. People keep asking me what it was like, but the time travel part didn't feel like anything, just the blink of an eye… the strange part all comes afterwards. I'm not sure I can really explain this, but it's like every day that I'm back and she's not, I'm aging and experiencing things and I know she'll still be exactly the same as she was when she returns. So, it's like every day that we're apart, we're less and less like twins. Unless you're a twin yourself you just can't understand how wrong that feels."

Sarah is a server and hostess in the West Toledo area. She was recovered at the train station a few blocks from her workplace and suffered a sprained wrist upon reentry when she became disoriented by the sudden disappearance of the crowd of commuters around her and slipped on the stairs, but was otherwise unharmed. She has been relocated to Columbus and is staying with friends.

* * *

Name: Jayleen Thomas   **Age at the time of the Event:** 3

Reentry date: April 2nd (322 days in the time stream)

"They said Mama and Daddy are on a trip and they're coming back soon." Jayleen is the youngest of three children. Her family lives in the northern Birmingham neighborhood and none of them have yet returned from the past. She was found at the local school, and had been attending her brother's art night with her parents when the time irregularity occurred. She pointed out her brother's picture for authorities from the school's records, and from there her family and identity was confirmed. Search and rescue teams have prioritized setting up remote cameras and other devices in locations like schools and hospitals that have high traffic, and the location where Jayleen was found had been recently outfitted with updated motion sensory equipment that helped alert authorities to her reentry.

* * *

Name: May Reinhart   **Age at the time of the Event:** 88

Reentry date: estimated May 29th (estimated 14 days in the time stream)

"The nurses here are very nice, nicer than them over at the place I used to be at. That place used to be good and then they just up and left us one day, and I called and called but I couldn't get any of them to even bring me over to check on Charlie. We got married on the 6th of July, and we drove up to Niagara Falls for our honeymoon. My mother always said you could

65

tell a lot about a man by the way he travels, and my Charlie was always a good driver and took good care of his car. He works up at the Chevrolet plant here in Detroit and all the workers come into the sweet shop across the street where I work after school. He comes in so often that I thought he must love chocolates, but he says really, he just loves me. Isn't he just the sweetest thing?"

May is a widow who suffers from dementia and had been a resident of The Oaks Retirement Community for the past six years, which is where she was discovered by rescue teams. Due to her reappearance so soon after the Time Event, when volunteers were first being dispatched, it took several days before she was found. Due to her preexisting medical conditions and general disorientation, she was severely dehydrated and malnourished when found, and this was used to estimate her reentry date. She has been moved to a facility in Ann Arbor for her long-term care, as she has no remaining family in the area.

* * *

Name: Rev. Henry Ethan Gates   **Age at the time of the Event:** 36

Reentry date: July 14th (60 days in the time stream)

"Back before we thought time travel was real, I think most people accepted that premise in a book or a movie as just part of a plot device and didn't think about what it would actually mean if it happened in real life. Now that it is a part of our reality, I know some people see the time glitch as something to fear, while others see it as a miracle. In my opinion, it is neither. Think of all the many things that we do not understand about the natural world; if every time mankind discovered a new fact about nature we considered it a miracle, science and religion would be only one thing. The question I was asked was whether the Time Event has changed my views on God, and I honestly can say that it has not. God is good, and this is a test. I'll just do my best to pass."

Henry is a Lutheran minister in the Toledo area, and was hosting a meeting about an upcoming church picnic when the Time Event took place. He has been able to identify at least a dozen others that were in the building with him at the time, none of whom have reentered from the time stream yet. However, there is another member of his congregation who also emerged from time just eight weeks after he did, and they have both now relocated to the Cleveland area.

* * *

The future of Toledo

One year ago today, the world was changed forever with the discovery that time travel is possible. Although the circumstances remain a mystery, our hearts remain with the citizens that were pulled forward and scattered through time.

We offer remembrance for those that did not survive the journey, and as for the survivors, they continue to be an inspiration to us all.

CHAPTER 12

First Lieutenant Briggs, Alpha Team Four – 4 years, 2 months, 17 days after the Event. Time populous: 271,493

"These survivors are really starting to fucking piss me off, Briggs!"

Corporal Simmons scurried into the temporary shelter they had hastily erected to get out of the sudden storm. Half the team was already crouched inside the field tent, just a three-sided structure tucked beneath the underpass of an exit ramp, while the rest were still briefing the Beta team that had just arrived to transport the survivor back to base. Briggs looked at Simmons shaking water out of his helmet and thought sardonically that he looked like a half-drowned Pekingese with those ears and that shaggy haircut. She missed the military high-and-tight; some of her squad looked like they were in a goddam boy band with those mops, but of course fashion wasn't a high priority for any of them right now.

"What's your problem now, Simmons? It's not like the guy had a choice on when to reappear, it's not his fault the weather's shit." Briggs finished marking her notes on their time and location and hunkered down to wait for the all clear.

"No, it's not the weather. It's these guys that demand an explanation the minute we show up, which you know damn well we're not supposed to give them… but then anything we *do* say, they try to argue it with us!" he said, punctuating his speech with sprays of water as he gestured wildly. "Like we're the time police and can just send him back when he came from! Don't we all fucking wish! I thought that guy was going to take a swing at Harris, honestly!"

Simmons was really worked up, but then again, he was always worked up. Briggs didn't try to answer him (he clearly wasn't in the mood for either a lecture or a pep talk yet, and they all knew from experience it was better to let him vent his steam valve a bit first). She wasn't sure he was really cut out for this kind of work, even though he'd been with her team almost since the beginning. But even after four years, he was still firing off complaints every time a rescue didn't go by the books. And the thing was, nothing really ever went by the books. Every single rescue was different, even when they'd been crisscrossing over the same stretch of territory now hundreds of times.

Sure, they encountered certain situations more often than others; it was relatively normal to get a tip from base from people calling 9-1-1 from their homes or office, but usually only from older people who still had landlines in their homes (government money kept all the landlines functional and accounts paid up). Young people all relied on cell phones these days, but unless their device was on their person at the time of their disappearance, the battery would be years dead when they returned. Even if they managed to keep ahold of it, people just tended to start calling and texting people they knew, which was worthless. Younger people were also more inclined to start wandering the area (by car or by foot), and were more likely to be alarmed or threatened at the appearance of an Alpha team. Despite the big Red Cross patches emblazoned everywhere, they still looked remarkably like a black ops team from a video game. There had even been a few instances in which returning time travelers, seeing the city half destroyed and all the people missing, thought they were in a Mad Max situation and immediately started collecting weaponry.

There were a lot of gun owners in Toledo, or people who knew gun owners, so there had been several situations over the years with standoffs that had to be deescalated when the survivor attempted to fight off rescuers from their homes. Barricades on the doors and windows – the whole shebang. The first few times they'd been pretty unprepared for it, something Briggs was still kicking herself for not adding to the procedural manuals from the beginning.

After a few serious injuries to Alpha and Beta teams (no casualties, thankfully) it became standard practice for rescuers to carry stun guns and basic weaponry for self-defense (only as a last resort) and they had all had extensive training on how to subdue and calm as the primary goal. In fact, the whole training program (*which had a required yearly re-certification that was coming up soon... damn, one more thing to add to the list*) was adapted from hostage negotiation training. She couldn't really blame Simmons for being salty when they were just trying to do their jobs, and they'd had a string of belligerent rescues lately including one guy who had reemerged and immediately gone for his hidden stash of methamphetamines in his home. He was high as a kite by the time they'd found him, and without any warning at all he'd pulled an 8-inch bowie knife and had taken a swipe at Simmons, and that was just in the last week. Not to mention the run-in they'd had with looters maybe six months ago. Luckily that didn't come up often and generally those groups weren't heavily armed, just looking for a quick score snatching and grabbing... but it was just another thing to contend with.

"*The trouble with this job is that we all need to be unicorns – a perfect, extraordinary thing that doesn't actually exist,*" thought Briggs while she watched Simmons rant. The rest of the team gave him a nod or two to show they were listening while they worked, but they too didn't interrupt this flow – he'd calm down once he'd expelled some of his bile. "*Everyone here has to be all things to all people... soldiers, trackers, technicians, paramedics, crisis negotiators, emergency responders... every year we're at this, the list of skills we need to have gets longer and there's never a break from training.*"

The light at the end of the tunnel was that she wasn't the only one concerned with how many hats the teams were being asked to wear. At her last command meeting they'd gotten word that there was finally approval to begin a specialized training program specifically to prep college-age recruits for Time Zone rescue, and that both Army and Navy were on board with the collaboration, now that the Alpha, Beta and Delta teams servicing Toledo were officially designated as a special force under the U.S. Military (though they still had police and civilian contractors in some roles). "Wormhole U" was the moniker being bandied about for the new feeder program. That might not increase their pool of talent right this minute, but it at least gave them some hope for the future. The program was intended to be an intense 2-year course that would give college credit plus count as time served for those who made it through, with another couple of years of classes to take while working part time in the field with their units, giving them on-the-job experience plus some classroom time for training.

God knows they needed some fresh blood. Her team was the best of the best, but Briggs was still tired to the core. They'd rescued a lot of people over the years and knowing that felt good, but they'd also seen their share of losses and it was hard on all of them. It was really just the luck of the draw where people were when the Time Event happened; it wasn't fair, but if you were in an airplane that was anywhere but parked at the terminal, casualty rates were 100%, and that was just the way it was. Not even considering the survival rates of a regular plane crash, you just couldn't reappear into thin air 10,000 feet up and survive, and there was no practical way to catch someone moving at thirty knots even if they had been able to predict when they would be arriving. Thank Christ they hadn't pulled airport duty in their territory; that was thankless and messy work for sure (at least there were fewer people in that situation than on the ground).

71

They were fortunate that out in the neighborhoods their success rate was close to 75%, which was a lot better than she'd experienced after the earthquakes in Indonesia they'd worked when she was fresh out of basic training years ago. The rest of her team hadn't seen that kind of casualty rate ever, and it was her deepest wish that none of them ever would. Scratch that; one member of her team had. Her K9 officer Duke was going on his 8th year of duty and had a few major tornados with high casualty rates under his belt, though his latest handler was less experienced. Specialist Yui was a competent handler from what she'd seen the past few months since he joined to cover for Yates who had torn her meniscus and was doing rehab back at base after surgery.

They were lucky to have gotten a replacement for Yates at all, considering how scarce trained staff was to come by these days. Part of the issue too was that adding more personnel on the ground wasn't necessarily helpful. There wasn't much opportunity to train in the field; they still needed to work in small teams to minimize their footprint in the volatile space. There had been several close calls over the years; in fact, just a year ago a returning survivor materialized practically on top of them, mere yards away. No one said it outright, but no one ever wanted to see what would happen if two human bodies tried to occupy the same space at the same time. It hadn't happened yet, but there had been travelers who lost limbs (or their lives) after they were unwittingly merged with rubble upon reentry, and one ghastly incident that they all heard about where an apparently young and healthy returning traveler had mysteriously dropped dead upon reentry and an autopsy revealed he had happened to get a passing dragonfly directly embedded inside his heart. *"Speaking of luck,"* thought Briggs, with an inner shudder.

At least they'd recently gotten some new tech to help them with safety. They had twice as many motion detectors and cameras (*and twice as much training to learn how to set them up*) than they had at the beginning.

Since people didn't rematerialize high up on walls, telephone poles, and other vantage points, it was relatively easy to set up a systematic grid to catch pop-ins. After all this time the science teams back at Sadler were still nowhere with predicting arrival times for travelers, but at least the field teams were getting better at catching up with them after they'd arrived.

One thing that wasn't improving was the aging of the city itself, and in fact it was top of the list for feedback she intended to bring up at the next council meeting. The Delta squads had done an amazing job over the years clearing out rubbish and fire damage, but it was sometimes hard to tell debris from things that had been in use at the time of the Event. Aside from actual casualties, many of the minor injuries sustained by returning survivors came from people who had been up on ladders, moving escalators, or other things of that nature that caused falls upon reentry… so in seeing this come up more and more, Briggs couldn't help but wonder what would happen in a few decades if apartment buildings, bridges, and other large infrastructure started to fail? Four years isn't too long without road-side maintenance with so little traffic since the Time Event, but multiply that by a few decades and they were eventually going to have a problem that she'd prefer to get ahead of now. Not to mention, some of those structures weren't starting off in good shape to begin with. Maybe she'd be long retired by the time it became a problem, but she'd rather have it discussed sooner rather than later.

"And another thing…" Simmons was running out of steam now, and the team almost as a unit started damage control (*add therapist to that list of skills* thought Briggs with an internal sigh).

"C'mon, Simmons, the rescues can't all be cute kiddos and beautiful women with a hero-worship complex," said Sergeant Jonas. He slapped Simmons affectionately on the shoulder. "I know you want to pose for another photoshoot but some days are just the dog's ass and that's the way it is."

That was one way to cheer Simmons up; he'd been featured in the news a couple years back carrying a survivor against a backdrop of smoke and flames, looking like a bona fide hero, and he loved to be reminded of it.

Simmons snorted, still looking a little sour, but he couldn't help but smirk a little and when Yui tossed him a granola bar he shut up and ate it without further complaint. The other half of their team (Lieutenant Harris, Private Kryztak, and First Sergeant Martinez) joined them under the bridge while the Beta team took off in the small helicopter with the survivor on board. It had stopped raining now, but they were soaked through and started shaking out their gear once Briggs nodded to them. They should eat more than just a snack while they were here, and regroup.

"How'd he take it?", asked Jonas. He kept the tone casual, but he gave them all a look that said 'watch it – Simmons is on a roll'. They showed no reaction at all but they understood…the mark of a well-oiled team thought Briggs with another inner smile.

"Not bad once we gave him a little shot to calm him down," said Harris, just as casually. "Nothing we couldn't handle. I'll put down money though that he'll never really accept the whole "time travel" story though, he seemed like a conspiracy theory guy to me for sure."

"You can say that again," said Kryztak with a laugh. "I think he said 'bullshit' a record number of times in an hour. We ought to call Guinness. He'll be a time-denier for sure."

Jonas snorted and started pulling out supplies for dinner. "Yeah, well if you think he needed a shot of calm-down juice out here in the field, just wait until he starts his rehab and they show him that video with the animation of the 'time scatter'. Even I thought that one was too sci-fi to be plausible." Jonas was the only member of this Alpha team who was a time survivor himself; he'd been back almost three years now and had accepted the situation so well that he'd been cleared for field work almost

74

immediately. If they hadn't been so short staffed that might not have gotten approved, but he had a stellar service record prior to the Event and had been training to be a Navy Seal, so they weren't going to look a gift horse in the mouth when he'd expressed interest in pausing his efforts and joining the Alpha teams instead.

"You mean the one with the David Attenborough-wannabe narrating?" asked Harris. He put on an over-the-top accent and posed dramatically for his re-enactment. "Now we ask ourselves, what is time? A line? A temporal distortion? Here now we see the Time Event, and as the fabric snags, the people within are scattered like so many grains of sand into the void. How now shall we pull them back to rejoin us in the present?"

He gestured with a flourish and bowed. His performance drew scattered applause and laughter from the group, and Simmons had stopped scowling. With everyone beginning to tuck into their food Briggs gauged it was time for a pep talk and a reset. It had been a hard day; first with a messy casualty found on the highway right at the top of the shift and then this latest guy causing drama.

"Okay team, let's take a half hour here to eat and repack. The weather's cleared up and we'll have about an hour more of daylight and then two more until we switch shifts so we just might find someone else out there who's less of a pain in the ass to end our day." Scattered agreement and an "amen" muttered from Simmons.

"Look, you guys are the elite, and we all know that the work we're doing is important so I'm not going to lecture you," she said between bites. "Just try to remember that we're stone-cold pros at this by now, but for every single one of these people returning from time, this is brand new information. They blinked, and their whole world disappeared – of course they're scared shitless and not very cooperative, and any explanation we give them is going to sound like total bullshit. Would you have believed it if it happened to you?"

"Hell no, ma'am," from Jonas, with fervor. Not even with a hint of sarcasm.

"Who says we believe it now?" came with a grunt and a grin from Martinez. He rarely said much but he was a calming presence on the team. Completely unflappable.

"I sure didn't believe it until I saw it with my own eyes," said Kryztak with a grin. She had been on the team for almost three years now, but the first time she had actually seen someone appear out of thin air in the field was two years in, and she had definitely been surprised. Willis and the whole base team still gave her grief for yelling "holy shit" into the field radio and would never let her live it down.

Harris, Yui and Simmons just nodded their agreement, and Briggs fixed Simmons with an extra look just to make sure they were on the same page. He barely nodded to show his understanding; that was the Simmons' version of an apology. He was a great soldier, but he needed to work on the compassionate part of the role for sure if he wanted to keep that unicorn status.

Duke, already finished with his own dinner, barked his agreement, and that loosened the tension once and for all as everyone smiled and relaxed and contributed a bite of their food to his dish. "For a service professional you sure are a greedy thing," Yui told him affectionately. For all his stolid demeanor, Yui was definitely an animal person, and Duke was more than just a search and rescue K9, he was also a certified comfort animal.

"*Even the frickin' dog has to be a unicorn,*" thought Briggs. She was proud of this team, and Simmons would come around, he just needed more coaching. And they could all do with a series of good saves instead of all these aggressive assholes they'd gotten lately. "All right Alphas," she said aloud. "The kiddos and pretty girls are out there waiting to be rescued. Let's go get 'em."

CHAPTER 13

Trevor – 5 years, 3 months, 14 days after the Event. Time populous: 268,740

"Hey, kid!"

Trevor looked at the man warily. He didn't have a windowless van or anything, but Trevor wasn't taking one step closer regardless. He had his baseball mitt and a bat, and he was pretty sure he could outrun this chubby man if necessary. He had sprouted six inches this year (on top of the four he'd grown the year before that) and he was getting to be pretty fast, even if he was still a little awkward while growing into his new, lanky self. This guy looked like he was trying too hard to look harmless, and that's never a good sign.

"Yeah?"

"You're one of them time travelers, right? From the city?"

"What's it to you?" With that, Trevor kept on walking towards the ball field, with the guy doggedly following, but at a distance. He wouldn't normally be so rude speaking to an adult, but he already knew where this was headed. This guy was probably some kind of reporter looking for a cheap sob story, or someone looking for a spokesperson for a product with some kind of time pun in the name, or just a salesperson trying to sell some scam saying they could get people out of the time stream or whatever. He's heard all these before. Every family with a connection to Toledo has heard these pitches a thousand times by now.

"Just wondering. I saw you in the public database."

"Uh-huh." He knows the database is necessary, but sometimes he feels like his whole life is on display for the world to see. Like he's a circus act for people to point and gawk at.

"So, like, did the government do experiments on you guys and stuff? Like trying to see if you were affected by the wormhole? *Are they still tracking you now?*"

Oh geez, this guy was the worst kind – some kind of conspiracy nut looking for answers. They popped up every so often, writing emails and letters, either trying to prove that the whole thing was a hoax or that there was some deep truth being hidden by the government or something. He might be a kid, but even he knew that was just ridiculous. If he had been experimented on by the government, it had been a pretty low-key experience. Other than make him eat some vegetables and clean himself up, the soldiers and scientists at Site Two had just asked him a lot of questions, and played board games with him for a few weeks until he'd been sent here to his foster family. Hardly some big conspiracy. If it was, it was the most boring conspiracy ever.

"That's classified." He was joking, but the guy instantly looked so horrified that he felt bad and said so.

"Oh."

"Look, I don't really know anything. There's really not much to tell – if you were caught in time, you just came out of it. Everyone else knows more about what happened while we were in it, ya know? To us it didn't feel like anything."

"Yeah… I was just curious. I've got a couple cousins that are stuck in there. I'm trying to figure out if there's anything I can do for them, while they're in there, or after they get back. Like if I need to find a lawyer or something."

"I don't know, man. I don't know who they'd sue though, Mother Nature? It's not like anyone knows where the wormhole came from."

The guy scowled at that and Trevor veered a little further away as he walked. "That's just what the government wants you to think. I'm pretty sure *they* opened it up somehow, probably doing some kind of experiment that went wrong. There's always someone to blame, things like this don't just *happen*."

Trevor almost asked what other "things like this" the man would lump in with a rip in the fabric of time, but decided it wasn't a good idea to encourage more conversation. He didn't look particularly threatening, but you never knew with strangers.

"Uh-huh. Well, good luck, I hope your cousins get back. I gotta go – my practice is about to start."

He jogged off quickly, diagonally across the park, hoping the guy wouldn't be persistent enough to follow any further, and he'd tell Coach to watch out for him once he got to practice. It was weird enough having telemarketers soliciting him as a time traveler, but he really didn't like being asked about it by strangers on the street. He was just starting high school and had been nervous about it, but no one had really pressed him for information at school. Probably because the kids from his junior high already knew he was a traveler, and he wasn't the only one in the school anyway. It wasn't all *that* unusual around here. Adults were the ones who made it weird... like this guy expecting a teenager to spill government secrets or have legal advice to give, or people looking at him with sympathy like he was some specimen in a museum. Other teenagers didn't really seem to care. He supposed they all had teenage problems of their own without the mystery of a temporal disruption to add to the mix, and that was fine with him.

Having foster brothers and a sister around his same age helped too. They had deflected any kids who tried to bother him too much or wanted to make stupid comments or tease him when he first arrived. He was still confused as to why some people thought the time stream was funny; sometimes there would be a sketch about it on a television show, or in a podcast, or a TikTok... he wasn't trying to be overly sensitive about it, and he wasn't crying about it or anything, he just didn't think it made a very good joke. But then again, Trevor's kind of serious for someone his age.

It's been five years since he left his old life behind, and his foster family is very nice but he's already thinking about what he'll do when it's time to make it on his own. Maybe it was those three months of living wild in Toledo that solidified it, but he's always been an independent sort, and not really interested in what's popular. Aside from the baseball team, almost all his hobbies are solo activities, and he can most often be found at the library immersed in a book.

Nowadays, everyone just scrolls e-books, but Trevor likes the quiet of the library, and he likes being surrounded by the books while he reads. Virtual libraries just aren't the same. And of course, psychologically, the Birmingham library was his home away from home during a pretty tumultuous time in his life, so no wonder it's become a core memory.

No, Trevor's not going to be pushing his story on TV for fame and fortune, or playing center field for the Yankees either for that matter. He's not looking to be a star. He's looking for a future where he can be part of the story, but not at the center of it, and he'll figure it out soon enough.

CHAPTER 14

Grant Hutchings – 5 years, 3 months, 14 days after the Event.
Time populous: 268,740

Grant scowled bitterly as he watched Trevor Martin run off towards the baseball field. He'd found the name and location easily enough in the database, and he'd been banking on getting more information out of a kid than he would from an adult, but apparently even children had been trained on how to be suspicious of questions and cover things up. Typical.

There was no way in hell something like time travel just happened spontaneously, he didn't give a damn what the so-called scientists were saying. It had to be an actual time machine. The whole thing reeked of a government cover up.

Whether it was something created by a private citizen that was now being hushed up by the feds, or something they had actively been working on themselves that had gone wrong, it was obviously something they would want to keep top secret and they would probably make up any lie to keep the truth from coming out. It seemed like a homegrown conspiracy; if it was a foreign government doing it to try to destabilize the United States, they would have chosen a more high-profile target, like Chicago or New York, where it would have caused more chaos. This was probably those crooks that were always trying to subvert freedom in our own house, those goddam politicians and their little minions. They were supposed to be protecting and serving this great nation. What a crock. They didn't care about people like Grant, who just wanted his rights left alone and not constantly under attack from people who wanted him to pay more taxes every year to help freeloaders looking for a handout. Probably this whole thing was some secret government branch trying to build some kind of machine to go back in time and change what they wanted in favor of the current crap administration, or some other selfish bullshit. He wasn't discounting for one moment that it wasn't some intentional creation they'd actually been working on for decades.

The real question was, was the Time Event something they had planned to happen now, or something that had happened off schedule? Probably an accident, and if so, it was a lucky one because they had been forced to show their hand. But if there was even a small chance that it had been planned, he needed to get ready; they all did. Because if the government could just press a button and make whole populations disappear, anyone who didn't agree with them on anything would be in danger. People like Grant could just *conveniently* be silenced whenever their voices got too loud.

In fact, now that he thought about it, this was even worse than he had originally thought – every time there were protestors, or lawsuits, or rallies of people they didn't like, they could just start making them all disappear. If there was a close election coming up, they could just start weeding out people who wouldn't vote the way they wanted, or even get rid of counties in every swing state to rig things to their advantage. They could rig any election and just remain in power forever! In fact, they could still do all those things right now, while pretending they were just as perplexed by the sudden influx of wormholes as everyone else. And those sheep out there would just accept it. People like him, who could see through their lies, needed to take action before whoever had control of the machine really gained momentum.

He needed to figure out what to do. He could gather stockpiles of arms, ammunition and supplies to outlast even a nuclear event, but all that prep wouldn't do a lick of good against a time machine. Whoever controlled it had a leg up on literally everyone else; reveal yourself as an enemy and apparently, they could just send you a thousand years away and shut you up for good. Who knows how many patriots like himself might end up banished to some other time, and probably locked up as madmen if they tried to warn others. But he had to try.

CHAPTER 15

Journal of Dr. Raj Anil, Senior Researcher – 7 years, 5 months, 1 day after the Event. Time populous: 263,612

October 16th

Today is a momentous day for me, and I hope you will indulge me a moment of self-congratulation. I officially defended my doctorate thesis and am now a PhD in the field of theoretical physics. It took me more years to complete than I originally had set my heart on, but with the amount of practical work I have been handling with Sadler in conjunction to the writing of my dissertation I think I can be forgiven for not being on the fast-track. Of course, the content of my paper is closely tied to theories around the time anomaly, so I have also had to revise it several times over the years as we have learned more and both rejected and put forth many new theories.

At present, we feel we have a more dependable roadmap of averages in terms of the number of returning travelers and estimate that if the rate of return remains consistent, we will be seeing spontaneous arrivals for probably another hundred years. There is, as of yet, no consistency in reentries in terms of physical location or their personal demographics (age, sex, race, etc.) or other measurable characteristics, but I can confirm that by averages, survivors follow the general makeup of the population of Toledo (median age of 34 and 37 for men and women respectively, etc.). For casualties, the demographics are slightly skewed because the majority come from people who were commuting at the time of the Event, so fewer minors and elderly people (who tended to be safely at home), and an elevated percentage of working-class citizens and minorities. But these statistics have nothing to do with the time stream itself.

I am still assigned to Site Two by name, but we long ago expanded our operations from the temporary facilities to more permanent headquarters erected a little further west and closer to the city. Luckily there is a certain amount of forest preserve and undeveloped land that was unpopulated and considered low risk to occupy, while the inner city and suburbs remain unstable. I have heard rumors that there is a plan to build a supernatant city that will float upon the lake and create a more permanent base outside the Time Zone's impact.

I can imagine it will be some time before that reality is achieved, but I remember years ago seeing a documentary about the airport built off the coast of Japan and I imagine much of the structure will be modeled the same way. As I recall, the whole island the airport sits on is man-made, and designed to be earthquake-proof thanks to huge pylons that can be adjusted to keep the ground stable, but not rigidly connected to the sea floor. It was truly a marvel of engineering when it was built, and I imagine the facility here, should they continue to pursue it, will be as well. We should have the funding to do so now that the assets of all non-returned citizens of Toledo have been consolidated by the government to continue funding for scientific research and rescue operations.

Technically, those still lost in time (the "time populous") are not considered to be deceased, although the statute of limitations for declaring missing persons as legally dead has long passed. In this special circumstance, the time travelers have been given a status of *ad intermin* ("in the meantime") that suspends their debts and legal obligations, but also seizes the liquid assets in their bank accounts ("temporarily", but for an indeterminate time) to be used for the good of the many. From what I understand, it's like a mandatory pooled savings account or 401K to generate interest that can be used for funding. I know this has been a controversial legislative move and I hear that specific laws are being drafted to ensure that upon return to the present there is some recourse for the survivors, but to be honest I have not personally delved into this complexity. I am definitely not a lawyer... but as of today, I can say that I am a doctor of letters. With this latest achievement I have been promoted to the head of my research team, the work of which I have been doing now for years but needed the accreditation of a doctorate to officially receive.

Although "time off" is a phrase we have all almost forgotten the meaning of here, I will be taking a brief respite for the weekend to meet my parents in nearby Cleveland to celebrate. I see them so rarely and they are growing old, and we miss each other very much, but all of us have accepted that the work being done here is too important for me to abandon my efforts even for an extended holiday. Over the years, Cleveland has become the easiest mid-way point for us to meet, though of course they are coming much closer to me than I to them in Boston.

As a teenager, adept at math and science and coming from a family of medical professionals and actuaries, I strove towards acceptance at MIT as if it were an end goal. When I reached it, I was almost consumed by a feeling of uncertainty when I realized it was actually just the beginning, and I recall as if it were yesterday how I felt overlooking the campus from the window of my freshman dormitory, having just seen my parents on their way, and feeling the exhilaration and trepidation of being on one's own for the first time. "Now what?" I wanted to shout... I realized I had never thought beyond the "getting there" part at all.

Looking back, I see now that my hard-won undergraduate and graduate work was all merely a stepping stone, and I suspect my doctorate will prove the same as I move into the next phase of my journey in life. Already I see that same pattern in my time here with Sadler; there is always another goal to reach for, another hurdle to overcome, as we work with breakneck speed... but towards an end goal that is undefined. Until

86

we know the parameters of the wormhole, the rip in our temporal plane may stretch out to eternity, and I may find myself shouting "Now what?" into the void for the remainder of my life.

My mother worries that I have committed too narrowly to the time project, and I think my parents would be happier if I moved to another field and just settled down and had a family, or at the very least tried to have all of these things at once. But I cannot bring myself to do so; I think both my work and my family would suffer from my split attention, and both things would be too important for me to treat them so unfairly. I am still young enough to change my mind, but I am old enough to know that I can most likely add more value to the world where I am. Sorry, mother.

I remain grateful for the many brilliant minds I have encountered on my path and look forward with clarity to the future. -RA-

CHAPTER 16

Tom Mitchell – 10 years, 1 month, 8 days after the Event. Time populous: 256,775

Tom had done a lot of hard work to curb his extreme anxiety over the years, but by the end of the day he felt as if he might fall to pieces at any moment. They had treated him for a severe panic attack, and presently he was huddled under a warm blanket with an IV drip and an oxygen mask in a quiet room where they had left him alone to get his bearings. The people working here were all being kind, and he appreciated that, but it also made him feel like he was being sullen and ungrateful, because in truth he was still very upset.

As far as he knew, he had been just getting home from work on a beautifully warm evening, and he was looking forward to having dinner with Rachael and then maybe taking a walk down to the riverfront to get some ice cream and see if there was any live music playing. A nice, relaxing evening for newlyweds who wanted cheap date nights before they had children to take up their time, but keeping their money saved for the eventuality. It was part of the reason they had stretched their budget to get a decent rental home so near the river; the walkways and squares were always filled with festivals and events in the warm months, and being within walking distance they were spared the hassle of parking and traffic.

He'd just put the car in the garage, grabbed the mail, and stepped in the front door. He had kicked off his shoes, and Rachael had waved and called to him from the back patio that she would be done in a minute. He caught just a glimpse of her through the sliding door as she set down a tray of plants for the garden, looking beautiful as always. And then, like something out of a horror movie, Rachael simply vanished. He had been looking directly at her when it happened and it was instantaneous. He was still standing in his own entryway, but it was instantly almost pitch black now, and freezing. His immediate irrational thought was that somehow, they were about to be hit by a meteor or something blocking out the sun, and he yelled out her name and stumbled right into the table by the door and practically broke his kneecap as he tripped and fell.

The next few moments were complete chaos to his mind, as in falling to the ground he dislodged about an inch of dust from the table above straight into his own face and effectively blinded himself. For a moment it was all pain and burning eyes and coughing, and when he had finally collected himself enough to see again through streaming tears, he half-crawled into the kitchen and could clearly see the full moon framed in the window. Feeling extremely foolish about the meteor thing, he croaked out Rachael's name and got nothing. His throat and eyes were still filled with dust and he washed his face in the sink before doing anything else.

The screen door was ripped, and he stepped through in his socks to the porch calling again for Rachael. He couldn't help limping and realized his pants were actually torn and his knee was bleeding badly from where he'd fallen. Feeling suddenly dizzy, he sat down on their porch swing to get his bearings, and only when he had collected himself sufficiently did it occur to him that there was frost on every surface, and the sky was getting brighter. It wasn't night at all, but just before dawn, with the full moon still in the sky. His hair and shirt were wet from the sink where he'd washed out his eyes, and he was cold now, and could feel water dripping slowly down his back and soaking his shirt.

At this point he may have lost consciousness briefly. He couldn't clearly remember how he got himself inside, but the next thing he knew he was frantically combing the house from top to bottom and hollering for Rachael. It wasn't a large place and he looked in every crevice twice (which even in his panic Tom realized was crazy; as if she would be hiding from him, crouched in a cupboard?). Eventually he stumbled back to the front door for his phone and realized he'd left it in the car. Outside, he stopped short; it looked like no one had cut their grass in about a year – the whole neighborhood looked like a mess, and he practically had to wade through it to get to the garage. There he found his backpack and his phone (dead). He could charge it here from the car, but the car wouldn't start. What the hell was going on?

He limped next door to see if he could borrow a phone... no answer. No answer, no answer, all down the block. Nothing but a few birds chirping in the silence. He was starting to feel like he was going crazy at this point, and the sun was fully up now making the foot-long, frosty grass glisten all around, and his still-irritated eyes could hardly stand the glare. He stumbled around aimlessly for what seemed like an eternity, calling out "help" at random intervals, feeling more and more pathetic as he did so. At the corner where the coffee shop was (the one that made the fancy lattes with the pictures in the foam that Rachael loved), he noticed a huge emblazoned poster taking up the whole shop window that made him pause.

"ATTENTION," it read in huge letters, with small variations in several languages below. "You are at the corner of Main and Maple. If you find yourself here alone, please come inside this building and use the landline phone that is on the counter to call 9-1-1. Do not leave this location. There are emergency supplies inside."

He looked around the square and saw other similar posters on various buildings; all were old and peeling slightly in the corners, but he was positive those hadn't been here last weekend when they had come for breakfast. But he was tired of mysteries already, and his knee hurt. Looking down at it in the sunlight there was really actually quite a lot of blood now and it had soaked his whole pants leg through down to his sock. He felt a little sick just looking at it; he had never liked the sight of blood. Pushing the sticking door open with some for force, he stumbled to the counter and found more instructions about calling and what to do if the phone was out of order, and some bottled water and packaged snacks next to the phone.

He pulled up a stool and sat down at the counter and actually put his head down even though there was more dust, because he was seeing little black stars now and he was pretty sure he was about to faint, or puke, or maybe both. He took a small sip of water to clear his head and then picked up the phone and dialed. The last thing he remembered was stammering his name and where he was to the dispatcher who answered, but then he really must have fainted because the next thing he knew he was being jostled around and there were people shouting instructions. He was strapped to a stretcher and it was loud and windy and that was the last thing he could recall for a while.

He awoke in a warm, well-lit room with a distinct hospital smell and with his leg still throbbing. It had been bandaged and elevated, and his glasses were next to him on the bedside table within his reach, along with his watch. His work backpack was on the floor so he guessed that he had been clutching it the whole time he had been wandering the neighborhood without even realizing it. His voice didn't seem to be working and he was just debating whether he could try and get out of bed when the door opened and a young doctor and an older nurse came in.

"Ah, awake now Mr. Mitchell! How are you feeling?" asked the nurse, smiling a quick, tight smile at him and adjusting his pillows efficiently. She patted his arm and didn't seem to actually expect a response, but immediately started taking complicated notes on the readings of the various machines next to his bed and ignored him. There seemed to be quite a few machines; too many for just a swollen knee. He felt the first prickle in the back of his hairline, the one he knew was the precursor to the hot feeling and the elevated breathing that his anxiety had used to bring him regularly. He hadn't had a full-blown anxiety attack in several years, but he automatically started his counting and breathing exercise and almost didn't process the doctor's opening introduction, he was concentrating so hard.

"Mr. Mitchell, my name is Dr. Xiang, and I'm here to give you some information about your situation, and to answer your questions. This is going to be a little confusing, but you're here in a safe place and you'll have the best of care, so I want you to just relax and try to listen, ok? Let me just confirm first that your name is Thomas Mitchell? Is it all right if I call you Thomas? Or is it Tom?"

Tom nodded. He didn't trust his voice right now not to quaver, but he tried to sit up and look alert so that the doctor would know he was paying attention.

"Thanks Tom. So, first off, you're here in a facility near Toledo, so you're still close to home and you're safe here with us. Don't try to talk too much just yet – I can see on your chart that you had some allergic reaction that we treated you for, and your eyes and throat are probably still a little sore. And that was quite a cut on your knee also, you needed twelve stitches, but no broken bones there. They're giving you something for the pain in that IV but let the nurses know if the pain starts to get worse." He made a quick check mark on his list and continued.

"Now, I know you're injured so you may still be a little disoriented, but you may remember something strange happening." Tom nodded vigorously at that and the doctor nodded back sympathetically.

"According to your driver's license we found you near where you live; is that where you were when it happened?"

This time he croaked out a "yes" in response and the doctor made a note on his tablet. "Good. Just try and remember what happened and give me a nod if this sounds like what you experienced. Did it seem to you like there was a moment when the world suddenly changed? Maybe it seems to suddenly be the wrong time of day, and a person or people around you seemed to vanish?"

"Yes. Rachael –", he almost choked on her name, and his whole scalp now was prickling hot and he could feel his heart pounding and the machine nearest to him started beeping. "What happened to her?"

"Try and breathe deep, Tom. As far as we can tell Rachael is okay, but what I'm going to tell you now is going to be upsetting so try to remain calm." Dr. Xiang looked at him carefully before proceeding. "What you experienced was something we have come to call the Time Event; an anomaly in time. What that means, in simple terms, is time travel. I know it sounds unbelievable, but you, along with many others, seem to have been pulled forward in time and it has been ten years, one month, and eight days since that moment you last remember things being normal."

"You're saying... what, that I've been asleep for ten years or something?" Tom had a sudden vision of himself with a long white beard, Rip Van Winkle style, which was stupid because for starters he was only 27, and anyway this doctor wasn't making any sense. How could it have been ten years?

"No, not asleep, and not a coma. To you, this happened instantly. You are still the same age you were and nothing changed about you. But to the rest of the world, more than ten years has passed." The doctor sat back a little and glanced at the nurse, who came around the bedside with a cup of water for Tom that he took almost automatically and didn't drink. Now that he looked more closely, he wasn't sure she was a nurse at all; she had on a lab coat but it was more like a scientist's gear than scrubs. Was this doctor even a doctor? Either way, this was the stupidest thing he had ever heard, but they looked so serious that he just couldn't think of anything to say and just opened and closed his mouth a few times lamely. His hand shook and he set the cup down.

"What about my wife? I want to talk to her."

"Mr. Mitchell, your wife, Rachael, isn't back yet. She is still lost in the time stream, like you were until today. We have no records that she has returned, but if she was at your residence with you at the time of the Event, we know where she will be. Someday."

"What do you mean 'someday'? You said that she was okay. What the hell are you talking about? I want to talk to her." He could feel his voice and his temperature rising, and it felt like two hot spots were moving up his cheeks to settle right behind his eyes. The machines behind him were beeping up a storm now, and a second nurse (a real one this time, in pink scrubs) came in with a tray and started fussing with his IV bag. He was really hyperventilating now, and seeing the black spots again. It had been years since he'd had an attack this big, not since high school actually. He lost track of things for a few moments after that but suddenly the tight band in his chest seemed to snap and he could breathe again. They had fitted him with an oxygen mask as well, and he could feel the fresh flow across his nose and mouth.

"There now, that's better, isn't it Mr. Mitchell?" The new nurse smiled down at him, plump and pretty, and seemed so understanding that he unexpectedly felt tears well up in his eyes. She reminded him of his mother and how seeing her looking down at him after an anxiety attack when he was a kid had always been what felt like it was really over. Maybe that was why he stopped having the panic attacks after she had died; he couldn't bear to have one without her around to make them be over. He took a shaky breath and nodded, and tried to uncurl from the tight ball he had made of himself in his bed. His knee was throbbing like a bass drum now.

Dr. Xiang was still there, hovering with what seemed like genuine concern. "Don't rush yourself, Tom. It's a lot to take in, and everyone has a hard time accepting it. Just relax and try to get comfortable again, did you jar your knee? What's your pain on the one-to-ten scale?"

"I'm okay, thanks. I just need to sit still for a minute." They stepped back and gave him his privacy while he took a few more deep breaths and watched the not-a-nurse taking more notes from his machines. He was quite sure now that she was some kind of scientist, or a fake one if this was all some kind of strange trick they were pulling on him. "What are you writing?"

"Not to worry," she said, this time with a real smile. "We monitor all the vitals for everyone who returns from the past just to make sure there are no ill effects, but the journey doesn't seem to affect people physically. You seem to be just fine overall. Though I don't imagine you feel that way with your knee so banged up."

"Well, to be fair I could have done that any time just by being clumsy. I'm not sure it was my 'journey'." He was being sarcastic there, but she didn't seem to notice.

"Maybe... but the shock of reentry from time is disorienting for a lot of people, and minor injuries from disorientation are common and nothing to be ashamed about. In any case, Dr. Xiang will tell you more now if you're ready."

Ready? No, he wasn't really ready to hear more sci-fi nonsense, but he could hardly get up and storm out with his leg like this, so he just nodded in acceptance, or perhaps defeat. He might as well hear everything they had to say, and then maybe he could go to sleep and when he woke up, he would find the whole thing had been a dream.

Rachael was the one who liked *Star Trek* and *Quantum Leap* and those types of shows; maybe he should have paid more attention after all, but he'd never been able to get into them. He liked shows like *Breaking Bad*, and *Yellowstone*, and *Snowfall*, and podcasts about true crime. She liked classic sci-fi, and BBC dramas, and quiz shows, lots of quiz shows. They both disliked horror films, and liked live music and comedy, though not always the same performers, so festivals were a better fit for them. It was one of the ways that they were actually perfect for each other, because they respected each other's tastes and had agreed that in general, TV and movies were things they would just enjoy separately without trying to force genres on each other. Even when they were first dating, they had both joked about the type of couples who morphed into a singular being with no separate interests. Now he felt like somehow, he was trapped in his least favorite type of plot line.

Dr. Xiang nodded to the nurse and the not-a-nurse, and they both left. The doctor resettled in his chair near the bed and pulled out a second tablet and a charger from his lab coat pocket.

"Listen Tom, I know what you're hearing from us sounds ridiculous, and it will take a while for you to process things. Definitely more than a couple of hours, and you've had a rough day. I'm going to leave you a tablet, which has some pre-programmed videos and FAQs that you can scroll through when you feel up to it, and tomorrow after you're rested, we'll answer any questions you have. I'm going to plug that in right here on your table to use when you want to, and I'll leave you a notebook and some pens in case you want to jot any questions down." He arranged everything neatly and brought over a spare blanket and extra water bottles as well.

"If you get hungry or need to use the facilities just press the call button here and someone will come and help you. Don't try to walk on that knee without help. Get some sleep, Mr. Mitchell, and we'll see you in the morning." And with that he went out and closed the door behind him.

Tom felt an immediate rush of relief to be alone again, followed by a sharp pang of panic to be alone again. He couldn't ever remember feeling this tired in his entire life, but nevertheless he reached for the tablet and began to scroll through the menu options. Probably the type of thing where you should start at the top and watch them all, but he skipped straight to one that said "6:32 PM, the day of the Time Event".

The video had a brief explanation that the footage came from various surveillance videos and CCTV recordings, and was unedited. There was no sound, and the clips simply showed people walking around, at the train station, at the park; and then suddenly disappearing from the screen and a few cars skidding off the road. The whole thing looked so fake. In fact, it looked like it came from a television show with a low budget, or a movie so old that the special effects didn't hold up. For some reason, the thought actually made him feel better because clearly this whole thing was just some kind of joke. If his knee didn't hurt so much, he would have been looking around for the hidden cameras long before this. But Rachael wouldn't have gone along with a practical joke like this; she thought practical jokes were mean and not funny to begin with and this one was definitely not funny at all.

But right now, he didn't think he had much more in the tank, whether this was a prank or not. He got himself under the warm blanket and got comfortable on his side so that he could watch the tablet while lying completely prone, and hit play on the first video up at the top of the list.

"...what is time? A line? A temporal distortion? In this 3D visual representation, the graph shows both time and space. The Time Event is represented at this point here. Before that point, time is represented as a line. Now imagine that this line contains everyone in Toledo, and each person is a grain of sand, all here in this time and place together. Suddenly, like a snag in fabric or the flick of a finger, the grains of sand are propelled forward in time, scattered into the void. How now shall we pull them back to rejoin us in the present? Alas, we cannot. And yet, despite their wide scatter pattern on this plane, which represents time, they all land on the same plane they departed, that represents space. Thus, though we have not yet discerned when all of the missing will be reunited with us in the present or future, we are confident that it will be here, where they call home."

He intended to watch at least the first few video clips, but fell asleep to the narrator's soothing voice almost immediately, and slept without dreams.

CHAPTER 17

Dr. Xiao Xiang, Clinical Psychologist – 10 years, 1 month, 8 days after the Event. Time populous: 256,775

"I'm pretty certain I fucked that up."

"No, you were fine! The first few are always the hardest. Really, it wasn't bad."

"Are you *sure*? I feel like I panicked and just rushed right through the whole speech as soon as you left the room. That guy must think I'm crazy."

They were in the staff lounge, doing an informal post-mortem on Dr. Xiang's first lead onboarding with a survivor, Mr. Thomas Mitchell. Rebecca Not-a-nurse had been there to discreetly observe in the room (although she'd really been taking the readings from the machines as well), and then from the camera view in their observatory room.

"Xiao, seriously stop worrying. You got through all the main points, and you left him in a good place, you saw that he started looking up videos right away instead of storming around trying to escape like some people do."

"Only because his leg is about to fall off."

"Ha! Well... that may be true, but it's not your fault he has a history of panic attacks, that's just bad luck on your first solo. Besides, even without that a lot of people take it worse. Don't sweat it."

"True. I remember seeing that video of Thompson's first time. That guy hit him in the head with the tablet."

"Yeah, I'm going to be using that one in my training talks for a long time. But really, you need to count today as a win."

"Ergh... I guess I just hyped it up in my head too much and got nervous. Thanks, Rebecca."

"Sure thing. Remember, you're just one out of a dozen people who are going to be coaching him through this, starting tomorrow. And since you're first up with him in the morning, you can smooth out any bumps. Okay, I've got to go finish that report. See you in the A.M., rookie!"

She grinned at him as she left the room. She was a good mentor, especially for someone like Xiao who tended to doubt himself. Rebecca had been at Sadler almost ten years before the Time Event unfolded, and she'd been training staff in general for at least a decade before that. She wasn't any more well-versed in time travel than anyone else had been, but she had the project management mindset needed to get technical researchers, doctors, scientists, and other staff up to speed on what to say, and the soft skill training needed on how to say it. All the smarts in the world didn't make a difference if you couldn't explain it to a layperson; and that's what the majority of the reentries were.

Xiao was one of those with the smarts, but needing some refinement in the people skills. He'd come highly recommended, fresh from the research lab at the University of Beijing, and he spoke all four of the most common languages spoken in the Toledo area (English, Spanish, Chinese, French-Canadian) fluently and with barely any accent, which was a highly commoditized skill with the counsellors' office. Culturally, he'd grown up partially in China and partially in San Francisco, but was struggling with "loosening up" in the Western mindset enough to speak to the survivors at a personal level, instead of sounding like the clinical psychologist he was. He would get all the practice he needed here in the field. Rebecca had a good feeling about him.

Meanwhile, Dr. Xiang doesn't have a good feeling about himself. He's all nerves right now. But he's also finding his groove, and making friends here. He's a likeable guy, and good at ping-pong and chess, which are favorite staff stress relief activities, and tomorrow he'll have a breakthrough with Tom over a game of gin rummy. In fact, he'll end up pioneering a whole new onboarding path of breaking news to people over chess, or cards, or their favorite type of game or puzzle; he'll correctly hypothesize that both the familiarity of the game and the mental engagement stimulating the brain make for optimal absorption of new information like time travel facts and figures. But all of that is down the line; at the moment, he pours himself another cup of coffee, and sits and frets about how maybe he really did fuck this one up after all.

CHAPTER 18

Trevor – 11 years, 1 month, 6 days after the Event.
Time populous: 254,396

Trevor's looking sharp in his dark gray interview suit and bright blue tie. It's not the most expensive brand, but it's well tailored and he's a handsome young man. At least, that's what his foster mom always says when she presents him with new clothes that she's altered for him. She's great at that kind of thing, and he's so tall and gangly almost everything needs alterations to fit him right. He's had jobs before this of course, but not the kind where you need a suit for the interview. He's been a waiter, a camp counsellor, a soccer referee, a gym receptionist, and in college he worked both in the science lab feeding and cleaning up after the test animals, and at the coffee bar on campus. This is something entirely different.

He celebrated his 21st birthday with a few close friends just a couple of weeks ago, but nothing big or fancy. He'd never met anyone else whose birthday was on the exact day of the Time Event, and every year all the tributes and 'in memoriam' speeches didn't make him want to celebrate anything. His birthday just made him think about the people who hadn't come back yet, and all they've missed. He also hasn't been back to Toledo since they had found him living feral at the museum and existing on junk food and novels.

He's back today – not inside the city itself of course, since that is still off limits, but at one of the Sites (not the one he'd been rescued to) to interview for a counselling position with the Sadler Group's outreach program. Being a survivor himself... although, he always felt strange saying that since he was one of the first ones back and barely even experienced any time distortion at all. It felt like cheating. And when people say "oh, how many days were you journeying? I was gone X many years" and he has to say "they estimate maybe a day or two", it sounds phony and then people always gush over how they've never met someone who got home so quick and how lucky he is and on and on. He can't be annoyed with them for being curious, but it's just like how as a very tall person he constantly has to hear about how tall he is, and oh my and do you play basketball and how's the weather up there and will you reach me that from the top shelf and wow how do you find pants... eventually it just gets old. But yes, being a survivor himself, he's hoping to contribute to the project by becoming a counsellor to people in similar situations. He's always felt like he was one of the lucky ones, and it seems like he should pay that forward in some way. Altruism aside, it's a stable job to have. Over the past 11 years since the Event there have been thousands of people who have returned and need support in many different ways.

From the practical perspective, there are the tactics of finding them a nearby place to settle down; helping them reconnect with any family and friends outside the area who by good fortune have returned (or by even better fortune, never left); guiding them through the mountains of paper-work needed to secure their return status to qualify for benefits; testing them for job proficiencies and finding them work and/or training that can help with rehabilitation. Counsellors with Sadler assisted with all of those things; as a case worker, they were assigned survivors and followed their files for functional support and regular check-ins.

For the support staff, the psychological impact of time travel was becoming more of a concern each year. Counsellors needed to not only help reentering citizens understand the situation enough to accept it, but became de facto therapists to them as they faced the many ways that the consequences of being a time traveler impacted their new lives. And the situation was always evolving; in the early years, the people returning felt

103

that the time they lost was almost inconsequential compared to the people they were missing. As time went on, and more people have returned, there is more grieving for those who didn't make the journey safely, but also a heightened anxiety around the amount of time lost. Looking ahead, the Sadler group is anticipating that this will become even more jarring in another decade, and another after that, and so on. So, counsellors are in high demand, with growing opportunities and competitive salaries.

At first, only trained therapists, psychoanalysts, and psychiatrists were fulfilling these types of roles, but there weren't enough to go around anyway, and over time it became apparent that survivors valued a friendly face and a friendly ear more than a clinical diagnosis. As one politician voting against continued funding for high-dollar personnel had famously (and controversially) put it, "the people are returning to a crazy situation, but *they're* not crazy, and they don't need crazy amounts of our money". Although the wording wasn't necessarily politically correct, a lot of people did agree with that sentiment.

Where the counsellor role stands today is less formal. More approachable. Sympathetic. Detail-oriented. Sensitive to cultural and socio-economic disparities. Patient. College degree required. Higher education preferred. Bilingual a plus.

When he was first brought to Site Two, as a scrawny malnourished kid, Trevor had been fascinated to see so many people after so much time spent completely alone. It was as if he had forgotten what noise and conversation and hubbub even felt like, and it was overwhelming. There had been soldiers everywhere, like something out of a movie, looking so sharp and in control. He'd watched them carefully and for a long time after he wondered if he could be like them someday. In fact, throughout his teen years the idea of eventually applying to become an Alpha, or a Beta, or even a Delta squad member was always at the back of his mind, but something about it just didn't feel right. He knew he didn't have the right mindset to join the science teams; he loved science as a class and he was good at math too, but Trevor liked people more than he liked data. He wanted to be involved with people's narratives, not just their stats.

His foster parents had always been supportive of him. He'd been sent to them after a couple of months at the site and he'd been really, really lucky to get to stay with one family this whole time and not get bounced around like some kids did. His foster brothers and sister were really welcoming, and it felt like he was a part of their family after only a little while. In his junior year, when he started researching joining the training program at Army, they had backed him completely as he started running and lifting weights in preparation. Joining the search and rescue teams was no cake walk of course; the recruiting materials made it very clear that the roles were physically and mentally exhausting. Successful Alphas, Betas, and Deltas all got military training and needed to be prepared to act as emergency responders at all times.

And then they showed survival statistics for reentries to make it clear this was difficult and grueling, and it suddenly hit him like a ton of bricks. What if he became an Alpha, and one of those casualties they found out in the field was his mom? Or DJ? Or his teacher, or one of his friends from school? What if he did all the training and got back to Toledo and he had to find all the people he'd been dreaming about saving and it was too late? It wasn't as though he'd never thought about losing them, but honestly, he'd thought of it in terms of 'what if they didn't return'… not in terms of 'what if they did, and it didn't matter'. The truth was, he didn't know exactly where anyone was when the incident happened; Mom and DJ had been out getting ice cream, and his friends could have been anywhere. What if they were all out on the road at the time? The survival rates weren't great for anyone who had been in a moving vehicle. And for the first time it really occurred to him that if that was the case there was literally nothing that he could do about it. Even if it didn't happen for fifty more years, their reentry could kill them whether he was there to welcome them or not.

He just couldn't face that, and the realization that Wormhole U wasn't in the cards for him after years of assumption about his future really threw teen Trevor into a spiral of shame, and then anger. It felt now as though his cowardice in not wanting to personally witness their deaths is what would kill everyone he cared about. He knew that didn't make sense but he still felt guilty, guilty, guilty. It was only when his stepmother had suggested he pursue the counsellors pre-training program instead, which many colleges had incorporated into their offerings, that he snapped out of it. It was technically still field work, and it was a necessary, challenging career that would benefit society and still give him a connection to his lost hometown. He remembered reading the pamphlets she had quietly brought him and feeling such relief. It was as if she had suddenly just brought all those people back from the dead, or at least spared him from having to face their deaths for a while longer. A reprieve.

After that, his natural curiosity and confidence returned. He got into the college program without issue, and found he actually loved the coursework. It was a truly interesting blend of science and people skills, and he got top grades from the start. He was a natural at the case studies and, as for people training to be educators, there were practical internships starting in his sophomore year. His classmates too were a blessing to him – it wasn't the type of program that attracted people looking for an easy major. Everyone there was interested in the wide variety of situations that the time flux had created, and interested in the science of time, and interested in helping people, and a few of them were even travelers like himself. No one training to be a counsellor found the over-sensationalized and mostly invented stories they ran on TV as "entertainment", and that type of exploitative behavior was universally panned by his new friends. They were required to watch some of the shows, and analyze the actual situations, and discuss in class how they, as counsellors, would help those people rather than manipulate them.

Trevor had been approached by those types of shows before, and when he was still a kid several producers had come knocking on his foster parents' door. He distinctly remembered his foster father (normally a laid back, humorous man) scowling and telling them to get the hell off his porch. "Barbara! Get my rifle!" he had shouted over his shoulder, and they had left very, very quickly. Then the family had all laughed until they cried, because there was no rifle to get and Dad certainly wouldn't have done anything with it if there was. Now that he was older, Trevor still occasionally got email offers from tabloid-type journalists looking for stories. All survivors got that kind of thing all the time; since their names were all public information it was just like any other type of direct marketing ploy or spam.

With his degree in the pre-counsellors' program (with top grades), and of course his personal connection to the Time Event, it's no wonder that Trevor got a call to interview immediately after graduation, and at one of the prime locations too. All of the Sites have counselling programs, situated near large metropolitan centers around Toledo to accommodate the people who have been relocated and their regular check-in meetings. But those are satellite offices, just connected to the Sites by name to keep the paperwork orderly. Sadler's main office is still located off the lakeshore, and the plans to build a floating city on the lake were just officially announced. This is where the counsellor's headquarters will be located after the facility is built, and the excitement around it is high. If he's lucky, he might get to work in the fanciest of high-tech facilities in the world someday soon.

He arrived a little early today so he's been waiting now for a while, trying to not reveal his nerves to the receptionist at the front desk. He took his time filling out the paperwork (basically the exact same info in hard copy that he had submitted online – welcome to the world of bureaucracy, Trevor) just to have something to do. "I don't want to look too eager," he worried to himself. "But if you're not eager enough, they'll think you don't really care and they won't hire you." That's when he noticed the motto emblazoned on the lobby wall.

"We are all migrants through time."- Mohsin Hamid

Like magic, the nerves disappeared; the people who come to work here are helpers. This is right up Trevor's alley. He's got this in the bag.

CHAPTER 19

Captain Briggs, Alpha Team Four – 13 years, 6 months, 10 days after the Event. Time populous: 248,140

"Up about ten more feet and hold," Martinez confirmed. He was perched on the roof across the street using a surveyor's optical level and a scope, relaying instructions to the team below. The Deltas had brought in the new equipment and the materials, and the Alphas were running point from the high ground. So far, they had had no incidents with reentries in their work zones and they were placing the last of the ten experimental weather barriers being piloted in high traffic outdoor areas. It had taken all week to get them all in place, but their timing was perfect because there was bad weather in the forecast for tonight so testing conditions would be textbook.

Briggs had high hopes for this latest test model. After several years of injuries and even deaths from weather in a reentry zone (a well-placed piece of hail, or even a large amount of rain entering the blood stream of a reentering person could easily kill them), Captain Holmes and his specialty inventors' squad had come up with a better solution, and about time. It seemed so unfair to survive the wormhole and then die from a little precipitation.

"Put this one in the 'so simple it's brilliant' category," she thought as she watched them adjust the final pole and start hoisting the sail. The whole thing was basically a giant umbrella. But it had taken a few years for Holmes and team to develop a fabric that was light enough to be manufactured at that size, and durable enough to withstand the elements; early attempts were too flimsy and just blew the rain in gusts. Once the fabric was developed, the problem became how to frame the canopies so that the wind didn't merely tear them loose (one early experiment almost became an impromptu hang-gliding experience for the unlucky tech trying to get it rigged); but finally, the weather shields were ready for field testing. The premise was essentially a large tent erected between rooftops to defer rain and snow to the side, letting it run harmlessly down special gutters that ran straight into the sewer systems. Some precipitation might still get through, but every bit kept out improved the safety rating significantly. Obviously, they couldn't blanket the entire city with them, but at least in high traffic outdoor areas like this one right by the main entrance of a major public transportation hub, they were giving the survivors a better chance for safe reentry.

"Cap! Can we camp rooftop there?" Simmons was pointing to the higher corner building with the water tank. "I think we'll be able to get cameras on three locations from there, and the forecast still says rain."

Part of the pilot was to get some footage of the test sites in situ, with video from above and below, but it hadn't rained more than a drizzle since they put up the first one earlier in the week. This was a good night for a test, if the weather cooperated, and Simmons was right – the corner building would give them the right long-range footage of multiple sites. She gave him the thumbs up and he and Jonas started pulleying up the supplies.

She'd put them up top with the video and radar, and the rest of the team could camp out on the ground level of the Northside building. It had been under renovation when the time ripple had occurred, and had been confirmed as unoccupied, so they could spread out without worrying about a reentry coming in right on top of them. They'd be a lot more comfortable than Simmons and Jonas up on the roof in a thunderstorm, but someone

110

had to do it, and she'd probably take the first shift herself under the barrier to take measurements on how much got through during the storm. It was days like this she missed having Harris running point, but he had command of his own team now and was doing a bang-up job from what she'd heard.

She wouldn't put Yui out in the storm (although of course if she asked, he'd just leave Sheila inside and take a shift; but K9s get antsy during high weather and Sheila was still only two years old and in training, so it wasn't worth risking any setbacks), so Kryztak and the newbie Private Greene could switch off with her on the ground. If the barrier worked, they shouldn't be too uncomfortable.

"Greene!", she hollered.

"Yo!" His response came from somewhere below her feet. Leaning over the rail, she saw him looking up at her from the fire escape two stories down. "Finish putting up those cameras in the corners and check 'em, will ya? I want to test them all before dark and then we'll test again after we switch to night mode."

"You got it, Cap!" He was a good kid, full of energy, and fresh out of the training program at the Army branch of Wormhole U. They'd had some strong recruits from there over the years, and if Martinez really did decide to switch over from field work to training duty in a couple of years, she was hoping he'd get a role as an instructor there. He'd been favoring his right shoulder a lot more the past six months, and though he never complained she could tell it was starting to bother him. Not that she was a spring chicken herself these days. Someday they'd all be old and gray and training bright-eyed, bouncy-tailed recruits from a classroom simulator, and meanwhile people would still be popping up from the past left and right with the same confusion and difficult path ahead of them. They'd still be arriving long after she was in her grave, probably.

Speak of the devil; the radio suddenly crackled to life. "ALPHA TEAM FOUR RESPOND. REENTRY ALERT AT 5TH AND WESTERN. PROXIMITY ALERT TRIGGERED. OVER."

"That's just two blocks away. On it, boss," called Simmons. He and Jonas were already disappearing from sight down the stairs. Within minutes the whole team was assembled at street level and moving out. Sure enough, they found their time traveler still standing next to the emergency call station, looking completely confused but not visibly injured.

The newer call stations were much better than trying to rely on landline phones. Completely photovoltaic, the solar panels, battery, and componentry ran independent of a grid, making them an easy setup almost anywhere in the city. They were quick to erect or dismantle, and could be attached to existing streetlights and telephone poles, so they weren't adding matter to spaces where reentries could occur. Adding a simple button to push and some audio instructions for use, they had set up thousands throughout the city and suburbs. For a time, lithium for the batteries was in short supply, but through some cooperative manufacturing efforts overseas and some creative materials substitutions, the problem had been resolved. In public areas like parks, these devices were now the most common ways for the Alphas to receive alerts.

"Hi, sir! How are you doing?" Kryztak called out with a friendly wave. Their survivor had instinctively backed up against the wall when he saw them coming; they'd learned long ago that the sight of their team in their tactical gear could be alarming, so they tried to make the initial contact friendly and casual. This poor guy was clutching his gym bag like it was the last lifeboat on the Titanic.

"I'm Jennifer. What's your name?"

"Howard Feeney. Who are you people? What happened here?" He sat down abruptly on the ground and Jonas moved in swiftly with the med kit.

"Whoa, buddy! Take it easy, we're here to help. Let me just take your pulse real quick, ok Howard?" Jonas was an old pro at the soothing voice and quick hands thing by now. Technically they were all trained as medics, but Jonas had a real knack for the bedside manner. A few months ago, Briggs would have said Yui was the least experienced on her team, since K9 handlers tended to specialize more in tracking than the medical side of Alpha training. But he'd surprised her when he'd performed an emergency tracheotomy in seconds; calmly and by the books, and barely batted an eyelash. The child in question had returned from the time stream mid-bite of a hot dog and had gotten an unchewed chunk straight down her throat in the shuffle. Luckily, she set off a motion detector in the reentry process and the team was close by; she was already blue by the time they arrived and Yui worked his magic. Actually, now that Briggs thought about it, she herself was probably the least experienced medic on the team nowadays since she'd been in a command role so long that she rarely had a call to execute a procedure on her own. You just have to be grateful if you live long enough to see yourself become obsolete – that was what her first commander had told her. She was really starting to get old if she was identifying with that old fossil's pearls of wisdom.

"Hey man, you're okay. Take some deep breaths for me, alright? Get that blood pressure down. Can you tell me what happened?" Jonas was still taking vitals, and she could hear Simmons already calling in the Beta team for transport. This guy would be all right, he was just shaken up. Official policy was still to keep the reentering Toledoans calm, but not get into debates in the field. The doctors and counsellors at the Sites would get into the explanations of the time anomaly once they were safely out of the city limits.

113

"I don't know." Howard still looked panicky. "I was just leaving the gym and I got in my car parked over on 5th and I think I fell asleep or something? But then all of sudden I was just sitting on my ass in the middle of the street."

Briggs sighed internally. She knew the decision had been made very early on for the Delta teams to completely clear the streets of parked vehicles for a reason; the argument at the time had been that if the vehicle wasn't moving anyway, people returning from time would just reappear in a harmless empty space, and in theory it would make it easier for search and rescue to possibly have more room to maneuver. What hadn't been realized at the time was that it exposed returning travelers to more weather (hence the giant umbrella pilot), and it also disoriented the hell out of people like Howard. What was done was done though; putting the cars back in place would have been impossible. One positive thing, at least, was that the Delta squads had documented the location of each car, along with VIN numbers, before removal, so they did at least have records of where their owners might possibly reemerge, or go looking for their ride when they appeared.

"Yes, that's odd," said Kryztak soothingly. "But you're not hurt, Howard, that's the important thing. Was anyone with you in the car?"

"No."

"Anyone you know with you at the gym?"

"No... just regulars I see there sometimes, but I don't really know their names. I usually have my headphones and don't really chat with people."

"All right, that's fine. Listen Howard, it's supposed to thunderstorm in a little while, so we're going to have some folks give you a ride to somewhere safe, ok? And they'll check you out to make sure you're all right and they'll answer your questions." Kryztak was adept at nudging them to the handoff point with the Beta teams smoothly.

A medicycle had just pulled up; Briggs guessed that with the storm coming and no visible injuries they hadn't wanted to send anyone by air. The medicycles were a specialized design that had been engineered just for use in the Time Zone; they were technically still vans, not motorcycles as the name implied. They had a very narrow single-driver cab up front with a swivel connection to get around tight corners, and the back was thinner than a regular ambulance, but with the same functionality. The idea was to have an emergency response vehicle with a smaller body, which could move anywhere in the city easily. They were used more for transporting survivors and not severe trauma patients, but were very handy and speedy for simple transfers.

They saw him safely into the back and had barely turned around when the radio squawked to life again with another proximity alert a mile south. It was really unusual to have two reentries so close to each other (both in distance and time) and the team gave each other a quick look of surprise.

"Fuck me! It never rains but it pours," declared Simmons, looking up at the cloudy sky with some apprehension. "Let's go check it out before the real party gets started. Briggs, do you want me to have the Delta team stick around in case we're not back to start recording that pilot data?"

She glanced up at the clouds herself. "Yeah, better do that. Good thinking Simmons. At this rate we might get lucky with a third or fourth return right in the test zones tonight. Go back to the last site and give the Delta team your instructions, and log in the details for that Howard guy. Meet us at the secondary location. We'll head that way now. Move out, guys. On the double."

They fell into their standard single file line, with Yui and Sheila leading the way. Their destination was near the riverfront. If she recalled correctly there was a big gazebo in the square that they had rigged with spot lighting to encourage reappearing citizens to gravitate towards it. After more than a decade of this work they'd been over every stretch of their territory so many times over they almost didn't need their maps anymore. Almost. Certainly, they all remembered the specific locations of really memorable rescues, and a few horrible misses too, like the poor bastard who'd come back on the operating table with the heart destined for his transplant wasted years ago in the past – there was nothing at all they could have done for him even if they'd arrived in time. Maybe it made her a chickenshit, but she was glad they had arrived after he'd already expired… it would have only been a few moments and he was sedated, but as horrible as it was to come across later, it would have been harder to witness his last moments in person while they were completely helpless. Luckily, most of their territory was more residential in nature and their maps were just a reference guide, but she still kept her laminated copy in her pocket at all times. It was standard procedure to carry it, but also more convenient for a quick check than pulling out a digital handheld to check by satellite.

They were taking a major thoroughfare as the most direct route to the alert. They'd seen some bad casualties on this stretch since traffic had been going at high speeds when the Time Event occurred, but they'd also put in some experimental cushioning in this area about a year ago when the new funding had rolled over for the year. It was another pilot, which so far didn't have any recorded reentries to validate the testing, but the labs had done simulations and thought it should work. They were passing the test section now, actually; the premise was a thick spray foam that went directly on the road's surface, which swelled and dried as a semi-firm polyurethane coating about six inches thick. The formula was porous, not easily degradable, and softer by far than bare concrete. In theory, a person returning from the time stream at high speeds might still be injured severely falling onto this coating, but it might increase their chance of survival as long as they didn't hit their head. They had laid the coating in a one-mile stretch on the road itself, leaving the shoulder clear for themselves and medicycles to get through. The cost of the special foam was too high to cover the entire city's roads, but a few key areas might benefit if the tests proved successful.

The last several years there had been a boom in new tech to try; funds had really expanded after the personal property of those still missing in time had been pooled to fund their rescue efforts. She had read recently that new inheritance laws were also being drafted and were a controversial topic out in the wide world, but being in an Alpha squad didn't leave much time for the outside news these days.

"I see movement, Briggs. She's flagging us down." A teenager with bright pink hair and matching sneakers was waving both arms at them from the steps of the square. She wasn't hard to miss.

"I see 'er. Greene, hop on the comms real quick and tell them to stay put. There's a speaker right on their six, you should be able to broadcast." Briggs gestured to Martinez to get out the rappelling gear, and he grinned at her briefly – it would be a lot faster just to lower themselves down from the overpass here than to jog another half mile down that long, winding exit ramp ahead. They didn't need more exercise, they got that in spades. Plus, they all liked to rappel when they got the chance.

You had to have a little fun in life.

CHAPTER 20

Traveler Onboarding – 14 years, 1 months, 10 days after the Event. Time populous: 246,200

Section 3: Setting alerts

This section covers how to set alerts for specific names as related to reentry status, common connections, and general news. The alert system will notify you when certain public information is published.

The Sadler alert system is a change detection and notification service that allows you to set up notifications to receive information. Setting up and editing these alerts is easy, and to get started, all you need is access to the public database from an internet connection and a valid email, phone, or other account at which to receive alerts.

1. From your computer or mobile device, go to Sadler Research/ alerts and create your account.
   a. You will be sent a one-time verification code.
2. Go to "Create Alert" and enter one or more names you wish to receive alerts on (up to 20 per request. Additional names can be flagged in subsequent requests).
   a. If you do not see the name you wish to set the alert for, you can open a Help Ticket to request more information, or check our database of residents.
   b. If you do not see the names you wish to set the alert for, and you believe the person was in the Toledo area during the Time Event but is not a permanent resident, please log their information here and an inquiry will be generated.

c. Nicknames, use names, and aliases may be added to full legal name for reference here.

d. If you have a social security number, driver's license number, or other legal identifier besides legal name, you can look the person up and set an alert using this information by entering it here.

3. Once you have entered up to 20 names, Sadler allows you to customize your alerts (per name, or for all names entered within the request).

- Click "Show Options" and choose customized alert features by pressing the up and down arrows:

- Alert frequency: Choose to receive an alert as it happens, once a day, or once a week.

- Language: Select a language in which to receive notifications.

- Delivery method: Select which account will receive your alerts. You may cc additional accounts to receive your alerts.

- Location: Receive notifications from all regions of the city, or choose a specific town, street, company name (specify current employees or past and present employees), school, or church that you associate with the person you wish to set an alert for.

- Degree: Flag specific names as close friends and relatives to prioritize alerts, and to identify yourself (optional) to others seeking proximity connections.

- Proximity connection: You can choose to receive alerts for close relatives and friends of people you have created alerts for.

4. Click "Create Alert" when you are finished.

5. Edits can be made to your existing alerts at any time by clicking "Edit Options".

6. You may create additional alerts (up to 20 names per request) as needed. There is no limit to the numbers of names you can request overall.

The Sadler alert system is designed to share information on people who have returned from the time stream, including their survival status, reemergence date, and connections. Certain personal data and private medical information will not be distributed through the public forum, but can be requested by family members upon proof of relationship that can be submitted here.

Information received through the alert system may be upsetting to viewers, including reports of death or injury. By signing up for alerts, you are agreeing to our general release terms that absolve Sadler and affiliates from liability for injuries caused from shock or surprise stemming from alerts and the information contained within.

Help us make our database more complete; if you have additional details that you can provide, please fill click "Supplemental Information" in the main menu and follow the prompts to add information or upload files.

CHAPTER 21

Dr. Raj Anil, Assistant Director – 14 years, 11 months, 3 days after the Event. Time populous: 243,907

April 18th

Today's big event went as smoothly as I could have ever hoped for. The official unveiling of our long-awaited floating city went off without a hitch, after so many years of planning. It seems like only yesterday that we had our "groundbreaking" ceremony on the shore, and yet simultaneously that feels like decades ago. I remember my mentor Dr. Lansing posing for the press photos that bright, sunny day, and heartily wish he had lived to see his vision come to fruition. But alas, his heart was not as strong as his mind, or his deep devotion to Sadler and the project.

I had the honor of leading one of the first tour groups for the grand opening. We were fortunate to have perfect weather, so from the starting point, where I met my group on the shore and guided them by shuttle to Lake City's main lobby, the whole experience was portrayed in its best light.

Not to complain, but I find the small shuttles a little claustrophobic. They only hold a dozen people maximum and it's less than a mile out into the body of the lake to travel, and yet I find their softly buoyant undulations slightly nauseating. The entire island is controlled by remote sensors that adjust to the lake's conditions, so the waves lap on the "shores" just like a real beach. Luckily the city itself has no discernible motion once you are on "land".

Lake City is over two full miles across, and was constructed in the westernmost part of Lake Erie, and intentionally positioned so that it would cross the "border" that technically divides Michigan and Ohio within the lake. This was to ensure that both states would have resources like the Coast Guard available and accessible to the floating island. Although not close enough to the Canadian border for emergency services, shipments of supplies are transported by rail and then through various U.S. and Canadian ports off the Great Lakes directly to the Toledo area.

The ports for supplies are on the north and west sides of the island. The east side dock is where the Beta teams bring newly found reentries for their welcome and onboarding. The south side dock is the shortest distance from shore with the shuttle tracks, and it is for daily visitors like my VIP group, employees, and survivors coming in to meet with their counsellors and for the standard physical check. So far, we have not discerned any lasting health impact from having been in the wormhole itself, but the collection of that data is still important to have.

My VIP group was comprised of a few local politicians, bigwigs from three non-profit agencies that contribute to our funding, recruiters from several universities looking to expand their pre-counsellors' curriculum, and a reporter and videographer from a national agency. Those last two had special permission to get some spoken blurbs from me and a few other staff members after the tour. Their main production team was here on site yesterday getting some B-roll footage of the facility, and some footage of the technicians who operate the buoyancy and oscillation equipment. I hear they have been working on a scientific documentary of the designing and building of Lake City, and that the footage they are taking now will be the finale. I am excited to see it when it is complete; we are so busy that entertainment is scarce, but it will be fascinating to see it from an outsider's perspective since we're all so close to the project.

The science may be a little dense for the average viewer, but the amount of engineering it took to develop all this is pretty impressive in and of itself. Although we still have facilities on shore, those are mostly used for the housing and storing of equipment for the Alpha, Beta, and Delta squads. As time has gone on, we have also needed more space to move things out of the city limits, although in fact much of the metal and other materials used to build this island was recycled from there. Just having this workspace so close and accessible is a real convenience, and the fact that it sits on man-made land that didn't exist before means it is one less thing we are "hogging" with our project. Although all the neighboring cities have been supportive ever since the time anomaly, there is only so much influx they can take, and there is some growing resentment regarding how much space and how many resources we have diverted over the years. This unique setup gives us more autonomy over our work, with less impact to the surrounding towns.

The main facility that the island houses is 3.5 million square feet of combined research laboratory, emergency medical facility, and rehabilitation center for newly discovered reentries. Going forward, time travelers that are found with reentry injuries will be treated in the field and transported here for long term care; but even those who return from time unscathed will spend between six to twelve weeks here receiving guidance and support from our counsellors and medical staff.

Many people have a hard time understanding what has happened to them so we have grief counsellors and therapists, but also teachers and scientists that try to make it comprehensible for different age groups, with varying levels of education and different cultural viewpoints on science. The program we have developed has been successful as a whole, so this new state-of-the-art facility should enhance that further. We find that once people can grasp what has happened (i.e., that time travel is real; no, this is not a joke; no, we cannot send them back), it is easier for them to think ahead. Many find comfort in learning to use our search databases to look for status updates on their friends and family, and to set up alerts for people not yet returned. The more the years go by and the more people that have returned, it is more likely for them to find connections who are in the present, who will be able to visit them until they are ready to be relocated. Unfortunately, it is also more likely for them to find people they know have died, or to find more shocking age gaps with those who returned earlier.

All of this and more was explained to the tour group, as I led them through the facility and showed the ways the design of the building is meant to help the time travelers. For example, there is a whole library with classroom settings for those who might wish for a more robust scientific explanation – charts, 3D modeling of time theories, scientific readings dating back over a century, and more will all be accessible to anyone, and our experienced staff will be available to review the material with those who wish to delve deeper into the science (though even the researchers have no real explanations for the origin of the wormhole yet). Other parts of the facility have areas for exercise, games, therapeutic activities, and even sensory deprivation equipment for those who may need a distraction or a place to think privately. But we will continue to encourage group counselling and activities. Many reentries find that talking through their personal stories is the most helpful step to acceptance of the time fluctuation.

The new counsellors' offices are modern, comfortable, and have friendly décor to encourage people to relax and express their emotions freely. The private rooms where the travelers will sleep are similar to luxury hotel rooms which are full of amenities. Senior counsellors, scientists, doctors, and other staff who choose to live at the facility rather than commute from the mainland also have quarters here, and I am one of those.

Even the lighting throughout the facility was designed with optimal lux and color conditions to encourage regular sleep patterns for health. All of this is designed to encourage those returning from time to face their situation with a positive outlook.

The medical portion of the facility is also up-to-the-minute in technology, with emergency and health equipment to handle everything that a major hospital can. We are very careful internally to only consider those with medical injuries as "patients"; we do not want to refer to those returning from time that way as a whole, since there is nothing physically or mentally wrong with the majority of them and we do not want them to feel that there is. Mostly we call them travelers, or survivors, or even "time refugees", and there is enough room at this huge facility to house many of them while they make the adjustment to their new lives. Moving walkways and small shuttles are placed throughout the huge facility to help those with mobility issues, and to quickly transport people between sections as needed.

The main building is mostly comprised of a single story, with a large atrium in the center for recreation and relaxation. The low, spread design is intended to minimize any structural issues from rough waters on the lake. Although of course not as volatile as an ocean, Lake Erie does see occasional swells, which will be mitigated by the adjustable pylons that connect the island to the lake floor. None of the buildings in Lake City are more than three stories high.

I had practiced many times reciting all of these facts and figures in preparation to leading this tour, and yet I still found it exciting to describe. We have created Q&A videos that have much of the same information to show future visitors, but these are the first people from outside Sadler to hear it all in such detail. We began in the main lobby for a ceremonial ribbon cutting and some press photography, and even that was more fun than I had expected it to be.

By the end of the day, I was quite exhausted, and now that my duties as host are complete, I have settled down in my new quarters to enjoy my tea and relax. I moved into the staff section of the facility about two weeks ago, and I have a pleasant eastern-facing view looking over the lake. I can just see part of the dock to the far right from my window, and one of the gardens that is designated as "staff only" is a short walk down the pathway. I anticipate many mornings having my breakfast there in comfort. Only staff quarters have exterior doors; although of course the time travelers are not kept here against their will, for safety reasons they are asked to visit the atrium for fresh air instead of the exterior of the island. The atrium is very large – over 50,000 square feet of garden space with a wide variety of fully-grown trees, vegetation and even a small river. Dotted with benches, gazebos and pleasant grassy knolls, it will be easy for those who want privacy to have it, and for others to meet with friends both old and new.

Tomorrow and the day after are also designated for tours and then the rest of the week will be dedicated to final staff training and review of emergency procedures. And then the week after, the first Toledoans will begin settling here (both those recently found that are still receiving rehabilitation services and anyone who reappears after we are "open for business").

I hope that once things are running smoothly, we will get permission for civilian tours and guests. I would love for my parents to come and see what we have built (though my mother gets very seasick and will hate the shuttle in from the mainland even more than I do). Until then, I have sent them many photographs (with strict instructions not to share them on social media or even with friends until after our grand opening is complete) and they are very excited to hear how the tour goes. I will call them in the morning; for now, I can barely keep my eyes open. -RA-

CHAPTER 22

Grant Hutchings – 15 years, 3 months, 10 days after the Event. Time populous: 240,817

Lake City was going to be their "in". It would take a few more years for Grant and his friends to get the right people in the right roles before they could make their move, but it was doable. The city of Toledo itself was too locked down to infiltrate right now... his surveillance team had confirmed that there was tech and Alpha teams all over the place, so the idea of just searching for clues in the city was too risky. And it was unlikely the time machine itself was even still there – most likely the government had moved it the moment their secret had come out fifteen years ago. But if they could identify where it had been deployed, or who had invented it, or by luck even get access to the notes on how it had been done, then they would be in business. And that information was probably in that floating city the government had built using his tax dollars.

They'd built the whole thing suspiciously fast, too. The average person was too stupid and gullible to see the truth... they were too busy mooning over the marvelous city and its fancy technology that they were pretending was brand new, but had probably been cooked up in some government lab ages ago and just kept from the public so they could dole it out as they wished instead of sharing it with the world. Selfish pricks.

Grant had been careful not to raise any red flags for the past decade, and had operated completely under the radar. And he had been busy. At first, he'd just kept watch from afar on his own, gathering as much information as he could about the Time Event, and keeping a close eye on people who had reemerged for clues. But he didn't trust any of their fake stories, and it was clear from the television programs that they were just trying to gain sympathy from the masses. People would fall for anything melodramatic. What he needed was real, first-person testimony from someone he actually trusted.

Then, after years of watching and waiting, his cousin Steve had come back. As Grant had feared, they'd wiped his memory. It made his blood boil to watch them pretending to do their "counseling" – treating Steve like some helpless little bitch, and trying to convince him that they were there to help. What a joke – they'd taken all his money, his truck, his house, and given him nothing but excuses and some measly monthly handout like some poor welfare piece of shit. But he'd held his tongue, and together he and Steve had started talking to other, like-minded individuals who could see through the hoax.

They kept off the internet as much as possible. There were some conspiracy groups out there that had the right idea, but were dumb enough to blast their opinions out there for everyone to see, and there was absolutely no question those fools were all on some government list somewhere from day one. Grant tried to make everything word of mouth as much as he could. Now, several years into their real efforts, they had a strong group assembled (31 members so far), and although they had expert hackers on the team, they weren't going to waste them on something stupid like a chat group.

Grant and Steve were still waiting on their other cousin Carey to return, and many of their other members had relatives who were still missing too. Until they knew for sure whether it would put their families in danger, they'd keep themselves underground and well hidden, but they were prepping all the time so that they would be ready when the time came to strike. They had some ex-military members with connections, so in terms of equipment and weaponry they were making progress. The hard part was getting in the right position to act. Once they had that time machine in their possession, they could demand just about anything and the government would give it to them. It was too dangerous, and too valuable for them to be ignored if they controlled it... and even if they never even turned the damn thing on again, the threat of doing so, or maybe even just threatening to destroy it, would give them all the leverage they would ever need. And then they could call the shots to get to the bottom of this whole charade. If by some chance they could save the citizens of Toledo and restore the city to its former glory, they would be heroes... and if Toledo was lost forever, at least they could make sure that it would never happen again while they rebuilt the country the right way.

The plan had been for a few select members of their team to get positions at the new Lake City facility and then lay low for a few years. Infiltration was key; if they picked up actual secrets on site that they could feed to the outside, that would be the best and most undetectable way to get information. But if that didn't start to happen naturally, eventually one of them had to get enough clearance to get deeper access to the real information they wanted – where was the machine, who had invented it, what the long-term plan was, what experiments were being done on those who had returned and whether those who didn't "survive reentry" were just being shut up. All that information lived in that facility. They just needed to be patient.

CHAPTER 23

News headlines –
20 years after the Event.
Time populous: 230,749

'It seems like just yesterday': U.S. marks the 20th anniversary of the time distortion

Anniversary events mark solemn moment that upended America 20 years ago

Photos: remembering those we lost to the time stream

'He returned home a different man': a survivor's story

Benefits program for surviving orphans is flush with funding

World leaders pay tribute to the victims and survivors of the time incident by the Associated Press

NEW YORK CITY, NEW YORK USA – Americans remembered the fateful May 15th event in Toledo with tributes to those still missing in time, the survivors, and the ones who lost their lives upon reentry from the time stream. The New York Stock Exchange was closed to commemorate the event.

In Cleveland, citizens and dignitaries gathered for the unveiling of a new record-keeping tool that will provide continuous digital updates to the public on those who have been confirmed as returned. A ceremonial ribbon-cutting was attended by survivors, families, and friends, with speeches and remembrances from several well-known survivors who have publicly shared their stories.

"It has been two decades, but for some us it was almost literally yesterday," said Michaela Malenko, a refugee from a war-torn country that had been relocated to Toledo just weeks before the Time Event took place. She suddenly returned after eighteen years to find that the conflict she had been fleeing was long over, but that her hometown and its people had been almost completely destroyed while she was away. Since her return, she has become a well-known advocate for others affected by the Event. "We may never know what actually happened that day twenty years ago, but we cannot forget, no matter how many years have passed," she added.

In direct and indirect ways, there is a fear that the world's consciousness of the Time Event is fading. Although the anniversary of the temporal disturbance remains a point of reflection for many, there is also a growing generational divide between those who grew up with existing knowledge of time travel versus those who remember the time before the Event, when such things were in the category of fairy tale.

The still unexplained glitch in time spurred a worldwide interest in both scientific study and emergency response training, and created a sense of pride and unity amongst science fiction fans who chose to see the positive potential in the proof of time travel rather than the immediate downsides of its impact. Despite the excitement that the Event originally generated, it has also opened time survivors to a certain degree of resentment in recent years from critics who feel that too much government funding and development has gone towards the recovery of such a specific niche segment of the population. The ongoing debate has become more heated as no major breakthroughs have been made by the Sadler Group regarding identifying how the wormhole originated, what caused it and whether it was natural or manmade, or even confirming whether it was an isolated incident or merely the only one recorded. Others feel that the reasons may never be known, and are less concerned with the mystery than the fallout.

"Whether we understand how it happened or not, the ripple in the fabric of time was an attack on our very being," said Senator Richard Ottoman, who lost his brother to reentry injuries twelve years ago. "Everyone should remember it, and until the many thousands still missing are recovered, we should not abandon them."

"With the return of each survivor, we are reminded of what we have lost, and what we have recovered," stated the President, speaking at a press event at the Pentagon. He vowed that the country would continue to support rescue and rehabilitation efforts for the citizens of Toledo. "No matter how long it takes, we will not forget our brothers and sisters, and we have a duty to defend and protect them... now, or in any era they reappear."

Spontaneous tributes around the globe included personal photos, postcards, and mementos from the Toledo area from those who had visited in the past, along with personal messages for survivors, and poignant accounts of milestones missed by those lost in time. Some Americans joined in volunteer projects on a day that is federally recognized as a day of service and remembrance, and schools have commonly designated the anniversary date to host science fairs and demonstrations to raise awareness and funding for time-related research.

To commemorate the second decade since the Time Event, the International Physics Olympiad (IPhO) has received special permission to hold their upcoming annual competition in June at Lake City, a location normally off-limits to civilians. This year's competition will emphasize the theory of relativity as a main category, and a special program guide for the contest will be sold to raise money for increased science curricula development in secondary schools.

"It took something no one previously imagined was possible to unite us," their website announcing this year's competition details stated. "It should be proof that anything is possible."

In addition to commemorations, the 20th anniversary has been marked by some protests groups who feel the city of Toledo should simply be abandoned and that any rescue services should be 100% automated. These groups have taken to picketing at tribute sites, proposing that there are too many others in need of emergency services, and that the tech being used in Toledo should be used to better the lives of disadvantaged people here in the U.S. and other countries.

"No one thinks that being caught in the wormhole was easy, and we know it wasn't their choice, but we're talking about a very small part of the globe that is getting special treatment," said one protestor outside an event. "We're talking about millions, if not billions, of dollars in funding that is helping only a select few. We need to consider the many, and where else that money could be used."

Officials from Sadler and the U.S. government have refuted comments like these for years, pointing out that the liquid assets pooled from all private citizens of Toledo while they are lost in time are largely being used to fund their own rescues. The interest generated on this account, along with Sadler-owned patents and royalties, is what covers a large portion of the research laboratories, and the developing tech coming out of these labs has been adapted for use in the wide world, to the benefit of many who are outside of the Time Zone.

Supporting Sadler's position on funding, recent economic reports and market research studies indicate that the time-related tech field has a current market value of $14.5B (USD) with a projected compound annual growth rate (CAGR) of 6.5% in the next 5 years. Purely from a business perspective, the time anomaly is considered to be an economic booster rather than a drain, and has helped spur manufacturing for original equipment manufacturers (OEMs), connected systems, and products from various industries worldwide. The increase in patent submissions is also considered to be an indicator of upward growth potential.

Today, on the 20th anniversary of the Time Event, American and global citizens look back in remembrance, but tomorrow as the third decade of impact from the time wrinkle begins, they also speculate about the future.

"We have been preparing for the possibility that we will be dealing with reappearances for decades or maybe even centuries to come," stated an official press release from Sadler. "Our teams are examining long range plans to prepare for multiple scenarios that may extend further into the future than we had previously imagined."

Announcements about the next stages of expansion to Lake City are expected to be revealed at the end of the fiscal year.

CHAPTER 24

Tom Mitchell – 20 years, 3 months, 9 days after the Event. Time populous: 230,056

Dear Rachael,

It's been a long time since I wrote a letter by hand, but it's supposed to be therapeutic according to my counsellor Trevor. He's a good guy, so I'll do what he suggests, but I don't know why I couldn't just type it. They want us to write out everything; all these notebooks and exercises and lists... list our regrets, list our goals, list our promises to ourselves. All by hand, because apparently when it's digital you just delete the mistakes or change your mind and it's gone for good, and supposedly by writing it out you get to see your own thought process better. And they say it's all about slowing down and that somehow forcing yourself to do it by hand makes you open up about it more. Clearly though they've never seen how slow I type, ha ha. I know that always used to drive you crazy but I'm still a henpecker, sorry babe. Also, best of luck reading my terrible handwriting. It's even worse than it used to be when you'd have to call me from the store to decipher my scribbles on the grocery list.

We're supposed to write these letters as often as we want, as long as we want them to be, and say everything we want to say. And there's so many things that I want to say to you, but I just couldn't figure out what to write for such a long time. Honestly, the first few years I just refused because writing to a future you... it made me feel like I was giving up on ever seeing you in person again, but I told Trevor I'd give it another try now. I started and stopped a bunch, and threw away a lot of drafts, but then realized I was having trouble because I was just trying to explain to you what had happened, and that's dumb because I don't know anything about the scientific part. And you'll get onboarded just like I did,

135

and people a lot smarter than me will explain it better. So here I am trying again to write only about how I feel, but it's harder than I thought.

It sounds too simple just to say that I miss you. I can't believe you've been gone for twenty years (ten years to me) and I feel like without you I'm not myself at all any more. It's like I'm half asleep all the time, and I just want to go back to the way things were. I know that can't happen, but I just feel like if you were here, we would pick up like we left off, even though I'm ten years older than you'll remember and maybe a little fatter and grayer. I'm hoping you'll think "distinguished" and forgive me if I'll be an even worse tennis partner than before since I haven't practiced since you've been gone, and my knee isn't what it used to be. I don't do softball leagues any more either. I tried a few years ago but it wasn't as much fun playing with all strangers and made me miss my friends more than ever.

I catch myself all the time waiting to do things thinking you would like to do them with me, and hoping maybe you'll be right back... so I should just hold off one more day, one more week. In the group sessions the counsellors tell us we all have to learn to move on, but I can't. I just can't.

I had my backpack with me on the day they found me, so I've got all our texts and pictures that were on my phone. Some people don't have much of anything unless it was in the cloud, because once you've left the city limits no one is allowed back in to gather personal items. I look at those pictures every day, even the ones that don't mean anything important, like how big our tomatoes were that first year we grew them on the porch, and all the screenshots you sent me of dog breeds you wanted to consider. I have so many pictures of corgi butts, thanks honey!! They say I should think about getting a puppy actually, for my mental health, and to keep myself busy.

I have a nice little apartment in Lansing now, it reminds me of the place you lived at when we first met – on the top floor with the little balcony that was just big enough to squeeze out on. I know you loved that place but remember *what a pain it was to get your furniture down all those stairs when we moved in together? No elevator at this place either, which is the main reason I haven't gotten the dog yet. I'm not sure my knee can take going up and down all day to take one out, but I'm thinking I'll apply for a ground floor one soon. It's a pretty quiet neighborhood and the whole complex is technically government housing and everyone's a time traveler. We have all these social activities they host for us so I've met most of my neighbors over the years, plus we have group counselling and Trevor comes out here every few months to meet with a bunch of us in person instead of virtually. I like going to his office better, even though that's only a couple times of year when they do our physicals to see if there's any discernible effects of being in the time stream. I don't know what they're looking for, maybe they were hoping we wouldn't age or something but if so, they'll be disappointed because I definitely have. But I like getting over to Lake City; it sort of feels like a vacation.*

Living here is kind of like being back in college in a dorm, except no one has roommates. If you're lucky enough to have family or friends who are also back from the wormhole, there are bigger apartments and townhouses you can apply for, and of course you can pay for one yourself at any time if you have the means. Meanwhile I've been here almost ten years now and I hate when people refer to these apartments as bachelor pads and I hate this feeling like I'm single again, because I'm not. We have a whole life together, just waiting for you, which is why I'm saving money still living in this tiny place. When you get back and finish the onboarding, we can look for a new, bigger apartment, maybe by another riverwalk just like we had, with a yard for our little dog that I'll go get any day now. My job lets me work remote three or four days a week so we can choose a spot anywhere you like, or we can go to a new city and start over, just us. All this counselling isn't mandatory, and I won't need it any more once I have you back.

They say they'll keep these letters we write in a box for as long as it takes for you to get back, as many as we want to write, even if it's every day. But who would want to come back from the time stream and have years' worth of one-way correspondence to read? Or maybe a whole box of letters from every single person they knew if someone had a lot of friends who are better at this than I am. They'd be reading novels instead of living their lives. So... I'll try to write them, but I'll try not to do it too often or be too boring.

In fact, this really is stupid now that I think about it, why am I even writing all these little details down about where I live and where I work? You're going to be here soon and I'm going to show you or tell you all of these things myself and you won't need to read any of this rambling. Please, please come back soon.

Love,

Tom

CHAPTER 25

Clarissa Fitzsimmons, producer and film director – 21 years, 8 days after the Event.
Time populous: 227,702

"Are we rolling? Give me the mark."

"Director's cut interview with Clarissa Fitzsimmons, part three. Mark."

"So, Clarissa, we know the end result of *Temporal Disruption* was critically acclaimed, but tell us a little bit more about the preparation your team did leading up to the film that won you the Oscar."

"Well, we were definitely making arrangements for almost three years before the 20th anniversary itself. By the time we actually recorded the interviews we knew we had way more footage than we could actually incorporate, so deciding on the final compilation is where the real work lay. As the producer, my team and I were combing through survivors' stories looking for the right mix for months, but more options kept cropping up so storyboarding was happening right up until the end."

"Are these stories people were submitting to you, or…?"

"Oh no, we did get approached by a few agents trying to pitch specific stories to us once word of the project was out there, but anyone who had an agent lined up in advance didn't pass the smell test for us. They tended to be highly embellished tales of wannabe influencers, and would be more appropriate for the old television programs that used to sensationalize reentry stories, and it's just not the format we were going for. To genuinely have the weight that we wanted to portray, to make the interviews really speak to their emotions, we needed people who were shy, or even hesitant to talk about their experience. Everyone that we connected with for this film really poured their hearts out to us, and to do that they had to trust us. In the end, we only filmed with each person for a day or two at most, but we spent time getting to know all of them months in advance so that they would feel comfortable opening up to us."

"So how did you decide then on whose stories to choose?"

"We searched the public records looking for certain criteria that make up an interesting angle for a story, and then reached out to learn more about them… but nothing about the interviews was scripted. We tried to have them hold off on telling us details until we could actually get them in the studio."

"So, no scripts at all… genuinely, the interviews we all saw were exactly what your team heard for the first time when they were recorded?"

"Absolutely. We prompted people a few times to tell us more details throughout, but everything you saw on screen was a first and only take. It's what makes the whole film so raw, and different from what we've seen in the past for documentaries about the Time Event."

"There's really no comparison to be made between a film like yours, which is really gut-wrenching and inspirational journalism, versus things like those scripted television programs of the past. But of course, they too left an impression on the industry; what would you say their long-term impact was, and did it affect a work like yours at all?"

"You and I have both worked in entertainment a long time, and we know that different genres have to be judged by different standards. But I think it's fair to say that some of the first stories coming out of Toledo were just premature; there wasn't enough history for people to really appreciate what it is like to rejoin society as a time traveler when so little time had gone by, so they had to embellish to make the stories seem more dramatic.

And by doing so, I think they lost the interest of the public too quickly. The format became very predictable, and I think it cast a lot of doubt with the average person on how hard the Time Event really hit those affected. It became more like a running gag. In the real world, it destroyed a lot of people's lives and that shouldn't be made light of."

"Even at twenty years from the event, it's a completely different experience than it was for the early reentries."

"Completely. And in another twenty years, or fifty, or more, it will only become a richer and more complex story. Depending on the circumstance, you have tragedy, comedy, motivation – all of the things that move the human spirit."

"Art."

"Well, if I can be immodest, yes, I think what we ended with can be considered art."

"And the decision not to attach a recognizable narrator for the story…?"

"We had a lot of top tier talent very interested in being involved in the project, but in the end, we opted for the faceless interviewer and focused on the people themselves. We didn't want to distract from their stories with a famous face or even voice. We had just a few written lines at the start of the film to set up the format, and the short epilogue. And we purposely steered away from the science; the public has seen a lot of that over the years already, and we felt like the average person understands it as well as they're going to."

"Some of those educational pieces have also had great acclaim."

"Definitely. But that wasn't our objective; even the great mathematicians and physicists of our time are still stumped by the time anomaly, so our focus wasn't on rehashing the theories of *why* but instead focusing on what it's meant after the fact. How do people react? How do they move on? How do they reconcile their past with their new future?"

"Guys, let's cut here and reset; we'll go into a few of the individual stories next to get Clarissa's commentary. Do you want anything?"

"No, I'm good."

[...]

"Ok, let's begin again. Action."

"Interview with Clarissa Fitzsimmons, part four. Mark."

"We'd really like to get your reaction to some of the specific stories that you felt had the most impact; the ones that have stuck with you and your team the most. Is there one that stands out to you to start?"

"Well, of course every story affected all of us, even the ones that didn't make the final cut of the film, but one of the earliest ones we recorded ended up being one of the most inspiring. The woman we interviewed had been a drug addict before the Time Event occurred and she was in a bad place, from both a mental health and medical standpoint. In the past, her child had been taken into protective services, and she wasn't sure if she was ever going to see him again. It was really a bad situation, and she was desperate to get her son back but it was honestly very unlikely to happen with her track record. But then the time shift happened... she reemerged about ten years after, and was under the kind of scrutiny she wouldn't have gotten in her own time."

"She was just a statistic in the past."

"Exactly. But when she reemerged from time, there was no drug dealer to go back to and no community of other addicts influencing her to relapse. Doctors were examining her for effects of time travel, so she was more exposed to medical treatment than she had been before. She was essentially forced to go straight, and really cleaned up her life. It's a strange thing, because even she admitted she struggled to come to terms with this... but while she missed her family and friends and still had love for them in her heart, she knew that really, they hadn't all been good people, or a good influence on her life, and she felt really guilty and selfish for being *glad* they weren't here with her. It was really poignant to hear her talk about it, and I think it really spoke to me because I do understand that sometimes you can really love someone and still know that objectively they haven't earned that love. It's illogical that you love them at all, but it's very relatable."

"When you first recorded her, her son hadn't reemerged yet from time, had he?"

"No – the interesting thing was that she had had all these years to turn her own life around, get sober, get a job, grow accustomed to a new life on her own... and then her son reemerged from time about three months after we first interviewed her. And we were able to capture a part two interview with her after she'd been reunited with him, and she was going to be allowed to regain custody, with supervision, and she was just so happy she could barely speak to us coherently. It was just night and day. Of all the stories we heard, and all the interviews we did, this was one of the only examples of someone who actually benefitted from being in the wormhole. It was as if the universe had just shuffled to the side to give her a second chance. Her experience is an outlier, but our whole production team really took heart from it. Most stories aren't nearly so inspiring."

"Give us an example of one that was more difficult to film."

"Well, the detective was hard."

"The one who had the open murder case when the Time Event happened."

"Yes. It was just horrific to begin with, to hear him talk about the gruesome details of the very violent and disturbing crimes that had been

143

committed, and everything that had led them to the suspect. They had literally been about to get the guy in custody but then of course they all got lost in time; and even though the detective was now back, all the evidence itself was stuck there in the city, with the crime scenes possibly destroyed or contaminated."

"Is there any way to verify that?"

"We tried to see if the search and rescue teams could check on the locations and status, but the Alpha policy is pretty clear that the teams are there to assist people returning from time only. Personal property, company assets, even official documents that are within the city are all off limits – no side projects. But with all the cleanup the Delta teams have done over the years, the chances of the crime scenes not being compromised is virtually nil. So, here's our detective, who was closing in on a killer, and has the suspect that he likes for it with really strong evidence, and the only things he has to prove it are out of reach."

"Not to mention the suspect himself."

"Right; law enforcement has an alert open on the guy, although that can't be in the public records database (innocent until proven guilty) but the Alpha squads would get a red alert if they happened to pick him up when he pops back in to the present. But that could be a thousand years from now for all we know so it's hardly a given that would even be possible. And even if you pick up the suspect, it doesn't help you recover the evidence. There's a very real chance he could get away with all of it on that technicality."

"There's no statute of limitation on murder obviously, but it also brings up some interesting questions for lesser crimes."

"Yes, and no matter the severity of the crime, what do you do about witnesses still not reappeared? Citizens have the right to a speedy trial so you can't just make a suspect returning from the time stream wait decades in prison for you to make your case. On the other hand, you definitely can't just pardon major offenses like murder the way they have with minor things like parking tickets and debt forgiveness, which was enacted over a decade ago."

"And your detective was really letting this eat him up."

"That was what made it so difficult. It was like we were just watching him have a nervous breakdown in real time while we were filming. Not only did he have some PTSD from pursuing this very grisly case, he was just fixated by the idea that this killer, a really disturbed individual, would suddenly reemerge from time and evade capture and resume his reign of terror... or that he might be found but end up getting away with it due to contaminated evidence or some other loophole caused by the whole situation. He clearly felt responsible, and that he was letting down both the families of the victims, and future victims this guy might have. It was painful to watch."

"Had he been placed with a new precinct after his reemergence?"

"No, he hadn't been cleared for duty because of his extremely high stress levels. That meant there was nothing to distract him from this one case, and he was... well, not even *borderline*, I would say *firmly* in the camp of obsessed. Even without access to all his original notes and case files he had a whole notebook that he had recreated and was essentially trying to make the case as tight as he could on paper and share every detail with us, in case he wasn't there to see the guy come to justice. We knew he wasn't well. I think he chain smoked for about six hours straight and just looked wretched the whole time, but we still should have seen the red flags when he kept asking us to promise we would tell the victims' story."

"It was before the film came out that he took his own life, or after?"

"Just before. I think he waited until the trailers were out and it was certain his interview was in the final cut before he did it, but he just couldn't bear it any longer. I wish it hadn't ended that way for him, but I do understand why he made that choice. I think it would have been even worse for him if the suspect actually had returned from time and walked. By taking his own life, this way he could let it go with some hope that justice would eventually be served even if he wasn't there to see it. And as he said in his suicide note, he knew that if the guy returned and wasn't charged, he would probably end up taking things into his own hands and he didn't want to be remembered as a murderer himself."

"I imagine that your whole crew took his death very hard."

"We did; he was a challenging person to get to know, and he really kept us at arms' length both during the shoot, and after shooting had wrapped. A lot of the other interviewees have kept in touch, and have said they found telling their stories therapeutic, but clearly not in this case. I'll always regret not being able to do more for him."

[…]

"Let's cut here and take a break. Thanks Clarissa, we'll pick up with you tomorrow afternoon if we need any more."

"Got it."

"Folks, this afternoon let's get some reactions on the more upbeat stories from some others from the film crew, and then tomorrow, critical reception for the film itself. Who do we have up next for after lunch?"

"We've got her cameraman John talking about the three teen brothers where the baby of the family is now the oldest – they're the funny ones that had the whole crew in stitches all during filming."

"OK good, we need something light to clear the mood."

"Then we've got the makeup artist to talk about the old lady who didn't think she would live to see her only grandchild grow up, but now is actually able to meet her *great*-grandchildren…we're getting some B roll of her and the kids this weekend for the director's cut promos."

"Got it, sweet old lady. And what's the third one for today?"

"Ummmm… associate producer to talk about the best friends that were both eleven years old when the Time Event happened and now one is an adult who adopted the other one when she came back from time. It's not exactly a smooth story as there's a lot of tension in the relationship so we're going to focus more on how the custody laws work and we've got some stats on how many minors have been affected from that parental rights group."

"Great – funny, sweet, educational. We'll pick up at 1:00. That's lunch people."

CHAPTER 26

Vlog from political analyst Harvey Trent – 23 years, 11 months, 6 days after the Event. Time populous: 219,727

Say, did anyone else notice that we almost had a war on our border this month?

I realize humanity is preoccupied with itself as usual, but this is a troublesome development so just maybe people can pull their heads out of our collective ass and focus on this for just a minute.

Armed conflicts in Brazil and Mexico erupted following protests across the region as the decision to reject a deal for economic integration with the Manufacturers Union were met with a crackdown by state security forces. Increased pressure to produce the goods and services that the U.S. relies upon to fund the Toledo Project have rendered many Latin, Central, and South American countries in competition with South Asian nations for years, and have also caused growing resentment between countries in the region vying for control of this lucrative economy.

For the people in the back, quick reminder that a couple of decades ago most manufacturing hubs were centered in the Asian market, but Lake City's demand for technology equipment and the need for less time spent in ocean shipping brought a lot of new demand to Mexico and Brazil. The closer proximity to the U.S. creates some supply chain advantages, but also a lot of pressure on the region.

Inadequate infrastructure to handle large-scale manufacturing facilities have caused rolling blackouts in some areas, sparking protests from citizens, while economic destabilization from hyperinflation of specific raw materials has eroded the savings of the middle class and increased resentment of U.S. and LATAM relations. This pressure has helped certain foreign time-denier groups' propaganda that put blame on the U.S. for the increased economic strain, and have motivated some countries to adopt nationalist trade policies to protect their domestic industries from foreign competition. While such policies can be beneficial on an individual level, they also reduce international trade and encourage protectionism. In short, not everyone is pleased with us and our continuing high demands.

Higher tariffs and recent restrictions have burdened certain Central and South American countries without access to raw materials, and more protests broke out over the lack of free trade. Government officials across the region are meeting in emergency sessions to discuss treaties that can smooth over hostilities and find solutions to the economic instabilities before they spill over into further political instability.

Experts agree that there is the potential for an even greater economic boom in Latin America, and an opportunity for the region to become a more prominent powerhouse of industry and move away from isolationism... if the infrastructure issues and logistics costs can be adequately reduced to support the demand for services. Traditionally, Brazil has an inefficient transportation infrastructure that dominates their logistics costs compared to other companies operating in the Americas. This has led to problems related to communications and cybersecurity breaches along with manufacturing. If these problems can be overcome, there's a real opportunity for the continued needs of the project in Toledo to spur economic growth, maybe even improve international trade worldwide... but failure to iron out some of the rough patches could also precipitate further tensions.

U.S. officials have increased security along the Southern border, but have not yet issued any official warnings or sanctions. It is my belief that the current administration will allow our neighbors to the south leeway to resolve this conflict without intervention, while quietly shifting some of the demand for goods and services to other regions to alleviate pressure until there is resolution. Playing nice in the sandbox and spreading out the wealth to parts of the Middle East and Asia could help soothe some tensions, but is it too little too late?

In my opinion, it is a mistake for the U.S. to remain silent on this issue while hoping it just fades away. The situation at hand has the systemic makings of a much larger conflict akin to the events that became the precursors of the stage that set off the World Wars of the previous century. We must answer to these accusations that we are overburdening our neighbors to the south, before reparations are demanded and our silence is interpreted as acceptance.

In the coming weeks and months, I will be reporting regularly on the escalation or (hopefully) de-escalation of this crisis on our border. But I have to stress again that this could be a very, very big problem for us all, and people need to wake up and pay attention.

CHAPTER 27

Trevor – 24 years, 2 months, 1 day after the Event.
Time populous: 219,287

Today the weather was gorgeous, so Trevor had had all of his meetings out by the shore instead of in the office or the atrium. All of the counsellors do that when they can get away with it, even though strictly speaking they're supposed to maintain the clinical setting for interviews. But most of his case work these days is with people who have been back a long time and know the drill.

Newer counsellors get the ones who have just returned; unless there's a complaint or a problem you keep your cases forever, since the whole point is for the travelers to have someone familiar to deal with while they're adjusting to their new lives. Of course, the longer they've been back, the more spaced out the checkpoints are, as long as they're making progress.

And today was too beautiful to spend indoors. Like most counsellors, Trevor's on a rotating schedule and travels between the main hubs where his reentries were relocated to after they reappeared. The first week of the month he's at his office here at Lake City headquarters, planning and confirming scheduling for the month and catching up on paperwork. Weeks two and three he goes between cities, taking the ferries across the lake (which are faster than skirting the Time Zone by land), visiting people and checking in with them. Some need help with paperwork or to set up new job training or things along those lines, but mostly it's just a wellness check to make sure they're adapting as much as they can. The ones that have trouble acclimating get checked up on more often, or maybe even get invited to come do a retreat at Lake City, which is where Trevor also spends the last week of the month (running sessions and training other counsellors while doing some virtual check-ins as well).

He wished Gary would consent to come in for one of those retreats. As a close relative, he isn't allowed to be Gary's counsellor of course, but he touches base regularly with the person who is. She keeps trying to convince Gary, for Trevor's sake if not his own. It's been six years since Gary reemerged. He was still at the house after all; and was pretty confused to find the remains of Trevor's "nest" in the living room (under about a foot of dust probably) and he turned out to be one of the people who just refuses to accept the facts of the time anomaly. Oh, not to say that he's a time-denier, but he wants to just carry on with the way he knows how to do things, and is as belligerent as possible at every turn when he has to make any kind of change.

The plant he had worked at was now defunct; not only had it been locally-owned and abandoned since the Time Event, the machinery he was certified on was long since obsolete and the tasks he had done were performed by AI robots in all the new factories that made similar products. So, Gary just point-blank refused to train for a new job. Technically, anyone reemerging from time in Toledo qualified for enough government funding and housing to get by without a job, but most people at least tried to rejoin society, either just to keep busy or to earn better money. Gary said no thanks. He started spending most of his monthly allowance on liquor and cigarettes and God knows what else, and he had become thin in the past few years. It had been a shock already when Trevor saw him for the first time after he returned; he had always thought of Gary as a big guy but it turns out he wasn't even very tall. Trevor had about six inches on him at least. Now, after years of neglecting his diet and drinking like a fish, Gary wasn't even muscular any more. He'd also been diagnosed with a type of 'black lung' that time travelers sometimes got when they materialized into a place with a lot of dust or mold; it was treatable, but clearly Gary wasn't keeping up on his health anyway, and wasn't taking his treatments. When Trevor last saw him, he looked like he'd aged decades in just the few years he'd been back.

Gary had lived in Toledo his whole life; everything he knew was there. It just wasn't an option to go back there and he was furious about it. Twice now he'd been flagged by Alpha teams for trying to sneak back into the city, once on foot and once on a small motorbike that turned out to be stolen. He'd gotten a slap on the wrist for that (for time travelers unless the offense was serious the courts tended to chalk things up to stress and look the other way) and was still on probation. Trevor was frustrated with the whole thing; he was an experienced counsellor but whenever he tried to talk to Gary, he found his temper too near the surface and all his training went right out the window and they would argue. The last time they had spoken was after the hearing where the probation was handed out, and that was eight months ago now.

"You know the whole city is covered with motion detectors and seeing-eye sensors anyway – what would you have even done even if you got inside? Go sightseeing?!" he had raged at the time. Gary had merely folded his arms and scowled, which just made Trevor even angrier. He had always remembered Gary as being so quick to argue, so quick to criticize anyone else – and here he was acting like a child and refusing to use his words. It suddenly made Trevor want to laugh, because he realized Gary looked just like a sulky old-man version of DJ whenever she was in trouble and pouting about it. Gary might not be his real father, but boy was he DJ's; it was almost worth it to argue with Gary to get that little glimpse of her here in the future. His counsellor sure was earning her salary dealing with *this* every month he thought wryly. But Trevor still left that day angry, and he was still angry now.

Thinking about it here on the beach of Lake City on a sunny afternoon, work completed for the day and just relaxing, he sighed and felt bad for being so frustrated. He never got mad at his own case files. He was nothing but patient with all of them, even when they were exasperating and didn't want to face facts, and were sometimes just as stubborn as Gary was being. He took a deep breath, and forced himself to think clearly.

Ok Trevor, stop avoiding this. Take it out and really look at it. And be fair. Why do you let him get under your skin?

You know why.

So yeah, he was kind of a bully to everyone when you were a kid. A lot of kids don't like their stepfathers. That's a separate issue from the wormhole. And the way things turned out, you got to grow up without him on your back after all. All that was a long time ago. Is it really worth resenting him for it now? He can't change the past any more than you can.

Probably not, but he's not even trying to change for the future.

What does it matter to you, really? You don't have to deal with him if you don't want to. If DJ came back, he wouldn't get custody of her without his counsellor's sign off and you know he wouldn't get it. Physically and psychologically, he's a no-go. If Mom came back, she'd either whip him back into shape or get time annulled since it's past the gap period. Legally, none of you are bound to him.

All he does now is hang out with those couple loser friends of his that made it back from time, even though they're practically old enough to be his father now.

What's it to you? They're familiar to him. They're not exactly great guys, but you don't have to hang out with them. They didn't bother you when you were a kid – they're just guys, and it's none of your business. If someone told you who you were allowed to hang out with, would you listen? No.

No, but…

But what? Be honest.

I just want him to TRY to be better than he is.

Do you? Do you REALLY? Or do you just want to win?

YES. FINE. I want to be right. And it's not enough that I AM right, that I was a good kid and he acted like I was nothing and he was wrong. It's not enough that I "won", and that he's such a loser now. I want him to admit it, and he's not going to. I deal with all these people who are learning life lessons, and seeing what's really important are the people they've lost, and missing them, and realizing they took the time they had for granted. Every one of them, even the ones who don't really make it here in the future, have those feelings and regrets. And this jackass wants to act like everyone else is to blame for his misfortune instead of everyone being in the same boat. Do you remember when I first told him who I was after he'd been at the facility a few weeks? He grunted. GRUNTED! That's all I got! And then he said "my wife back yet?" – not even "your mother"… "MY wife"… like he needs to still remind me he's not *really* my family. I'm the only relative he's got who is alive and not stuck in a wormhole somewhere and in six years he's never once even said he was glad to see me.

Take it down a couple notches. You see this with reentries all the time. What do you tell people when they're disappointed in the reaction they get from others – try to look at it from their perspective. Gary remembers a kid. You're not that kid anymore – maybe he really would be glad to see that kid if that's who was here. But you're an adult man; you're as old as he is, and you're a professional and an authority figure; you're not his friend and you're not someone he trusts. You're nothing like him.

I was never anything like him.

And that's just it, you've spent your whole life trying not to be like him, and you've succeeded. You're not. He didn't meet you until you were already five years old, and even at that age you were suspicious of him, and he wasn't

155

experienced with kids at the time so you never bonded. You didn't like doing the things he liked to do, and vice versa. And when you got older, it was more and more clear that you weren't going to grow up to be like him at all. So, you didn't, time stream or not. You grew up to be what you were meant to be, and that's not a bad thing but you're also not a person that Gary is ever going to understand. You better just acknowledge and accept that, or journal it, or whatever. Because nothing is going to change that. Stop trying to make him be better than he is. It has to come from him, or not at all. You know this.

Trevor sighed, looking out over the water. He did know that. And he actually did feel kind of better now, just putting into words even if it was just for himself. It was tiring to be so angry about something he couldn't do anything about anyway. Maybe now he could let it go.

He spontaneously picked up a small rock on the shore, weighted it in his hand (*this rock is my anger – I'm getting rid of it forever*) and sent it skipping across the calm water. The ripples spread, ebbed, lingered, then disappeared without a trace. The lake had accepted his sacrifice.

CHAPTER 28

Excerpt from the White House press release −26 years, 3 months, 2 days after the Event.
Time populous: 213,421

Today marked the official signing of the Treaty of São Paulo, an accord to cease all conflict in the region following the stabilization of the region and codified peace terms between Brazil and its neighboring nations.

The underlying issues causing conflict were resolved when in an unexpected move, the United States agreed to fund infrastructure repairs and rebuilding of major transportation hubs in Brazil to better support the manufacturing pipeline and international trade in the region. The agreement will shore up failing wind, water, power, and communications, eliminating many of the pain points of the citizens that were the cause of protests for months before violence erupted. In return, stabilization in the region allowed the return to free flow of trade and raw materials at high outputs, benefitting the U.S. and other regions that have come to rely on the Latin mid-region for trade.

Funding was sourced mainly from an endowment from the Sadler Group, as much of the technology that supports both search and rescue operations in Toledo and the structure and maintenance of Lake City relies on a strong supply of goods and services from the region. In recent years, diversification away from Asia and Southern ASEAN countries has sparked some resentment in those regions, but globally all regions have seen some benefits as international trade has increased worldwide in recent decades.

In addition to the economic concessions made, as a show of goodwill the U.S. has made an exception to the ban on international travel for returned time travelers that were foreign nationals and visitors to Toledo from Central and South America at the time of the Event. Provided that they continue to stay in communication with their counsellors to document any lasting effects from their time in the wormhole, these refugees will be allowed to return to their home countries, and the Treaty has laid out provisos for their return.

The Treaty marks the end of a sensitive period, and while there was no escalation to outright war and hostilities, tensions have been running high. We are pleased to put an end to this situation and look forward to many years of cooperative relations and the free flow of trade through the Americas pipeline in cooperation with the Manufacturers Union.

CHAPTER 29

Site Two Parade Ground Event – 27 years, 10 months, 22 days after the Event. Time populous: 207,994

"All right, thank you all for coming, or for tuning in remotely from the field. First Lieutenant Simmons here. I'm not much of a speaker, but I'm honored to give this speech today to recognize Captain Amanda Briggs, the leader of Alpha Team Four since its inception almost 28 years ago.

It seems like only yesterday when we began, and it's been a privilege to serve under the captain's command all these years and to follow in her footsteps as your new leader.

As one of the original founders, Captain Briggs has helped to build this search and rescue organization from the ground up. The coordinated efforts of Alpha, Beta, Delta, and in recent years Epsilon squads, were only made possible by leaders like her, who had to envision a sustainable system in a matter of weeks after the Time Event. The fact that we are still using their foundational work today speaks to the strength of their determination, and ours.

Now, it's been almost three decades, and some of you younger recruits weren't even born when it happened – "

Hoots and wolf whistles from the crowd.

"Settle down, sweet children. As I was saying, some of you have lived your whole life knowing that it is possible to skip forward in time, but it cannot be overstated that on that day, the world was turned upside down. The disappearance of over a quarter million people in a single moment was not only a mystery, but something that could have induced panic all over the globe. So, take a moment to appreciate that those involved with the first iterations of our entire operation were essentially flying blind, trying to contain a situation that was very much out of control.

As a testament to the United States military branches, first responders, and scientific community, the response to the situation showed the courage and fortitude we are built on today."

Thunderous applause from the crowd.

"We hate to see her retire, but we almost lost her altogether and that was too close a call. So as Captain Briggs now goes to her well-earned rest from field work, her contributions to the procedural materials at the academy will continue to be invaluable for generations to come. There's a lot of us here in this room who she trained herself, on the field and off, and we are forever in her debt."

More applause from those assembled on site, more solemnly this time. The captain had almost been killed in the field from an explosion at an old factory during a sweep. Officially, it was classified as an accident involving some corroding storage containment that had been missed in routine cleanups over the years. Unofficially, the sweep had been ordered after a series of small explosions and chemical fires in that sector in a short period of time had raised suspicions from above; they reeked of sabotage. The Alphas had enacted a more thorough sweep grid of the industrial district ever since, and increased surveillance dramatically in that area but had yet to determine the culprits. Briggs had made it through rehabilitation and physical therapy, but she had known her career in field work was over the moment the explosion had happened. She'd resisted taking a higher commission for years to remain in the field, but her time had finally come.

"I'd like to bring to the stage Major William Holmes, and Dr. Raj Anil, Director of the Lake City Research team, both liaisons to Sadler's

Board, to present Captain Briggs with this medal of commendation for her many years of hard work and sacrifice."

The teams murmured amongst themselves while handshakes, congratulations, and photographs were arranged, with applause again as Captain Briggs took the podium.

"Thank you. Thank you very much. I won't keep you standing out here long, as I'm not one for long goodbyes, and you all have work to do. But I truly want to thank each of you, whatever squad and team you are a part of, for however long you have served.

It's been the honor of my life to serve with you all, and I see a lot of familiar faces out there in this crowd, and there's a few missing that I know we'll never forget. We've been through a lot together – from slogging through the rain placing pilot tech and slapping instruction posters on every surface (that's right kids, analog posters and landline phones back in the day), to the remote sensory nets we've just about perfected in recent years. It's amazing that just within the span of my career we've been able to improve the survival rates of reentries from the past by over 25%, and reduced the number of injuries by 50%, from the first five years.

I know we're no closer than we were at the beginning to solving the puzzle of the catastrophe that brought us all here together, but that was never in our purview for those of us in the field. I know it's a shock to all of you that I'm no theoretical physicist..."

Laughter now from the Alphas. Briggs had said that before to all of them often, usually as a cue to shut up and leave her alone.

"...I'm just a simple solider. But after all these years in the Time Zone, I've come to the conclusion that it doesn't actually matter how it happened, or why... it's like any other adversity the human race may have to face.

Historians can tell us how a conflict brews into a war, and science can tell us about the conditions that created a devastating earthquake or tsunami. Maybe no one can tell us what causes a wrinkle in the fabric of time, or maybe someday they will… but the fact is, when those things happen, people still get hurt, people still need rescuing, people's lives are still ripped apart. Knowing the *why* doesn't mean anything if we can't save them. And that's why we're here. These teams right here are who you call when you don't need an explanation, you just need help."

The crowd murmured agreement.

"The team I have now is truly amazing, but I'd like to extend my thanks to all of my squad members past and present, who have saved not only thousands of time travelers, but each other, and myself, on countless occasions. From high-wire acts, to building collapses… it's been like living in a high-octane action movie watching these squads work, and I could not be more proud of you all. Now… with this new robot leg they gave me I could probably still outrun any one of you…"

"Yeah you could, Cap!"

"HOO-RAH! ROBO-CAP!"

"…but I think I'll hang up my hat while I've still got 75% of my original limbs. And let this be a caution to you all to watch your backs, because although the medtech these days is truly amazing, and this technological marvel of an artificial leg can probably just about do my job without me even attached to it, I'd prefer none of you have to experience it for yourselves.

I hope that someday, the work we are doing will no longer be necessary because we will have recovered every soul lost to the time stream. But until then, I'll continue to be grateful to all of you for your dedication and service. Thank you."

CHAPTER 30

Grant Hutchings – 28 years,
5 months, 12 days after the Event.
Time populous: 206,007

Grant was furious. All that fucking planning... YEARS of fucking planning... and they'd been scooped by some disorganized band of foreign terrorist bastards who couldn't even make it into the building without being stopped. And now everything was in shambles – Lake City was on high alert and under scrutiny like never before, and all their careful plans were ruined.

He had obviously known they weren't the only game in town. *Of course,* there were other groups trying to find out the real truth about the time machine and get their hands on it. But his boys had been smart about it. They'd been patient, and they'd put in the time to blend in, and above all, their mission was the true one. They were out to find out the truth, and force those cowards in the government to show their true faces, and admit that the whole Time Event was just way to cover up the billions, maybe even trillions, of dollars they were funneling into their other projects and being used to control the masses. It was no coincidence that those leftist bastards had won almost every election since the Event had occurred.

He was so sick of the sympathy the whole world was showing for something that was just a fabrication, a web of lies, and not even very well done lies either. His team was trying to save America for the real Americans, and the rest of the hippie-dippy population with their feel-good bullshit about rehabilitation could fuck right on off to Canada or wherever would take them.

Last year, they'd finally reached a point where they were ready to make their big move, and they'd even succeeded in sneaking in some explosives to the industrial part of Toledo, which they planned to set off to distract attention away from their real attack site. They had the tools, the underground network, the funds, and the people in place. He and Steve had things under control and they were almost ready to deploy.

And then, a series of mishaps. Due to chemical instability, several of their booby traps had detonated early and raised suspicions. And right on top of that failure, their cousin Carey had reemerged from time and conveniently been "killed in reentry". As if they wouldn't have seen right through that bullshit – clearly, he had been one of the ones who wouldn't cooperate with the lies and had been silenced, aka murdered. But it had put the spotlight on Steve, as a blood relative, and they'd had to pause their plan while Steve pretended to mourn the "accidental" death normally, so that his coworkers at the facility wouldn't suspect anything. He'd gotten a maintenance job at Lake City almost as soon as it had opened, and had worked his way up to a position where he had the right keys to the right areas and had just been biding his time.

And *then*, right when they were ready to deploy again after Carey was safely remembered (not that they would even release his body to them – they were still experimenting on the dead, those sickos), that fucking idiot Joey had gotten himself killed in a stupid motorcycle accident, and he had been a vital player in the plan too. Not that they didn't have contingency plans, but there was just that additional small delay of a few weeks while they ironed out the details… and that was just enough time for some commie bastards from God knows what shithole little country to come bumbling in, trying to cyberattack the city and getting themselves caught. Of course, he was *glad* they hadn't been successful –he'd rather see their whole plan burn to the ground rather than some foreign enemy bent on taking over the U.S. of A. getting the win – but now they'd have to rethink everything from scratch all over again.

Those morons had put a spotlight right exactly where he didn't want it shone, God DAMN them. Meanwhile, the government was hushing up the whole attack to cover their own asses – of course they wouldn't want the stupid public to know they were vulnerable in any way. The whole incident was being called a "training exercise" and probably the men they had caught red-handed (who should have been buried in an unmarked grave by now) were actually being sent back where they came from for billions in blackmail money. The only good thing about it all was that the foreigners were being blamed for the booby traps in the industrial zone, so he could breathe a little easier.

Grant was getting too old for this. He was sick and tired of having to play it safe for appearances, living a double life for the mission and getting thwarted by chance at every turn. Almost he wondered if the government knew about what he was doing and had infiltrated his own group, and was undermining it from within… but no… he'd known most of these guys now for decades. He trusted them like his own flesh and blood now, and he would die for them if he had to.

He would just have to start from the beginning, and come up with a new and better plan, something those goddam sons of bitches wouldn't be expecting. And he'd better talk to Steve about recruiting also… none of them were getting any younger, and unless they could get their hands on that machine after all, they were running out of time.

CHAPTER 31

Engineering Quarterly, Issue 134 – publication date 30 years, 5 months, 24 days after the Event. Time populous: 200,243

In recent years, the field of micromobility has grown by leaps and bounds, becoming one of the most prominent modes of short-range transportation for commuters worldwide. Micromobility refers to a range of single-passenger lightweight vehicles operating at speeds typically below 50 km/h (30 mph), or multi-passenger vehicles operating at speeds below 25 km/h (15 mph).

Decades ago, micromobility vehicles mostly referred to scooters and cycles, powered by batteries that could be charged at stations. Their popularity quickly spread as the public found that they offered more flexibility than public transit options and were sustainable and more affordable than cars for short trips. Parking and the density of traffic in neighborhoods was also a factor, and many cities worldwide began to support these devices with infrastructure that took accessibility for such technology in mind.

Alongside this boom came safety challenges; lithium-ion batteries, especially when uncertified, posed fire hazards that threatened to outweigh their advantages, but after the technology was adapted for search and rescue efforts in the Toledo project, the converging of technologies and safety concerns were more adequately addressed.

Sadler's tech division replaced the lithium-dependent power sources with greener options and developed more powerful solar collectors that had less volatility, stricter regulations for recharging, maintenance, and the managing of end of lifecycle. The result was more powerful micromobility choices, with significantly decreased risk of thermal runaway incidents and fires. In parallel to these developments, new vehicles were being engineered for both land and air micromobility options. Sadler's interest centered on having compact, electric land vehicles that could move easily around the Toledo area without needing to use the standard roadways and high traffic areas where reentries could occur. The frequency of returning survivors needing quick transport and medical care out of the city limits also spurred the need for redesigned medicycles and "lake hoppers" (small, lightweight air transports that use far less fuel than traditional helicopters).

In populated cities, new traffic laws, roadway signage and markings, and safety rules have been developed specifically for ground micromobility vehicles, similar to bike lanes that were incorporated as far back as the late 20th century. Sadler and its affiliates hold the patents for several designs that experts say have the potential to revolutionize air travel in a similar way in the immediate future, and several lawmakers have proposed personal air traffic laws as becoming necessary to supplement outdated guidelines meant for unmanned drones and other novelty items.

This may well become a watershed moment, when technologies and the material needed have advanced so far as to be affordable, safe, and practical enough for micromobility to permanently replace many outmoded types of public transportation (such as buses, subways, and commercial airplanes) for short personal journeys. Sustainability experts project that the benefits would include a dramatic drop in the use of fossil fuels, though large shipping vessels on land, sea, and air would likely still be necessary for the transport of goods and materials for large-scale manufacturing.

CHAPTER 32

Tom Mitchell – 32 years, 1 month, 4 days after the Event. Time populous: 195,379

Dear Rachael –

Please don't read this letter until you've been back from the time stream for a while, at least until you have gone through the rehabilitation process and it's been at least weeks or months, and not just days for you. It's been 22 years to me, and 32 years since the Event happened. I hope you've read some of my other letters first, too, and if you haven't, go back to the beginning because this isn't the one to start with.

I promise that I have never stopped thinking about you, and hoping you would come back to me, but it's time now for me to let you go. NOT letting go of the hope that you will come back – I still desperately hope that you will. But I'm about to turn fifty years old and if you came back to me now, you wouldn't even recognize me as the man you married all those years ago. I don't want to disappoint you, and every year I get older I just picture you coming back from time and being stuck with this sad old man. And I know if I'm not the one to let go, you'll refuse to leave me and that's not fair to you. You're going to come back still young and beautiful and smart and full of energy, and there's no reason you shouldn't be able to start fresh when you return from time. If you still wanted to see me, I would love that more than anything, but it will be without obligation. And I won't write any more of these letters, because if I keep writing, I'm not really moving on.

Trevor says it's healthy for me to take a break, even though it hurts, because if I do this now, I may still be able to do something later in life that brings me joy instead of always looking back like I've been doing for so long now. I'm not sure if he's right, but if I wait five more years to do it, why won't I wait ten? Why won't I wait another twenty? And then I never will.

I know we said 'til death do us part', but I've come to the realization that the time anomaly killed all of us really; no one is the same person they were, no matter how long they were gone and how long they've been back. It killed so many hopes and dreams. The world is different than it was, and I hope that you come back to a time when people you know are also returning so that you don't have to go through this alone. No one we were close to has made it back, though a couple of friends-of-friends are around now. Your sister isn't back yet either. I'll keep alerts on for both of you, whether I'm writing letters or not.

I promise that in my heart I will never really let you go, and I will remember everything that led me to you and made me the luckiest person alive for those few years we had together.

I still love you, and I always will.

Tom

CHAPTER 33

Dr. Xiao Xiang, Assistant Director – 33 years, 4 months, 6 days after the Event. Time populous: 191,391

It had been a difficult day. A long, tedious, frustrating day. No, week. And even longer.

People were always so impressed when they heard his job title, Assistant Director at Sadler Research, but if only they realized how unglamorous such a position could be! Even his wife, who had worked here in the medical section herself for over a decade before moving to a private practice on the mainland, seemed to just assume he was some sort of king with loyal subjects to do his bidding at all times, but nothing could be further from the truth.

The Director was a good man; Dr. Xiang didn't begrudge him his status or title in the least. But there was no denying that being the *Assistant* Director was a grind. The Director needed to be highly visible; the majority of his time was spent speaking at panels, in tense meetings with government officials and world leaders, publishing whitepapers to represent the institute and their mission... all of these things were hard work too. But the Assistant Director got the hard work that was the thankless, invisible kind; stacks of bureaucratic paperwork; invoices up the wazoo that needed approvals in triplicate; difficult choices to make on prioritization of resources for training, staffing, technology upgrades, building renovations and more; decisions to be made on personnel and their benefits, their lodging, their engagement scores and performance. Even environmental concerns to address regarding the city's impact on Lake Erie and its natural inhabitants, pollution levels, and waste containment systems. And that wasn't even scratching the surface of all the top-level security measures that had been put in place in recent years; checkpoints and an entirely new badging system for the staff; additional safety and training courses to take; new protocols to adhere to. He wouldn't even be surprised if they handed him a mop and a bucket and told him to clean up a spill in the staff room next. He missed the good old days when he could just come to work, do his job and do it well, clock out and go home for the day.

One moment he would be looking at high level budgeting for the next fiscal year and wondering where he could fit the mandatory building maintenance into the P&L with the budget reductions (in the millions) that had been put in place to finalize the São Paulo Treaty funding ahead of schedule to save on interest rates. That treaty may have won them the Pulitzer Peace Prize, but it was also a real money pit. Right on the heels of these high-level decisions and the next minute he was dealing with staff complaints about the poor quality of the current coffee machines and whether that constituted unacceptable working conditions for those housed on site. From the most critical points to the most minor facilities issues, the Assistant Director was the funnel through which all things eventually came.

Of course, his direct reports handled a huge amount of the workload as well, but he was also taking on too much himself in trying not to overburden them, because he couldn't afford to lose any of them to burnout at the moment. Considering the size of the place and the complexity of their operations, they had things pretty well in control, all things considered with the recent tightening of the belt in the budgeting. Each wing of Lake City had separate managers over Research, Medical, Counselling, Technology & IT Services, Facilities & Human Resources, and Media Relations, plus Site Liaisons to coordinate with the Alpha, Beta, and

Delta crews and their military chain of command. All together, they made up the staff that reported into him as the Assistant Director, he reported in to Dr. Anil as the Director, Dr. Anil reported in to the Board, and the Board was a contracted extension of the U.S. Government.

Today had been a day of difficult conversations regarding that tightening of the belt. They'd all been hoping that there would be a respite coming with some discretionary funds that could help move the needle on a few of the most urgent projects, or at least be used for some low-hanging fruit that could boost morale. Unfortunately, word had come down from the board that there would be no leeway on budgetary spend (for the third year running!), and the staff was frustrated. Most of the grumbling wouldn't come directly to his ears of course. Instead, it would trickle in, insidiously ruining his days bit by bit. He imagined himself to be a complaint magnet, with little complaints inching towards him as he scrambled higher on a narrow peak trying to escape them. Gah... he was losing his mind.

At least he had a few days' rest coming his way. He had been staying in his office bunk for the last two weeks to work late nights so that he could get ahead enough to take the much-planned and much-needed vacation with his family. His wife had confirmed over Zap that the kids were excited to be visiting their cousins in San Francisco for the week and clamoring to get in the air; they would be staying at his sister's house and his parents were driving in from Santa Barbara also. They had already offered to watch all of the children (his three, plus three of his sister's) over the weekend so there would be a couple of nights at a fancy spa for the adults to look forward to, and some relaxing rounds of golf during the day if they were lucky with the weather. They might feel a little guilty leaving all six of the kids (with more energy than a litter of puppies) with their mild and serene grandparents, but not guilty enough to refuse the offer. Xiao's sister and brother-in-law were both knee-deep in the tech world and were rich beyond rich, but probably had just as little free time as he and Mai had. They just had a nicer house and better scenery to be busy in; Lake City was pleasant, but he missed the stately hills of the Bay Area where he had been raised.

Plus, his parents were looking forward to it. They had been hoping Xiao could get clearance to bring the family back to Guangzhou to visit relatives there, but senior staff from Sadler had international travel bans still in place after the security breach five years back.

It hadn't been entirely out of the blue, since everyone working in Lake City had yearly drills and safety training to adhere to, but there had been a rogue group of time-deniers who were convinced that the entire organization was a front covering up a plot to control the world stage, and they had somehow booby-trapped parts of Toledo and later attacked the facility itself looking to find proof of their theories inside. Luckily, security had been on the ball, almost immediately flagging the unauthorized vessel that docked in the drop off zone, and the group that had attempted to infiltrate through the staff entrance had been quickly detained.

Armed with false credentials and staff badges that were at least close to the real thing, they had planned to enter the facility and gather evidence, leaving through the shuttles at the end of the weekend shift. All that was clumsily executed, and they were rounded up within minutes of entry, but what was more worrisome was the corresponding attack on the cybersecurity system, which ended up being traced to part of the connected system that controlled the HVAC system in the medical wing. Although the interoperability protocols locked down the smart system as soon as the attack was detected, that assault had come from outside the city itself and was later proved to be facilitated by a group of foreign investors who were funding the time-deniers group, and who also had strong ties to an international terrorist organization. This was sufficient for the entire situation to become classified to avoid an intercontinental incident, or spur rumors.

There were still world governments and leaders that remained suspicious of the United States after all these years, wondering if the incident in Toledo was part of a larger experiment and what the real intentions might be. Not everyone was wowed by the pure science and moved to cooperative efforts.

With the help of their government counterparts, keen on avoiding a panic or sparking another world war, Sadler had hushed up the on-site situation (telling the staff it had been just a drill to spot weaknesses in the security system) and had taken the opportunity to retrain on protocols. Higher-level management like Xiao had had more extensive work to do to disguise the costs of new security measures that were put into place within the budget. Although they had to cut some spending in other categories, so far, they had been able to camouflage the extra spend as mandatory upgrades for the facility, but that was why the double whammy of being hit with the São Paulo costs was such a blow, even years later.

Most of the Sadler staff didn't know anything of sinister plots that had been vanquished, and the U.S. government had quietly increased cybersecurity support of Lake City in subtle ways. In the meantime, due to the foreign interference and still-unresolved influence with the time-deniers group, certain countries had been flagged as no-go zones for Sadler staff who were over a certain security clearance. Lower-level employees were allowed to vacation where they wished (though the scrutiny on their travel plans would increase dramatically behind the scenes), but higher levels were barred from such travel – both to eliminate them as security threats, and to protect them from being molested by unfriendly groups while abroad. Even domestic travel had to be sufficiently secured well in advance, and although his family would be unaware of their presence, he knew there would likely be undercover security staff watching over them the whole trip.

Just one more stack of papers and he could sign-out for a few days, guilt-free. He took the last swig of his cold coffee and grimaced at the bitter aftertaste. The staff was right; they needed new machines. This at last was something he could fix, and if he could just find that expense request here on his desk, that was one that was getting signed off on today. He might not be able to decipher the mysteries of time, prevent infiltration from a nefarious foreign enemy, or solve decades of infrastructure problems in one fell swoop, but he could provide a beverage that didn't taste like swill. He was the Assistant Director. He had the power.

CHAPTER 34

News headlines –
35 years after the Event.
Time populous: 185,672

'How long before we see the return to normalcy?': U.S. acknowledges the 35th anniversary of the time disruption

The scientific community demands more answers from the Sadler group

After the Time Event, manufacturing hotbeds are growing into superpowers while the U.S. fixates on containment, experts say

Photos: glimpses of the abandoned city

With survival rates up, benefits programs are stretched to capacity contributed by Reuters

CHICAGO, ILLINOIS USA – All over the United States, commemorative parades and gatherings paid tribute to the historic May 15th event in Toledo, Ohio with acknowledgements to those who have returned and those still pending their return from time.

Due to the dramatically increased survival rates in the past decade as new technology and improved safety science procedures have made reentries less volatile, the number of surviving Toledoans needing government assistance and funding has also gone up significantly. In addition to welfare, housing, and medical support, the further away from the Event people return, the more likely it is that their employment qualifications have become outdated.

"The fact is that after a 35-year hiatus in time, many of the people of Toledo no longer have marketable job skills," said the Vice President on Friday, speaking at a technology conference in Frankfurt, Germany. "We need to give them accelerated training to catch up to speed if we want to reintroduce them into the American workforce in anything but menial roles."

With close to 100,000 of the time populous now confirmed as returned, there are still a large number of citizens yet to account for. The exact number has never been determined, since a fair number of false reports were filed in the early years from people attempting to collect survivors' benefits or steal identities, and there were visitors to the city (both foreign and domestic) that were also pulled into the time stream. The neighboring cities in the American Midwest have been taking on the influx of Toledoans now for decades, giving the survivors easy access to counselling services at Lake City. In recent years, proposals have been made to make counselling services substantially more automated rather than in person.

"Our virtual reality simulations are so close to true life now that there is no need for one-on-one counselling to be bounded by proximity," said Roy Cao, founder and owner of Vtech Industries. "We've been lobbying our legislators for years to shift some of the funding for counselling to more pragmatic solutions."

Certainly, the topic of funding has been top-of-mind in Washington DC as the next presidential election looms. On both sides of the aisle, candidates have brought up the Time Event's funding as a pain point for their constituents in early debates, and it is expected that high-level proposals for improving the program will be a cornerstone for the platforms of several candidates. Some are calling for dramatic reductions in funding, while others are focusing on reallocation of funds. Either way, the path forward may well be decided by politics over policy.

Supporters of the Sadler program point out that much of the technology used to build Lake City and to generate the equipment needed for time travel simulations has resulted in patents that also pay for a large portion of the research done by the group, independent of government funding. Members of the Sadler Board stated that there is "a prevailing myth that we are totally backed by government monies, but the study of the Time Event is funded by a combination of federal funding, private grants, and the patented technology owned by our non-profit group." The Sadler Research Group has also stressed that the funding they do receive from the federal government is highly regulated and that individual lawsuits regarding private property and ownership do not fall under their purview, and that decisions on how to distribute the funding for individuals does not come from them.

Critics of Sadler claim that it has too much power over the proceedings in the Time Zone and that as a private company, even one commissioned by the government, it should have more accountability to national and international bodies.

The government's involvement with the Toledo time glitch has always been controversial. From the initial decision to strip personal property and assets of those lost in time to fund search and rescue efforts, to the complicated inheritance and property laws put into place to handle the affairs to those who are still missing and those who have returned, an entirely new specialty of law had to be developed to regulate these decisions put in place by federal mandates. One leading firm that specializes in time law says that before the event Toledo was only the 79th largest U.S. city in terms of population, but that it now accounts for 50% of their inquiries looking for representation.

In addition to the pooling of financial assets, which the harshest critics compare to a communist state without the rights of property ownership, reemerging Toledoans have also become more vocal about needing compensation for loss of personal items. Upon their return, the funding they qualify for covers the value of housing, car, utilities, workers compensation, and other categories – but all based on average values. Individuals who had amassed more personal wealth, such as real estate and property, have always balked at the idea that their monthly stipend only covers more modest housing than they were accustomed to before the Time Event, although others have argued that since property within the Time Zone has been rendered essentially worthless, property ownership in Toledo is no longer a deciding factor in wealth at all.

Custody battles affected by the time variance are another specialty law category growing in recent years. As more minors and their parents have returned from the wormhole, the complexity has increased. While in early years, sending children to foster homes to await parental returns was a standard practice, there are now more cases of adoptive families suing for custody, citing abandonment clauses due to the length of time between the Time Event and parental returns. Complications have also arisen from older teens claiming independence from returning parents who are sometimes ill-equipped to handle the responsibilities of older children.

"I was just a baby when we both disappeared; and my mom was only 21… but I got back first so now I'm already almost 18, and there's no point in her becoming my legal guardian right now," said one minor suing to remain with her foster family. "I'm preparing to go to college and need to focus on setting myself up for my future. I'd rather stay with the family I've known for years for now, and am taking legal action to do so."

The issue of parental rights has sparked considerable debate in recent years as returning time travelers find themselves without the means to support the children they still desperately want back, both financially and from a community standpoint. One advocacy group that specializes in helping reentries navigate being reunited with their children says this problem is at the heart of why their organization was founded. We spoke with the founder of The Village Trust, Deborah O'Dea, who returned from the time stream after 16 years and is still awaiting the return of her husband and three children (aged seven, four, and two at the time of the Event).

"When I first got back and found out that I was in the future, it was overwhelming but I very quickly tried to just accept that this was a fact, and began preparing for when the children returned," she told us. "But very quickly I realized that the time ripple hadn't just disrupted our family by separating us physically, it also removed the whole support system that I had in place. My husband and I both worked full-time jobs and daycare is expensive, so we had arrangements in place to do remote one day a week each, and my mother-in-law watched the kids the other days. We had a daycare for emergency scheduling conflicts, and my sister was available to pick them up most days if necessary. And this was our game plan, at least until they were all old enough for school. But when I got back from time, I realized that while I was praying for some miracle to bring the children back to me right away, if that were to happen, I would have three children to handle on my own with none of that backing and it would be virtually impossible to continue on in the same way. So, I founded The Village Trust to help rebuild communities of people who have lost the necessary pillars of support that their childrearing plans were based on to the time flux."

Disparities in economic status in regards to post-Event action steps have also come under criticism. Although the search and rescue teams do cover every part of the city methodically and technology is dispersed by population in each area rather than socio-economic factors, accusations have been made that experimental tech has been disproportionally concentrated in more affluent areas of the city over the years. There has also been more vocal disapproval of the execution of relocation of survivors to neighboring towns and cities, with some claiming their neighborhoods are being inundated with lower-class people that raise crime statistics, while others dismiss these claims as racially-motivated bias.

Groups such as the United Way and the ACLU have pledged support to program efforts aimed at overcoming these biases and educating new communities to accept a wider range of inhabitants with a variety of special needs related to their survivor status. "People whose lives were disrupted by the Time Event lost their social and economic status, but that does not make them a future detriment to a community," stated Sean Cullers, CEO of Community Begins Here. "Even if they were poor or disadvantaged before the Time Event, their reemergence is a chance to start fresh, and we help them to do that."

As the world marks the 35th anniversary of the time disruption, there are many unanswered questions about survivors' rights and whether the outreach programs can support a higher rate of return for decades more to come. Sustainability experts have been tasked with creating new predictive models to map the trajectory of the costs for the immediate future and are expected to release a report later this year. It is expected that one part of their recommendation will focus on the logistics of allowing returning time travelers to apply for permanent visas in other countries.

Cases of fraud and identity theft rose dramatically in the decades after the time disruption as cybercriminals took advantage of the confusion with data that needed to be manipulated to incorporate time-related information (ad interim status and etcetera). So far, to avoid the rest of the world from having to adjust their record-keeping systems to factor in the complexities of reporting relative ages and birthdates on international passports and in regional databases, reentries from time have thus far been limited to national travel and U.S. residency since the event. The nearby Canadian cities of Windsor and London, just across Lake Erie and still accessible by ferry to the counsellors' headquarters, are rumored to be trial areas for international resettlement of survivors in the near future.

With the immediate needs of search and rescue now under control, and no major breakthroughs in reversing or recreating the science of the wormhole to date, focus is shifting to more long-term plans for accommodating the returning citizens of Toledo without continued disruption to the rest of the country.

CHAPTER 35

Dr. Raj Anil, Director – 37 years, 9 months, 16 days after the Event. Time populous: 176,921

March 3rd

Today is a bittersweet day, the last official day of my employment with Sadler. In some ways, I have been looking forward to my retirement, and for the past several months since we came to our agreement and it was officially announced, I have counted down the days with a growing sense of excitement. I would have liked to see things through longer, but I feel the transition period to my replacement Dr. Xiang has been successful. I have faith that he will be a strong and empathetic leader, and that with creativity, he will be able to meet the financial challenges we are currently facing.

I regret being unable to find a better solution to mitigate the expenses needed to maintain and upgrade Lake City's facilities and that the resultant reduction in staff is one of the unsolved problems I am leaving my successor. In my own defense, budgetary constraints have worsened in recent years and there is no "easy" solution. The cost of preserving this facility, especially as our infrastructure and equipment require maintenance and upgrades, is no small thing to manage and we have had to cut corners somewhat.

Still, despite some personal regrets, I choose to focus on positivity. As a team, we have accomplished so much together over the years, and though we have not yet resolved any of the mysteries of the time distortion itself, I can almost set this aside as a secondary consideration to all of the lives that we have helped rebuild. The physicist inside of me still yearns for understanding, and I hope that in my retirement I can return to the science and perhaps, with concentration, even find something that has hitherto been missed. Some of that is, admittedly, pure vanity to think that I could discover the secret of time travel when the most brilliant minds of our generation have been occupied with that task now for decades with no resolution. But still… it won't hurt to try.

Months ago, when my retirement was first announced, I distinctly remember sitting at my office window, mulling things over and idly watching dozens of squirrels running about the island burying nuts for the winter. For the hundredth time I was wondering how squirrels and other wildlife even got onto this artificial island in the first place. They appeared so gradually that none of us really noticed; maybe stowaways on a ferry since the bridge from the mainland is quite long, and always has shuttle traffic on it that would deter animal life looking to migrate here. Birds of course were the first to appear, that was no big mystery. But you see squirrels now everywhere, and occasionally rabbits as well.

In any case, the squirrels were busy preparing for the winter, running about frantically and burying things every few feet. I remember having heard that thousands of trees are planted each year in the world by squirrels burying acorns and forgetting where they are, and that fact has always stuck with me as such a charming idea. Then it struck me; each squirrel was so diligent in his efforts – Focused! Determined! Busy! – and yet the majority of their work would be abandoned the moment they left that location, and if their nut was ever found, it would likely be another squirrel who dug it from the ground and benefitted. It made me realize that I am like these squirrels. I am always busy, always working. I am putting my whole heart into my tasks, which are for the metaphorical preparations for winter! Most of these efforts will be forgotten, even by me, but they

184

can still contribute to the betterment of society... either from the lone, starving squirrel searching for sustenance in the heart of winter who stumbles across this treasure, or perhaps not recognized for hundreds of years until the forgotten seed has grown from a small insignificant sapling into a mighty oak that houses other squirrels. The squirrel who planted it is simultaneously irrelevant and necessary.

Ha! I am suddenly reminded of another "wildlife" story, one much less philosophical. It was when this facility was still relatively new, and one of the many ways that survivors were being rehabilitated was through the use of support and comfort animals in their therapy sessions. Due to concerns about allergens, it had been determined that the dogs and cats (and other animals – we had domestic rabbits, geese, and even a few miniature pigs!) would be brought in daily by their handlers, rather than living full time in Lake City (a decision that was later reversed for convenience, and to offer "after hours" support to those who needed them). Although there were food and water stations throughout the facility for them, the animals lived on the mainland.

No one is quite sure how it happened (and as far as I know, no one ever owned up to it), but somehow there were some un-spayed cats that got loose in the facility and had litters of kittens in one of the storage areas. Suddenly, we were all spotting random streaks of fur out of the corners of our eyes in the halls!

For weeks there were attempts to catch them all and take them back to the mainland for adoption. Some staff members even used to opportunity to test new motion detectors at the food and water stations; but every time we thought that surely, they must have gotten them all, another litter would appear! It was an annoyance to some people, especially the operations managers who were tearing their hair out trying to figure out where they were hiding (in the ceiling it was later found), but it was also vastly amusing for the rest of us. Most of us who had chosen to live onsite rather than commute in daily were missing the idea of having "pets" and this was a source of entertainment for us. The small tabby who very solemnly marched into the background of a livestream interview with the very serious and foreboding-looking facilities director of the time soon became the stuff of legend.

My friend and I were off duty and playing table tennis in a staff lounge when we heard peals of laughter from next door. We poked our heads in to find a dozen of our colleagues in tears watching our boss trying not to break character, while also attempting to scoop up the recalcitrant feline with one hand. He clearly thought his attempts to grab it were off camera, as with a completely straight face he continued to answer very somberly (the man had a deep, rich voice that always sounded very serious and in ten years working for him, I don't think I ever heard him laugh aloud - although he was not a bad boss at all), while to the side we could all see him gesturing to make the cat come close, and signaling to his assistant to grab it.

The interviewer was unflappable and kept asking questions, but the cameraman must have had a wicked sense of humor because he made no attempt at all to zoom in on the Director and cut the cat out of the shot. So, we (and everyone watching the broadcast) all saw the top of the assistant's head as he chased the cat on hands and knees right in front of the podium. We laughed so hard!! Rebecca was actually rolling on the floor; it was one of the funniest things I have ever seen.

That prompted weeks of the Sadler staff having an underground competition of cat-themed memes, and reenactments of our Director contending with progressively aggressive cat behavior (playing with yarn, fetching a dead mouse, presenting its backside to the camera, and so on). It was very immature of us, but it was a much-needed respite from our more serious work.

Ah, it feels right to wrap up this journal entry on that lighthearted note, remembering the good times with friends instead of feeling sad about this chapter of my life closing. Although the work we have done here is of course a serious business, there were so many small moments of happiness had here in Lake City, which I have long thought of as home.

My personal belongings have already been packed up and transported for me, and I think that in the coming weeks the 'settling in' process at the small cottage I have waiting for me will be a welcome distraction. My new "digs" are in a small community with many retired members of the Sadler staff, so I will enjoy getting to visit with some old friends and colleagues, planting my own garden, and taking up some of the hobbies I have never had time for. For now, I sit in the bare apartment/office that has been my home for most of my adult life, just taking a moment to record my thoughts before I begin my rounds of the facility saying my farewells to the staff. There is a party planned for this afternoon; a 'surprise', though of course I know about it.

I imagine this room will be a peaceful space for someone else now, and so I leave behind just one memento for the next tenant; an engraved quote by the great Albert Einstein, set in a polished stone paperweight and gifted to me by my dear parents many years ago. *"Learn from yesterday, live for today, hope for tomorrow. The important thing is not to stop questioning."*

I take that advice with me everywhere I go. -RA-

CHAPTER 36

Film review – 40 years, 3 months, 15 days after the Event. Time populous: 169,579

Title: *Temporal Disruption: 40 Years*

Critics Score: 60%

Audience Score: 45%

Movie Info: *Temporal Disruption: 40 Years* is the long-awaited follow-up to the critically-acclaimed, Oscar-winning film that explored the individual stories of select time travelers and the impact of their journey through the wormhole twenty years ago. At forty years after the Time Event, this sequel merges breathtaking cinematography with must-see revolutionary footage of the abandoned city with the personal stories of new survivors from the time stream. Shot partially by drone, and partially with special permission and the cooperation of the Sadler group, this film combines a first-person POV with voiceover narrative from multiple survivors' voices.

Genre: Documentary

Running time: 180 minutes

Director: Clarissa Fitzsimmons

Producers: Clarissa Fitzsimmons, K. Lansing, Theodore Roberts

Distributor: Channel 42 Productions, Lighthouse Entertainment Group

Critics reviews:

"Visually, this is a stunning display. The special permissions given to the film crew to capture the empty city from the ground are some of the most intense footages released to date, and give a poignant reminder of what we have indeed lost."

"Despite its flaws, this film is worth watching, especially for those who love the exotic visuals of the abandoned, apocalyptic-style settings. It doesn't stand up to its predecessor in its impact, but surpasses it in visual storytelling."

"A cinematographic masterpiece, but lacking the connection to the individual time travelers. Although I appreciate the director's attempt to separate the style and tone from the original, the end result seems to be asking lightning to strike twice. The finished work is executed well, but doesn't seem likely to recapture the influence of the original."

"The three-hour runtime is too long, lacking tightness and precision. The film coasts along and is crafted reasonably well, but the point is never quite made and leaves you feeling unsatisfied and without conclusions. In this way, it is a very apt and accurate portrayal of how many people feel about the temporal event itself and the lack of resolution even after all these years."

"Although the first-person POV genre adds an interesting element to the film, and the narrative voiceover is still raw with emotion, the stories being related feel recycled. In truth, a strong musical score or soundtrack may have been more effective than the disembodied narration, which feels like a gimmick that otherwise spoils the masterfully crafted picture being painted."

Audience reviews:

"It's somewhat interesting, but there is no tension in the storytelling since the individuals featured are rehashing similar incidents that we all have heard many times before. It's unclear what the film wants to say beyond that the situation is still unresolved."

"This is visually interesting, but overall, not compelling. It's ultimately derivative, and obvious in its thematic execution."

"Conventional, but worth it for the glimpse into the ground-level view of the Alpha teams."

"As an educational piece, this documentary may stand up as a snapshot in time to how things have progressed since the Time Event occurred forty years ago, but I can't imagine wanting to watch it a second time since the content is derived from the same news we have been hearing for years. I was expecting some sort of reveal that never came."

"Unless you saw the first film when it was first released and remember its impact, you can't appreciate how much stronger it is than this iteration."

"Now that the survival rates are so positive, the stories people share are less impactful than the ones highlighted in the original film. Not that anyone wishes for more tragedies, but the tone of the narrators in this film seems more confused than anything as they bemoan their personal struggles. The viewer tends to become bored with their repetitive reactions, and three hours is far too long to stay engaged."

CHAPTER 37

Trevor – 42 years, 2 months, 9 days after the Event. Time populous: 161,073

"*Dear Trevor,*" he read.

"*Look! After all this time, I'm still writing things out by hand just like you always nagged me to do… I think finally I can admit that you were right, it does force me to slow down and it is strangely satisfying to put pen to paper rather than just Zapping you virtually.*

I know officially I've "graduated" out of the program so there's no more check-ins required, but you were one of the few people I could talk to for a long, long time and I felt like I owed you a status update. And there's been a lot going on with me these days.

Last time we spoke (has it really been five years already? Too long) I had just met Amelia, and we've been married two years now already! We chose not to do a big ceremony or I would have invited you, but we just went down to city hall. After all the complicated paperwork of arranging both our time annulments we just wanted to get it over with. It was sad in a way, to put a period on the end of that chapter of our lives, but a relief also. If you remember, Amelia reemerged about four years before we met and we're about the same age on our personal time scales. It's strange to think that my wife was actually born thirty years before me, but she's only a couple years older than me now! Certainly, it makes for some weird conversations because we grew up in such different eras, but we can laugh about it. I call her "old gal" and she calls me "whippersnapper", and it makes for a good story.

Not to be too sappy about it, but I remember you telling me years ago that the time ripple was a mystery, and maybe a gift... if we wanted it to be. At the time I thought you were just spouting philosophical advice to keep me from getting too depressed and sorry for myself, but I know what you mean now. If I'd met Amelia before the Time Event, she would have been just a nice lady about my parents' age and nothing more... and yet here she is, the most important person in my life. Like you always used to tell us – "however it happened is how it should be".

Although we're too old and tired to chase infants and toddlers around, we did decide to foster older children who are waiting on their parents to come back in time. We talked a lot about what we could do to help others, and we agreed that children seem to have gotten the shortest end of the stick so it's what made sense to us. The first kid we had was actually someone I knew; my old friend Andy's daughter! She's off at college now, but she keeps us in the loop and Zaps us with updates on how she's adjusting. Her dad was a good friend of mine from work, and unfortunately neither he nor his ex-wife are back yet, but I'm sure they'll be proud of her and how hard she's been working to adapt once they make it back.

Right now, we have a 13-year-old girl, Meghan, who's been with us about a year; and Jose, an 11-year-old who just arrived about a month ago straight from the onboarding process, maybe you know him from Lake City. The agency says they might send us a third kid in a few months if we have the capacity, and I think we can rearrange the den to become another bedroom if they don't mind the laundry being right there. The ones we have now are both nice kids, and making friends at school pretty quick. The school district we're in has a great continuing counselling program for the kids – there's a lot of survivors in their classes – so they don't stand out in that way.

Meghan's quite an artist – she's filled up whole notebooks of drawings of her family and friends, since she doesn't have access to very many pictures (just what was on her social media at the time that she can get from the archives now, and I guess her mom was pretty strict on not letting her post too much personal stuff). She gets good grades at school and is in some sort of club that shows kids how to make the most of all the alerts they can set up on the people they're waiting on. It's so much more complicated than it was when you first showed me how to do it – she's brought home some tricks to show us. She has a huge extended family, most still lost in time and others who didn't reemerge safely back in the early days, but I think it's just a matter of time before someone comes to claim her.

It's crazy how far things have come since the early days! I remember you patiently waiting for me to wrack my brains for the last names of people I worked with and people I hadn't seen since junior high – JUST IN CASE – but now that everything is digitized you can just put in your name and the search functions find all sorts of connections you never would have even thought of. When Meghan first showed me how to optimize my search flags, right away the database found two guys from my old softball rec league that were back from time already, and although they weren't close friends, I did recognize them right away (one from a team we used to play often, and one who subbed for us a few times). Jerry lives out in Boston now, so we've just chatted a few times, but Phil is here in Cincinnati just a few miles away! We tried joining an 'Over Fifty League' together, but after the first season he pulled his hamstring and my knee started acting up, so now we just get together for poker nights or to watch the big games on 360VR, and that's nice too.

Meanwhile, Amelia and I just asked Jose if he wants to join a little league team this year and he says he would. He's a pretty quiet kid so I think this will be good for him and he says he and his brother used to play, so I'm checking out the local organizations and maybe I'll get a chance to do some coaching this summer. Do you remember that team (God, what was it, twenty years ago now?) that I did some assistant coaching for, the one I used to make you come watch their games when we should have been doing official counselling sessions? I felt like we both needed the break, and I turned out okay even if we did skip a few sessions just to watch. That was a fun couple of years with that team, I wish I'd gotten to do that kind of stuff with kids of my own, but I'm making up for that the best I can now.

I still keep an eye out for Rachael in the alerts, and I really hope to still get to see her again one day and know that she got out of the wormhole all right. I know she will forgive me for moving on with my life, now that I'm too old and gray and "out of range" even for her understanding heart. Amelia's Frank would forgive her too, I'm sure, even though he'd still be in our age group; but they were on the outs even before the Time Event happened and I like to think he'll embrace a new start of his own if he makes it back. One of his sons from his first marriage is back from time eight years now, and although they were never that close before (since he and his brother were adults already when Amelia and Frank met), he sometimes visits us and sends cards for the holidays and keeps in touch. He's about to get married next month, to a nice guy he met from Chicago who isn't a time traveler, and the wedding is there so we're in the midst of preparing for a little family vacation coming up soon. As soon as we find a dogsitter willing to take our crazy mutts Goober and Mr. Fluffernutter for the week we'll be all set.

Well, that's all the news I have for now. I miss you buddy – it's been too long since we talked, and I promise to reach out more often now that I'm officially retired and have more free time. Maybe now that I'm out of the program you can just stop by for a BBQ or something next time you're in my neck of the woods. I'd love to introduce you to Amelia and the kids. You're probably the hardest working man in Lake City, and you deserve a break.

Hope to see you soon!

Tom"

Trevor grinned as he folded the letter and put it to the side. He was glad to hear from Tom; he was always glad to hear from any of his cases who were no longer in the program, but usually it was just a quick Zap, not a full letter. "Snail mail" had been a thing of the past even when he was a kid, but the resurgence of handwritten, personalized correspondence and even calligraphy, had made its way back into fashion over the years, and he loved that. He loved that, as a counsellor, he had contributed to that trend. What Tom had said was true – the counsellors were always big advocates of handwritten journals, where people couldn't just delete unfinished thoughts and forget about them. And he had personally always loved making lists; he was one of those people who feels real satisfaction in checking things off of them. "Make your to-dos your to-dones" his mom's notepad on the refrigerator had said – he still remembered that after all these years.

Funny, the little things like that he remembered, about the house and the neighborhood, even though of course he hadn't seen it since the day he'd hitched up his bike and started for the museum. Maybe if he had known it would be the last time, he would have looked around the house and fixed it in his memory more before he'd left on his big adventure, but he hadn't. Little details like the notepad came back to him in flashes.

Trevor in his fifties isn't that much different than that kid who loved books about adventures and dinosaurs. He's still an optimist, and he still loves libraries and museums. Whenever he was doing case work in Chicago he would stop at the Field Museum, or maybe even meet with people there – but nowadays most of the check-ins are done through virtual reality rather than in person, at least while budgets for travel are still slim. It was harder to connect with people when it wasn't face-to-face, but it did let him stay in one place most of the time, and that had its advantages too. He and Val had a nice little place near the helipad, so he had given up his quarters in Lake City and switched to commuting. The new lake hoppers made it a quick 5-minute trip, and no one used the slower land shuttles on the bridge any more, except guests to the facility.

He could do most of his work remotely now anyway; he only went in to the office occasionally, and it was usually just to meet new hires or catch up with his buddies. He was planning on meeting a friend there on Friday for lunch, actually. Enchilada day at the Lake City café.

He didn't miss the facility as much as he missed traveling to see people like Tom. He'd always liked getting a glimpse of them in their new lives; he was glad Tom was happy, and that he was getting a chance to be a dad finally. Trevor had never had time for kids himself, though it would have been nice if DJ had come back from time sooner… although he wouldn't have been able to care for her while living the dormitory life in Lake City anyway. He was a lot older now, but that meant he had more money saved too, and although the house wasn't huge it had a nice yard, and they had a spare bedroom for when DJ joined them. And if either his or Val's mom came back first, they had the spare bedroom plus a small office they could give up if necessary. He kept hoping it would be necessary.

He put Tom's letter aside and went in search of a snack (still the same old Trevor) so that he wouldn't get too bogged down worrying for the thousandth time about whether they would ever get here, and wishing they would hurry up and come back already, and thinking about how many things they had already missed. He still had work to do today, and if there was one thing he had learned from being a counsellor all these years, there was no point worrying about the past.

However it happened is how it should be.

CHAPTER 38

News headlines –
45 years after the Event.
Time populous: 151,717

'History continues to repeat itself'; A new generation reacts as the U.S. marks the 45th anniversary of the time incident

Survival rates are dramatically improved by artificial intelligence in search and rescue functions

Demands for the science community to find a solution to speeding up reentry rates grow

Descendants of Toledo's elite file a class-action suit demanding inheritance laws be reexamined

Photos: drone footage of Toledo's crumbling infrastructure

Featured editorial by Dr. T. Parsons, PhD

Opinion piece: We are running out of time

When the snag in our universe happened that fateful May 15th, forty-five years ago, Toledo, Ohio was a relatively unremarkable city in the heartland of America. The modest metropolis, home to over a quarter of a million citizens, was, in an instant, completely abandoned by the human race. The world was captivated by the mystery and came to the aid of the lost city in an unprecedented and cooperative effort.

Although the almost immediate return of some of the missing time travelers was verified within weeks, and the very proof of the theory of relativity confirmed, it took years to forge the complex system developed to handle both rescue efforts and scientific research.

The emergency response portion of the Sadler program saw significant gains in successful rescue statistics for years, but was heavily challenged two years ago when large portions of the program were outsourced to an automated control system. There was concern that the new methods for training and more high-tech paraphernalia introduced to encourage automation combined with a reduction in staffing would upset progress, but in fact the numbers have improved greatly in a very short time. This is both welcome news and a cause for some alarm. Although improved survival rates, shortened rescue and evacuation times, and reduced staffing costs are short term wins, there have also been reports that those reemerging from the time stream report more disorientation and less acceptance of the situation after the fact. Mental health concerns have risen over the years as a result, with increased counselling support needed for counterbalance.

Drone footage has revealed increasing problems with the city's infrastructure due to initial damage and overall lack of maintenance, and an influx of technology that has rendered the city streets almost unrecognizable. This is further emphasized by the mass removal of trees over the years to cut down on leaves and branches blowing through reentry zones in high winds and creating potential hazards for travelers. Those reentering from the wormhole are experiencing not just the instantaneous disappearance of people, objects, and structures around them, but the sudden appearance of highly sophisticated, futuristic gadgetry all around. Combined with limited funding for rehabilitation programs, analysis of the survivors shows increased initial levels of shock and stress compared to earlier generations of returns, and a lengthening period before acclimatization into society. These statistics, though they do not affect the actual survival rates, are worrisome and indicate a need for more support.

At the same time, onboarding programs have been shortened in the past decade due to lack of funds. Although as more time has passed since the initial event it has become extremely likely that travelers' understanding of both professional and household technology has gaps, the programs that would support reassimilation have been reduced. This can only lead to frustration from the public, with many saying that the people returning from time are a burden to society.

It is clear that the public's goodwill towards the city of Toledo is rapidly waning. The success rates are so much higher than in the early years that there is less sympathy for survivors, and their individual stories have been relegated to the 'thoughts and prayers' category that social issues like poverty fell into years ago. It is my belief that if the scientific community does not make a concerted effort to rapidly draw the standoff with time in Toledo to a close, within a few years we will see funding dry up even further, and those who return will receive considerably less care after their initial rescue.

The fact that even after all these years the world's best scientific minds have been unable to unravel the advent of the time anomaly or pinpoint its origins is a continued source of concern. Although there have been no additional reports of any time ripples outside of the Time Zone in which Toledo sits, the possibility still looms that this catastrophe could be repeated, perhaps this time in an even more populous area. The idea of such an event happening in a place like Shanghai, with over forty million residents, rather than a small urban center like Toledo is unthinkable. And yet, the public is weary of the cautionary side of time travel and seems reluctant to even consider the potential impact of a reoccurrence.

Just as it was when Einstein first published his theory of relativity, the pure science remains above the level of the common man's grasp. What brought people together (in understanding) following the Time Event was not the science, but the human connections that were disrupted and our collective empathy for our fellow man. For a short time, the situation in Toledo brought the reality of time travel to the world's stage, but with the continued inability to recreate, reverse, or even understand the effect of that lone incident, we are on the cusp of forgetting all that we learned as human beings from this tragedy.

In my opinion, it is an extremely dangerous time for mankind to become forgetful. With almost 130,000 Toledoans returned from time, we are still not even at the halfway mark to recovering the full contingent of the city. Those returning still need our help. Though we, on the outside looking in, have all long since accepted the situation, to them it is still something out of science fiction, and they will be just as scared and lost as those who returned years ago. Although statistically they are more likely to know other survivors now in the present than those in the first generations of returns, they are also more likely to have shocking age gaps and cultural divides that have grown up between them, which will be both alarming and potentially harmful to their lives as they attempt to assimilate.

Furthermore, I believe that a lapse now in keeping up progress with the returning travelers could prove detrimental if the rate of return fluctuates in coming years. Although it seems unlikely to happen, would any of us be remotely prepared if the remaining residents suddenly reappeared all at once, or in large groups? Conversely, what if returns ceased entirely with half the disappeared still missing? Any major shifts in the data would be worrisome, which is why the collection of that data is still vitally important even if firm conclusions cannot as yet be drawn.

For those of us who grew up after the Time Event, we have seen the illustrative models in school and in the media our whole lives, and know that there are various comparisons to scattered grains of rice, ripples in a pond, wormholes, etc. Most of these models, paired with simulations that take the finite population of Toledo as the one constant variable in the equation hypothesize an end date in which all missing people have been accounted for. But what if indeed the Time Event has a start, but not an end at all, and the ripples in the fabric of time extend out to eternity? No matter how weary the public is of the topic, we are not yet at a point in time where we can abandon the pursuit of understanding.

I urge us all to stay engaged with this problem longer. It is my honest belief that we have the capacity to solve it.

CHAPTER 39

Beverly neighborhood, Toledo – 48 years, 7 months, 7 days after the Event. Time populous: 139,225

"You're positive – POSITIVE – we're not showing up on their scans now?"

"Fucking ask me again, Darryl. I've told you ten times, I fucking sniped it. We're clear."

"NO NAMES, remember? I don't care if we're off the comms, you don't need to yell it. There could be other kinds of recording devices all over this neighborhood. Who knows what new tech they're testing out around here."

"Both of you shut up then. Get up to the main gate. Our window is only about another hour and then we need to haul ass to make the edge of the zone on schedule."

"Yeah, yeah. We're going."

The other members of the snatch and grab team were already in the house. It was a very risky business just passing the border, and ten years ago it wouldn't have even been possible with Alpha teams combing every neighborhood and the latest model of Orien iSpys® everywhere in sight. But the newest tech worked off of an unconnected grid. Although in theory this type of smart system was superior in that it was solar powered with a continual backup battery for emergency charging, it was also easier to hack into.

The old models, which worked off of lidar tech, had a limited range but transmitted their data directly by satellite; the new systems used a different type of connectivity that was more energy efficient, but had interoperability issues. It was complicated, but doable, for a talented Hacksaw to introduce a glitch into the system that temporarily caused a blind spot in a small area while the system ran a self-diagnostic check. In small, concentrated doses, these were not enough to set off alarms from the main system. It was normal for the system to do these self-checks regularly, which is what made the system sustainable and low-maintenance. As long as they were careful to come in slowly and leave slowly by a different route (sometimes multiple diagnostic checks too close together triggered an alert), they would be virtually invisible. It was like a slow game of chess, moving forward in a set pattern according to certain rules.

Looting in Toledo was a very serious crime. But a lucrative one, if you could pull it off. Aside from items with intrinsic value that were just lying around waiting to be picked up, the underground market for "antiquiuities" coming from the lost city brought incredibly high prices. On the downside, you had to be able to authenticate the exact locations of your find with recorded documentation of where you had recovered it from, so if you got caught, you were basically handing in your confession to the authorities with all the evidence needed to put yourself away for about ten years minimum. And that was for a first offense. Pretty steep penalty for what would be considered petty theft in most parts of the world, but considering that the value of anything coming out of Toledo would be ten times its original worth and add in the charges of endangerment (in theory, any time traveler not yet returned was put in "imminent danger" by your unauthorized presence) and trespassing... those charges added up. There were no appeals, either.

Despite the danger, the money was so tempting that crews were constantly looking for ways around the tech that was now the primary guardian of the city. They still had to watch out for live ground crews, but they were much more spread out than back in the day.

The previously more densely-populated neighborhoods, which got the most scrutiny due to the higher number of reentries, also tended to be poor or middle-class. The pricey neighborhoods like Deveraux and Beverly with their big lawns and houses (spaced well apart) meant less time travelers arriving home, less traffic, fewer pedestrians, less public transportation. All this meant less tech watching over the area. Add that to the fact that the houses could contain luxury items that would have fetched high prices even without the connection to the lost city, and this was a profitable heist if you could swing it. It was ironic that back when the city had been populated, these would be the areas with the most security, but in a world where human lives were prioritized over possessions, looters benefitted from that irony.

The plan was straightforward; use lake hoppers to clear the initial border. The team, usually no more than six, to continue on foot, following the mapped path made by their Hacksaw to the target. Scavengers enter and forage, opening safes and lockboxes. Gather the goods and let the Authenticator make the selection (small, portable items like jewelry and collectibles that fetch a high price in the black market are preferred) and make the official recordings for the authentication. Pickups pack it all up for removal. Everyone carries it back, everything in half-grav packs to keep things manageable; a different route on foot, but back to the original lake hopper location and out. No weaponry – get caught with that in the Time Zone and you'd double your sentence for sure. Most teams wouldn't even take antique weapons out for that reason, no matter the price they'd fetch.

"What do we have this time?"

"Jackpot in this place. The jewelry alone is going to pay for this trip."

"Diamonds?"

"Emerald ring and a diamond necklace with matching earrings. Big ol' rocks. Plus, some cheaper stuff in the regular jewelry box that will still sell – pearls, semi-precious stones."

"Easy to carry out too. What's that thing though?"

"Some kind of map case, full of some art prints that might be worth something. And the flat box has a pretty good coin collection."

"Heavy."

"Expensive. We're taking it."

"You're the boss. Ready to head out?"

They hoisted their packs and slipped out silently. This group is one of the lucky ones that will make it out; that jewelry will sell fast to some wealthy collector looking for a piece of the lost city. These are non-violent offenders, ordinary thieves – hardly the marauders that used to plague the Alpha teams with vicious clashes decades ago, or the persistent looters of the early days.

Most of these small teams sneaking in and out are looking for a quick payout; but there is a rumor that a few have been specially commissioned by survivors looking to recover specific personal mementos from their abandoned homes. The possibility that there is an actual time machine and that its inventor might try to recover it is another reason why survivors are not allowed back into the city for personal items, but most people don't realize that that's part of the concern.

In fact, there are some that argue that the Delta teams should be tasked with doing the very same thing these petty burglars are doing... going house by house to collect all valuables to sell, using the profits to continue to fund rescue efforts rather than using the tax dollars of hard-working Americans. Is it really that different from emptying the bank accounts of those still lost in time to pool resources for funding, something that was done decades ago?

Critics of the continued quarantine of the city argue that personal items (with or without intrinsic value) should have been collected and held for the returning survivors offsite years ago. Counter arguments say that emptying tens of thousands of households and procuring storage (and protection) for decades would not be cost effective, nor would it further the mission of saving lives.

The argument continues that for households where all parties have been accounted for (as survivors or as confirmed fatalities), there should be no need to preserve the locations or the property within. The counter argument dryly refutes that the Delta squads are not professional movers, and that the rescue teams are not preparing for a flea market.

But what is the long-term plan? Wait until *everyone* is back from time and then let people go loot their own houses? Imagine desperately needing something you can't currently afford on your survivor's welfare, knowing damn well there's one just sitting in your house rusting away... fifty years from now if they let you have it back, will you be grateful? Maybe we should just wait for the whole city to crumble, call it an archaeological dig, and go looking for buried treasure. Maybe by the time all the time travelers are accounted for the city *will* have crumbled, and this whole society forgotten, and future archaeologists will puzzle over the remains.

It's a common debate; from friends around the dinner table talking in hypotheticals to politicians looking for realistic new avenues to collect funding from anything of value. Certainly, the question pokes at some of the fundamentals of human nature. What makes a house a home? Is it the collection of things you own? Is it the people who live inside? Why can't it be both? At a very philosophical level, this aspect of the Time Event reveals cultural differences; if the anomaly had happened somewhere besides the United States, already viewed as overly materialistic by much of the rest of the world, property questions might not even come to the top of list. And yet... isn't it human nature to collect and gather the things we like? Your books, art, clothes, knickknacks; they are all a reflection of you. Can you hold them in your mind, their essence? Sure, if you are a Zen Master. The rest of us need the actual stuff.

CHAPTER 40

Alpha Team Two – 50 years, 7 months, 3 days after the Event. Time populous: 132,490

"I can't see a damn thing, Gordon! I repeat, ZERO VISIBILITY!"

"Get under cover, Happ – we're too exposed here – due north, 200 meters, into the station!"

"Grab Taggart and Juarez! I've lost comms, we've got to get out of this wind!"

They staggered across the courtyard and into the relative safety of an alcove. Happ found an entrance and they tumbled into a pitch black, but blessedly quiet, lobby. Pulling out emergency lighting from their packs, they checked their equipment first, then went looking for a warmer area to take stock of the situation.

The blizzard had hit suddenly, from the north and east. A rare combination of polar vortex and sub-zero temperatures from one direction and a series of humid, warmer storms moving up from the southeast met, merged, and dumped 37 inches of snow directly on Toledo in less than 48 hours.

Whiteout conditions made routes impassable for the Alpha squads, even if they had been able to wade through the drifts that were already higher than their heads due to high wind conditions. Beta teams couldn't fly at all in this weather, and medicycles were useless without passable roads. And snow removal was impossible for the Delta crews – there was literally nowhere to put it, and it was coming down faster than they could clear it anyway.

"We're lucky this kind of storm hits about once every hundred years and not all the time," said Corporal Taggart bitterly. "We'd have a casualty rate of 100% from October to March every year."

The four of them were tucked into a small corner office of the fire station, which luckily had an emergency generator, but they still had every dry layer of clothing they had on, and had ransacked the station's emergency supplies for heat blankets too. Power had been out for hours and it was negative twenty degrees outside, according to the satcom. The storm was still messing with the radar and the rest of their equipment, and they'd had to turn off the motion detector and iSpy alerts altogether because there was too much precipitation flying around to make heads or tails of anything, and they couldn't mobilize to get to anyone calling for rescue anyway.

Official word from base was for everyone in the field to just find shelter and stay put. They would just have to hope that any returning time travelers would be lucky enough to emerge indoors and do the same. Even the state-of-the-art OLED polymer emergency lighting that had been laid a few years back to guide people to safe routes was worthless in this kind of storm; their electroluminescence needed carbon and hydrogen to convert electricity into light, and that didn't work under feet of snow.

"Jesus Christ – the wind's got to be ripping those weather panels right off the roofs," exclaimed Juarez, as a loud grinding noise right above their heads made them all jump to their feet. "They're not meant to withstand gusts above about fifty miles per hour at best. Not that they're going to stop any of this weather anyway, but they're probably all going to need repairs once this is over."

"Assuming we can even salvage them – if they actually dislodge, they could fly all the way to the lake," Taggart muttered, settling back down on the small sofa.

Lieutenant Gordon snorted in disgust. They were so short-staffed these days, the last thing they needed was more maintenance assignments. That was supposed to be Delta work, but those teams were even more under-resourced these days and their backlog was so long that it just made more sense to have the Alpha teams do the small items as they went. Gordon thought bitterly that nowadays he felt more like a handyman than a soldier. And they were working in teams of four instead of eight now with the latest round of budget cuts. At least that meant fewer of them caught out in this crap. He'd eat his hat if they got less than twenty inches of snow tonight.

"Every single damn camera is going to need recalibration too. All of the tech will need a full rework; the snow shouldn't damage the actual guts of them, but the wind probably has all the gimbles out of whack."

"Urgh, stop adding to the honey-do list." Happ flopped back down on the floor and started pulling out the camping stove to make coffee.

"Hey man, I call it like I see it. All I'm saying is all the tech in the world won't do the job if it's not configured right, and we're going to get stuck with fixing it, you know we are."

"Shit."

Juarez was right, and he was their Tech Specialist, so he would know – it would probably take weeks if not months to get everything back in order. Assuming the snow could even be cleared quickly; the longer it took the longer it would be before they could start checking all the gadgetry. Maybe this would be a chance to clear out some of the obsolete gear at least. Over the years more technology had been added in layers but was rarely removed from site while they were short-staffed.

They'd honestly been lucky for a long time, with mild winters and snowfall that was more of an inconvenience than a serious danger. Other parts of the world had seen some record-breaking storms due to climate change, but they'd had good fortune, as though the universe figured they had enough going on for now in the Time Zone, thanks very much. Things like surface heat coils to melt mild snow and other advancements had been made over the years to minimize things that could be in the way of people materializing during the winter months, but those things wouldn't stand a chance against a storm like this.

"Gordon, do we even have enough squads to do a full sweep of the territory on foot, or do you think we'll need to bring in auxiliary groups?"

"Geez, I doubt we'll have the manpower without them... probably it'll be all hands on deck. But before we even think about sweeps or repairs, we'll have to find a way to move the snow. Maybe down into the sewers. And I don't want to think about how many returning travelers we're going to find buried out there in those drifts. Poor bastards will be frozen stiff by the time we get to them, and they better watch it with the heavy plows too, or we're looking at a bloody mess for us to deal with."

Taggart gave a little shudder. He knew they probably wouldn't even be conscious of what hit them, but he'd never liked to imagine the particulars when they found mortalities. Their success rate was so high these days that it wasn't very often at all; he wouldn't have made it as an Alpha back in the day when it was more common. He wished he could have been there during the K9 unit days though – he would have gone for that track at Wormhole U for sure. Dogs made for better companions than iSpys. But that program had been defuncted by the time he'd enrolled. He had an uncle who'd been an Alpha way back when, and he'd gotten the bug hearing his stories as a kid, but times sure had changed since then.

Happ passed out the coffee; there was nothing to do now but sit and wait, and try to keep warm. He wasn't going to complain if no one else was, but he was freezing his ass off even with the generator starting to do its thing. Being from Houston, the winters here were harder than he'd grown up in, but he'd been in the program for four years already (two as a Delta, just over two as an Alpha Private First Class) and this was the worst winter they'd had; there was probably more snowfall in the last hour than the past several years combined. Hurricanes were more of a problem where he was from, and he couldn't imagine trying to do a job like this in a city with regular hurricane damage. Toledo saw an occasional tornado warning, but that was usually about the worst of it. Imagine having to work the Time Zone in a place like Florida, or California – droughts, mudslides, fires, hurricanes, tropical storms, earthquakes – what a mess. Really, it was lucky it had happened here in the middle of the country where nothing much happened. Of course... it would have been even better if it happened in the middle of the Canadian Rockies or something... you'd have a few time traveling moose wandering around, but that would be about the extent of it. Although to be fair, for all they knew there *were* Time Zones all over the place and the moose were all wondering what in the hell was going on.

As a kid, Happ had been obsessed with the idea of the wormhole. His friends were bored to death of hearing about it; just a boring thing talked about in history class at school and something that was always on the news that only adults paid attention to; but he thought it was fascinating. The idea of skipping from one moment to the next... sometimes he'd imagine that when he blinked, maybe he'd time traveled ahead five minutes. Would anyone notice if it was just five minutes? Maybe they were all time traveling at random intervals all the time, but in little chunks where people didn't realize it. Maybe when he went to sleep, he skipped forward each night and he wouldn't even know it. Every time he felt tired during the day, he wondered if it was because he'd actually skipped over his sleep time.

When he'd qualified for Alpha, he was pretty stoked – he would have happily remained a Delta. The money was good, and it was interesting to see the mysterious city he'd been hearing about his whole life up close. But as a Delta, they never really saw any travelers; both survivors and fatalities were evac-ed before his team would ever show up. Since the streets had been cleared of all obstacles before he was even born, mostly they were just cutting back trees and lawns, repairing infrastructure, fixing or adjusting tech. In reality, it was pure maintenance work.

He'd liked Delta Team Six fine, but when they started seeing layoffs at budget time and some of their work being shifted to the Alpha teams, he thought it might be worth trying the Alpha test. He knew he couldn't be a Beta, because he hadn't done any of the forensic coursework, or the piloting modules. The Epsilon squads, after a short-lived stint specializing in animal control (the city had seen a surge in the pest population that was now largely eradicated), had been disbanded, and their duties merged back with the Deltas anyway. It seemed like a long shot, but he had done the prerequisite courses back at university, and he was fit enough to pass the physical training test for Alpha. He knew he was weak on the medical side, so he was still taking some side classes, but the requirements were less stringent nowadays, when there wasn't much call for anything more serious than basic first aid in the field – the hoppers picked reentries up almost immediately, and the Lake City hospital could deal with things better than they could anyway. To be really honest, being an Alpha wasn't much like what he thought it would be; he'd imagined finding people constantly, and carrying them to safety like in all the training videos (of course those were exaggerated – but still!) but mostly they just patrolled up and down, up and down the city. In the buildings, out of the buildings. Respond to alerts, record the locations. He'd still never even seen a reentry with his own eyes – it was always an alert after the fact. Sometimes the Beta teams even beat them to the reentry sites.

He was still cold, and got down on the floor to do some pushups to warm himself up. The rest of the team groaned at him – they teased Happ constantly for being such a gym rat, always lifting and measuring protein powder and making notes. He just laughed them off. He might not have the medical creds and maybe he was just a dumb Delta who got lucky... but if he was going to be an Alpha, he was at the very least going to look like one.

Outside, the blizzard raged.

CHAPTER 41

Excerpt from the Ledger – 50 years, 7 months, 13 days after the Event. Time populous: 132,411

State of Emergency Declared as Winter Storm Alice Wreaks Havoc in Toledo Area

DETROIT, MICHIGAN USA – Official statements from the authorities are grim regarding the impact of the massive storm front that devastated the already vulnerable area last week. Snow drifted as high as ten feet in some areas and the massive weight of ice and snow has collapsed two bridges and caused structural damage to many buildings throughout the area.

Although it will take weeks to completely clear the city and tally the full impact, there have already been 48 casualties in the Time Zone confirmed and only two confirmed survivors from those who reemerged during the storm itself and in the days immediately after. This shockingly low survival rate marks this week as one of the deadliest in Toledo since the Time Event, and more injuries and fatalities are expected while immense amounts of snow and ice blanket the reentry zone.

Most of the fatalities recorded appear to be the result of exposure to the elements from those who reentered outdoors in the storm, or from freezing temperatures indoors. The power has been out in Toledo since last Friday, and although the temperatures outside are now rising, there was little that could be done during the storm itself.

Very unfortunately, three of these deaths are children under the age of ten, including a three-month-old baby found frozen in her crib in her family home. Even more horribly, both her mother and father have been recovered from the time stream and had been eagerly waiting for her return. A recorded statement was issued on behalf of the family and was shared millions of times on social media platforms within hours.

"We were fortunate to both return from time only a few years apart, and we've been praying for almost ten years for our little girl to rejoin us so that our family could embrace a new future together. We are grateful to still have each other, and will honor her memory as best we can." The family asks that their privacy be respected as they mourn, and asks that any charitable donations go to the search and rescue fund. They thanked the Alpha teams in their message for saving so many, and many more to come.

"This tragic loss of so many lives is even more horrible when you realize that if they had they rejoined us at any time other than this particular week, their families would be celebrating their survival," read an official statement from the Sadler headquarters. "We are expediting our efforts to clear the city and hope to find more survivors, but there is no denying that the death toll from this storm is unprecedented, and that in the weeks to come, the amount of structural damage to the city may cause more injuries to those returning from time."

At least one death appears to be a result of a roof collapse due to heavy snow, with at least two others officially confirmed as accidents caused by ice and wind. During the storm, at the Site Three checkpoint, 67-mph winds guests were recorded, ripping much of the protective weather tech from buildings, causing damage to the structures and shorting out over 50% of the sensors used for motion detection. In the days since the storm, the disruption of the tech has forced the program to call in auxiliary teams and volunteers to manually comb the city for survivors and to help clear snow.

"I've been through the training and I've been on the volunteer list since I turned 18 last year, but this is the first time I've been called into an exercise inside the city limits," said Ben Argos, of Detroit. "It's a shame to finally get to see it under these circumstances."

In recent years, the staffing levels of the Alpha, Beta, and Delta squads have been significantly reduced due to improved AI and technology designed to automate rescues, but in the aftermath of this event there is a renewed need for boots on the ground. Much of the snow is being plowed inward towards the Maumee and dumped into the river to clear the streets, but each load must first be checked for bodies that may have reemerged during the storm.

In addition to the time travelers, there has been one reported casualty and three serious injuries of Alpha team members caught out in the storm. All four were attempting to get under cover when a section of the overpass collapsed from the combined weight of snow and rusting infrastructure on the bridge that was backlogged for Delta maintenance.

In Washington, lawmakers called for renewed emergency funding to be directed towards the Toledo area.

"A storm of this magnitude qualifies as a natural disaster, and in truth, if this were a different city with a full population, the death toll might be even higher," stated the Senate Majority Leader. "The distressing thing is to realize that although there were very few people in Toledo during this horrific storm, those travelers who were unlucky enough to reemerge during it and its aftermath had under a 5% chance of survival."

Reports also indicate that parts of the Lake City facility were damaged in the storm, with the weight of the ice and snow affecting the pneumatic lifts that keep stability on the manmade island that supports the counsellors' headquarters and medical facilities. Although there were no serious injuries reported on the island, most of the staff and residents have been evacuated to the mainland while the damage is fully assessed. Repairs to the underwater supports will be delayed by the amount of ice and snow in the lake itself, and the researchers and counsellors are preparing to host survivors in emergency locations on the mainland until order can be restored.

In nearby cities outside the Time Zone, people are still struggling to clear the snow in their neighborhoods. Transportation has come to a halt across much of the Midwest, although the snowfall in these areas was considerably less than in Toledo itself and heavy-duty equipment has been brought in from Chicago to help clear routes for supplies.

Gusting caused the biggest issues, with drifts up to two feet in parts of Detroit, Cleveland, and Ann Arbor. Snowfall was officially recorded between four to eight inches in these locations.

CHAPTER 42

Grant Hutchings – 53 years, 1 months, 7 days after the Event. Time populous: 129,289

Finally. FINALLY, they were ready.

It had taken years for them to work out how to get around the increased security measures that had been put in place after the cyberattack by those commie foreigners, but there were young guys on the team now (including some second-generation members who had been training for this their whole lives) who were tech geniuses. They were ten times smarter than any of those fake scientists that were always being paraded around as time experts, talking about things they didn't even understand. And they were about a million times smarter than those time-deniers that had attacked last time, too.

Grant was no time-denier; the disappearances were real. Anyone who thought they were faked was just fucking stupid – how else would people be coming back at the same ages, decades later? Fake video footage wouldn't cause a child to remain five years old for fifty years, and his group had personal connections who had returned to back that up. No, as far as conspiracy theories went, time-deniers didn't have a leg to stand on. The real secret, *the whole point*, was who was controlling the time machine itself, and for what ends. Whoever ended up with it was going to have all the real power, and he intended that to be his side.

Maybe he wasn't a tech expert or a scientist, but he understood things just fine. The world had gone to shit since the Time Event had happened, and those responsible were going to pay for it now. His cousin Steve hadn't lived to see their full mission through, but Grant would make damn sure all the sacrifices they'd made wouldn't be in vain, not after all this time. They had already waited decades longer than he had ever thought things would take.

Sure, they'd made some progress in the early years, just gathering followers and planning out the things they would do once they had the machine. But they had hit a brick wall when they just simply couldn't find it. The assumption had been that once they had a few undercover plants employed at Lake City, the secret of where it was hidden would quickly be revealed... but they'd searched and searched for evidence of a top-secret bunker, or a heavily-guarded lab, or even just a hidden safe somewhere on the premises... and they'd come up empty. Steve and the others they'd carefully gotten into maintenance or security jobs had gotten into almost every nook and cranny of those buildings and their computer systems over the years and there was nothing to find in Lake City after all that prep.

They'd been stumped for a while (it could be ANYWHERE!), but the breakthrough had come when it had dawned on Grant that the safest place for the government to hide the time machine would be putting it back in Toledo itself. Lake City was too high-profile, but Toledo proper was chock full of hiding places. There were hundreds, *thousands*, of unoccupied buildings; and whether the machine was large or small, hidden or in plain sight, there was simply no one there to see it. All their bullshit about the tech to supposedly catch reentries was probably mostly just to keep people away from the site of the machine. The government could do all their research and time experiments from there, and continue to greedily rake in the cash from their patents, and all the while they had the whole country, the whole *world*, on a fucking leash that people were too blind to even see.

Once they'd realized Toledo itself was their real target, Grant and Steve had forged the plan to attack, and then that unfortunate series of bad luck had stalled them once again. But they hadn't panicked; they let the foreigners take the blame, and then they took their time and started a whole new campaign. Although they were patriots, and no goddam cowards, before they went full scorched-earth they'd tried to hire snatch and grab teams to find the machine quietly, or at least help narrow down the search area. Of course, they didn't *tell* the hired help that was the intent; they pretended just to be looking for Toledo treasure like any greedy thrill-seeker would. It made more sense to let some random group of looters, who wouldn't be able to give away their mission secrets if caught, take the risk of sneaking around the Time Zone for them. He had combed through thousands of hours of their body cam footage, but nothing definitive emerged.

Selling the antiques that the looters brought them took care – getting caught selling on the black market would ruin all their plans – and to be honest, many of the younger guys in the group became too obsessed with building their wealth this way. This wasn't the damn mafia, and Grant had no desire to become some greasy crime lord, running stolen goods and money like some stereotypical movie villain. He was a simple man, who wanted his God-given rights, that was all. Enough with honest people like him getting crushed under the bootheels of crooks in some far-off capitol cesspool, watching their freedoms get restricted again and again and again. Enough giving handouts out to every pathetic person, organization, and country that couldn't cut it on their own, sending beggars to their borders on the daily. His original group of followers felt the same way, but he was starting to worry that the younger generation had lost sight of their vision.

In his mind, the whole campaign outsourcing through the looters was turning out to be a bust, and Grant had been working to phase it out despite opposition from within the group. In the end, it had taken years longer than he wanted to convince his generals that they'd wasted too much time with those losers who weren't even part of their organization. He should have known if they wanted it done right, they would have to do it themselves. He was only able to convince the others once he had made a powerful friend who would solve their funding problems once and for all.

Grant had always handled most of the black-market transactions himself, despite his distaste for the process. People like Steve needed to maintain their innocent personas as Sadler employees with clean slates, and he didn't trust his foot soldiers to be as cautious as he would be. In his underground dealings, he'd run across a buyer who seemed likeminded, and tried to recruit him to their cause. His intention had been to gain just another member, but as it turned out the gentleman in question was actually very, *very* wealthy, and had plans of his own.

Mr. Billionaire had been subtly using his wealth and power behind the scenes to get key friends and allies into key leadership positions in several states and countries, and had spent years creating a network beholden to him, and it was almost ready. When the time was ripe, he planned to run for the country's highest office and win.

His proposal to Grant was simple. He would secretly bankroll all their preparations, trusting only Grant with his identity. When he gave the signal to take action, Grant's troops would secure the time machine and start making demands, and the current administration would look weak while *he* would swoop in and negotiate a resolution. He would win the election handily, and then for years they two could strike public deals to "avoid time catastrophes" that would all be orchestrated according to their secret plans. He would be a hero in the eyes of the nation, and in times of disaster, things like regular election cycles would go out the window – emergency powers would be granted, and laws changed. He would be a new kind of ruler for this country that could once again be the greatest on earth. All the while, Grant and his group would be the fall guys if they were found out – that part of his plan he neglected to mention – but first they had to get ahold of that time machine. Everything depending on that.

They both agreed it must exist, and it really worked, so having it under their control instead of under the control of the current government was the key.

Grant was no dummy. He knew damn well the billionaire was a slippery son-of-a-bitch who intended them to do his dirty work and then reap all the rewards. That wacko wanted to set himself up as a king – he was no true American. That's why he'd take the guy's money, but had no intention of actually handing over control of that machine once they had it. Like any rich asshole out there he thought he was so smart, but not smart enough to see a double cross right in front of his eyes. Rich people always assumed money could buy them anything, but it never bought true loyalty. He was just like any other worthless politician who wanted lies upon lies; Grant wanted the truth out there once and for all, and his loyalty was to the mission. Once they had that machine, Mr. Billionaire just might be the first one to disappear.

But first he would get what he needed from that bastard. The preparations took time and money, and there was a lot of work to be done. First, Grant secured some land out in the western desert, far from prying eyes, and had set it up to look like he was building a dirt bike track, lodge, and shooting range for vacationing campers and outdoorsy types. A few 'opening soon' signs and some fake construction vehicles, and it had given them a base camp to work out of for the next decade. No one ever went out that way anyway, but it was smart to camouflage it as much as possible. Using funding from his new rich friend, his boys had built the flight packs and submersibles they needed for the plan from raw parts, disguising them as sporting water vehicles. Most of the weapons they would need had been cleverly smuggled cross-country in RVs as part of his fake tourist destination already. Low-tech, false-bottomed smugglers' holds would end up winning against all that high-tech Alpha bullshit in the end.

Grant had enough troops now to really mobilize; and though they had a few tricks up their sleeves to keep their attack under the radar while they were getting in to Toledo, they weren't going to be putting all their hopes around some cybersecurity attack like punks. This was going to be an old-fashioned cage match; they were going to get in, take control of the city, seize that machine, and then make their demands with the whole world watching. No more government coverups and no more secrets. Finally, the truth would be out there, for anyone smart enough to see it. All they had to do was get a foothold where they could lay up within missile range of major cities and they'd be able to demand pretty much whatever they wanted, including stalling for time while they gathered more followers. Once they could get their message out to the masses, he was sure there were enough real Americans left who cared about the truth to rally to them.

The hard winter storm a few years back had stalled their plans yet again. The city was crawling with people doing repairs and replacing tech for years afterwards and they'd had to put things on hold for a while until things settled down, but that was all in the rearview mirror now. The city was repaired enough to have returned to normal levels of activity, and those phony bastards at Sadler were feeling sorry for themselves and licking their wounds, and preening themselves for having public sympathy again. It was the time now to take action.

They would send a crew to Lake City on the off-chance that it would be less guarded and an easy take, but the real action would take place on the shores of Toledo itself. Grant and his senior staff would coordinate the initial attack from their command vessel further out on the lake to the north, coming in from the Canadian side where there was less security. If their troops took the city as planned, they would move in and set up camp. If their plan failed, they would send out their manifesto from the ship as their final act of defiance. They'd already promised each other they wouldn't be taken alive, and by their lives or deaths, they'd expose the truth for the world to see.

Grant was relieved it was finally time to take action. One way or another, everything would be out in the open, and their mission would finally be completed. There was no turning back this time.

CHAPTER 43

Lake City. The Siege: Part I – 53 years, 1 month, 8 days after the Event. Time populous: 129,277

It was fortunate that the weather had been stormy all week, and the lake rougher and choppier than was usual at this time of year. Those slightly higher waves had delayed the attackers from docking by just a few precious minutes, but those were long enough to sound the alarms.

The attack on Lake City came from across Erie to the north and the west and was largely ineffective; the corresponding attack on the Toledo Harbor came from the east through semi-submersibles, and was unfortunately, somewhat more successful.

Everyone who worked at Lake City was put through the standard safety drills every quarter for fires, floods, tornados, active shooters, biohazards and contamination (plus a litany of procedures specific to the floating city regarding evacuations of staff and patients by air, land, and sea routes); but a full-scale assault of the city was something not often seriously considered. That being said, the security measures held. Unlike the relatively clumsy cybersecurity attack years ago, this one was of a more violent nature, and instead of a motley crew of time-deniers, this was a more organized and coordinated pseudo-military affair of some size.

After the fact, the attack would be traced to a domestic terror group looking to challenge the American government for supremacy by gaining control of the unoccupied Toledo and the Lake City facility itself. The plan was to take the area, knowing its position in the center of the country would be prohibitive of nuclear or biological warfare in retaliation against them. Their proposed strategy was to gain control of a major artery of the nation and squeeze. It might well have been the start of a long and grisly civil war on American soil, but as it was, it was thwarted by the alertness of a few, the bravery of many, and luck.

* * *

Dr. Xiao Xiang's day had begun much like any other; as the Director of the facility, he had learned to be an early riser, getting in his jog and morning coffee before the sun and taking his personal hop-pack to the employee landing zone. The security staff on the roof greeted him cheerfully by name, but even after all these years Terry wouldn't open the door for him until his bio-scan reading cleared. It was protocol.

He made his way down directly one floor to his office and settled in at his desk. Normally he might take a stroll through the atrium this early, but on such a cloudy, drizzly day it was hardly worth it. Instead, he would get ahead of his meeting schedule. Ho hum. But first, something that was different from his normal routine was a scheduled call with an old friend. Dr. Anil had been enjoying his retirement in Grand View, just along the western side of the lake, and within view of the facility from the back deck of his small cottage off the shore. He too was an early riser, so they tried to touch base every month or so – it was nice to commiserate with someone who understood firsthand all that the Director's complicated position entailed. They were having a nice chat and were just deciding on a time to play a round of golf that weekend or next, when Dr. Anil surprised him with an exclamation.

"Since when do the Alpha teams come in from the north – and with such speed? You must have some flyboys trying to impress someone. I can see the spray they're kicking up from here!"

Dr. Xiang glanced through his office window – there were close to a dozen skimmer-skips coming at dangerously high speeds, beelining for the northern dock, and those were definitely not Alpha vehicles. They were too light for the rough waters, and they were spraying like white-water rafts, with a few practically capsizing on the swells. Alphas used heavier combat and transport-skips that barely made a ripple even in choppy seas. He barely had time to register the sight when he suddenly heard a deafeningly loud whine of air vehicles above and immediately knew these were way too heavy duty to be personal packs, the only kind allowed on the employee entrance pad. Multi-transport hops went to the east pads. Something was wrong.

A quick shiver went up his spine, and without further thought he slammed his hand through the emergency glass that protected the panic button in his office. The entire building would go into immediate alert, and every exterior door and window would already be locking. In his office, rolling shades were already cutting off the windows, and he heard sharp popping noises above. His office had feet of concrete and silicate between floors, both to dampen sound and provide security, so he knew whatever was happening above was much louder than what he was hearing.

"Raj, listen carefully. I think we're under attack. I've started the lockdown protocols now."

He hung up without further explanations; Raj would understand what was about to happen next. The head of security was already on the 4D screen, barking orders and calling off checkpoints. Xiao pulled up all the security cams and saw staff rushing to their designated areas for emergency protocols, and security moving at a run through every wing. The cyber-scans were running but weren't showing any alerts yet – this appeared to be a low-tech attack, which might prove to be more effective. Sadler had the best cyber system that money could buy, and then some, since it had been designed by the Orien Institute that employed some of the most brilliant minds on the planet.

"Director!" His security chief was visible on the comms right outside his door, putting in his bio-scan info, and Xiao entered the code from within that would let him enter. His office had a special revolving door that would allow only one person at a time to enter or exit during lockdowns, complete with a bio-scanner to enter the door, and a stop-gap to detain them within it if the second bio-scan within raised any alarm. In case of emergencies, both the Director's office and the security offices in each wing functioned as bases of operations for quarantine measures. Captain Gordon was pushing his way inside now, entering another code to double-seal the exterior door.

"Director, we've sealed off the visitors' lobby and we have a whole crew manning the exterior doors and the entrances to the wings, which have also been secured. Travelers and medical patients are being moved to the designated safe zones. All exits and entrances have been sealed and secured. Rooftop cameras have been disabled from the outside; we're switching to satellite cams and drones."

"I thought I heard gunfire above me just now."

"Yes sir, I'm afraid there are armed crews attempting to penetrate the building at three different rooftop points, but you hit the panic button in time to get the primaries and secondaries in place. So far, they're holding."

"What about those skimmers? Why didn't the alarms go off for them?"

"They've found a way to disable our remote warning system. It might be an inside job, and we're on high alert until we can confirm. A dozen vessels landed from the north, at least ten more from the east. We've got a couple dozen armed insurgents on the island so far, and they've taken out some of the exterior comms with some kind of jammer, but we've still got eyes from above that they can't touch. They'll likely try to hit the underwater comms links next, but the Deltas have a few tricks up their sleeves that will hold them off."

"Alpha deployment?"

"It took us a couple minutes to get through, but they've now confirmed the city proper is under attack also. The Alphas are coordinating at the harbor and along the riverfront. They'll contain the situation and come for us as soon as they can."

"Jesus. So, we're on our own for now. You've got the mainland on alert?"

"Yes sir. We had initial trouble getting through there too, but police, fire, coast guard, and national guard are all securing their borders now. You name it, we pinged it. Canada's pulling out all the stops along the northern shores. I'm not sure what the escape route was for these guys but if we can close the net on them, we will."

"All right. Any ideas on who we're dealing with?"

"One moment, sir." Gordon's earpiece was blaring and Dr. Xiang could see the reflection of scrolling images and data through the side of his goggleset. He gave a few orders verbally, and his fingers flew over his wrist cuff, sending instructions to various teams. "Sir, all checkpoints verified as secured from within, and the shields are up and running. I'm afraid we have a few casualties from dock and rooftop security, and a few unlucky folks who were out in the gardens that got caught in crossfire. We're not sure yet if there are any hostages taken, they're taking a look at the footage now. But it looks like at least some of the people that were outside when the alert went off made it inside in time, or hopefully got to the emergency bunker entrances undetected."

The bunkers were a recent addition, maybe installed a year ago, and not common knowledge even amongst staff. For obvious security reasons they didn't tunnel into the facility, although that had been the original proposal. Instead, each had secret trapdoors to underground spaces that had air, food, water, and supplies to last up to five days for ten people and were accessible only from the maintenance garages above them on the surface. Although the staff was put through exercises regularly for tornado and active shooter drills, these bunkers weren't part of the normal training.

"Sir, I'm needed in the security office. Don't leave the room or let anyone else in."

Another bio-scan to exit, and once Gordon was out, Dr. Xiang added the locking protocol that would keep any changes to the system from happening unless he was the only person in the room. This was to prevent him from being taken hostage and being forced into action by his assailants; no matter what they did to him, the system would not allow itself to be breached while another living person was in the room. As the Director, he needed to lock certain parts of the system down with his personal codes to add layers of cyber protection, and these would remain locked until the all clear had been sounded and could not be lifted manually. As soon as that was done, he would need to do a verbal check with his direct reports for status. The procedure was to not reveal your location in the complex even to internal leaders. They would use the coded responses that only he and they individually knew to communicate.

Casualties and possible hostages. Remembering the gunfire on the floor above, Dr. Xiang felt a deep stab of worry for Terry and the rest of the rooftop crew, but he had a checklist of his own to get through right now. All transmissions would have gone to emergency mode to avoid interceptions, but the panic button should have sent out secure coded messages to all staff, emergency responders from neighboring towns and cities, and the field teams automatically. Gordon was right, it might be an inside job – but for now, he just needed to hang tight, and do his job while they did theirs.

CHAPTER 44

Toledo. The Siege:
Part II – 53 years, 1 month,
8 days after the Event.
Time populous: 129,277

While the attack on Lake City was largely subverted before it had even begun, the corresponding attack on the city proper gained more traction. The attackers had successfully found a way to keep their skimmers and semi-submersibles undetected by the security system, but more importantly, they had found a way to stall the automatic messages to the Alpha, Beta, and Delta teams that the Director's alert should have triggered. The field teams would have been blindsided, and their attackers had been relying on that element of surprise to win the day.

As it was, a single low-tech alarm was raised, and it made the difference.

* * *

Dr. Raj Anil stared dumbly at his phone. Xiao had just hung up; the facility was under attack. It was a Director's worst nightmare. He breathed a quick prayer for the safety of the staff and residents; how frightening for the people just arriving into the future to find this as their new reality! But within seconds, his logic overtook his panic. There were protocols in place, of course, to deal with such situations. He didn't need to take any particular action – he was retired. But still… just in case… he had an old scanner in his office. It wouldn't hurt just to check.

He pulled it down from the bookshelf. It was dusty but still in working order. It had been mainly a decoration in his office for years, to be used only in an emergency. As a former employee of high rank, he had been told there was a slight possibility of him being kidnapped and ransomed by some evil agency bent on taking down Sadler. At the time this had seemed far-fetched to someone like Dr. Anil, who held a slightly naïve belief in the innate goodness of people. Now, it looked like that might actually be happening. He had been briefed on the possible scenarios and procedures upon his retirement, and technically he was still eligible for a security detail when out in public; but since he rarely left his small gated community, there was hardly any need and he had declined. Suddenly it occurred to him he might want to turn on his house alarm for the first time in years, just in case.

But first – the scanner. He tuned to the Lake City frequency and, as expected, got the emergency protocol messaging. Good. That meant things were in motion as they should be. Nothing more he could do there. Next, he tried the Alpha base, but heard only normal, daily chatter. Not good.

"Um… hello?" He knew that wasn't the correct way to speak on comms, but he wasn't a soldier for god's sake. He was an old man. And his nerves were just about shot.

"Alpha Team Five, Harbor Base. Identify yourself please." The voice was crisp, and somewhat annoyed, or maybe just astonished, to be addressing an apparent civilian on what should have been a secure line.

"Soldier, this is Dr. Raj Anil, former Director, security code 43901 Franklin Alpha Bravo. I have reason to believe Lake City is under attack. Do you copy?"

"…"

"Soldier?"

"Copy that."

The transmission went dead; or rather, the external comms protocols had been enacted. Finally. Now there really was nothing more he could do now but wait. And perhaps set that house alarm after all. And then perhaps a nice calming cup of strong tea.

* * *

Meanwhile, the Toledo Harbor was under a full-fledged attack. Dr. Anil's message had reached the base too late to stop the initial onslaught, and there were several killed or wounded out on the docks themselves, but the alert was raised in time to meet the next wave. Within minutes the Alpha and Beta teams were in a defensible position at the base and fighting back. There were close to 100 of the attackers that had made it past the harbormaster's office, with others popping up at several points along the river where their semi-submersibles had come to the surface. They were armed to the teeth and wearing heavy tactical gear, and had clearly come ready for a fight. Meanwhile the defenders in the field had mainly stun guns and batons; things used to subdue panicked time travelers, not fight a major battle.

If they had maintained the element of surprise, the terrorists might have overcome the base, and it would have been difficult for the teams scattered throughout the city to recover for a counterattack; but those few moments of awareness were enough to lockdown the headquarters and open up the armory. Heavy duty ion guns were rapidly dispersed, and the Delta crews were already putting up barricades all along the main route and reinforcing them. The attackers were stranded on the narrow half-mile strip of harbor and the outlying buildings and would be hard pressed to extend further into the city from that point without a fight.

The squads that had already been out in the field had now received the alerts and were meeting at their designated checkpoints to receive weapons that the Delta crews were running underground through the sewer systems on the double, as they had been drilled to do. The sewers themselves had been expanded and cleared out over time; since no time travelers were expected to arrive underground, the system had become a primary avenue to move small to mid-sized equipment throughout the city with no risk of reemerging accidents. Once armed, the Alpha squads were converging on the riverfront, picking off the attackers as they tried to extend into the city streets. Within minutes there were standoffs all over the waterways, and some of the assailants were making a strategic retreat back towards the main lake entrance.

Meanwhile, the Betas were locking down their base of operations at the coroner's building to the west. There was additional weaponry there, but it was also the docking bay for most of the medical air transports. These light crafts weren't well-suited for combat, but in emergencies, they needed to be the eyes and ears above the city. Beta crews were rushing to get their arms and were taking off to form a grid over the city; so far, there didn't appear to be major drone activity or missile sightings according to the scans, but nothing was to be taken for granted.

Though in reality the coroner's office was merely a drop off point for processing, there were rumors out in the wide world that the secrets of the wormhole and the experiments being run on casualties was handled here, so the building itself was considered a high-risk target and had extra security and lockdown measures in place. That being said, the actual contents of the building would have very little use to someone staging a takeover – therefore, those rumors had been allowed to persist in order to draw potential attackers to a low-stakes location that could draw fire without substantial loss if it were to be captured. Again, part of the protocol.

Near the Harbor Base, the firefight had begun in earnest. Although they were somewhat surprised to be met with resistance where the lack of alarms should have given them the element of surprise, the terrorist group was unwilling to give up the fight for the city, or perhaps had never intended to retreat at all. If all of the Alpha, Beta, and Delta crews met them in force they would be far outnumbered (even now, with staffing cuts, there was a fair contingent to reckon with), but they had squirreled themselves away in the row of brick buildings (former garages and boating supply companies), which had few windows and were ideal for cover in a siege. Continuing to pop off rounds and electron grenades periodically, they were clearly setting up recharging stations for their ionic rifles and would be more dangerous if additional semi-submersibles were able to bring them reinforcements and equipment from the lake side.

Fortunately, comms had been reestablished with the Lake City security team at this point, and while they knew they would eventually need to come to the rescue of the facility, the leaders here in the city proper knew that Lake City was currently still in the hands of the staff and holding its own. Word was that there were definite hostages, civilians and staff, that had been captured. With their whereabouts unknown and the threat of harm to the hostages as their attackers' only negotiation tactic, it simply wasn't an option at this point for the Alphas to blitz the besieged buildings at either site. It might come to that in the end, but first they'd see if there was a less risky resolution.

* * *

A few hours later, Captain Juarez and his Alpha team were hunkered down near an alleyway along the main drag. They were running point for this section of the besieged harbor area. The Deltas had hurriedly put up a 6-foot barricade consisting mainly of materials from a nearby bridge that had recently been torn down. The infrastructure in this area was weak; but right now, it made for a good, strong barrier. Large sections of concrete and rebar made for solid, thick cover, but allowed them spaces to peek through and assess the situation. Lieutenant Lillian was flat on her belly along the top, shielded behind a jut of the wreckage. She had the scope out and was rattling off a series of measurements to Taggart, who was keying them in. As more data was added, a 3D model blueprint of the buildings being surveyed was forming on screen.

"I'm not seeing any movement from the west quadrant, but there's a heat signature coming off the corner there, three degrees from center. Looks like maybe an ion cannon."

"Shit. That's gonna be a problem for us out on the streets if they get that charged. We don't have enough shields to cover everywhere."

"We'll jump off that bridge when we come to it, Taggart. Steady on."

"Sarge, throw me that infrared scope. I think I see troop movement along the roadway."

Sergeant Patel handed it up, and pulled out a second one. She and squad leader Captain Juarez took the angle; they really needed another squad here to cover this section – it was too exposed on the west side.

"Yup, looks like about ten more of them, moving in from the harbor to building one. Call it in."

Taggart relayed the information to the base, just as a team of Deltas came up from the alleyway with some additional equipment and began setting up a breach shield. Placing the sensors every six feet or so, once in place the shield could withstand several blasts from an ion canon and most small arms fire for an extended period, and even gave overhead protection within a limited range. Everyone breathed a little easier once they had it up and humming.

"Thanks, fellas."

"You got it, Cap. There's another Alpha squad en route now, and we're your backup team for the evening shift. You want us up top?" He indicated the rooftop of the building behind. Juarez took a look at them;

they were fully armed, but they didn't have anything with the range to reach the enemy on them, and up there they'd honestly be sitting ducks for that ion canon. He didn't want Deltas as backups; they weren't trained the way an Alpha squad was, and he didn't want them put in danger.

"Nah. You're safer at ground level with us. You can take the center point here and we'll take the west point. When the other squad gets here, they can take the east. Tell your team to keep their heads down and within the shield range. None of us is putting so much as a fingertip outside it until I give the say-so."

"Roger that!"

"Patel, you take point. Lillian, stay up top and keep the chatter going. Taggart, stay on comms. Delta leader…?"

"Jeffries, sir."

"Jeffries, a word please."

They moved down a little way to a viewpoint and crouched behind a screen of rusting rebar.

"What're you hearing from your end? Are the Delta squads all out-fitted for the field now?"

"Yessir, every armory has been opened up and the enemy hasn't been able to get near any of 'em to go shopping on our dime. Our squad's been running underground the last few hours making deliveries while extrusion teams are pushing barricades. What about you, any word on who these a-holes are?"

"Negative. Some rumors about people looking to find the time machine and steal it but that's got to be bullshit. Even if we knew where it was or how it worked, I doubt anyone would think we're dumb enough to just leave it lying around in the empty city, but maybe these jerks are crazy enough to think so. They hit us harder than Lake City, which appears to have been more of a sneak attack at small scale. So, whatever they really want is here."

"Foreigners again?"

"Can't tell; haven't heard any of their chatter at all. Their communications about the hostages have been all sim reads, so no accents or syntax to detect. They don't seem to be particularly high-tech with their attack methods, but they *were* able to temporarily block out our alert system, so who knows."

They felt a sudden shudder as the attackers leased a round of ion blasts from their cannon. The shields held handily, but it was a disconcerting feeling. Even through a shield, ion jolts sent a little electric shock you could feel in your teeth. It was an odd, nervous feeling.

"Easy, team. Everyone good?"

The team did a quick sound off. Everyone still sounded loose, but on the alert. The second Alpha squad rolled up and took their positions. They were ready now if those bastards wanted to try and push forward, but Juarez was guessing they wouldn't try it tonight. It looked like a good old-fashioned siege to him, and they'd see who would blink first. He knew it wouldn't be his squad.

"Captain, what happens to anyone returning from time during this mess? Are they just on their own or what?"

Juarez gave him a friendly look. Jeffries was a good guy. Here they were in the middle of a war zone, and he was still thinking about the travelers. He certainly didn't envy anyone who would reappear from time at this particular juncture – what a shock!

"Not to worry, the Beta teams are still monitoring the iSpy network and every motion detector outside the attack zone. They'll extract anyone to an emergency location until Lake City is back online. The only ones who would be in danger would be anyone who reemerges right here in the hot zone, but we can't worry about that right now, and it's unlikely from the statistics."

"Yessir. Hopefully it'll be over soon and we can get this junk moved out again. Last thing we need is all this debris right in the field of entry. Those bastards are making of mess of my Time Zone."

CHAPTER 45

Lake City. The Siege: Part III – 53 years, 1 month, 10 days after the Event. Time populous: 129,261

Counsellor Diana Kowalski and survivor Shauna Mayes had been just in time to reach the bunker. Diana had been giving Shauna a tour of the gardens. It was only Shauna's first week out of the wormhole, and Diana thought the fresh air would do her good. It had been a windy, drizzly, gray kind of morning and maybe a bit bleak for a walk, but Shauna had said she felt cooped up in the counsellor's office and Diana had thought a view of the lake might make a nice change of pace from the enclosed atrium.

They had only been outside for a few minutes when the alarms had gone off. Diana had practiced the protocols along with all the staff on how to respond to this alert. She'd always been indoors for the trainings though – the outdoors seemed so much more exposed. She whirled towards the door and saw the flashing light that indicated the inner rolldown door was already in motion. Things were moving a lot faster than a typical drill. They were already too late to go back the way they had come.

"What's going on?" Shauna looked more confused than panicked, which was something to be thankful for at least. On her first day back, when she'd first learned about the time stream, she had hyperventilated to the point where they had needed to sedate her briefly to get her into a bed; she was an asthmatic, and not a small person. Diana was pretty fit, having swum and rowed crew on her college teams only a few years ago, but she knew she couldn't carry Shauna to safety if she collapsed in the same way out here in the open.

"Probably just a training exercise. Don't worry." But she herself was worried; it wasn't time for another drill yet this quarter and if this was a real alert, the back doors would be closed already too. There was no point going around to the main lobby as that was the first place they would lock down... and now there were shouts in the distance and something that sounded like gunfire.

"Over here!" There was a man at the door of the sheds waving them over. The wind seemed to push them along as they hurried towards him. She recognized him from the garden; Jim... Pierce? Price? It was something like that... from the tech group. Usually, he was already working on his schematics when she brought her coffee out to the staff area on sunny days, and he always had a sunny smile to match.

The moment they were through the door, he closed it, and pushed them towards the far back corner floor. Pressing a code into an innocuous-looking wall panel, the door slid open, revealing an underground stairway with a hidden bunker beneath. There was a fake cabinet (or rather, a real cabinet that was nailed to the floor) to hide the sliding door; once they were inside, it would close seamlessly to camouflage their entry point. She wasn't particularly claustrophobic, but she suspected Shauna might prove to be. She hesitated.

"*Hurry!* I saw a bunch of hoppers landing on the roof. They're not ours."

He ushered them down the stairs and closed the hatch. Diana heard a pneumatic hiss, and felt air flowing. She was about to ask if he knew what the heck was going on, but then saw the look of panic on Shauna's face and knew she needed to deal with that first. She put on her best clinical poker face and calm smile and settled her in on one of the bunks, murmuring reassurances that it was likely just a safety drill, and that the facility had them all the time, and that she would check things out. Nothing to worry about! Shauna just curled up and nodded and shut her eyes tight. She was breathing heavily, but didn't seem to be in immediate danger, and she had her inhaler already clutched firmly in her hand.

Meanwhile Jim had security feeds up and running on a bank of monitors. By the time Diana joined him he had already connected with the security center to confirm their location through the established one-time code and been verified.

"What is this place? Can you see anything happening out there?" She kept her voice low, to keep Shauna from hearing. Let her just keep calm while she could.

"Can't tell. There are short-range cameras up above on the inside and out of the shed, but the range is really small. We don't have a view of the other areas from here… they're designed that way in case the wrong people get in here. That way they have a limit on what can be accessed if we're infiltrated."

"Instructions from security?"

"No, these bunkers don't have real comms and we can't send anything out except that initial verification code – it's a one-way security protocol to keep us from being detected. Nothing that will let them hack into the mainframe from here." *Or to keep us from being captured and forced to give false information to our security team,* he thought to himself.

"It's Jim, right?" He nodded. She glanced at Shauna and lowered her voice further. "Diana. Do you think we're actually under a real attack?"

He ran his hands through his hair and over his beard and let out a 'woof' of air before answering, which she knew meant yes before he actually said anything. "Yeah. Those hoppers definitely weren't ours, and I saw guys running up the beach too. I think… I think they were shooting. I saw someone fall."

"Staff?"

"Yeah. I couldn't tell who."

On screen, there was movement that made them both sit up straight. There was a team of people all in black creeping through the gardens. It was clearly a military formation; they were sweeping systematically. She counted ten of them, and three more approaching from the rear entryway. Worst of all, they had hostages with them, people they were forcing forward with their hands on their heads. She didn't recognize any of them, but from Jim's quick intake of breath, he did.

"Shit. That's Frank, and Toby. New guy I just hired. He hasn't even made it through safety training yet. Poor kid probably hasn't even heard about these bunkers yet."

At least he can't tell them where we are then, she thought grimly, but obviously she didn't say it aloud. On screen, the team was retreating into the shed above them, hostages in tow. They appeared to be unharmed, and the militants backed them into a corner and set a guard, but didn't appear to be engaging with them otherwise. Jim commented that they couldn't be heard from their soundproofed space below, but she held her breath anyway.

"Do we have sound up there? Can we hear what they're saying?"

"No. Too risky that they might pick up a signal so the feed we're seeing is just CCTV that's not transmitted back into the base. Even having the micro-cams to get this video is somewhat of a risk, but it's the latest tech and supposedly undetectable." He saw her questioning look. "I helped install these bunkers last year. Special project. I'm one of the few people who know where all the air, water, vents and tech come and go from."

Hmm. That might prove useful. She took a closer look around the space; it was actually quite large. One big open room with bunks all along the back wall and a curtain on a rod that could screen them from view, a full conference table and chairs, the bank of monitors they were seated at, and at the far end a galley of sorts and a doored cubicle that she assumed was a bathroom. It wasn't exactly a palace but it could easily accommodate them.

"Where does the air come from? And the water?"

"They're both part of a refiltration system that connects to the lake itself. There are pipes that go down through the false island bed… you know how this whole place is built on those semi-flexible panels?"

"Sort of. I've seen the models in the lobby that they show tourists but I never paid much attention."

"Yeah, it's basically like a large jointed raft with a thick layer of rock, soil and concrete attached to the top for building on. Underneath, there's columns every few feet that loosely attach down to the lake bottom, and have adjustable springs so that they can slightly move the island as needed… for the waves, wind, etc."

"Okay… so they dug the bunkers down into that layer above the raft."

"Right. So already we're a lot closer to the faux bottom than even the basements in the facility. which are more like crawl spaces just for pumps and plumbing and things. But those also go directly into the lake at some point."

"The electric too?"

"Most of what we use is solar and stays on the surface. Backup generators also on the surface level, but there's an emergency power line that goes through waterproof piping to the closest point on the mainland."

She had a sudden disconcerting thought. "It can't flood down here, can it?"

"No. Our plumbing and everything in this bunker is one-way, straight to the lake. Since this shelter is for emergency use only there's no septic tanks, it's not meant for long-time use. Our air comes from an underground fan room; it comes in through the vents there," he said, pointing. "Then it moves outward through the other vents there. There's a pump that works to keep the hatch moving air outward towards the lake. Even if we lost all power, it would automatically seal that hatch and two backups before water could come up it. Basically, it's like we're the bubbler in a fish tank, aerating the lake with our recycled air."

"Is that hatch big enough for a person to go in and out?"

He looked at her with surprise; she thought like an engineer. Or a survivalist.

"Yes, technically. There's emergency lighting and some breathing apparatus that maintenance uses to service the pipes in one of the cabinets over there. If we really needed to, we could go out the hatch. But it would literally put us under the island into freezing cold water, with only a few minutes of air." He glanced over at Shauna on the bunk. No way that lady was going scuba diving in the middle of Lake Erie.

"Right. Well... good thing you're here with us, and you know so much about this place."

* * *

The first day, they merely waited; staying quiet, staying hidden. Up above, they had pictures without sound. They could tell that their attackers were attempting some sort of negotiations using their hostages, of which they now had over a dozen. The maintenance shed they were occupying was essentially a large pole barn, full of tractors, lawn mowing equipment, tools, and workbenches. The militants had moved all of the large equipment near the windows (probably to block snipers), and moved the workbenches to the outer edges of the room to give themselves space to spread out their own gear. They slept in shifts. There were at least 20 of them.

Jim said there was an identical bunker on the other side of the shed – two per maintenance barn, four barns. So, there could be others that had made it to safety like they had. Maybe. Luckily, with it being so early in the day and not the greatest weather, most people were safely indoors when the attack had happened. Probably. They had caught Shauna up to speed on the situation as best they could, and although she had cried a little and needed to put her head between her knees to keep calm, she had taken it fairly well. They just needed to wait things out.

By day two they were making other plans.

The scope of the feeds in their view was frustratingly limited, but it was clear that their attackers held the ground between the dock and the gardens. There hadn't been a surge of Alpha teams storming the beaches, which they'd all been privately expecting and hoping for. Instead, there were only bad guys assembling a worrying amount of weaponry, and the occasional hostage being dragged in front of a camera to give some kind of message. At the end of the second day, they executed two of them as a show of their power, and that was their undoing.

Jim Price wasn't a soldier. He was a builder and a technician. But seeing two of his friends and coworkers gunned down in cold blood awoke something protective deep inside him he hadn't known existed. He turned away from the grisly scene while Shauna was still sobbing, and went straight for the scuba gear in the cabinet. He was going out that hatch.

Diana wasn't a soldier either, but there was more to her than met the eye. Aside from having spent most of her adolescence in the water, she was probably one of the most stubborn people on the planet; it was part of what made her a good counsellor. She knew where to poke at a subject to get to the real issue – and she wasn't going to be deterred by a grouchy response, outright rudeness, or even open hostility. More than anything she hated being stuck in this bunker, where nothing could be done. She was going out that hatch.

Shauna definitely was not a soldier. She was soft, unathletic asthmatic, but even she wasn't going down without a fight. But she wasn't going out that hatch, because she couldn't swim.

Together they made a plan; the next morning before dawn, at the start of day three of the siege, unless there were signs of a counteroffensive or a signal from security comms, Jim and Diana would go down the emergency hatch with a copy of the latest video feed from the maintenance shed. The plan was to come up within the lake and make an attempt for the mainland shore away from Toledo Harbor, which was likely also under attack. They would give themselves three hours to try to reach a friendly zone and communicate with the Alpha base or the National Guard stationed on the mainland.

At the three-hour mark, Shauna would set off a series of traps in the ventilation system that Jim had rigged up. All she had to do was light a match, close the tube and seal it, and press the code he had written down for her into the computer. Due to the underground nature of the bunkers, each one had an emergency secondary system that connected to the maintenance shed above; the piping and mechanisms were well hidden and made to look like part of the regular HVAC system of the building, but wouldn't stand up to intense scrutiny. Normally, the secondary system only kicked in if the primary system had a catastrophic failure, but Jim had recoded it to accept a system purge upon command. Using materials and supplies in the bunker galley, he had mixed a sort of bomb that would have no real effect other than thick smoke and an unpleasant odor – but the hope would be that it would appear to be something much more dangerous, and drive the terrorists out of the building and into the open. If all went well, their arrangements with the real military teams would have long-range snipers standing by and ready to engage.

They didn't know how many other hostages there might be, or what was going on in other parts of Lake City. They weren't even sure if the facility had been breached or not. But all of them agreed, maybe it wasn't a great plan but it was better than just sitting in a bunker watching innocent people die on CCTV.

And besides, any plan that works is a great plan.

CHAPTER 46

Lake City. The Siege: Part IV – 53 years, 1 month, 11 days after the Event. Time populous: 129,252

It was the morning of day three, and they were getting ready. Besides the breathing apparatus, there were goggles and a sort of plastic to wear over your clothes in the emergency supplies. It wasn't anything like a wet suit – more like a giant glove to put over yourself – but once on, it had a button that sucked in air and vacuum sealed the plastic to your body, and kept in body heat (and apparently kept water out). It was tech that had been developed for the Delta teams working in the underground sewer systems, and had a wider range of motion than a regular hazmat suit when used for the same protection and sanitation purposes.

There were also waterproof LED lights attached to wristbands and headbands in the cabinet, and some emergency floatation devices with miniature propulsion jets that were worn like belts. Worst case scenario, the devices had homing beacons. Even if they didn't make it out alive, the footage they carried might be found that way and be of some use to their side.

"Here. Take this too." Jim passed her a long, serrated knife in a hip holster. He had one on already, and was fitting it with an ankle strap to the exterior of his boot.

"Should you be wearing boots? You're supposed to kick shoes off if you fall into deep water."

He shrugged. "These wet suit things keep them from filling up, which is what makes them heavy... I guess I was thinking if we have to make a run for it once we get to dry land, I didn't want to do it barefoot."

It was time to go. They reviewed the plan one more time. Shauna set the timer for three hours – she would have no way of knowing what happened to Jim and Diana once the hatch was closed, but three hours from now the terrorists would be getting smoked out regardless. Whether that proved to be a turning point or merely an inconvenience for them remained to be seen.

The hatch itself was narrow; basically, just a long, sloped tube with various apertures near the top forcing the air downwards. With the top hatch open, the bottom one that opened to the lake had automatically sealed and the flow of air had stopped. There was no ladder or anything sticking out of the tube walls, just small indented grooves to be used as handholds and footholds for maintenance. Jim had explained that he would enter first, go down about ten or fifteen feet and hold; then Diana would enter. They couldn't go out too close to each other without risking running into each other. When they gave the signal, Shauna would close the hatch and seal it, which would automatically reopen the bottom hatch and restart the powerful flow of air that would carry them down and out, sort of like a water slide at a park, but with air. They would hold on to their breathing apparatus until they hit the water, to be sure it wouldn't be torn off, and with any luck they would emerge somewhat near each other out in the lake. In theory, the service tubes were propelling the air downward and away, so they should pop up in open water, not underneath the edge of the faux city.

Much like a tsunami, or a whirlpool, there was a chance they would be propelled further than they thought and separated, or that they could drown, or that they could emerge directly into the hands of the enemy. They had determined that if either of them made it to the surface they shouldn't waste time searching for each other, but spend all their energy attempting to reach the outside teams.

They took one last look at the monitors. The hostages were huddled together, sleeping, while the terrorists stalked around the building. Diana imagined them preening themselves, feeling pretty proud of themselves for dominating unarmed people. She felt anger boil up inside again; all for the sake of what? Power? Control? The secrets to time travel? The most brilliant minds on the planet hadn't figured that out in over fifty years, and these cretins definitely weren't scientists. They were probably just guns for hire, looking to capitalize on a vulnerable place in the U.S. to take hold. Well, they'd get what was coming to them. Diana had grown up in a military family, and if there was one thing her brothers had always said, you did not fuck with the United States armed forces, or their baby sisters. She was ready.

The three of them shook hands and nodded at each other, but none of them could think of anything inspirational to say. What they were attempting was a long shot on top of a long shot. Jim lowered himself into the hatch, then Diana. She cleared her throat, to give the count loud enough for both of the others to hear, and grasped her goggles and breathing tube in either hand.

"Ready in three, two, one, MARK." The hatched slammed shut, and with a sudden rush of air, Diana felt herself speeding downwards. She remembered to keep her toes pointed, to better penetrate the water, but she still felt the jolt in her whole body, and then a mad rush of gurgling, and she felt like she was being spun in a washing machine, every which way. She finally opened her eyes and saw through her goggles a faint light above, and kicked towards it. Almost she hadn't even needed the breather; she was already at the surface and broke through already at some distance from Lake City. She was shocked at how far, actually.

The lake was still choppy with waves, and it was freezing cold, but the plastic suit helped and the goggles were protecting her eyes. She didn't see Jim anywhere; she did a quick turnabout and then headed for the shore as they had planned. She hadn't swum this far in a long time, and certainly not in open water. In college her longest event was the 400 meters, and she wasn't as conditioned as she'd been back then, but she settled into an easy stroke she thought she could maintain and concentrated just on getting to the shore.

What followed seemed like an eternity, and she didn't dare check her watch because she knew that she really couldn't go any faster whether she was on schedule or not. All it would do is raise her stress levels, and she needed to focus on her breathing, and her stroke, and her kick, and beelining for the shore. Just get to the shore.

She knew she should have made Jim take off those boots. She hoped if he had made it to the surface, he had the sense to just activate his floatation device and homing beacon and wait for rescue. She was a strong swimmer with years of training, and it was all she could do to stay afloat and on track. Her parents had been so proud when she'd gotten that scholarship to swim at college. Her brothers were all Navy by profession, but they'd only been moderately good at the sporting aspect. Diana had won more awards than any of them, and still held most of the records in her high school conference. Not that she kept track of such things, but her father cheerfully did, and regularly informed her. She still swam for fun and exercise, and Lake City had a decent pool for the staff and travelers to use. She would kill right now for a calm, smooth lane of water to cut through. But she was almost there.

When she reached the edge, she had a retention wall to contend with rather than a beach; the swells helped her there, bringing her high enough to reach and grab at the chain link fence. Although she scraped both knees and the palm of one hand, she had just enough energy left to pull herself up and over and to the side of the roadway. It was just over the two-and-a-half-hour mark. It was a high traffic area and clearly, they were already under an alert because a state patrolman came screeching up almost immediately, demanding she identify herself and explain her situation.

From Diana's perspective, her role in the siege effectively ended with the handoff of information to the authorities. The Alphas had the ball now, and they would run with it.

CHAPTER 47

Lake City and Toledo. The Siege: Part V – 53 years, 1 month, 11 days after the Event. Time populous: 129,252

Armed with the information provided by Diana about the smoke bomb plan, and the basic knowledge of the number of assailants and hostages in the shed above, there was just half an hour left to take action. With the confirmation that no other bunkers had submitted occupancy codes, the Alpha teams would just have to take the calculated risk that the attackers had a significant portion of their Lake City hostages in that one maintenance shed and that the rest contained only enemy troops. Views from the satellite confirmed that the rooftops remained clear; the terrorists had shot down a few guards, but after multiple attempts to penetrate the secure doors had failed, they were simply keeping a few unmanned watchdogs circling in the air, ready to shoot down aircraft or drones coming in to investigate.

With the help of mainland authorities, it was arranged that snipers would enter at the waterline by personal submersible, and pick off the captors emerging from the maintenance shed once the smoke began pouring out of it. The S.W.A.T. teams would take down the aerial threats while the Coast Guard would rush the northern dock to draw attention away from the firefight on land.

Upon confirmation of the safety of the remaining hostages, the Alpha teams would sweep the other maintenance sheds and rooftops until Lake City was deemed clear, and then the Alpha teams in Toledo would be given the all-clear to bombard the harbor buildings with stun grenades and move in to detain anything still breathing. It was a risky plan in some ways, needing both coordination from multiple groups and the unavoidable danger to the hostages themselves, but in actuality it went down exactly as drawn up on paper. "We didn't have time to think about it long enough to screw it up," Security Chief Gordon would famously recollect in later interviews.

Inside the facility, three members of Sadler staff had been detained that morning for questioning after they had aroused suspicions that they might be in cahoots with the attackers. So far, they had admitted nothing, but it seemed likely they were the ones who had stalled the initial trigger alerts. Meanwhile, the moment the Alpha forces protecting the Toledo Harbor got news that Lake City had been secured and the hostages had been rescued, their counter-offensive at the harbor began in earnest. Armed with personal ion shields, they were given the order to storm the waterway buildings.

* * *

"Move, move, move! Taggart, Patel, get down, we've got heavy artillery on the left!"

Lieutenant Lillian winced; Juarez had apparently forgotten his parade-ground voice was too intense for comms, and he sounded like he was about a millimeter from her eardrum. But she could hardly blame him and his adrenaline when they were all antsy with it for three days now, and finally getting to take some action.

The other Alpha teams were swarming along with them, while the Delta teams like the one Jeffries commanded were trailing them from afar, sending out longer range anti-ion blasts both to deflect fire away from the Alphas and to deter the enemy's ion canon from fully charging. Being exposed in the open, she could see a couple soldiers on the ground from their side, but it was clear that they outnumbered the terrorists. The attackers had been firing heavily at first, but now they were weakening, and one building in which they were hiding had already partially collapsed into a cloud of cement dust while others were aflame.

"Cap, we've still got movement at ten o'clock!" Patel was firing calmly and rapidly from one knee, shielding Taggart who was struggling to get a MediCuff™ over her left calf from behind. With a shock, Lillian saw that was where Patel's leg ended in a splash of crimson; her foot was entirely disintegrated. She didn't even understand how Patel was still upright with a wound like that. And Taggart was covered in blood, but she couldn't tell if any of it was his own or not. Already Deltas with additional ion shields were charging in to protect them both and pull them back towards the rear. She pushed forward.

"Lillian, on my flank! Move it!" Juarez barked, while she and the remainder of the Alphas in the formation tightened up and pushed the full power of their shields to the front. Patel must have gotten an unlucky stray bouncer, because the ion shields were supposed to protect from the ground up.

They were almost to the edge of the buildings now, and there was so much smoke that they had to switch to infrared. There was still sporadic fire coming at them, but it was noticeably less than when they had surged forward, and Juarez signaled them all to crouch down along the alley while he confirmed how far the eastern offensive had penetrated. It wouldn't do to have friendly fire at this stage.

"Shit! Get down!"

The whole team ducked as a spray of bricks rained down on them from above; there was now a gaping hole just above their heads, and several of them felt the quiver as their shields lost power. That had been a close-range blast from a canon, and if it had been aimed straight at them, they would have never even seen it coming. Lillian couldn't believe their luck; if they hadn't just crouched, that shot would have taken off all their heads in one go. As it was, it basically gave them a tailor-made window for stun grenades, which at Juarez's command they started pumping into the building.

For a few minutes it was nothing but smoke and the thud of grenades hitting the far wall, and shouting over comms. But then a pause; silence and no returning fire. They were given the go ahead to enter.

* * *

The Alphas moved into the buildings one by one. The insurrectionists had been overcome. The siege was over, and though there were twelve casualties of staff and residents at Lake City and twenty-seven Alphas and Deltas at the Toledo Harbor, the terrorists failed to establish any real foothold.

An hour later, a suspicious vessel drifting near the city was boarded by the Coast Guard, which was found to contain the bodies of the insurgents' leadership. They had taken cyanide pills down to the last man only minutes earlier. Almost everything that was eventually known about the assailants and their silent funding partner was gleaned from Grant Hutchings' final communication, a sharing of his manifesto and decades of notes on his theories of the government cover-up of the time machine. His surviving foot soldiers, including the three members that had been discovered embedded within the Lake City workforce, knew very little other than that their mission was to "expose the truth to the world", though they seemed unable to clearly articulate what that truth was.

Ironically, the siege that the domestic terrorists had planned in order to spread their message far and wide had a different effect that they had intended. Grant's paranoid manifesto and bizarre theories, combined with national pride in the defense of Toledo and bravery in the face of the sneak attack, elevated the reputation of the Alphas for years to come and probably drew in more recruits than the past several decades combined. Like so many other events throughout time, history was written by the winners.

During the three-day siege there were only a couple dozen reentries within the Time Zone and all but two were recovered safely by the Beta squads while the other teams held down the defense of the city.

Jim Price's body was found floating two miles off the shore of Lake City the morning after the siege ended. It was determined that he had clipped an underwater support beam in his path of propulsion, breaking his collarbone and knocking him unconscious. His breathing apparatus had come off in the surge, and they assured Diana he wouldn't have felt anything. He was given a hero's funeral, and the fountain in the main garden bears his name to this day.

CHAPTER 48

Recruiters' training manual –
56 years, 3 month, 12 days after the Event.
Time populous: 123,161

WELCOME TO WORMHOLE U

The skills and hands-on training you'll gain in our joint program between the U.S. Army and U.S. Navy cannot be matched anywhere else. You'll help maintain the search efforts in the Time Zone, identify threats both foreign and domestic, provide safety and medical support, and rescue reentering time travelers. So, whether you work with intelligence, technology placement, or civilian affairs, you'll have an integral role in the salvation efforts in Toledo, Ohio in the heartland of our nation.

Our mission is to care for those lost in time as they rejoin us in the present, from integral safety to reassurance and support.

In recent years, the tragedy of the hard winter and the attack on Lake City and Toledo proper have generated a renewed emphasis on recruitment for our program. We are hiring, and we need you, and your commitment, to save lives and further our mission to help those caught in the time stream.

CAREERS AND BENEFFITS

So, you're interested in a career in the Time Zone. Here are some jobs that you might pursue.

Alpha Team Member: As the first responders on the field teams, this role spans everything from technology setting and repair to search and rescue responsibilities, and crisis handling. These elite squads are known as the boots on the ground within the Time Zone, and are the first contact for reentries from the wormhole. If your passion is helping those who are lost find their way, this is the role for you.

Beta Team Member: Combining the skills of a pilot, the stealth of a soldier, and the services of an investigator, our Beta squads are trained to assist in the rescue and transport of all surviving travelers and to seek answers for those who are lost to reentry. This critical function is paramount to the success of the program.

Delta Team Logistical Specialist: This role encompasses everything from civil engineering to labor and freight moving. You'll perform maintenance management in order to maintain and repair infrastructure within the Time Zone, and oversee incoming supplies and equipment, as well as sustainability and recycling programs for tech development.

Cyber Network Defense: We will train you to respond to cyber security attacks and analyze network activities to detect and protect against unauthorized activity in cyberspace. You will be trained on specialized computer network defense duties, including maintaining infrastructure and testing new tech developed for the Time Zone and the safety or reentering travelers.

Research Data Analyst: As an analyst, you'll be responsible for providing our partner branch of the Sadler Research Group with crucial and reliable information about patterns within the collective data of reentries and potential areas of convergence. You will analyze and assess tactical findings, as well as create, document, organize, and cross-reference intelligence records and files.

LEADERSHIP AND YOUR FUTURE

When you join our program, you receive more than just a paycheck or a career. We give you the tools needed to become the best version of yourself, with advanced military training and specialty schooling to learn specific skills that are transferable in the private sector. Take on more responsibility as an expert in your field with advanced collegiate courses and practical field training that certify you for multiple careers in the future. Join our growing team today!

CHAPTER 49

Trevor – 58 years after the Event.
Time populous: 119,534

Today is a triply important day for Trevor. For one, it's another May 15th, the 58th anniversary of the Event – but that's something for everybody, not just him and the other survivors. For two, it's Trevor's birthday and he's feeling old, old, old. Sixty-eight is too old to be still working... which is why for three, he's officially on his last week before retirement. When the facility had been attacked, he'd been safely in the counsellor's wing. Good thing too, because he was too old to be running into bunkers and being a hero like his sorely-missed friend Jim. After the siege was when he had started seriously considering his longer-term plans for life outside of the job.

His coworkers are excited for him. They know he's been looking forward to getting to travel more (maybe even outside the U.S.) and worry less... even though he'll still worry about DJ until she's back, no matter where in the world he's traveling. He and Val still have that spare room, and he's not giving up on her. He can't... he'll be all she has left, with Gary gone and Mom not making it through her reentry a few years back. The rules on releasing remains from reentries had finally been relaxed, so he'd scattered her ashes in the same place where he had scattered Gary's years ago, doing his best to send her off right.

But he's not going to think about that right now, because he'll get upset, and people keep Zapping him to say congratulations. Some of them are meeting him for lunch to celebrate (in the Lake City café of course – most businesses on the mainland still close early for the Day of Remembrance so people can get home to BBQ with their families or watch the parade). They've also got something extra special for him – a combined birthday present and retirement gift; by pulling some strings, and date-dropping his super-early reentry status (he's still listed in the official books as one of the possible first reentries since they've never been able to pinpoint the exact time and date), his friends have arranged for an Alpha team working the area to get him a live stream of his old neighborhood and his actual childhood home, and by some miracle they've arranged to have him on the live comms talking directly to the team.

As a counsellor, he's been able to access official sweeps before, so he's seen glimpses of his neighborhood in bodycam clips as teams went through, but nothing like this – he can ask them to open up a drawer, pick up a drawing (not to remove from the Time Zone, of course, since that's against regulations, but to examine) – maybe his action figures are still there guarding the house for him... it'll be a short window, maybe 15 minutes tops, but something special that most survivors won't get, and an interesting way to get closure for his long career.

The last weeks have been very busy. He's got more casework than ever since the survival rates are so high, and each of them had to be individually contacted and introduced to their new counsellors, and any pending paperwork that needed to be completed and Zapped off is getting wrapped up now so that the follow-ups go to his successors. He might be old, but Trevor has pristine case files; he's trained more counsellors than anyone else in this office, so they all know he won't be leaving them with a mess, but it's still a lot to take in. And speaking of training, he's got three fresh counsellors in their 90-day probational period that he still needs to make recommendations on and pass to a new mentor. After a lifetime of effort, it feels like a lot crammed into just three weeks, but he'll miss all this when it's gone, he knows that well enough.

The plan is to wrap things up here and then relax at home for a couple of weeks – sleep late! Drink coffee! Catch up on his reading! – and then their big trip out to Yellowstone in August. They're choosing to drive, even though that's a long time for old bones to be sitting even with the autocar doing most of the work... but he's looking forward to that special road trip feeling that's different than regular talking and snacking and scenery. He'd always loved that road trip feeling, by car or by train, going out to do counselling in the satellite cities, before most of the work became virtual. He did some of his best thinking on the road; it wasn't the same feeling you got just sitting still and concentrating while at home on the couch. And he's never been to Yellowstone before, the furthest West he's been is to Colorado. Most of his casework was in the Midwest and the East Coast, and he's been through New England many times over the years; a lot of Toledoans had connections there where there are big cities, so there were a lot of relocations in Boston, New York, Pittsburgh, Philadelphia... even a few in Maine and Vermont. All great places to road trip. Now he's ready to see some Badlands and bison and geysers, and for once he just wants to forget about time.

And when they come back home, he'll be getting the house and garden ready for autumn, and putting up decorations for Halloween (Val's favorite holiday). Then maybe he'll finally start writing his book. He'll be writing about the Time Event, of course, but only the positive things, because it will be for DJ's eyes and he doesn't want her to think about all the people who have been hurt, or died, or killed themselves, or had their hearts broken by time. He's known too many people like that, who just couldn't handle being refugees in time. DJ will still be just five and a half years old when she comes back, and she'll learn about all the science and conflicts and history and facts at school and in the news for the rest of her life. He wants what she hears from *him* to be about the friends he's made – people who he never would have met if it wasn't for the wormhole – and funny things that happened, like the league softball player who had just swung the bat when the Time Event occurred, and would never know where the ball ended up but chose to believe it was a home run. Or the daughter, mother, and grandmother whose reentry dates so perfectly aligned that they all ended up the same relative age and later became famous for their cooking show.

He would write about Julia, a virtually unknown local artist who came back to learn her mural on a Toledo restaurant wall was featured in the early news footage of the Time Event and had subsequently become one of the most recognizable pieces of art in the world while she was away; and Veronica, who was convinced her cat (with very distinct markings that even he couldn't argue weren't the same) had been using up his nine lives for decades so that he was still there at the shelter to find her when she reappeared; and Ernesto, who had been thrilled to reemerge after fifty years just in time to see his favorite team win the World Series for the first time since he'd been gone. And he'll talk about small things over the years that made him smile, like reading Tom's long letters, and glimpsing how much Gary looked like his daughter, and describing the last birthday cake Mom had made him and how it was the best one he'd ever had and how he got to eat the whole thing himself, after the Event happened.

He'll tell the happy stories only... and if DJ comes back before he's gone, he'll read them to her. And if she comes back too late, she'll have to read them for herself.

"Trevor! They're ready for you!"

They've got him set up with a 360VR view, in a private tank room, and his Alpha contact Lieutenant Happ has him on comms. They're all his for the next fifteen minutes, and they're at the front door of the house already, ready to make their sweep.

"Happ here – whenever you're ready sir – go ahead and walk us through." He's not prepared, and the "sir" threw him off, too. He had the vague idea of having them just move around the house to jog his memory,

266

but for a moment he's overwhelmed seeing the place that's at once so familiar and yet almost forgotten after so many years. They can't take anything out, but suddenly it hits him. Everything they are seeing right now can be lifted and reproduced from the live feed!

"Stay here in the living room, to your left. There should be some photo albums in the cabinet under the television. Yes, those big books right there, that's them. Can you open them up and just page through?"

"You got it, chief."

Suddenly, his mother's picture is right there in front of him – he didn't have one with him when he was removed from the city and he's almost forgotten what she looked like. And there she is – younger than he ever knew her in real life, but smiling and happy, and a little blurry because it's a picture taken on an old camera from some remote time before he even existed. Her high school graduation picture, and her with her friends, young and laughing, posing in front of a big building he doesn't recognize. And there's his grandmother, holding him as a baby. She's a short, wide woman with a huge smile who he barely has a conscious memory of other than her soft humming while she rocked him as he drifted off to sleep, but it all comes back just seeing the grainy photo. Baby Trevor, toddler Trevor. Looking serious on the first day of school. Dressed up for Easter church, when Mom had her hair long and braided almost down to her waist. He remembers the tiny little beads that used to click clack as she bent over to talk to him. Mom and Gary on their wedding day. Mom and Grandpa dancing. A baby shower full of relatives and then fat little baby DJ, with big brother Trevor grinning with his front teeth missing and holding her on the couch the day she came home from the hospital.

Trevor and DJ, DJ and Trevor. Bath time. Snack time. Dressed up for Halloween. Dressed up for Christmas. With aunties and uncles, neighbors and friends. Gary throwing a laughing DJ up in the air. Mom and DJ playing in the kiddie pool in the grass of the front yard. The memories are flooding back, but he tells the Alphas to just keep flipping – don't pause to look closely right now. He can get every picture they show on screen printed, and there's just eight precious minutes left in his window. When DJ gets back from the time stream, she'll have a whole reproduced album just like this one waiting for her. He'll label every picture as best he can to say who's who and where they were, and all the memories he can muster. She'll never be in danger of forgetting all their faces, no matter how many years it's been, or how long they've all been gone when she comes back.

School pictures. Trevor holding a baby duck at the petting zoo. DJ eating cake, covered in frosting. Mom sewing something and laughing. Gary and his friends trying to put together DJ's playhouse and looking confused. Trevor in his little league uniform. Another school picture day. Trevor and DJ on the swings. And that's it, that's the last page.

"Sir, anything else in the house you want us to try and hit? We've got to move on in a minute…?"

"No, thank you guys. This is all I needed. Thank you."

"You got it, sir. Congrats on your retirement. Out."

They disappear from the screen with a friendly wave, and Trevor grins and wipes his eyes and sends the recording off to a friend in the reproduction room who he knows will do him the favor of printing them up. This is the best day he's had in a long, long time.

CHAPTER 50

Obituary for Dr. Raj Anil –
60 years, 4 months,
2 days after the Event.
Time populous: 113,920

Dr. Rajesh Anil, PhD, of Grand View, MI passed away peacefully this Tuesday, September 17th from lingering complications after a heart attack last year. He was predeceased by his parents, Dr. Naveen Anil, and Disha Anil.

A private celebration of life will be held in his honor for friends and Sadler staff past and present on this Saturday at 3:30 PM at the Lake City facility, where he long lived and worked, first as a member of the science squad, then as a researcher, then as the Senior Lead of Research Wing, Assistant Director, and finally as Director before his retirement 23 years ago. Even after his official service had ended, his alertness on the day of the Lake City Siege saved many lives, and we are indebted to him. The memorial will be held at the Northeast Garden entrance, and at his request, his ashes will be scattered into Lake Erie at sunset.

We invite you to make a donation to any charity that supports survivors of the Time Event, something Dr. Anil dedicated so much of his life to. His passing leaves a gap in our community, and he will be sorely missed. The Sadler Group has announced that the Staff Garden will be renamed in his honor.

CHAPTER 51

News headlines –
65 years after the event.
Time populous: 102,242

'Reconnecting with those who have returned; remembering those we have lost'; the U.S. honors the 65th anniversary of the time incident

The 50-year Storm: how we rebuilt 15 years later

Addressing security vulnerabilities in the region: foreign influencers seek to divide America

Photos: Lake City renovations and expansion

Renewing the science: Sadler merges with the Orion Institute
by E. Gunther

May 15th

The Sadler Group commemorated the 65th anniversary of the Time Event at the Lake City facility with a special reception for local dignitaries and scientists from around the world, at which they officially announced their merger with the Orien Institute.

This long-anticipated merger between the two research superpowers will bring the substantial data about the individual time travelers and readings collected within the Time Zone from Sadler together with the award-winning AI-powered modeling software from Orien. The experienced physics and string theorist teams will work together to expand the deep-data analysis and accelerate deployment of 4D time modeling and scenario simulation.

Orien has laboratories in multiple countries, and is headquartered in Geneva, Switzerland. Launched close to 25 years ago, when their focus was on security technology, Orien has since invested in platforms that transform data into actionable scenario building. Using information about those who have reentered from time, the data can then be used to search and monitor key indicators for possible patterns and extrapolate conclusions about those still lost. In a 4D model, the fourth dimension is time; teams can visualize the timelines of individual survivors and casualties by mapping their points in the zeroth, first, second and third dimensions.

In layman's terms, Orien's models can track a range of people and locations, which combined with reentry data, may be developed into an algorithm that can possibly track a person of interest across the fourth dimension (time).

"The Orien team adds to Sadler's science and modeling expertise in the field of relativity, and we are excited to welcome them on board," said Dr. Jeffrey Badwell, Sadler's Director of Research. "The merger expands the specialization of our team, and with that, our goals to predict reentry times, identify a point of origin, and detect a conclusion date for the Time Event itself have been renewed."

Sadler's Lake City facility will welcome a team of approximately fifty research scientists, software engineers, and technical service team members from Orien, and the recently-expanded East Building will be reconfigured as their research headquarters. The welcome center, medical and counselling facilities will remain in the larger West building.

It is important to note that although many theories have been put forth over the years that the citizens of Toledo may be so scattered in time that a "completion date" with 100% recovery of the people lost may never be reached, this infinity theory has been largely dismissed by the scientific community. As more years have gone by, and almost 180,000 people have been recovered, the statistical data supports the calculations that if the rate of return stays relatively consistent, the incident will conclude about 100 years after the original event, or about 35 years from the present.

This hypothetical end date is another reason behind the merger. Officials from both Sadler and Orien have stated that with their combined funds and continued worldwide support from the scientific community, they have the long-range plans to ensure that their research and support services will be available to the citizens of Toledo for many years to come, surpassing the proposed 100-year anniversary date.

"Though of course if by some miracle the time anomaly would reveal its secrets to us and we could find a way to speed its end, we would rejoice," said Orien's Director Dr. Ilse Keller in her keynote speech at the merger ceremony. "Barring this possibility, one of our shared stated goals is to ensure our existence for as long as the time loop remains open."

Although public polls indicate that people are largely optimistic that the Time Event will in fact have a final end, maybe even within our lifetimes, there is a growing minority who are concerned that the closing of one Time Zone may open another. Widely considered to be a conspiracy theory, there are still indications that preparations for another doomsday Time Event are making their way into the mainstream.

Similarities are being drawn to cultural phenomena of Y2K (January 1st, 2000 A.D.) and the end of the Mayan Calendar (December 21st, 2012 A.D.). In both cases, there was a belief that a cataclysmic or transformative event would take place on the specified date, with some claiming there would be a worldwide catastrophe or even an ending of the world and human civilization. Scholars even at the time dismissed these predictions as pseudoscience, but doomsday theories of galactic alignment, geomagnetic reversal, and even collision with another planet sent by alien beings became a subject of popular speculation as the dates approached. Although these historical anecdotes seem ridiculous now,

Time Zone theorists today point out that the very concept of proven time travel would have seemed equally ridiculous to the people of the late 20th century when these theories abounded.

"Who is to say that this one rip in the fabric of time is a singularity?" says the introductory information on the website run by Zone Watch, a group that theorizes that Time Zones will begin opening regularly in the future. "For decades, the mystery of May 15th has been called an 'anomaly', but what if it were to become a recurring, or even common event? What if there have been many other such events in the past, when the science was not sophisticated enough to detect them?"

Although scientists say there is no indication that the Time Event has been replicated elsewhere in any recorded history, the idea of another wormhole in a more densely populated area is a major concern that needs to be at least considered. Government leaders have called on emergency responders to prepare protocols to handle possible temporal disasters, including an alert system that will warn nearby authorities (outside their own cities) of such an event. The Alpha search and rescue branch has long had training manuals to deal with 30, 60, and 90-day planning to organize and execute initial operations in the unlikely advent of another time disaster, and these plans have been shared and drilled with the militaries of various countries for training exercises.

"One positive thing about the Time Event, maybe the only one, is that it unified the world in the pursuit of understanding the science," said one pundit reporting on the anniversary. "Any economic or social advantage to be had from a disaster like the one Toledo experienced 65 years ago is outweighed by the negative impact to society."

The merger of Orien and Sadler is an inspiring example of cooperation in the world of science, and there will be additional plans to open a new satellite branch in Europe, in conjunction with the plans to renovate portions of Lake City to house the new staff and computing equipment.

CHAPTER 52

Rachael Mitchell – 70 years, 3 months, 25 days after the Event. Time populous: 90,135

She was bending down with the tray of plants, so she didn't see quite how it happened – but suddenly she fell right through the deck and smashed into the ground below. Immediately she felt hot, stabbing pains that radiated up both legs, and she cut off a shriek because it took all of her energy to just not pass out.

For a few minutes she didn't dare move (even moving her hand to her face somehow hurt way down in her feet) but just clenched her teeth and tried to breathe while burning hot tears slid down her cheeks into the dusty ground. Tom must not have heard her fall – he must have gone upstairs already – but he would come down and find her any moment, she could wait a minute. She didn't think she had the strength to yell for him, or even to open her eyes.

But he didn't come. Time passed and the hot feeling in her legs was spreading, not fading, soaking its way over her whole body. She imagined it as a red, pulsating blob settling over her, making even the air around her throb. She'd been hoping it was the kind of pain like when you stub your toe badly and it's agonizing for a minute, but then it fades away and a few minutes later you feel silly for thinking maybe it was broken. No, this was not one of those times. She'd never broken a bone before, but she couldn't imagine this *wasn't* what it felt like. Could she even sit up? No… not yet. She felt like she might vomit if she did. Start with just opening your eyes.

It was dusty in the dark below the deck. Sawdust and dirt swirled in a beam of light from a hole in the side of the porch, and she could see she was lying on a mess of stones and damp soil, littered with broken boards. It smelled musty under here, and although the pain was still horrible, it seemed to be slowly receding back down to just her feet and legs. She could breathe again, and could feel other pangs and bruises in other places now, and she could smell and taste blood. It was probably lucky she hadn't landed right on her head; some of these stones were big, and sharp. One of the broken boards had an exposed nail that had ripped the skin all down her arm and it was looking pretty bloody. The rusty nail was partially in her flesh and she shakily pulled it free and pushed it to the side weakly. She could feel blood trickling in her hair now also, and the side of her head felt hot and sticky.

Breathing through her teeth, she propped herself up tentatively on an elbow and moved her head just a little (her neck creaked but seemed intact) and looked up at the underside of the deck. There was a big hole where she had fallen through, and cracks where there were a couple of boards missing on the side also; the sunlight streamed through, highlighting the dust she had disturbed. Where was Tom? He had to come get her; even if her legs had been working properly, she was too short to climb out of that hole alone, and with her legs feeling like this she couldn't kick her way out the side.

"..." she tried to call, but started to cough from the dust immediately and had to put her head down again and pull her T-shirt up over her nose and mouth. Each cough made her ankle throb with dull fire.

"Just stay put – we'll get you out of there in a jiffy!" The woman's voice came from right behind her, from the outside of the porch, and almost made her jump out of her skin. "Just keep your eyes closed, this wood's rotten and probably full of mold. Yo, hand me that crowbar!" That

275

last was shouted over the shoulder, and she heard an answering shout over from the side yard.

She heard a few thumps and cracks, and suddenly light was streaming in from behind her and there were other voices that sounded like they were calling for medical help.

"Yup, looks like she's fainted – let's get her legs immobilized while she's out of it. Toss me another one of those splints!"

"Check out her head first, and get a neck brace on her. I see a couple of big rocks down here."

"A-ffirmative, boss. Doing a scan now."

The Medibot™ took a quick reading, projecting a miniature 4D hologram above the screen with various injury points flagged. None had an alert status above moderate except for the left leg, which indicated a fractured fibula, and the right ankle which had a broken lateral malleolus. Ligament damage as well. No damage to the spine. Minor injuries to arm, head, face, elbow.

The same tool was used to do a quick scan of the eyes; mild concussion; and with a barely perceptible needle, to take a minute sample of blood from her first finger. The DNA marker results would be instantly uploaded to Orien and be compared to samples from other confirmed survivors to look for relatives (as well as running matches through government databases like CODIS, Interpol, and others). The database was completely protected for privacy, though there was some controversy surrounding the requirement for all time travelers to provide DNA. That being said, the new algorithms Orien used were so quick and effective that they could possibly have relatives identified and alerted by the time the survivor was safely settled into the medical bay in Lake City.

"Yeah, that's a bad break... she's in for a few long weeks of recovery and physical therapy for sure, ankles are tricky. Stick a butterfly clip or two on her eyebrow there too, that cut's deep."

"Got it boss. The hopper just landed – let's pop her on the board and get her back to the city, they'll fix her up... lift on one, two..."

"...three. Hey, there you are! Just stay calm, we've got you now. What's your name, hon?"

There were three of them, friendly looking people in fancy gear peering down at her as they carried her quickly across the lawn. She could hear some soft thumping and caught a glimpse of what looked like almost translucent helicopter blades, or a dragonfly's wings, whirling lazily overhead. But she was strapped down to something, and couldn't move her head to get a good look. She had a moment of panic – an ambulance was one thing, but helicopters were for serious accidents – how badly was she hurt? And the hospital was only about 5 miles away, they could have driven... she'd heard ambulances were expensive, and who knows if their insurance even covered something like a helicopter? Or whatever this thing was – with those weird blades it really did look more like a giant insect.

"Rachael Mitchell. My husband Tom is in the house, can you get him please?"

"Not to worry, Rachael. Tom's not here, but we'll take good care of you."

"No, I saw him come in after work, did he call you? Or – "

"Easy now, don't move, that was quite a fall you had. Let's just get you settled in safely first. Let's just get a quick note or two in while they tuck you in safe. This is your house?"

"Yes, but – "

"Anyone here or in the yard with you today, besides your husband? Kids, neighbors maybe?"

"No…"

"What's the last thing you remember doing? The date, time?"

"The date? Today's the 14th, or the 15th, I think? And it was after 6:00 but I wasn't keeping track, I was planting out in the yard and left my phone inside. But Tom never gets home earlier than that, and he'd just walked in the door."

"All right, Rachael, that's fine. Now, this is going to be a quick trip, and this here hopper's nice and smooth, so if you start to feel a little dizzy just keep your eyes closed and it will be over before you know it. We'll just take care of things here, don't worry about the house or anything right now except getting better."

"Beta Team Three, accepting transfer. Helloooo there, Rachael! I'm Jody, your pilot today – we'll just have a quick flight, no more than ten minutes or so to the hospital. Let's get you a little shot for the pain, and we'll be off. Wheels up!"

She couldn't even move so she could hardly protest, but her head was spinning by now. The hot twinges in her legs were making her queasy, and these people were all talking and moving too fast, and everything was too bright and too loud. Obviously emergency responders were *supposed* to work quickly, but she felt like she'd been dumped in the middle of some sort of strange relay race, being passed about like a baton.

This notion was not dispelled when they arrived at Lake City just eight minutes later and she was whisked away to yet another efficient and cheerful team. They'd landed softly on a miniature helipad, and she caught a quick glimpse of water, flowering trees, and an impressively shiny white building that looked like marble.

"Orien-Sadler" read the logo on the whisper-quiet doors that opened to admit her gurney as they raced through the halls, the paramedics keeping up a steady stream of cheerful chatter that she didn't seem to need to respond to. She could see just out of the corner of her eyes, which still felt hot and dusty, and she blinked out more tears and felt them running down into her own ears. They were clearly in a hospital, but a fancy one unlike the local one in their neighborhood. Again, she worried about how badly she must be hurt to be rushed to a place like this, and whether Tom would be able to get here quickly. Eight minutes by fancy helicopter gave her no real idea how far that was to go by car.

At last, they seemed to be at a destination, a bright white room with a lot of beeping machines. The next few hours would be scan-rays and painkillers and a tetanus shot and bandages and ointments and stitches and medical history and more scans and finally casts and something in an IV that sent her, at last, to sleep.

CHAPTER 53

Kip article from National Geographic – 70 years, 5 months, 5 days after the Event. Time populous: 89,741

The winner of this year's photograph contest highlights the beauty of artificial rice fields in Lake Poyang in the Southeast Province of China. Using the principles learned from the civil engineering and construction of Lake City in the United States, construction of the partially floating islands began nearly ten years ago and this farmland is now one of the largest sources of food production in the region.

Constructed all along the outer edges of the 1,400 square mile freshwater lake, over fifty artificial land masses of roughly five square miles each house arable fields used for agricultural growth of a variety of rice variants (mainly Indica). The islands were initially proposed as a way to combat the effects of climate challenges faced in recent decades, in which a frequency of natural disasters and overuse of pesticides was contributing to a decline in fertility of the land.

The development of the islands took principles of horticultural sustainability techniques, new watering systems that utilize the fresh water below the islands and new solar lighting systems that maximize plant growth. Although rice production is still labor-intensive, and dependent on cropping and planting, transplanting, and seeding methods, the new man-made islands have increased the amount of available land for planting and the soil conservation methods being used have greatly improved outputs in the region. Employing techniques such as ratooning, an agricultural practice of harvesting a crop and leaving the roots and growing shoots intact to allow plant recovery, combined with greater control over pests and disease, crop outputs from the floating islands have been a major agronomic success.

In terms of exports, China still exports almost 5.75% of the world's rice and is now the fourth principal rice exporter in the world. Workers in the Jiujang area take small hoppers or ferries to the islands daily to maintain the fields and equipment, and to harvest. Agriculturalists and farmers in the province have bred genetic varieties of rice with more tolerance of the elements, with increased growth rates to speed production times. The integrated systems used on the islands, which include field measurement monitors to continually monitor the crops, allow the farmers to maximize available resources and pinpoint low-yield areas within their environmental footprint.

Construction of the first test islands began almost ten years ago, after several years of planning and international cooperation and bidding for supplies and labor, all of which boosted the economy of the region. The initial launch of five islands spread to the current fifty, adding 1,250 miles (over 300,000 hectares) of growing space within Lake Poyang alone. Similarly, in the Northwestern region of Qinghai, Ch'inghai Lake now houses over thirty artificial islands of usable farm land, with plans to expand. This region, being drier in climate than the subtropical area of Lake Poyang, produces mainly Japonica rice.

The lake fields have been tested by earthquakes, droughts, and floods, and have performed according to predicted simulations without substantial loses to crops due to the engineering employed to protect the floating islands from rough waters and winds. Considered a geotechnical engineering marvel, similar projects have been proposed in the Middle East and Africa to supplement horticultural and agricultural growth in areas where the population has the most need for succor. Development is underway for specialized islands to counter hotter climates and drier air conditions in the African continent now, with proposed sites in Lake Victoria and Lake Nyasa, where the governments of its bordering countries have agreed to allow test sites. Although the technology is dependent upon freshwater lakes, ocean versions are also being experimented with in the Baltic region and Mediterranean Sea.

Careers in agricultural economics and agronomy worldwide have grown significantly in recent decades, and crops and soil management and the development of new varieties of crops, analysis of soil structure and chemistry, and water movement within growth systems have come into more focus. The floating rice fields in China have attracted biosystems engineers and aquaculturists who have proposed adding underwater farming to the fields to increase fish and freshwater plant harvesting, and there are plans to test these in a select portion of the Poyang Lake farms.

In addition to all the practical benefits of increased fertile farmland, the floating rice fields are stunningly beautiful. The photographer who captured these breathtaking images, Naoya Fujinomo of Tokyo, Japan, shot the series at dawn from a small geocoptor rotocraft, using a photogrammetric camera with IMU and integrated lidar scanner.

CHAPTER 54

Epsilon Team One –
70 years, 6 months,
2 days after the Event.
Time populous: 89,472

It had been several decades since the last Epsilon squad had been assigned, but pest control in the city was becoming a necessity again. The last time had been far more unpleasant; a rat problem that had reached what could be considered epic proportions had begun interfering with the tech, most notably the motion detectors and iSpys.

Although foodstuffs had been removed from businesses and residential areas by the Deltas in cleanup efforts long before (with special priority placed on restaurants and factories), the resourceful rodents had immediately begun eating any and all organic materials and concentrated on expanding their territory. While people had long eradicated them in buildings when the city was populated, the lack of human presence (particularly in residential areas) now allowed rats to burrow into basements, crawl spaces, and into homes, walls, and furniture.

A few unlucky travelers had emerged into what can only be called infested areas, much to their dismay, and even the Alpha teams were threatening to strike if something wasn't done about the situation on the ground. Aside from their disgust, the Alphas were constantly having to replace chewed wires, recalibrate equipment that had been moved or damaged by the vermin, and contend with inhabitants of rat burrows when trying to place new equipment. It had been a nightmare for months.

Epsilon squads had been called in; they weren't military, but essentially exterminators with special Time Zone training. For over two years, they had moved systematically through the city, suburbs, and underground tunnels eradicating the rodent population as humanely as possible. It was an ugly job, but necessary. There was no point in saving the city for future generations if those were the conditions under which they would have to live.

Once things were under control, a select number of cats (spayed and neutered to keep the population in check) were released as sentries of sorts, each with homing devices on their collars that would keep them from triggering the tech. Eventually, with these measures, the Epsilon squads were no longer needed full time and were disbanded in a round of budget cuts. The fateful hard winter storm and the clearing of snow and ice through the sewer systems had also contributed to the final stages of cleanup for pest control.

Now, the latest round of Epsilons, recently reinstated at Orien-Sadler, had a new challenge to face. In recent years, larger wildlife such as deer, raccoons, woodchucks, skunks, fox, and even coyotes had begun moving into the abandoned city en masse. When there had been more Alpha, Beta, and Delta squads on the ground (and more ground transports moving through the city streets rather than just air patrols from above) they had been sufficiently chastened – but with the rise of more advanced tech and fewer squads patrolling than in the early days, the wild animals had deemed Toledo something of an extension of the forested area to the east. Although individually the animals were causing no major harm, the presence of large mammals, especially deer which tended to move in herds, were a danger to reentering travelers.

Epsilon groups had been tasked with moving them out of the reentry zone, and keeping them out. A new series of sonar equipment, attuned to species-specific wavelengths inaudible to the human ear (similar to a dog whistle) had been developed to place in a network in and around the Time Zone. The devices were designed to detect specific species and switch to the frequency most discouraging to that animal near that section of the net. So far, testing was successful.

Orien-Sadler held the patent for the tech, and it was being tested in various other parts of the world to protect herds of oxen and cattle from lions and other natural predators. It was considerably more humane than extermination, and more practical and safer than posting guards for protection.

In Toledo, the Epsilons were also reinstating sentry cats and dogs – but this time, of a digital variety. The network had the capability to project a holographic animal, complete with hissing or barking, to move wildlife on its way. These virtual sentries wouldn't trip any alarms or motion sensors, and could cover infinitely more territory than a live animal would.

There were only four Epsilon squads that needed personnel, but they had plenty of applications to choose from. The novelty of the position was a huge draw for those looking to join Orien-Sadler, but lacking a military, medical, or technical background.

CHAPTER 55

Rachael Mitchell – 70 years, 6 months, 15 days after the Event. Time populous: 89,450

"Have you been writing in your journal like we talked about?"

"No." She sighed; Diana knew she hadn't been, but she always asked Rachael this anyway. It made Rachael feel guilty, but not guilty enough to start doing it. She couldn't organize her thoughts well enough to put things on paper right now. She couldn't even concentrate enough to organize her thoughts inside her own head these days. She looked down so she wouldn't need to see Diana's critical look. She hadn't washed her hair in several days (Monday maybe?) and she knew she looked like a crazy, lazy mess, but she just didn't care. It was as if every day she was trapped in a dream she couldn't wake up from, and one moment she felt antsy and felt like if she didn't get up and pace *immediately*, she would simply lose her mind; but then she would just lie down and go back to sleep for hours.

Besides, she still couldn't pace all that well. Her left leg had healed decently but her right ankle still ached, especially at night. They'd offered her a sort of air-propelled cushion that she was supposed to wrap around her ankle when she walked for extra support, but she could barely reach over her enormous stomach to get to it any more so she just hobbled around stubbornly.

God, she felt disgusting. She'd put on at least 35 pounds already and she still had weeks to go. People had stopped trying to convince her she was glowing; she definitely was not. Yes, she was eating the healthy food and taking all the prenatal vitamins they put in front of her because it was easier than thinking about taking care of herself, so the baby was fine. Everyone here was constantly checking that the baby was fine, so she just let them worry about it for her. She was tired of thinking about it.

"How's the baby doing? Starting to kick a lot?"

She just shut her eyes for a minute so that she wouldn't snap and say something rude to Diana. She knew the counsellor meant well and was just doing her job, but her timing was just off. It was like she poked right at the spots that Rachael wanted to let be, every time, every session. Every damn day. They wouldn't just let her be alone for a while, everyone at this place was so damn gung-ho about rehabilitation and outreach. Everything was get ready, get ready... get ready for a new job, a new home, a new time, a new life. She didn't want any of it.

What she wanted was someone to bargain with. If she could just go back, and take a pregnancy test a couple weeks earlier so that she would have known in time... then Tom would have known too, and now he never would. She couldn't think about this too hard, or she'd make herself hysterical again, and the last time they'd had to medicate her and it had taken days to stop feeling nauseated from whatever they'd given her. She didn't want that again. She just wanted to have found out earlier, so she could have surprised him with the news and seen his joyous reaction; or maybe they would have found out together, like a cheesy couple in an ad.

She and her girlfriends had always thought those pregnancy test commercials were ridiculous; not only were the people always handling something covered in urine way too much, but they were always made from the viewpoint that pregnancy was 100% the goal. No one ever saw the two blue lines and said OH SHIT in the commercials. But she and Tom would have been the sappy, crying, happy people for sure. They hadn't been trying, but they hadn't *not* been trying either. Instead, she'd found out here at the facility, after she came to the next morning after her rescue with her legs on fire, and was told she couldn't have too strong a dose of painkillers 'because of the baby'.

She'd just stared dumbly at the nurse for a minute until he realized she hadn't known, and then clearly wanted to burst into flames right in front of her for his faux paus. Poor guy... she'd been so shell shocked with the news that the whole on-boarding about time travel hadn't even phased her. She'd just sort of numbly listened to their whole spiel and watched all their video clips on autopilot and barely even wanted to ask any questions.

Well... until they got to the bad news part. At first it had been like a strange, alternate universe science class, with their little charts and graphs and holograms showing her the dumbed-down version of relativity, all carefully packaged in a little welcome speech for people like herself. And although at the beginning she didn't believe a word of it, the moment it hit her that the reason Tom hadn't come when she'd fallen through the deck was because he wasn't there any more, she believed all the rest. Nothing else in the universe but a time warp would have stopped him from getting to her, not when she was hurt and scared and needed him. And for just a brief moment she thought *when he gets back, I'll have such a surprise for him...* and then she saw their faces and knew before they even said it that she was the one who was too late. Not just too late to pick up where they'd left off; she was years too late to even say goodbye.

Something had snapped deep inside of her when she heard that, and like a motor clanking and groaning and creaking to a dead stop, she felt like she'd never stop feeling broken again.

"Rachael, you have to try to do the journalling, or just some of the exercises. I know it's hard and you don't want to, but you have to try. For yourself as much as for the baby."

The baby... she knew it was a girl, but she hadn't picked out a name yet. She felt like if she just sat quietly and didn't think about it too much, maybe it would just come to her. It wouldn't be long now, and she wasn't ready. The staff here was trying their best to get her prepped… they insisted on breathing practice, and yoga, and she'd been assured she could stay at the facility until after the birth, and she'd dutifully read some of the books (at least turned the pages while her eyes scanned some of the words) and watched a few horrifying video clips (who on earth would consent to letting that be recorded?) but she still wasn't prepared. Every now and then she felt kicking, and tried not to think about it.

"Rachael. *Rachael.* They're saying you have a visitor. Are you up for meeting someone?"

"Who is it? Someone I *know?*"

She was simultaneously excited and ashamed; it was ridiculous to be moping around still in her maternity pajamas in the middle of the afternoon – if someone she knew had returned from the time stream, they certainly weren't going to be impressed with her right now. An old coworker? A neighbor? Maybe even her sister? But none of them were who she really wanted to see anyway, so what did it matter?

"No, someone who's a friend of Tom's. He'd like to come meet you in the west garden at 2:30, if you're up for it? He's at the reception desk up front, but he needs to make a stop on the way, he wants to say hello to a few people at the office first."

"Okay…" 2:30 gave her a little time. Maybe if she hobbled swiftly, she could take a quick shower, and not make an ass of herself meeting someone new. A friend of Tom's… someone who had friends here too. So, it must be someone he had known here, in the future where his new life was, or they would have said the name – she knew all Tom's old friends from back in the day. This would be someone who had only known Tom without her. That felt odd, and she had butterflies in her stomach, butterflies that felt different from a kicking baby, and not altogether pleasant.

But she felt better after the shower, and her hair felt strange and slippery hanging wet and clean in a ponytail down her back, and combed properly for the first time in God knows when. She didn't have anything to wear except more maternity yoga clothes, but she left her big sweater behind in her room. It was warm and fluffy and comforting, but even she was beginning to realize it was becoming more like a security blanket than an article of clothing, and it felt like progress to set it aside for a little while. She even made an effort and stretched down enough to get the air cushion on her bad ankle so that she could actually get out to the garden on time.

Outside it was warm and breezy, and there were hydrangeas in the garden. They'd been in her wedding bouquet also, and she shut that thought off quickly and stuffed it to the back of her brain. She didn't want a stranger to see her burst into tears right off the bat. They really had done a nice job with the landscaping (she told herself sternly to admire it and keep it together). There were nicely edged paths, with tiny stones that were easy to walk on even with a hurt leg; and tall, stately trees surrounded by clusters of groundcovers and variegated bushes, with large planters of jumbles of flowering plants everywhere. Benches were spaced far enough apart to allow for private conversations, and all with views facing outward over the lake. A large, graceful fountain. It was beautiful here. It was hard to believe the whole island wasn't a real island at all, but something they had built.

She sat on one of the benches facing the main arched entryway and waited. The bench she was sitting on had a plaque declaring it to be dedicated to the memory of a Dr. Xiao Xiang, Director of the Institute, from his beloved children and grandchildren. Looking around, she saw other small plaques on benches and on a few large boulders that had been decoratively spaced alongside the paths. It reminded her of the arboretum near where she had lived as a child; she and her mom had often walked there. She had used to like sitting on the benches and pretending the people they were dedicated to liked having visitors there at "their" bench. She hoped Dr. Xiang, whoever he was, was enjoying her visit.

There was a crunching sound along the path, and a tall, sharply dressed, elderly gentleman with a cane appeared and grinned at her like he was an old friend of hers, not just of Tom's.

"Ahhh, Rachael! You look just like your pictures. I feel like I know you already, though that's presumptuous of me to say." He shook her hand warmly, and settled down on the bench beside her. Somehow, he put her right at ease. Maybe it was just a relief to see someone who was just glad to see her, instead of looking at her with pity.

"My name is Trevor, and I knew your husband Tom for a long, long time. We watched each other get old, I'm afraid." He said this gently, but with a smile, reminiscing, which brought a prickle of tears to her eyes despite her best efforts.

"That was supposed to be my job," she said with a shaky almost-smile. Not quite, but almost. "But I guess I'm glad he did it without me anyway."

He nodded sagely. "Yes. I would always tell the travelers that no matter what happened in the future, they should be glad to have one. We lost too many in the early years, to accidents, or just not knowing enough about how to prepare them. Because unfortunately, making it back is the easy part. The hard part is every day afterwards."

"You sound like my counsellor."

"I should; I trained enough of 'em along the way," he said with a grin. "I've been retired now a good long time, but it never leaves you, I guess. It's in my blood now."

"You were Tom's counsellor?"

"I was… for, oh, over twenty-five years. And I saw him many times after he was out of the program, we tried to get together every year for a ball game, or a barbeque during the summer holidays. He was a friend."

"What… what was he like? When he was older? I mean… I read the stuff in his file. I know he had a family…"

She looked down quickly and couldn't get any farther beyond the lump in her throat. She wanted to know, but she didn't want to hear another word. She wished she'd worn her sweater after all; the sleeves on this shirt weren't long enough to pull her fists inside. Trevor turned a little towards her and put his hand out flat. It was a reassuring move, and without even thinking she put hers into it, and he covered them with his other hand. Sandwiched between his steady ones, her hands stopped trembling and she took a deep breath while he nodded at her steadily.

"That's right, breathe. I understand. You want to know all about it, but you don't, either, right?"

She nodded. This guy was good; he must have been a great counsellor back in his time. No one else here had been able to get her to focus like this in months.

"You didn't read any of the letters he left yet?"

"I… I couldn't. I saw the box, and there's so many but I just couldn't start. Not yet. But I do want to know. I want to know that he was okay without me."

"Yes, that's what we want for everyone we care about, isn't it? I know that's what he wanted for you, too. And I know he would have been so thrilled about a baby. Though I expect it's difficult for you to go through the experience without him."

She nodded through her tears but didn't try to take her hands back to wipe them.

"All right, I can tell you a few things now, and then you can tell me if you'd like to hear some more things later. What I can tell you first is that Tom was lost without you for a very long time. You know he had some anxiety issues in his youth? Yes, well, becoming a time traveler didn't exactly help with that. He had to do a lot of work on himself just to stop having the panic attacks, and he was pretty twitchy and hyper in our early sessions. He always said between that and the time jumping, he had become like that Dr. Who you liked to watch, but without the fancy accent."

She couldn't help but smile at that a little.

"Anyway, we spent the first few years really just working on his anxiety. I was a new counsellor back then, and still learning the ropes myself... he had someone else for the first year or so after he was back, I got him a little later – and he had only skipped forward about ten years, so he didn't really have to take any training courses to get a new job or anything like that. And he had hurt his knee in reentry so he gave up playing sports for a while. So, he had nothing to distract himself with. He became very fixated on the idea that he shouldn't do certain things without you. I think in our time we said "FOMO", the fear of missing out... this was like a mirror version of that. He was afraid of you missing out."

She squirmed a little, feeling a rush of guilt.

"Now, now, deep breath. Don't feel too bad about that; it was just his way of worrying about you, or showing how much he missed you. He got pretty dark there for a few years. But we got through it." He patted her top hand a few times while she got ahold of herself and when she looked at him clear-eyed again, he nodded and continued.

"It took me almost ten years to get him to start journaling and writing out letters for you. I think he thought maybe if he procrastinated on it, you'd just come back. Journaling can be very therapeutic though."

Here he cocked an eyebrow at her meaningfully and gave her a mock-stern look. She blushed, and he chuckled.

"Yes, Ms. Diana *is* a tattletale. But try it – it does help most people. Anyway, once Tom got over the worst of his anxiety attacks, we were able to get him to make some new friends. He volunteered helping with the local little leagues and things like that. He always missed you, that you never need to question, but he had a lot of things going for him, and he was happy."

A little more pressure on the hands. She knew the hard part was coming.

"It took him a long time, and he waited until he really honestly felt he had gotten too old for you before he moved on, but I know he never forgot you, and he wanted nothing but the best for you. He finally met a nice, older lady like himself, and they took in some foster children, and later adopted a few too, so he really made a positive impact on a lot of lives. And they had several dogs; he always included pictures of the dogs on their holiday cards. He was really happy for a long time and had a contented, long life, and he and his wife passed within just a few months of each other, and their adopted kids and grandkids really miss them. And that's the story of Tom. The short version, anyway."

He gave her hands a final squeeze and released her to wipe her eyes on her sleeves, and sob a few quiet sobs. He let her be and didn't try to interrupt her or distract her. That's what she realized had been bothering her about the other counsellors – they tried so hard to sidetrack her from her pain when she just wanted to wallow in it for a little bit. Trevor just let her cry and didn't try to put a shiny object in front of her to divert her. After a few minutes she felt empty and dry, but in a way that felt lighter, like she'd been violently sick but had gotten the poison out of her system. *Pull it together, kid.*

"It sounds like something out of a fairy tale book when you tell it. The story of Tom." She gave Trevor a tentative smile and he laughed at that.

"Yes. Maybe when you and I have our lives summarized into a few facts, we shall sound so lucky too, and forget all the little pains of living. Now... this has been a lot for you to hear all in one go and I'm sure you'll want some privacy to process things. If you wouldn't mind walking with me back to the facility...?"

"Of course... although you're probably faster than me, with this bum ankle." Not to mention I'm waddling like a penguin with this belly, she thought wryly. She'd better start trying a little harder at the yoga maybe.

"Not to worry, we can take it slow."

As they moved slowly down the path Trevor pointed out some of the names on the inscriptions and gave her small tidbits about his old friends. Eventually they came to the doorway and he gave her a slight bow and a cheerful tip of his cap.

"It's quite dull being retired, you know. So, if you'd like someone to talk to, I'd be happy to visit you again, while you're here with my friends at Lake City, and we'll tell some more stories. I love stories, and Tom used to tell me you do also. And perhaps once you're settled in your new home on the mainland after the baby comes, you can come visit with me there. I always have lots of snacks."

"Well, I *do* love snacks and stories."

They both laughed at that, maybe the first time she's really laughed in months. Her laugh feels creaky, like an old clock that needed to be oiled and wound, before the gears could start moving once again.

CHAPTER 56

A Moment in Time –
72 years, 2 months, 4 days after the Event.
Time populous: 85,165

"Thanks for joining us this evening, for this special episode starting our third season with Zing Social. I'm your host, Armani Graham, and tonight we'll be taking an in-depth look at the fascinating stories of two families, both with young parents reemerging to a time in which their children are *considerably* older than they remembered. We'll examine the different ways they're working to cope. Let's begin with John and Garrett Newsom. Now, John, you were a teen father, just graduating high school when the Time Event occurred, is that correct?"

"Yeah, I had a scholarship to play football at Kansas State and I had training camp about to start over the summer so I was about to leave. My girlfriend Jenna was going to do summer school and finish her GED because she had to miss the end of school to have the baby. Our moms were going to help watch him while she finished, and then in the fall she was going to move out to Kansas. We had it all worked out."

"But then the wormhole opened."

"Yeah. Jenna was only gone about two years and made it back, so when Garrett came back seventeen years ago, he went to live with her and got to grow up there. And then her mom came back about five years ago too."

"Now Garrett, that had to be unusual – to have your mom and grandma raising you, but with your grandma being the *younger* of the two?"

"Well, I was used to my mom being old, because that was how it had always been since even before I could remember. And people used to ask all the time if she was my grandma. But then Gram came out of the time stream, and she was only like 45 on her personal time scale, and my mom was over eighty years old by then, so people would get real confused."

"And now your dad is back, and the two of you are almost the same age on your personal time scales."

"Yeah, people always ask us if we're brothers."

"So, John, how do you reconcile being a father to someone who's basically the same age as you?"

"I mean... I kinda can't. There's no point trying to act like I'm in charge. He's all grown up, just look at him! A real linebacker! I can't even imagine trying to boss him around. I'm just trying to get to know him, so we can be friends at least. And it's not like I had even learned what it *was* to be a father yet, it was so new to me when we all got disappeared."

"Are you going to try to live in the same household, hang out together?"

"Well, Garrett just got accepted into Kansas State himself, and the university is making a special exception to still let me have a scholarship if I take some classes to catch up on the things I missed out on, and they said I can still tryout for the team at camp when I get there. So hopefully we're going to be teammates next fall, too, even if I can only make the prep squad. I can't play another year in high school, because I don't have any more years of eligibility, but the coach is going to let me practice with them so I don't get rusty."

"Garrett, how do you feel about all that? Do you feel like you're missing out on having a father?"

"Nah, I mean... no offense, but I grew up without one, and it was okay. There were plenty of other kids around who had parents still lost in time, or who were just divorced or whatever. It's cool that we can just be friends."

"Well, we'll hope to see you both excelling on the football field very soon. Now, let's turn to the Choi family, whose situation is a bit different, and even more complicated.

Helen and Edmund were young parents at the time the wormhole opened, both in their early twenties, and they were lucky enough to reemerge recently, almost at the same time! Their twin sons were two years old when the Time Event happened. Jimmy came back several years ago and is now seventeen, and their other son Donnie came back just a couple of years before they did and is now four. So, when you returned, Donnie would have been almost exactly as you remembered him, but Jimmy was already a teenager?"

"Yes, it was very strange, and hard to get used to. We're still struggling with it."

"It's been very difficult. He's our son and we love him of course, but we just don't know him very well yet. I feel like I should understand him better because I remember *being* his age not all that long ago, but it's so complicated."

"Jimmy, please give us your perspective. What has it been like since your family has been brought back together?"

"Sorry to be blunt, but it really sucks. They don't know anything about me."

"It's hard to reconnect sometimes?"

"They don't want to reconnect with me; I'm already too old. They just want Donnie, who they can raise just like they wanted to."

"That's not true—"

"No, Jimmy, really—"

"It IS true, "Dad"… give me a break! You're barely five years older than me; it's bizarre."

"It is, but we're trying to—"

"What? Go back to being a family? You're both being unrealistic. Donnie's still a little kid – you can bring him up and have a normal life with him. The three of you got lucky. I'm never going to fit in to that, it's like I'm some distant relative who's come to spend the summer or something. And no matter what, Donnie might be my "little brother" but he's never going to feel like my *twin*."

"Do you feel *any* closer to Donnie than to your parents?"

"I guess so. I mean, he was still only two years old when I met him so it was kind of like my foster parents just had a baby. It was fine, until *they* came back and wanted us all to go live together."

"I have to ask, just to be fair, your foster parents aren't all that old either. Why doesn't their age bother you as much as it does with your biological parents?"

"I guess… because they never tried to act like they were my actual parents. Like, they were nice, and I had rules and chores and stuff like any kid. But they talked to me more like… like I was a guest. And I had the safety net of knowing I could ask to leave if I wasn't happy… and someday when I became an adult, I could just do my own thing and not need anyone's approval."

"And you don't feel like your parents will let you do your own thing?"

"It's like, all of a sudden, I have this life-long *obligation* that they expect me to fulfill, and they keep talking about our ancestors, and family traditions, and it's like… I didn't grow up with any of that, but now I'm supposed to just immediately care about all of it and change my life to include it. And in the meantime, Donnie will just grow up with it and accept it, so he'll always be this perfect model child and I'll always either have to pretend to care about stuff I don't care about, or I'll be seen as this rebellious outsider who won't cooperate with their plans."

"We're trying to—"

"It's hard for us too—"

"I know, I KNOW. I'm not saying it's your fault. I'm just saying, it doesn't work for me to be forced into this weird-ass dynamic. I'd be better off living on my own until we get used to each other instead of trying to force us to bond. But we're never going to be the prototypical nuclear American family, so just accept that and stop trying to make *me* the bad guy just because I already have."

"Alright folks, let's take a break, and then we'll have some family counselling experts in to discuss some methods they use to help families like these that are struggling to reconnect. And make sure to join us next week, when we'll talk to Michael and Margaret, two Canadian citizens caught in the time stream that were initially prohibited from returning to their own homes due to the international time laws; and with Frederik, an international tourist who missed his connecting flight in Toledo on the day of the Event. He has reemerged to a time when no one he knows is still alive, plus the country he is from no longer even *exists* under the same name. We'll get his perspective on what it's like to be suddenly without a country and to be a last remnant of his nation. We'll be right back."

CHAPTER 57

United Nations General Assembly –
73 years, 8 months,
6 days after the Event.
Time populous: 84,101

On 21 January, the U.N. International Time Committee established pursuant to resolution 3201 held a formal consultation to consider the midterm update of the Panel of Experts to include a wider range of specialist fields. The Committee heard a presentation that was followed by an interactive discussion between Committee members and the Panel.

The presentation considered the ongoing threat of the existence of a man-made hypothetical time machine, and the commitment of the global community to eradicate this potential danger to the world through identification and containment. A renewed focus on finding the inventor of the time machine was proposed, with many calls from the Member States for the U.S. to ensure that, should such an inventor be identified, they will be disciplined for their actions.

Debate regarding the intentions of the inventor became heated. Some members of the General Assembly have argued that while the motives of the inventor are unknown and cannot be assumed as malicious until they are found and questioned, either way the priority must be on persuading them to explain how they achieved the opening of the wormhole for the scientific community, not on penalization. At this time, it is unclear whether the inventor is even aware that others were affected by their experiment; there is not even clarity on whether or not the inventor is still in the time stream themselves, or have returned.

The argument from other Members is that the very concept of altering the fabric of time is a very dangerous one and although in their own time, the inventor might have considered time travel as fictional or hypothetical, the fact is that they still endeavored to build a machine for their own use, without warning authorities or even their neighbors of their actions. There would be no way for them to know the impact of opening a wormhole, or whether it would injure or even kill others in its path. Genius or not, by indulging their own curiosity, they took the selfish stance that their own needs for scientific discovery were paramount to the safety of others.

As one representative expounded, the inventor should be held liable in some way for their actions; otherwise, others may be inspired to try and emulate their experiment. If they are simply excused as having made a mistake, with no legal or punitive damages, there are millions of people affected (not to mention the economic influence) that will not have closure for something that was forced upon them. It sends the wrong message to have no recourse; it excuses all scientific experimentation, no matter how dangerous, potentially exposing the world to the whims of inventors everywhere. There must be some accountability to prevent future irresponsible behavior, both from this inventor and others like them.

Setting aside the discussion of the fate of the inventor, talks turned to next steps regarding finding evidence of the time machine itself. An agreement was reached that a more targeted search should be conducted under the oversight of the U.N., as it was agreed that the U.S. government and Sadler-Orien have not done enough to ease the world's concerns about whether such a device may exist. This has bred mistrust and division, and the shadow of the threat of another Time Event looms larger since the Lake City Siege, when it became apparent that some would use the hypothetical machine as a tool of annihilation.

In the face of these threats, the global community must speak as one to decry the reckless use of a time machine that has the power to uproot human civilizations with the push of a button. For this reason, disarmament is at the heart of the recently launched policy brief on a New Agenda for Time Regulation. The agenda calls on Member States to reinforce the global norms against the use and proliferation of time machines, and pending their total elimination, renewed commitment to never use them.

Further discussion on what should be done with the time machine (if it exists and if it can be found) is expected from the Panel of Experts at the next session, when they will present their proposals for containment (including potential locations and facilities, safety protocols, and timelines for preparation). The Panel will also give recommendations on potential destruction methods, although there is still disagreement on whether such a critical scientific discovery should be preserved for study, either for a set time, or indefinitely.

CHAPTER 58

Dr. Samantha Estrada, Pediatric Psychiatrist – 74 years, 6 months, 28 days after the Event. Time populous: 83,571

"My momma told me to never go with strangers, and you're a stranger and I. Ain't. Goin'. With. You. I *ain't*."

The little girl crossed her arms, sat down on the curb, and glared at all of them. They could smile and laugh, like her sassy-pants attitude was just a game, but she'd *scream* if they tried to make her go with them – she would do it! She hated the kind of adults that treated kids like they were funny when they were mad. It wasn't nice, and it made her *more* angrier. She just didn't understand what had happened though, why these people were even here. They had just left the grocery store, and she had heard the door close behind her and then all of a sudden, she was by herself. Mommy wasn't right behind her, and the slidey door to the store wouldn't open back up. And now all these dumb grown-ups were here, trying to boss her around. She crossed her arms tighter and kicked at the curb with her heel in frustration.

Mommy had drilled her on stranger danger about a *million* times, and she wasn't about to get stranger-dangered today, no ma'am. Mommy had said never never never go with a stranger and don't be fooled if they say they know her mommy and daddy or it's an emergency unless they know the family password. If it's a policeman or fireman it's okay – but these people didn't look like the police and firemen that came to school every year to talk about safety and not doing drugs. She remembered what *they* looked like, and they had warned about strangers too. Teachers, and her Daisy Scout leader, and her karate instructor were always talking about staying away from strangers. Even Peppa Pig said don't talk to strangers. These people must think she's a real sucker, but she's not going *anywhere* with them.

Meanwhile, the dumb grown-ups were discussing how best to handle the situation, which was currently scowling at them all with suspicion. There had been thousands of reappearing children over the years, but most were upset finding themselves alone, and relieved to be picked up when they realized their parents had disappeared... or were too young to understand fully what was going on. This girl was not only extremely suspicious of them all, but she was adamant that she was not going with them peacefully – she had mentioned she took karate twice already, and they were unwilling to test it – and it wouldn't help her reentry process to start off with a bad experience bringing her in by force anyway. The Beta squad had taken a trip back to Lake City to get a children's specialist to come onsite to help, it would just take a few minutes for the hopper to get back. It was standard procedure to bring in an expert for children, unless it was medically necessary to rush them back, though the Alphas were well trained in negotiation tactics for adults who were reluctant to be transported. Being generally considered to be in a more fragile state, kids were to be handled, well, with kid gloves.

Not surprisingly, she wouldn't take any food or drink from them any more than she would have agreed to help them find a lost puppy or get in their van. Finally, they had offered their not-so-fragile problem child a tablet to play with, which she had accepted sulkily. And maybe she was right not to trust them since that had been a trick specifically designed for rescuing children in the field; the tablet was actually a Medibot with a game setting on. Pressing the start button for the game took a tiny blood sample needed to start the DNA trace (the needles these days were so delicate the prick was completely imperceptible). So at least they were getting somewhere, even while they weren't getting anywhere.

The hopper was just landing now, and the woman coming towards them certainly did not look like the pediatric psychiatrist she was… soft blue jeans, a fuzzy pastel sweater, low ponytail, white tennis shoes. She looked like everyone's favorite kindergarten teacher, by design. She gave them a cheery wave, both a greeting and a dismissal. The Alphas sauntered casually to the side to wait on events.

"Hi there! My name is Dr. Sam. Can I sit here with you?"

She got a suspicious nod, and sat down on the curb a few feet away. This one was a tough cookie, but Sam was in luck today; not only had the Medibot's search turned up a surviving relative, he had been immediately reachable, and more importantly, had given her the critical family password. But it wouldn't do just to run up and blurt it out; the best way to start the rehabilitation process for children was to make them comfortable first.

"Sorry if those guys were being pushy. I hate being told what to do, don't you?"

"Yeah. I'm not going with them."

"That's fine, don't worry about them. I'll chase 'em away for you." She pulled a mock tough look at the Alphas, which got a trace of a smile from the girl. Still suspicious.

"Were you here at the store with your mom and dad?"

"Me and my mom were buying ice cream. We've gotta get home or it's going to melt. Can you call her please?"

"We'll try to reach her, I promise. What kind of ice cream did you pick out? My favorite's cookies 'n' cream. But I like the kind with peanut butter cups in it second best. My little girl is about your age, and she likes mint chocolate chip. How about you?"

"I got Rocky Road for me, and Mommy got butter pecan. Strawberry for my brother and Daddy."

"Yum! Are you going to have it with chocolate syrup?"

"Yeah! And we got the kind of whip cream that squirts from the can."

"Ooo – that's my favorite! I always take a squirt right from the can when no one is looking. Shhh, don't tell!" That got a small giggle.

"Mommy lets me have an extra squirt in my mouth if I get out all the bowls and spoons and shake the can for her."

It was funny, all those years of training and study for her doctorate, and years of exams and licenses and thousands of hours of field work in mental health services, and Sam still found that people bonded over the simple idea of food easier than anything else; adults and children alike. Get people talking about their favorite cultural meal, or ask about their holiday traditions and family recipes and nine times out of ten people would open right up. She also truly loved cooking and sampling new cuisine, so her enthusiasm at their responses was genuine. Probably it just proves that we are all primordial creatures and not the complex pinnacle of evolution we'd all like to assume she thought wryly. But if it worked, it worked; she would use it shamelessly if it meant getting through to the travelers who were her patients.

Of course, society also has complex feelings about food, and eating disorders were still more common than most people realized… but in general she found thinking of something comforting like a favorite meal was an easy ice breaker, in a professional capacity or socially. In fact, she and her husband Jamie had bonded over food when they had first met, before the Time Event had even happened.

She was more than halfway through her PhD while he had been an undergrad at the same University, and they were both studying at a nearby bistro and coffee shop with free wi-fi so frequently that they couldn't help but eventually meet. He was very handsome with his wavy black hair falling softly into piercing blue eyes, and he had been very flirtatious with her the first few times they had crossed paths. Soon they had realized she was quite a bit older than him (fifteen years! the perils of looking too good for your age she had thought bitterly at the time), and without any actual discussion of it, romance was just off the table. Honestly, they both felt a little silly realizing what a big gap it was, and just chose to ignore it and pretend that hadn't been their intention at all to save face. But they both had actually enjoyed their chats at the bistro, and struck up a friendship that soon progressed as she began teaching him how to eat and cook properly.

He was an inordinately picky eater and that caused him to decline a lot of invitations out – probably one of the reasons he wasn't already spoken for. But Sam persisted, and soon realized he wasn't really all that picky, it was mostly just because he had grown up in a family that only made prepackaged foods and never pushed him to try anything new. Only by describing new foods thoroughly and enthusiastically was she able to convince him to move beyond chicken tenders and French fries. Through taste testing and analysis of what he did and didn't like (textures, flavors, spice levels, and so on), soon he was being more adventurous in what he would try, and before the year was out, he was becoming a regular foodie. By the next summer, he was the one making her elaborate dishes in his small apartment off campus, or suggesting new restaurants for them to try. The timing was perfect, because she was so deep in her doctoral thesis that she didn't have time to cook for herself, and was subsisting mainly off of dried noodles and coffee – a home cooked meal revived her in body and spirit.

And they liked so many of the same things; movies, music, sports; it was easy to ignore the age difference and just have fun together, and they hung out alone a lot of the time. It wasn't romantic at all – it was just nice to have someone to be with. He didn't have a big group of friends at school, and a lot of hers were recently married or first-time parents without a lot of free time (not that she had much of that either, trying to finish her dissertation – but he made for a nice distraction from that). This continued for almost two years, and while they weren't studying the same things at all, they were both "students" so it had still felt like they were in a similar stage of life, and the age gap was barely a concern.

She had had a small celebration party for having successfully defending her thesis, and Jamie had offered to cook for it, so of course, a few of his friends that she knew were invited to join them. It had been a strange cross-pollination of groups and seeing the span from undergrad party animals to nearly middle-aged parents in one room really highlighted that age difference more than their time alone ever had. Worse yet, suddenly that gap came into extreme focus as both sides gave them good-natured ribbing about cougars and sugar babies, which just felt gross to both of them. Strangers had always assumed them to be a couple, and it had never bothered either of them – but having a whole room full of people discussing it and sympathetically agreeing that "if only the timing had been better", they would be perfect together... somehow that made them both feel awkward as hell, and very exposed.

After that disastrous evening, they probably would have eventually gone their separate ways. He was about to graduate and was considering moving back home to Oregon, and she was about to start her first full-time job. But then the Time Event happened. The next thing she knew, she was being brought to Lake City, having an almost out-of-body experience as she was put through a rehabilitation program that was textbook for trauma patients... precisely what she had just finished her doctoral work on. And it was the future. Way, way in the future.

Her sisters and her parents were long gone; they were from Florida, and had lived out their normal, natural lives far away from the Time Zone, leaving her with a few letters and not much else but memories. All her friends from back home were gone, or in their final years in retirement homes across the country, and the ones from Toledo (and their spouses, and their children) were scattered to the wind. It had been 65 years since the Time Event, and depending on when they had reemerged, some were now middle aged, elderly, even deceased, while others were still in the time stream. But Jamie was back.

He had reemerged sixteen years earlier and trained to become a chef, and now lived in a tiny San Diego apartment with two roommates and a cat, and he had dropped everything to come back the moment he got the alert about her reentry. He had come to see her at Lake City, and when reception alerted her that she had a visitor and she saw his name, she had never felt more thankful in her life. They were both crying before he even came in the door, and it felt like just the most natural thing in the world for him to sweep her up and kiss her and never let her go again. It wasn't until they had been talking for hours that it even occurred to them that they were now almost the same age after all.

All that had been ten years and a couple of kids ago now, and here she was, Dr. Sam, getting to use her training in the field after all, and got to go home to beautifully cooked and plated meals on top of that. She worked with all sorts of people at the clinic, but she had been trained to specialize in children, since when she had gotten the job at Lake City, they had been short on staff in that area. After so many years since the Time Event had occurred, the return of minors kept getting more complicated, as it was more common for relatives to be elderly or deceased. That, combined with the fact that survival rates in general were higher than they had been in the early years, and the demand for fostering was higher and only going up.

In this case, little miss DJ Martin was one of the survivors who would likely end up in foster care. Although her brother Trevor was already back at Lake City eagerly awaiting their return, he was 85 years old now and only partially mobile – it was unlikely he would be able to become her full-time guardian without assistance. But either way, first they had to get her to the facility; at least she had stopped scowling now.

"DJ, I know you'd like to wait here for your mom, but do you think we could go somewhere and talk first? And maybe they can bring us some Rocky Road there?"

"How'd you know my name?" Suspicious still, and she was a sharp one to have caught that.

"I talked to your family, and they told me your name and the password. I won't try to make you come if you're not ready, we can talk here more if you want. But I'd really like you to come with me. Something has happened here in the city, and it's easier to explain it at my office, where I have a little movie about it and some stuff just for kids like you. It's just a short ride away, and we can go in that cool hopper there."

"Up in the *air*?"

"Yeah – unless you'd rather drive. It's okay if you're scared, I thought it was scary the first time I rode in one, but now I think it's really fun. You can see the whole city from up there! I can point out to you where the zoo is, and the river, and maybe we'll see your house from up above."

"Wellll…" She was tempted. None of the kids from school had ever flown up in the air before, except Suzie, who had been on vacation in an airplane – but this hopper thing was cooler looking than a regular plane. Next show and tell she would have something really good to talk about, and maybe Dr. Sam would take a picture of her up in the air ("pics or it didn't happen" stupid Suzie would say). If she really knew the password and all. "Okay, tell me what the password is."

Sam whispered it to her, and they walked to the hopper hand in hand. There, they took several pictures of her smiling in the passenger seat with the headset on (DJ even consented to let the Alpha team gather around with them for a selfie) and then they took off into the sunset.

Trevor is back at the facility waiting for them to arrive and ready to observe; but he's asked them to start onboarding DJ first, even though he'd like to see her right away. He knows from years of counselling that she won't believe her ten-year-old brother is now an old man, and if she's presented with that right off the bat she might shut down and refuse to believe anything. It's better if they introduce him in a couple of days as an old uncle (family, but someone she never met before) until she's ready to know the truth. She's just five and a half years old, and the stubbornest person he's ever known. It's going to be hard for her here in the future, and she'll fight the idea that her mom and dad are gone with everything she's got, but she doesn't need to know about that just yet. Trevor knows Dr. Sam by reputation, and when she called him just an hour ago with the news, he got a positive vibe from her right away. DJ will be in good hands, even after he's long gone.

Val passed two years ago now, and he sold their little house with the extra bedroom because his mobiscooter didn't function well on the stairs; but the retirement village where he lives is right by the west hopper dock. Trevor's been waiting for this a long, long time. He can wait a couple more days.

CHAPTER 59

News headlines –
75 years after the Event.
Time populous: 69,122

'Looking forward to a new era; the U.S. revisits 75 years of time travel'

U.N. Time Committee unveils detailed plans for the search for the hypothetical time machine

Photos: "Moments in time" memorial concert in the park draws musicians worldwide

Perspectives: A panel of the past

May 15th

LAKE CITY, USA – Orien-Sadler commemorated the 75th anniversary of the Time Event with a series of special exhibits set up on the mainland near the parade route, outlining the history and milestones of their organization and featuring video clips and even live talks from survivors recounting their experiences. Members of the public were invited to ask a panel of time travelers their questions directly.

"I really enjoyed getting to speak to the panel. I have a few neighbors who are time survivors too and I like hearing their stories," said 15-year-old Michael Devine, a student at Ann Arbor Academy. "It's weird to think that there are people who were actually born in the 20th century that are still here today in the 22nd and can tell us about our country's history firsthand."

One example that was brought up at the panel was what things in the future are most surprising to returning Toledoans, and one was that some of the cautionary measures they had come to expect in their own time regarding health care and supplies were simply not a factor now.

"When I was really young, I remember my great-grandmother having a large stock of canned goods in her pantry, and I asked her why she needed so many," recalled Liz Thompson at the panel discussion. "She told me it was because she had lived through the Great Depression*, which was so far before I was born it didn't make sense to me that her mindset was so altered even years later, and I honestly thought she was just old and crazy. But now I understand her better, because the people of today look at me the same way when I get uncomfortable in a crowd, or buy an extra pack of toilet paper for my house just in case. The Great Depression to me is what the pandemic** is to people today – something so long ago it barely seems real."

On a related note, regarding epidemics and disease, it is now a standard practice for those emerging from the time stream to be thoroughly scanned and treated for any lingering viruses or conditions after a minor outbreak ten years ago at Lake City proved to be a strain of rubella that had been eradicated generations ago. Doctors and researchers at the facility further refined their onboarding procedures to account for these checks, as the further away from the Event we get, the more likely it is that antique strains will be encountered.

"Part of the challenge of working at Lake City is that our assessment and action plans need to have a wider scope than a standard medical facility," explained Dr. Zachary Warren, Director of Medical. "We need to provide the latest medical treatments like any hospital, but we also need to be prepared to treat historical diseases and infections that a modern facility rarely encounters. Our staff gets special training for when a Medibot detection comes up, and our 48-hour quarantine period for treatment is enacted before the onboarding process begins."

On a more lighthearted note, the panel of survivors also agreed that one of the most jarring things about emerging in the future was seeing old fads from their past brought back by the cyclical nature of art and fashion. And of course, seeing their favorite television programs in their entirety, available on all new platforms with a much clearer sound and picture quality than they remembered.

"It brings a whole new dimension to binge watching when you have ten to fifteen years-worth of episodes to catch up on," joked panelist Andrew Voight. Others agreed, but also expressed some regrets knowing that there was no chance for additional seasons. "Seeing as how everyone on the show is dead or retired now, the best I can hope for is another reboot," said one panelist. "They already did one twenty years ago I hear – but I'm still working my way through the original series!"

The visitors to Lake City also had a chance to record Kips with their thoughts on the 75th anniversary, and as part of the festivities on the mainland, one local elementary school spent the year having students create 4D timelines to share. These interactive family trees plot out their relatives' reentry dates and comparative ages, and facts about their lives before and after the Event.

Another special display shared ideas submitted over the course of the last year for the eventual rebuilding of Toledo. High school students around the globe were invited to participate in the exercise sponsored by the American Time Association. The contestants were asked to provide an essay outlining whether they felt the city could be repopulated at all, and at what percentage of returns the threshold should be to begin this work; what factors they would consider for reuse, recycling, and reconstruction; and what they would envision the city to be like within their lifetimes.

One hundred finalists were chosen from the tens of thousands of submissions, and the ten scholarship winners will be announced next month.

This exercise is mirrored in the work Orien-Sadler has been doing for the past decade, with expert analysts tasked with preparing for the eventual rebuilding of the city.

"The impact of the Time Event may be with us forever," said one researcher. "But there also will come a time when all of the travelers are accounted for. It's the one firm variable we have to work with, that there are a documented, finite number of people who were pulled into the time steam. It's time for us to determine what will happen once they are all out again."

Although the Orien-Sadler group cautions that there are additional considerations and possible variances in return rates to factor in, after 75 years, roughly three quarters of the documented population of Toledo have been accounted for. Experts feel that it is fair to assume that equates to roughly 25 more years of reemergences, and although the efforts to find a way to speed up the process continues, the institute admits it is unlikely to find that answer in the remaining time allotted. Public opinion polls show some compassion fatigue after so many years of attention to the problem, but also reveal that now that the end is potentially within sight, many feel it would be better just to let things run their course.

"The worst thing would be to accidentally lengthen the process of returns, or somehow halt them," stated one commentator covering today's event. "Or to somehow increase the fatality rate, which has been steadily low for several decades. At this point, they should just leave well enough alone and collect people as they come."

Other experts have theorized that the secret to the Time Event may somehow be revealed after the wormhole is closed. The initial opening came without warning, so no specific metrics were captured, but the hope is that with all of the tech that has been put in place within the Time Zone in the years since, some measurable data will be recorded when the Event comes to a final close.

To date, returning survivors have been measured in every conceivable way that would not jeopardize their health, and organ donors among the casualties to reentry have been examined thoroughly, yet no physical mark of time travel has ever been discerned. No deterrent to the aging process has been confirmed, a widely-held theory that has gained momentum in popular culture, but seems to have no basis in reality.

As we are now well into the 22nd century, we remain hopeful that in this new era, we will finally see the conclusion to this time variance, and be able to put the past away.

*The Great Depression lasted from 1929-1939, and was a time period when an economic shock impacted most countries around the world after a financial crash that caused over one third of banks in the United States to fail within only a few years.

**The global pandemic began in 2019 and rocked the world with supply chain shortages, widespread deaths and infection, and a lack of medical resources. This historical tragedy is often cited by survivors from the 21st century as an impactful event in their lives.

CHAPTER 60

Rachael Mitchell –
75 years, 1 months, 2 days after the Event.
Time populous: 68,907

She had considered reading it on the actual 75th anniversary of the Event... but then she had decided that this letter, Tom's final, final letter, was something just for her and needed to be separate from all the hoopla that came with the anniversary celebrations. It still shocked her that they even called it a celebration; she had only been back from the wormhole five years, and to her it was still a tragedy, one that had stolen her whole life from her. But to the average citizen, it was just another holiday, like Memorial Day or Veterans' Day, or anything else from her own time had become. People rarely commemorated the actual thing they were commemorating – it was just an excuse to have a day off and get together.

Trevor had given her the letter a few months ago; it was something Tom had left in his will (it still felt strange to her to believe that), with instructions not to give it to Rachael until he thought she was ready for it, and settled into her new life. Trevor said he thought she was there now, although she wasn't as sure of herself as he was. But maybe this is was as ready as she would ever be anyway; Anna Marie was five years old and loving school. They had a nice, small apartment with a pear tree right outside the window and a little grassy area for Buster to run around and bark in, and she had made a friend or two at work. Best of all, her sister had recently returned, and she had someone who really understood her again at last – but of course she was trying not to burden Kelly with too much while she was still onboarding herself.

She didn't even realize it until Kelly had reemerged a few months ago, but she had been low key angry with her the whole time she herself had been back. Even though of course she knew none of them had wanted to time travel, she realized deep down she felt as if Kelly had just been ignoring her for five years, instead of being missing. And she felt the same way about her friends; it was as if they were all just in a fight and not talking, which was ridiculously untrue. And once she realized she'd been harboring this very strange, unfair anger towards everyone, she realized it was also why she couldn't let Tom go. In her mind, he was the only one she'd forgiven for leaving her and everyone else was just being uncooperative, so she'd clung to the idea of him like a lifeline.

Another thing that made it complicated to move on was how to tell Anna Marie about her father. She couldn't help but describe him as she had known him – how could she describe any version of him from a future she hadn't been a part of? – and so in telling even small stories to keep his memory alive, she had done too good a job and couldn't let him go herself.

No wonder she hadn't been able to bring herself to date, no matter how much people said it would help her move on with this new life. She had met some very nice, attractive people over the years, including other time survivors who were just trying to adapt like she was. And she hadn't been married to Tom long enough to forget what it was like to be flirted with by strangers… but internally she still *felt* married, and just couldn't process it to even consider taking it beyond the flirting stage. From the logical perspective, she knew Tom was gone. She had seen pictures of him aging (going from the familiar face she knew, to a slightly-chubby sort, and then to a thin and stressed version that made her heart hurt, and then to a smiling, distinguished older gent that made her smile) and the proof of both his life and death… but it still hadn't felt real to her. With Trevor's company she had finally visited Tom's grave in Cincinnati last year and that had been hard, but it still didn't feel like closure. It felt like the part in a movie when all seems lost, and suddenly it all turns around with some surprise. After all, the whole idea of time travel was basically fiction made reality. Was it really so ridiculous to hope for a miracle?

Plus, being a single parent took a lot of energy, and most of her money to be honest. She excused herself for her lack of a social life on that basis alone. But today... she was going to read this letter, and maybe it would be the closure she needed or maybe it would set her back, but she was determined to get it over with. She had prepared in advance. Anna Marie was staying the night at a friend's house, and she had tissues and chocolate stocked and ready. Buster had a tasty bone to chew, so he would leave her alone, but would definitely come to cuddle if she needed it. She was ready.

Her hands shook as she opened the letter, carefully sealed and with Tom's instructions to Trevor. His handwriting had improved over the years, she thought with a smile. All that journalling is useful for something after all. Before she could even begin to read, a stack of photographs spilled out, and she laughed with delight and surprise. Over a dozen snapshots of dog butts – this is what he had left for her. Each one was carefully labeled with the dog's name, age, and a memory.

Peanut Butter Cup, 14 years; my favorite activity was chasing squirrels and a close second was stealing mittens from unwary children.

Genevieve, 10 years; and my brother Corbin, 12 years; we came all the way from Iowa to our new home one Christmas day. We loved playing in the snow, and never missed a chance to dig a tunnel.

Goober, 15 years; I only had one eye, but I could spot a crumb drop from 50 paces. I got a special hot dog every birthday, with extra ketchup.

Thumper, 5 years; I was taken too soon, but the time I had was full of sticks and bones and chasing rabbits. I once peed right on a cat, and it was the highlight of my life.

Flops, ?? years; I was rescued from a kennel when I was already old, but I got to be a puppy again and be spoiled rotten. My favorite place to sleep was in front of the fire, and I would turn every half hour for an even toast.

Poncho Villa, 12 years; I was dad's first fur-baby, and I loved to run. I won third prize at an agility contest once, and got a whole basket of goodies and a trophy.

Roomba, 11 years; I was mostly blind, which is how I earned my name (both by bumping into things and turning around a lot, and for picking up every tidbit I encountered).

Badminton, 9 years; I was the smartest. You couldn't even spell words in front of me, I knew what you were saying. My favorite thing was w-a-l-k-i-e-s. My best friend was Birdie, 10 years; I was the dumbest (and maybe the cutest). I was always absolutely thrilled to do whatever you wanted to do, unless that thing was take a bath.

Luke Skybarker, ?? years; I was a stray, but I wanted a home so bad I jumped right in Mom's car and stowed away. I once stole a whole steak right off the grill pan. No regrets.

Max, 14 years; please notice my extraordinarily fluffy rear – I was a corgi-doodle mix and a particularly sassy thing.

Fat Alberta, 16 years; the kids named me, and I never forgave them. I am quite slender under all my fur, thank you very much. Every summer I would get a lion cut and be the talk of the town when we went around the block.

Snickerdoodle, 8 years; I had more energy than everyone else combined. I may have been the runt of my litter, but I could wiggle with the best of them.

Mr. Fluffernutter, 11 years; I was an escape artist of the highest degree. No crate or fence could hold me, and I was a bold and adventurous soul.

Polly, 12 years; I was the last of dad's fur-babies, and maybe the sweetest. I had the silkiest ears.

She laughed until she cried reading them all. It was a whole lifetime of dogs. Already her heart felt a little lighter, as she picked up the letter itself to read. It was short, but it said everything she needed to hear.

My dearest Rachael,

I know it will be hard for you to believe, but I'm quite an old man now and I'm making my last adjustments to my will and making some final arrangements, since my health has taken a turn and I suspect it won't be long now. My wife Amelia passed on a few months back, and I'm all on my own now, though our adopted children and grandchildren have been a great support to me. I wish that you and I had had more time together to have the family we always dreamed of, but I wouldn't trade the one the future handed me, and you shouldn't either.

I struggled for a long time in what to say to you, knowing this is a true goodbye, and wanting to express all of the things I could wish for you. In the end, let any wisdom I can pass down be done through the rumps of my dogs.

I loved every one of these dogs – every one, no matter how naughty, was a joy to me and my time with them was far too short. For many years after I reemerged, I was all on my own, and I put off making decisions like getting a dog because I was afraid of making any big moves without you. Looking back now, there should be even more fluff-butt pictures to show you.

Don't miss out on your life – whether it be friends, romances, trips, experiences, or sweet mutts like these. Give all of the love you have to your new life and never regret it.

Love always,

Tom

CHAPTER 61

American Scientific – 76 years, 4 months, 3 days after the Event. Time populous: 61,319

A recent study of returning survivors confirmed that their recovery time upon emergence in the present day is strongly influenced by their circadian rhythm.

For those who reemerged around the same time of day as the Time Event, their circadian rhythm was not negatively affected, but for those who reemerged at other times, the sleep cycle that the human brain works off of was more strongly distressed.

Since humans have evolved to have a 24.2-hour cycle, while the earth revolves on a 24-hour cycle, that extra 15-to-20-minute gap requires bright light in the day and darkness at night to reset properly, thus the circadian rhythm. Lacking the influence of the sun, people who spend many hours per day indoors require optimal circadian stimulus to help the melatonin levels in the brain stay within healthy circadian thresholds.

For time travelers, reemerging into a completely different time of day can upset circadian readings for days or weeks, affecting their ability to fully process cognitive learning about the time stream when they are first being onboarded.

Although some of the measurements used to record recovery time are subjective (speech patterns, content of counselling sessions, questions asked, speed to try learning applications, etc.), researchers at Orien-Sadler began to suspect that the initial entry time had some effect on the onboarding process. With permission from survivors entering the program, a special lighting system was designed and installed in their rooms at the Lake City facility, programmed to imperceptibly "catch up" the circadian rhythm for each specific traveler based on their reentry time of day.

Researchers reported that those using the special circadian system reported more overall acceptance and understanding of the Time Event in a series of questionnaires applied weekly, compared to a control group. Although there are many factors stemming from individual circumstances and characteristics, the results were promising enough to continue the test program and to expand it outside the Lake City facility.

In the private sector, testing has begun using the same lighting model, to help night-active people (people who work evening or night shifts and sleep during the day) "catch up" on their rhythm for the rest of the week, and to help people with limited sleep hours to adjust their circadian rhythms for maximum sleep effectiveness. Orien-Sadler stands to make billions in government contracts alone if this technology is picked up for first responders and military personnel.

While at Lake City the lighting systems in question are operated within controlled room settings (both the test subjects and control group have similar lodging accommodations with the same wall and carpet color, ceiling reflectance, type of lighting, seating/eye level for lighting), in residential homes there is no consistency. Further, occupants of residential homes have multiple people occupying the space, not all of whom need the same circadian stimulus. Therefore, Orien-Sadler has patented a personal circadian device for private use by individuals; a headset no larger or more noticeable than a pair of sunglasses that provides the correct stimulus.

While the headsets are still in beta testing, initial comments from test subjects are positive. The wearer programs their work and sleep hours into the platform and the headset creates the appropriate schedule for stimulus, and adjusts as the wearer moves indoors and outdoors throughout the day. Additional adjustments for the amount of sunlight based on weather conditions are also applied automatically.

After wearing the device for one month, 64% of test subjects reported that they felt better rested, or had slept longer without waking than normal. Test subjects also wore sensors that monitored their sleep and reported the amount of restful sleep they received. The long-term effects of appropriate sleep levels include an improved immune system, and reduction of common ailments that are worsened by immune system issues.

Less extensive devices for day-active people who just want better sleep cycles are also in development and testing. Both types of models will be launched in the marketplace at the start of the year, with customer reviews and data-driven reports to be made available this fall.

CHAPTER 62

DJ Martin – 77 years, 10 months, 12 days after the Event.
Time populous: 57,510

Dear diary,

My name is DJ and I am eight years old but I was born 83 years ago, and that is what my teacher Miss Lucy calls a Fun Fact About Me. My great-uncle Trevor got me this diary for my birthday and he says it is to tell stories so here is mine.

I am from Toledo and Miss Lucy says that makes me extra special. I live on Elm Avenue with my mom and dad and brother. Our house is blue with a white porch, and pink tulips in the yard. I picked them out. They were supposed to be red but they weren't and my mom said that is just how they grew and you can't always tell until they grow. Next time I will try to pick red again and see what color they come out as.

For now, I live on a street called Plum Grove Road. Mrs. Tanya says a plum is a fruit and she will buy some to eat when they are in season so I can try them. I live with Mrs. Tanya and Mr. Eddie and Bobby. He is twelve years old. They have a black and white cat named Boots who is also twelve. Bobby says he is called Boots because his feet are white and look like socks (but I don't know why they didn't call him Socks). The house is green and it has a fence. It has bushes and no flowers but Mrs. Tanya says I can pick some out in the spring.

My school is called Adams Elementary and I am in the 2nd grade, going into 3rd. My friends are Sophie, Shanna, Bryan, Anna Marie, Troy, and Gigi. We all live on the same street and we play at the park. I like riding bikes and using roller skates the best.

This year we learned about adding and subtracting and volcanos and we had a pet frog in class. When my mom and dad come back and I go home, I'm going to ask if I can have a frog because dad is allergic to cats like Boots and dogs, but Miss Lucy says people can't be allergic to frogs.

That's all I can think of for now.

Bye!

DJ

CHAPTER 63

Jamie Russell, cooking instructor – 79 years, 1 month, 1 day after the Event. Time populous: 54,409

Today will be something of an experiment; it's not technically part of the counselling program, but more of an auxiliary class, and I'm pretty excited to be the one teaching it. My wife Sam is a big shot at the facility, so I'm sure some people will think I'm just riding her coattails, but actually it was my boss George who suggested the whole thing a few months back.

George owns the brunch joint I work at on the weekends – mostly your standard breakfast foods and sandwiches, but he lets me do a seasonal menu with whatever's around at the marketplace that week. It's a good gig; during the week I do a couple of days of ordering and prep work before dawn, then hang out with our kids for the day while they have virtual classwork and Sam's at her Lake City office. Then on the weekends I work the brunch and lunch shifts and do some inventory checks for the week. The weekday chefs get a little break, I get a little creative work to keep me busy, and George gets a productive restaurant in a city hotspot near the commuter line (along with his two steakhouses, one in the business district, and one in the burbs).

Anyway, we have a lot of survivors looking for work in the industry. Since it's one of the few professions that technology didn't heavily affect in the future, it's something people can step right into if they've already had culinary training, no matter how long they've been lost in time. So already, we have a lot of loose connections in Lake City, and outreach programs looking to shuffle people into open roles.

Recently, we started to hear that people coming out of the time stream who had never had to live entirely on their own were looking for some basic cooking classes to take; not as a profession, but just to boost their domestic skills. Back in our day, a lot of us relied on mom's home cooking, or delivery and take-out food, so I understand. For those living exclusively off their time stipends, I can see why it makes more sense to cut back on luxuries like eating out. So, George proposed a cooking class, where we'll go into Lake City to teach people in the onboarding stage. He'll be able to write off the cost of my time as charity work, and he'll probably gain some customers who will look for us once they leave the facility and go it on their own.

This is the first week, with classes on Tuesdays and Thursdays for a few hours each morning, and we've got our kids set up with a tutor for the time I'll be here. It'll be interesting, commuting in with Sam instead of taking the visitor's shuttle for once – they've given me a contractor's badge so technically I'm "staff", and I don't even need to bring in supplies. Just a quick note to the facilities manager for the ingredients I'll need for the lessons that week and everything will be there and ready for me they say, with the stations set up for a class of twenty or so, working in pairs. I'll be getting paid top dollar to make easy stuff like scrambled eggs and joke about the Food Network and Iron Chef to a roomful of people who will actually know what I'm talking about, plus I get to fly to work on a floating futuristic city with my beautiful wife, but get to call it quitting time at 1:00 pm. Don't you threaten me with a good time.

I never imagined my life would be anything like this… I thought I'd get that bachelor of arts degree and go slog away in sales or marketing 8-to-5 daily, just something as a cog in the wheel of some large corporate collector of souls back in Oregon. I didn't really know anything else to do, and it seemed like that was all being an adult amounted to, really.

When I met Sam at the bistro all those years ago, I figured she was an undergrad like me, and boy was I wrong. She'd been through undergrad, her masters, and was heading towards the finish line of her PhD and here I was, this stupid kid trying to impress her with my 'oh woe is me I have a 10-page paper due tomorrow' routine. Pathetic.

My friends gave me so much grief over her at the beginning, because I'd made the mistake of talking too much about 'the hot girl' I was working up to asking out for weeks. To be honest, I started to suspect she wasn't as young as I had first thought as soon as we started actually talking, but I stubbornly kept at it. I didn't think it would be that big of an issue if she was just a *little* older, maybe five years, but it turns out my guess was still way off base. When it came out that I was way too young to be a serious contender, I remember the look on her face that just said *nope, sorry kid*. And we might have just left it there, and God knows what would have become of me here on the other side of time if we had.

But we had already bonded over food. So, we kept talking, and she brought me out of my shell… and although my friends never stopped teasing me for being besties with an old lady, they always liked having her around just fine. She was (and is) a chameleon of sorts; it's why the kids she works with now like and trust her just as much as the adults do. Meanwhile I always seem to stick out like a sore thumb, especially after I came out of the wormhole and decided to become a chef. Body art is a chef-y thing to do, so I've got vegetables and fruits tattooed all up the side of one arm, and cheese and bread and chops up the other side. It's colorful, and I like it, but since tattoos aren't a very popular thing these days, people really notice it everywhere I go. I had to find a specialty shop to even get it done out in San Diego, and it cost me a fortune (at least, a fortune on a time stipend). Young people nowadays just do holotatts, which are basically virtual tattoos that you can change every day and remove with the press of a button on the corresponding wrist or neck projector. Real tattoos are a thing largely left in the past.

I don't know, I guess I'm old school, but I feel like part of having body art requires the pain of earning it, but kids these days don't see things that way. In fact, they'd probably think that marks me as old and out of it more than the tats themselves; why on earth would anyone expose themselves to pain on purpose? Life is hard enough, you dumb ol' time guy.

And to be fair, life *is* hard enough. It's hard to be a survivor and look at the public database list and see all your friends (and for many, relatives) listed as missing, or deceased. It's one thing to know someone has died, but to see so many in a row, with details, is hard. And you're not an old, old man. These are people who were college students the last time you saw them – young and full of life and hope – and you see died on reentry; reemerged forty years ago and died of colon cancer or old age; still lost in time, and on and on. When I first came back, I looked up everyone in Toledo whose name I could even remember, and found very little left for me. My own family was back in Oregon, fifty years older or already passed on, and I had nieces and nephews that hadn't existed when I left that were already middle-aged. They didn't even know me. Sam was almost the only person I had an alert on at all, and I didn't dare hope.

At first, I was just scared and stupid, and took all the drugs I could get my hands on, and tried to just lose myself. But my counsellors kicked me in the ass a few times, and instead of just losing it completely, I moved out to the coast and threw myself into culinary school. I made so many gastriques, and Beef Wellingtons, mountains of hand-rolled pastas, and fancy pastries of all types, just trying not to think about anything but the craft. I'm relieved to say that it worked. I kept myself so busy with learning, and eating amazing food, and trying new things, that I stopped feeling sorry for myself, or thinking about Toledo almost at all. It was like it was this other life I'd had, something separate from what I was doing now, and

I realized I'd be all right here in the future because being a chef was what I was meant to do, and no one was going to force me to put on a suit and tie and drag me back to that dull, gray corporate future I thought I'd been destined for.

I did a lot of growing up in that 16-year stretch, 'coming into my own' as the expression goes. And just when I thought, if this is it and this is as good as things get, I'm going to be okay with that, the universe stretched out its hand and gave me a gift.

I'd never gotten a time alert before, but one of my roommates had had one the year before, and so when that distinctive chime sounded, all three of us whipped our heads around (all four of us, if you include the cat). I practically leaped over the couch (and would regret it the next day because at that point I was nearer to forty than thirty and my knees knew it even if my brain didn't) and was shout-reading the alert at the top of my lungs and sobbing before my roommates could even get up.

All three of us jumped around like maniacs there in the living room and then we practically howled at the moon while I ran around packing a bag and booking a skip-hop while the cat gave us all deeply disapproving stares from her perch in the corner before disappearing under the bed for some peace.

Those fellas still live in San Diego, but we make an annual trip to get together and they were my best men at the wedding just a year later. There was no point in waiting, Sam and I were made for each other. We just needed a little nudge from space and time to get us there. So, say what you will about the wormhole. I know it messed up the lives of nearly everyone it touched, but I'm selfish, and I regret nothing.

And now, it's time to go teach people that to make an omelet, you gotta break some eggs.

CHAPTER 64

Summary notes from the International Time Committee – 80 years, 2 months, 24 days after the Event. Time populous: 49,813

The United Nations General Assembly met to confirm that, to date, several suspicious devices recovered from Toledo have been relocated to containment sites for study. So far, it is unconfirmed which of the devices (if any) is the machine that caused the Time Event, and the U.N. task force lead by the Panel of Experts continues to search the area, independent of the Alpha teams' search and rescue efforts regarding time survivors.

It was long ago determined that the containment sites, the locations of which are top secret, should be situated in various countries rather than a singular location that could become a target for attack. As part of the planning for the eventual destruction of any and all time machines discovered, the Time Committee has put in provisos for the transportation of suspected time devices and outlined protocols for their containment and study. The Panel of Experts has decreed that the methodology for destruction can only be determined after extensive study of each machine and that extra precautions will be taken to make sure any device is not accidentally triggered in transport, during examination, or during destruction.

Confirmation of the identity of an inventor is pending validation of an actual device, though the Panel has stated that the emergence of the inventor may be the catalyst for identifying the correct machine.

CHAPTER 65

A Moment in Time –
80 years, 4 months,
1 day after the Event.
Time populous: 49,775

"Welcome back. If you're just tuning in, we first spoke with Ms. Rachael Mitchell, talking about how being pregnant during the Time Event affected her adjustment to the future, and the complications of raising a child who (until recently when their class action suit was won) did not even qualify for time survivor benefits. It's an interesting conundrum that has only affected a small percentage of survivors, but recently came into focus when the suit she was part of was settled out of court and the guardrails for the funding adjusted. Rewatch this story and others in full on Zing Social. Now, let's turn to our next guest, Ian Carr. Welcome to the couch, Ian."

"Thanks for having me!"

"Now, I see here that you reemerged just about a year ago, and that when the wormhole opened, you were an up-and-coming comedian. Tell us a little bit about that, and what you are doing now."

"Yes, so, "up-and-coming" is maybe a little generous. I was practically unknown, but I was giving it my best shot."

"How did you get started?"

"Well, I was about 32, 33 when I decided to quit my day job in an office. I had always liked standup, and I'd done a lot of amateur nights and open mics over the years, but I had never really had the guts to just throw myself into it fully. I'd always had that safety net of my "real" job. You know, where you pretend that you're a real grownup and in exchange they give you money and make your life miserable, which at least gives you material that you can use in your routine talking about the futility of life for a laugh from other people who spend their days pretending to be grownups for money. But one day I woke up, and I'd been out at a club the night before and gotten a lot of laughs, and I was exhausted and feeling cocky, and also kind of hung over, and I realized I had a Teams meeting about to start – "

"Sorry, let me just interject for our viewers that "Teams" was a virtual platform that businesses in the early 21st century used to use, similar to a Kip channel today. Go ahead, Ian."

"Yes, sorry... anyway, I realized I had to go to this meeting and I just... didn't want to do it. Not that anyone ever *wants* to go to a meeting, but that day I just felt like, if I don't stop what I'm doing and try for real to do something fun and interesting with my life, it's going to be too late and I'm just going to get older and fatter and more pathetic. And I figured I can do *all* of those things without *also* needing to join this stupid, boring meeting. So, I just rolled out of bed, sent in my resignation, and went right back to sleep."

"Just like that?"

"Yeah, it was either the bravest or the dumbest thing I've ever done, probably both, but it felt right. And I had a little money saved up, and I'd gotten an inheritance from my dad when he had passed away. He had always told me I was funny and wanted to know all about my gigs, but he never *once* asked to hear about my boring meetings... so I figured he would approve."

"Sounds fair to me! So, you started down the comedy route full time."

"Yes, and for about two, two-and-a-half years after that, up until the Time Event happened, I was getting by. I got a few semi-regular gigs and traveled around the Midwest and the East Coast with a group of my comedian friends, and to save money we had rented one tiny apartment just to keep all our stuff in. We were almost never all there at once so we didn't care about trying to make it actually livable for four people... which it was not... and on the rare occasion when we were all there it was like sleeping in a storage locker, and nothing but hilarious to all of us. And it was just the best couple of years of my life, just freedom to travel and hang out with some of the funniest people I knew, and getting paid to do it! Not getting paid a lot, granted, but it was just the most incredible experience and I wouldn't trade it for anything."

"And when the Time Event happened?"

"When the Time Event happened, Johnny Bang-Bang and I were home in Toledo for a few days between gigs, and Lee and Henderson were still on the road; they weren't in the Time Zone when it happened."

"Tell us about this... Johnny 'Bang-Bang'?"

"Yes, so Johnny was not (sorry Johnny) the most handsome man, but he always had no problem talking to beautiful women, and they all just loved him. So, he was "Johnny-Steal-Your-Girl", or "Johnny S-Y-G" and then just "Syg", and Lee (whose name is really Daniel but he became "Major Lee" after he revealed himself as a Six Million Dollar Man fan) thought we were saying "sig", like as in a "SIG Sauer" rifle, so he renamed him Johnny Bang-Bang. And "Henderson" was really Gene, but he (no offense and may he rest in peace) bore a striking resemblance to Harry from *Harry and the Hendersons* and had a penchant for wearing Hawaiian shirts, so his name kind of morphed from that."

"Uhhm...? You've lost me there, Ian."

"Okay, see, so you have absolutely no idea what I'm talking about, and quite frankly there is no reason why you should, since that movie came out before your grandparents were even born. And the *Six Million Dollar Man* is a show from probably before even your *great*-grandparents

336

were born, that was an oldie but goodie even in my time. I used to watch it at my grandfather's house in reruns. But it perfectly illustrates how hard it is to be a time traveler, especially if you are a comedian that relies on people understanding the context of your jokes. In your own time, you can have a joke that absolutely kills on stage, and here it's crickets because you'd need a degree in history just to get the reference. It's seriously a comic's worst nightmare."

"So have you tried to do any gigs at all since you've reemerged?"

"Not really, yet. I've mostly been just talking with other survivors, trying to revive my shattered ego and reassure myself I'm at least still funny to people who are from my own century... And I'm trying to rewrite some of my act to see what can be salvaged without those contextual cues, and also writing some new material. To be fair, some things are universally funny so it's not like every story you tell has to be scrapped, but all the transitions are off, and forget about at least 70% of one-liners. And it's hard, because I've also missed about 80 years-worth of other comedians doing great material, so I could write something new that I think is just killer, but it could be stepping on the toes of something popular I missed and people would think I was just being a copycat. Alternatively, I could be poaching off comedians from my time and most people now would never know, but as we've established, most people wouldn't get their jokes anyway."

"So, you're catching up first by watching 80 years of standup comedy?"

"Basically, yes. Not a bad way to spend your days, right? Actually, from what I've gathered, standup as a form went out of fashion for a few decades and only recently has had a resurgence – and all of that industry knowledge I missed, along with who knows what else. So now, starting from a place of ignorance, I just feel awkward and weird... which *can* be funny (that was Henderson's whole schtick), but on me is just awkward and weird."

"What happened to Johnny and Lee and Henderson, do you know?"

"Johnny reemerged long before me, and unfortunately passed from lung cancer a few years after he got back, but at least the three of them got to see each other again. Lee and Henderson were in Chicago when it happened so they never came back home to Toledo at all, but I wrote to their extended families and found out they both had long lives, though they never made it big on the stage."

"Would it be stranger for you to come back and see that they had become famous?"

"It would be strange, but amazing! To see someone, anyone, you knew "way back when" hit it big is exciting, but to see someone you knew wayyyy back when would be even more satisfying. You know, one of the things I think is hard to articulate, but... the best way to show how weird it is to be a time traveler to people who haven't experienced the time anomaly themselves, is looking away from your personal life which is too close... and just looking at famous figures. There are actors, musicians, artists, etc., etc. in your own time that you know all about because you see them in ads, in social media, in interviews, and in popular culture constantly. They're a part of your life whether you recognize it or not. And then, bam, a time skip happens and of course no really famous people just happened to be hanging around in Toledo that day, so they all went on with their Hollywood lives. And then you come around all these years later and you're like, 'I wonder what happened to my favorite actors?' And you look them up and find that the greats of your time got old and started making crappy pictures just for the paycheck; or were involved in some scandal that made everyone sour on them; or quit acting for politics or a charity or some other profession; or they petered out and stopped being famous and no one now even remembers who they were; and then on top of all that, they went and died. You read about that all in one go, decades after it happened, and it feels like such a shock. And it's like they let you down, because here you are this huge fan, and they went and forgot all about you."

"Not to mention it must be strange to see a celebrity crush 75 years older than you last saw them. I can imagine that must be jarring."

"Oh, definitely. You've always seen them in this idealized way that you don't see people from your real life, so that fall from grace is even more upsetting than you would think. And you should feel guilty that you're disappointed to see them as a little, old, shriveled up person when you should be congratulating them for having a long and hopefully full life. Really, you shouldn't even get to have an opinion, because a celebrity crush is already such a ridiculously arrogant thing... here you are making this presumption that this talented, beautiful person would have even give you a second glance if you had ever actually met them in real life. And yet you've harbored this vague idea that if only you had happened upon the right set of circumstances, you would have had a chance with them. And here you are, acting *disappointed* that they lived their life without you, like somehow you would have made them happier if life had put you in their path. Time traveler or not, that's just ludicrous. But somehow it feels worse that they moved on, more so than it does with the people you really knew in real life, doing that exact same thing... or maybe it's just harder to forgive the celebrities since you didn't actually know them at all, and just want them to exist as they were in your fantasy world forever."

"I never really thought of it that way, but I see what you mean. Anyone from your real life back in time you have had to forgive for getting old?"

"Just a few ex-girlfriends who were probably relieved not to have to run into me for the rest of their lives!"

"Haha! What about new girlfriends, anyone special here in the present day?"

"Not yet, I'm not sure someone born in the modern day would want to deal with me since I'd literally be born a century before them and that just seems wrong. And it's hard to connect even with other survivors really... some of us seem about the same age *now*, but depending on when we reentered and how long we've been back, we could still have been born and raised in totally different eras and that makes a lot of the normal 'small talk' harder. Even something as simple as music – forget that people in the present day have never heard of any band we grew up on – but you've got over a hundred years' worth of taste to accommodate all at once now. Hey, maybe instead of comedy I should bring back the forgotten art of radio and start a Golden Oldies station. All requests, all the time!"

"Hmm, well, I'm not sure what that all means, but I'm sure some of you travelers out there do! Well, thanks for sharing your story with us Ian, I think you've gained some fans tonight, and maybe we'll see you at a gig, or "on the radio" sometime soon. Tune in next episode, when we'll speak with Aaron and Sian, a couple who have stayed together despite the extreme age gap the wormhole created in their relationship, and both the criticism and support they have received for their connection that they say is 'stronger than time'. Goodnight!"

CHAPTER 66

United Nations Press Release – 83 years, 3 months, 20 days after the Event. Time populous: 42,503

Breaking news: officials declare they have recovered and verified the real time machine in Toledo, Ohio and finally have definitive proof that the cause of the Time Event was man-made and not a naturally-occurring phenomenon.

BASINGSTOKE, UK – From the general population to scientists specializing in string theory, the consensus has long been that the most likely cause of the time anomaly is not from a spontaneous appearance of a wormhole, but an occurrence created from a human-engineered device. The International Time Committee had successfully narrowed their search for an inventor to an epicenter of activity in recent months.

"For decades we had been seeing a trend in data that would indicate that 100 years is the likely span of the wormhole. The possibility of this being a completely natural phenomenon with such specific parameters was far less likely than the result of a specific, more calculated influence." said Dr. Gerard Pozzi, of the U.N. Panel of Experts.

Working off of various models of the space-time continuum and plotting different hypothetical scenarios, the Panel narrowed down the source of the time snag to an actual physical location. Initial models from Orien-Sadler proved to be flawed as they were using parameters that were too symmetrical. As the revised programs proved, the Time Zone is less of an even circle and has jagged edges. Researchers compare this as being similar to the way a piece of fabric pulled inwards from a single point has irregular ridges rather than a perfect outline, though of course this is a 2D/3D visual representation of a 4D concept.

Using a newly-adjusted algorithm, the recovery team on site in Toledo successfully located a notebook that contained plans and partial schematics for a time machine that correlated to a device found in the same location, which has since been confirmed as the most likely source of the wormhole.

This also confirms the identity of the inventor of the machine, which has been classified as top secret, though we are able to report that he has not yet reentered from the time stream. Although some calls have been made for transparency, the majority of world leaders long ago signed a pledge to ensure that every precaution would be made to protect the identity of such an inventor until they can be thoroughly interviewed.

The importance of understanding how the machine works and to avoid another time-related glitch in the future is paramount, including the suppression of the technology and/or elements that would recreate such an occurrence. It is unclear how the inventor was able to identify or manipulate the exotic matter that relativity theorists consider a necessary factor in controlling a wormhole at a non-quantum level. Although statistically unlikely, it is possible that the right conditions occurred naturally, and were only discernible when aligned in conjunction with a machine capable of channeling the correct circumstances to achieve time travel.

Some are already questioning the logistics of whether the length of time set in the machine correlates to the physical size of the Time Zone, and if any experiments will be done to try and define the parameters of the machine's workings before destruction, but experts have stated that there are no such plans to manipulate time fields in any capacity.

"The fact is that the human race is not equipped to handle another large-scale anomaly," stated Pozzi. "A larger Time Zone, or a Time Zone accidentally unleashed in a populated area, would be disastrous even with all we have learned in the past eight decades, especially as we are nearing the end."

More announcements are expected about a destruction date, and it has been made clear that the confirmed location of where the device was found within the city will remain classified information, to prevent an outside agency, government, or criminal organization from attempting to reclaim the inventor himself upon his reentry. The creation of a new time machine and the threat of blackmail not to use one would be effective and could wreak havoc on the world's stage.

CHAPTER 67

Rachael Mitchell – 83 years, 6 months, 4 days after the Event. Time populous: 41,254

Dear Tom,

I know you're long gone, and you know I've never been convinced about the afterlife. But after all the letters you wrote me, it seemed wrong not to write even one back. I'm bringing this to the place where your family has your headstone, and I just hope that somehow, you'll understand what I'm trying to say.

I wish I had had a chance to tell you goodbye, but even more I wish that when you had come home that day I had been inside, and spoken to you and kissed you hello. Instead, my last memory of you is just a glimpse through a window. At least you were the last thing that I saw before the world got turned upside down. Even more though, I wish you could have known that your daughter was on the way. I named her Anna Marie, for both our mothers, and she has your eyes, and my nose, and right now she's a perfectly rotten teenager and the best thing that ever happened to me.

Thank you for saving me the pictures of your dogs. I have them all up in a collage in my office, along with a picture of our Buster, who loves ice cream and sleeps with all four feet straight up in the air, and Goober II, named after your Goober, just because he looked like a Goober to me. Your last letter was just what I needed, right when I needed it.

At the time, they were denying Anna Marie time survivor benefits because she was born here in this time, and there was no real policy in place to deal with that. People like me were supposed to just figure it out for ourselves. So, I was struggling a little financially, and Kelly was newly reemerged and just adapting into her new life so quickly and so well that I was honestly kind of jealous, and feeling down. But your letter was the pep talk I needed, and the next week I started trying to find other mothers who had their children out of the time stream, and we started talking to a law firm that agreed to help us. And for a couple of years after that, things were a whirlwind, but we ended up winning our case and helping other people, and I made some of the best friends I have in that group, and now I couldn't imagine my life without them.

After we won, we were local stars in group therapy for a while, and I was asked to be on a Zing show talking about my experience, which was strange but exciting. And I met Ian on that set. And... this is hard for me to say to you, even though you're not even here... I just fell in love with him right away. He's not particularly handsome, or flashy, but when he talks, he just captivates me with his storytelling. And I know you would have approved of him – in fact, you already liked him – he's that comedian that opened at the Laugh Factory when we went for Scott's birthday, do you remember? You thought he was hilarious, with the way he kept laughing at his own stories. The whole time they were interviewing him on the show I just kept thinking he looked so familiar, and then I remembered you saying how comedians were the only celebrities you could really trust, because actors spend all their time showing you the characters they play, or their carefully crafted, perfect personas that weren't real... but that with a comedian you see the real person and all their flaws, because their whole job and appeal is based on telling you outright that they're an awkward loser who maybe had to poop in an unlikely place, or made a fool of themselves and will tell you all about how embarrassing it was, and that's why we all say "OMG, SAME, I'M AN IDIOT TOO" and bond with them.

After the show, I told him that we had seen him on stage back in the past, and he was pretty thrilled just to be recognized and remembered. I think that's something all of us coming out of time really crave and don't often get. Like, you walk through a crowd and you scan faces, and nothing jumps out, nothing at all. And it feels lonely to know that you're anonymous. Or that maybe you do know

345

some people in that crowd, but you just don't recognize them because their age is all out of joint with the last time you saw them, or it's been fifty or sixty years longer than you realize since the last time.

Anyway, Ian and I went out for coffee and pancakes at a diner, and we ended up talking and laughing all night. It was the first time I really felt like someone was seeing the real me in years. And the rest, as they say, is history. We're getting married this weekend, and even though officially our marriage was time-annulled before I even returned, to me it feels like this is the real end and I'm finally letting you go, but in a good way. I feel like you would be happy because I'm happy, and your mother's ring is safely put away for Anna Marie to have someday. I wore it on a chain around my neck all this time, but it's in the safe deposit box now, and to be honest I feel naked without it, but I'll adjust.

You used to tell me you wanted to be my last first kiss, which is still the sweetest thing I've ever heard, and I love you for it. And even though that didn't end up being true for either of us, I'm glad that we both found something special on the other side of time. So... I wanted you to know that I am taking your last advice to me, and embracing my new life with everything I have, but that I love you from the very deepest part of my heart.

Rachael

CHAPTER 68

DJ Martin – College admissions essay
– 86 years, 1 month,
3 days after the Event.
Time populous: 35,090

My name is Deborah Jean Martin, and for our college admissions essays we were encouraged to write about a problem we have overcome; describe a person we admire; or just to tell our own story. In my case, I can speak to all of these in one essay, because my brother was the person I admired most, and we were both time survivors.

Statistically speaking, I reemerged from time in Toledo at an ideal moment (75 years, 6 months, 28 days after the Event to be exact). It was during the later years when search and rescue had reached a sophisticated stage with a low fatality rate for reentries; the weather was clear with no meteorological complications; and although I was still a small child which made me statistically more at risk, I was not in a moving vehicle at the time of the Event, or in an area with structural damage. The Alpha team found me within a matter of minutes, and I was in no immediate physical danger at any point, although I was extremely put out by the circumstances and apparently quite sulky about it. My onboarding began immediately, though I scarcely realized it at the time, with the kindness of Dr. Samantha Estrada, now the managing Director of Lake City, but at the time a specialist working with children in the field.

My brother Trevor's timing was not so fortunate. As one of the very first reentries from the wormhole, he did not benefit from the help of any formal rescue teams for months, but survived on his own ingenuity in the empty neighborhood we grew up in. He was just barely ten years old, but managed to feed and care for himself, exploring the entire neighborhood while rescuing pets from locked houses, and kept himself entertained without electricity or any news from the outside world for weeks.

As an early survivor, he entered the new world we take for granted before any funding was in place; before Lake City was even conceptualized; before anyone knew what the Time Event even was. For those of us who reemerged in later years, a whole team of people was there to welcome us, and explain what had happened (or at least part of what had happened), and to ease us into our new lives with gentle guidance. Trevor had only himself and his own imagination to rely on.

Although the survival rates have gone up dramatically over the years, many, like my mother, did not survive reentry. Trevor and I were two of the lucky ones that made it. There are also many survivors who, even with the excellent support of the Orien-Sadler staff, find the adjustment to the present difficult, which is why even today there is a high rate of mental health issues, suicide, and addictive behaviors amongst survivors. My father turned to alcohol when he found the stress of reentry too great, and although he would have been long deceased before my return anyway, I wish for his sake that his life had been longer and happier.

I know that Trevor wished the same, and as a counsellor for many years, he dedicated his life to helping other survivors as best he could. Even after his retirement, he continued to informally counsel friends and neighbors, and even relatives of his previous cases, until the end of his life. His passing left a huge hole in the fabric of our community of survivors; an impact that feels even greater than the hole in the fabric of time caused by the time machine, at least to me and those who knew him best. His funeral was a massive event, with people hopping in from all over the country to pay their respects, and I was humbled to realize just how many lives he had touched.

When I first reemerged, they told me that my brother was my great-uncle, a relative on my mother's side that I had never met before, and I had no reason to disbelieve them. They felt that the truth was too complex for a five-year-old to comprehend, and they were right. I happily considered him to be my uncle, and my brother's namesake apparently, for years.

When I was ten years old, he told me the truth, having decided that I was old enough to understand and curious enough to figure it out soon enough on my own. I remember being simultaneously relieved that he was not still lost in the time stream and furious that he hadn't told me the truth sooner. We both cried, because finally we were truly reunited, but also because we realized how little time we really had left together as a family. I finally knew the truth… that my mother and father were already gone, gone before my time, and my brother, the hero of my childhood, was approaching ninety.

I had five more years with him after the whole story came out, so we were lucky after all, because his mind remained sharp until the very end, and he was able to tell me so much more about his life and the things he had learned. I feel as if I lived a part of that life with him, since he was such a vivid storyteller, and always could make everything sound like an adventure.

In the remote past, my brother Trevor had made up my bedtime stories each night… some of my earliest memories (in fact, some of my only memories of Toledo and life before the anomaly) are of him spinning elaborate tales with a flashlight under a homemade tent of a sheet and a box fan on hot summer nights. Here in the future, my "great-uncle" Trevor read to me from his journal, and showed me pictures of long-lost family and friends and brought them to life for me through his memories, and gave me a view of the Time Event that school just couldn't teach.

Going back to the prompts for this essay, it is easy to say that my brother is the person I most admire, and the problem I have overcome is how to best honor his memory – I plan to follow in his footsteps as a counsellor at Orien-Sadler, using the things I have learned through his guidance. Even after all the travelers have been returned, the impact of the Time Event will affect people's lives and counsellors will still be a necessary part of our society for years. Maybe someday, I can publish his journals as a book so that others can benefit from his unique and uplifting viewpoint as I have. And that answers the last question as well, how to tell my own story, because my story is his story, and the best stories live on and on.

CHAPTER 69

Delta Team One – 87 years, 4 months, 16 days after the Event. Time populous: 31,121

Now that the time machine had been found, the official rebuilding of Toledo was cleared to proceed, and things were underway. They were beginning from the most eastern point and moving westwards, with the ceremonial groundbreaking at the original Site Two headquarters three months ago.

Delta Team One was overseeing one of the first dig sites in the east. Originally designed as cleanup crews, the Delta squads had migrated almost exclusively to civil engineering over the decades, first to repair infrastructure that threatened to endangered emerging travelers, and in recent years to plan the rebuilding of the city itself. The outskirts were mainly remote forested areas and a few treatment plants, so the risk of encountering any returning survivors was very low. The plan was to begin by building residential housing and commercial and industrial space in these areas first, essentially shifting the city center to the east side of the Maumee and leaving more space on the west side for expansion later.

The harbor area was going to be expanded, and needed some repairs after the siege years ago that had damaged a lot of the docks themselves, but those were low-hanging fruit since the area had never fully been out of commission – Alpha, Beta, and Delta teams had been using them for decades as a point of entry for shuttles and hop-skips going to and from Lake City. The intention was for Lake City's state-of-the-art medical facility and counselling center to remain, but for the facility to be annexed to New Toledo once the Time Event was deemed fully complete. The

351

hospital on the mainland would be upgraded entirely as well, and a new site had already been picked for its location.

There was even talk of eventually building a time-related museum and also some professional sports stadiums on the west side as a tourist draw, as the Time Zone was still a worldwide curiosity and likely to remain so for years to come. Right now, the planners were just focusing on the essentials, but several private investors and firms had come forth making proposals in recent years. When it came time to seek funding, they would have takers.

Derrick Shay was the foreman of Delta Team One, and he was uninterested in museums and stadiums right now. Privately, he thought they were a good idea and likely to happen, but at present he was more concerned with the logistics of laying out new city blocks. Or rather, sub-urban blocks. The new eastern outskirts were progressing rapidly; they had marked where sewers and ion stations were needed and the latest street-lighting was all modular, so the telescoping pods could be placed as soon as the plumbing was complete. Likewise, in the designated public spaces and pathways, the underground Oubliette™ trash compactors and recycling chutes could be installed as soon as all pipes were in place. The site of the first of many apartment buildings and aeropads was being leveled, and this was the area he was surveying with his crew this morning.

It was strange, he reflected, to build housing, shops, and restaurants for a whole population that couldn't actually move in yet. It reminded him of a video game where a whole civilization went up layer by layer, not at all the normal way of handling a new build. And it was odd too, to have such a huge project without someone to buy the end result; everything they were touching would be populated using government funding for displaced people from Toledo first; with the housing market opened to transplants from other areas in a later phase.

He knew also that this early part of the planned community project would be the simplest because they were building on virtually unused land, and on the expanded shoreline that had been built out to increase the city's footprint using the same methodology that Lake City employed. Later, when they reached the old city outskirts, they would be dealing with more roads, bridges, and other infrastructure that needed demolition and cleanup in plenty before they could start fresh. But that wouldn't be for a while yet, and there were still lingering questions under debate about what to do with private property, some of which needed to be ironed out before they could proceed.

In theory, there were abandoned residences that had surviving owners, but after 87 years, it was hardly practical to expect that most personal items would still be useable, or worth collecting and documenting. On the other hand, it seemed wasteful to just trash it all, especially items that were considered high-value antiques in today's market. And there were socio-economic factors at play as well. Although the more affluent (i.e., traditionally white) neighborhoods might have more valuable mementos to preserve, the ACLU and other civil rights groups had pointed out that this created a potentially racially-charged situation where the personal property of some was being prioritized over others.

Personally, Derrick would be happy to just bring in the dumpsters and toss it all. He couldn't imagine it was really worth it to sort through a whole house full of junk looking for a few trinkets of value. He remembered well helping to clean out his mother's home in Philadelphia when she had been transferred to a retirement community, and it had seemed like an endless pile of boxes upon boxes of ancient shoes, abandoned crafts, worthless costume jewelry, cards from people she hadn't spoken to in decades, and junk mail. The idea of doing that house by house looking for hidden treasure might be someone else's idea of fun, but not his.

"They want to turn us into a bunch of goddam looters," he had groused to his crew over a beer one evening after work. "All those years keeping those bums out, they might as well have let them take what they wanted and saved us the trouble."

He didn't really mean that, of course. Looters were a pain in everyone's ass. There hadn't been many incidents in years, but he remembered way back to when he'd been new to the job there had been a band of looters that had nearly scared the life out of an emerging survivor who thought (rightfully so) that they were burglars and had called emergency services in hysterics. His friend on the Beta team that transported her confirmed that she would survive, but that she had to be treated for a mild cardiac arrest after the incident, and that those who had been detained would likely get more jail time as a result.

All that had been before the big siege. He'd been pretty fresh to the team when that had happened, and although he hadn't seen much action during those three chaotic days aside from moving in some barricades, it had given him an appreciation for why it was important to repopulate the city and not just leave it open to attack – from looters, terrorists, what-so-have-you.

Aside from the contents of the actual homes and offices (the decision to clear those out was easier as no one expected to find treasure in old file cabinets full of papers and reports, and they were unlikely to find any trade secrets that weren't already common knowledge hiding in such antiquated records), there were questions about what to do with retailers and industrial businesses where there was equipment to deal with. And for all areas, residential and commercial alike, there was the cleanup of decades worth of Orien-Sadler tech and gadgetry to deal with. The first challenge would be not to disrupt the essential feeds while emergences were still a possibility, but there was definitely some outdated equipment that they would need to collect rather than trash, since it could be upcycled for use in other parts of the world.

In some ways, the abandoned city was a true treasure trove of materials, and Orien-Sadler had created a whole new branch to deal with sustainability issues a few years back. This group had been set up in an annex site to the west, and processed the outdated tech materials, removing wiring, batteries, photovoltaic LEDs, housings, arrays, and other materials to make new systems and componentry. Using almost all recycled materials and adding in the latest wireless tech, and capabilities for Li-Fi, Vi-Cam, and AVM, new indoor and outdoor connected systems were ready for interoperability testing within weeks and were shipped to other cities looking to upgrade to smart buildings and public spaces. The sale of these services and goods had been a major contributor to Orien-Sadler's research funding in recent years, easing the burden on the taxpayers to almost nothing.

Derrick's team had already removed a few generations of old tech from the most populous areas of the city center, and the plan was to get anything that was wired into the systems out of the way before anything was touched in those areas regarding infrastructure. The latest gen models worked completely off-grid and were more reliable for everything, from motion detection and night vision, to their warning triggers and silent alarms.

"Boss, Delta Three's on the line. They want to coordinate for that pipe drop off zone."

"Okay, I got it."

The sheer volume of materials needed for this whole city expansion was staggering. He'd been working with construction crews and robotic automation his whole career but nothing at this scale before, building an entire metropolis from scratch. Amazing also to think that only a few years ago, this area, which was technically still within the Time Zone, would have been off limits to any of them. And now earth movers and equipment dotted the entire landscape, with mounds of dirt, gravel, sand as far as the eye could see. It was really a massive undertaking, and the goal was to have whole neighborhoods move-in ready within the next five years. It had been a major economic boost, here in the United States and their manufacturing hubs in the rest of the Americas, but also in other regions across the world that were providing raw materials by the ton. It was pretty incredible to be part a project so large in scale that it could be measured by GDPR, and Derrick was plenty proud to be involved in it, and proud of how much excitement his crew had for the whole endeavor.

Whenever he had been on a road trip as a child, passing through remote areas of the U.S., he had taken notice of small, sometimes abandoned, towns along the freeways and wondered about their evolution. Someone had once decided it was a good place to build, before or after the highways had been laid. Often the town was so small, and butted right up to the road, that he wondered what planner had decided to cram the buildings so close when they had thousands of acres of farmland, plains, or forest right there – why not move the houses back a few hundred yards from the noise and pollution of the highway? It was what had gotten him interested in civil engineering in the first place, thinking about how he would have done things differently.

That was what he was really getting to do now; he had been on the committee for the planning and layouts for years, and rethinking the entire city's architecture from aeropads to waterways and everything in between had been a huge undertaking. They had also been given the freedom to improve on public spaces, making more parks and common areas for all neighborhoods, and standardizing the quality of personal transportation hubs and housing options throughout the city. They weren't constrained by current market values or socio-economic predisposition; the new city could be just as diverse in its population, but without the institutionalized divide of the previous neighborhood lines.

Derrick hadn't eyed the plans from the perspective of future political districts, but other people on the planning committee had specifically analyzed their work with that in mind. In fact, various teams had been instructed to gauge the city plans with any number of specific interests in mind, with the goal of poking holes in the planning stages, which is why it had taken over a decade to come to the agreements. At the time, they had all felt some frustration over the bureaucracy of planning by committee, but since it had been previously agreed upon that they couldn't start until closer to the hypothesized closing of the wormhole anyway, there was no rush.

In the end, looking at their new city layout, he'd felt confident there was no "bad neighborhood", at least on paper. Once people started actually living there, certain areas would naturally be more in demand and property values would go up or down and there would be gentrification… but at least they were starting from a neutral place. He was really curious to see how this social experiment would go; it would be something for him to follow someday in his retirement years.

"Who knows, maybe I'll even settle down here myself someday," he thought comfortably to himself. Maybe as they built, he'd keep his eye open for a cozy spot to call dibs on.

It was a nice little city, after all.

CHAPTER 70

News headlines –
90 years after the Event.
Time populous: 25,105

'Nearing the end'; the U.S. commemorates 90 years of travels through time

Status of the rebuilding: the coming repopulation of Toledo

Kip carousel: sharing photos from the construction zone

Featured article: Debating the future by Emerald James, correspondent for Kamata Global News

As the world prepares for the final decade before the expected closing of the wormhole in Toledo, Ohio, perspectives on the Event are more varied than ever before. Although it had been long suspected, the confirmation in the past decade that the way things transpired on May 15th ninety years ago today was caused by human intervention has drawn everything from ire to admiration.

In a special series of interviews, I facilitated conversations with everyday citizens in multiple global locations, gathering feedback on conflicting views about the inventor of the time machine. It is clear that some consider him to be a genius, albeit a careless one, while others assign him a more nefarious disposition.

Those who stress the amazing accomplishment of discovering time travel at all feel that the inventor should be remembered as an explorer, or pioneer. Others point out that aside from the damage done to the individuals pulled forward in time, all 22nd century citizens now suffer from having to accommodate these people (some with antiquated opinions and understanding of social norms), adding a burden to society. Still others are weary of the continued discussion of time travel altogether, saying they have been hearing about it their whole lives, and when the last survivors are accounted for, never want to hear about it again.

Personally, I feel that despite the negatives, the inventor of the time machine has given us as an exceptional viewpoint into history. Have we not, throughout the millennia, attempted to capture history through pictograms, written and spoken word, video and film? This is a chance for active conversation and debate between people of the modern era and people who are essentially our ancestors. This is a way to keep history alive – not just from their own time, but from the generations before them since they have living memories of relatives born even longer ago. Human memories normally have an expiration date, and the Time Event has extended them.

One thing that I found very interesting was that the people I interviewed outside of the United States still find the Time Zone much more intriguing. Particularly in Europe, many people expressed an interest in visiting the Toledo area once it has been deemed safe, to walk the streets that have been abandoned for the past century. In Asia, the underground market for antiques from the lost city (and forgeries), still draw interest, and many people in these regions seem to have built up a romantic view of Toledo, even so far as to replicating landmarks from the city in virtual theme parks for people to visit. It is clear that once the Time Zone is reopened, visitors from all over the world are anxious to see it with their own eyes, much like the lost city of Atlantis or some other mythological location of the past.

Several people also expressed admiration for the longevity of Lake City and the technology employed there, and I agree with them. It is a fact that several countries, along with most of Florida and southern California in the United States, faced eroding coastal land and flooding that threatened populated areas. These have since been restored (and even expanded) using the building models perfected in Lake City to create new floating coastlines that have saved whole neighborhoods and cities from displacement. Though the time travelers themselves were negligible in the creation and development of these technologies, many feel that the world owes them a debt of gratitude nonetheless.

In closing, I will note that another point commonly raised during my interviews was the concern that the time machine has not yet been destroyed by the International Time Committee (as far as we in the public sector know). Although some felt it should not be destroyed at all, most seemed to feel that it should be, for reasons of public safety, and the debate centers on whether that should have been done immediately after it was found, versus not until the inventor returns and can explain how it works. Opinions appear to be divided based on people's thoughts on the inventor himself and his intentions. It has become clear to me that the debate will continue, and when that mysterious person who is responsible for the Time Event emerges, it will be to a very divided reception.

CHAPTER 71

Anna Marie Mitchell – 93 years, 7 months, 22 days after the Event. Time populous: 15,830

"Happy birthday, honey!"

"Thanks Mom!"

"Where are you calling from? The 4D looks a little distorted."

"Sorry, I'm right near the electron ledge. I wanted to call you before we got to the jump zone. I've only got a few minutes before I have to check in though."

"Not a problem – you just missed Ian, he took the dogs to the vet, but he says happy birthday too. We'll make your cake when you're home next week."

She had splurged on this trip, a graduation present to herself, and the parahopper tour of the mountain's summit was the highlight of the whole thing. She had waited to call until she was close to their scheduled departure time, partly to give her mom a glimpse of the spectacular views the hololodge atop Everest offered, but also so that she could keep the call brief. She didn't mind sharing all the details about the trip when she got back, but she wanted to keep it mostly to herself now, while it was happening.

It was something she had always struggled with as a time survivor; keeping the present in focus, wanting the past to keep within its boundaries. And yet, she wasn't a survivor... not really. On paper, that was her status, and she knew her mom and others had had a long fight to make sure children like her that had been conceived in the past but born in the future got the same rights as any other traveler. But still... she had never felt quite as if she belonged in that box along with the kids who had the 21st century birth dates to prove it. She definitely didn't belong in the past, but she didn't quite fit in to any box neatly in the present either. As a result, she had grown up resenting anyone who tried to include her demographic in their representation – she considered herself an individual, though she'd stick up for any survivor taking flak merely for being what they were. She had no patience for time-deniers.

Only once had she had a real problem with her paperwork, when a customs official had noticed that her passport had the traveler status stamp, but not the adjusted age field. He had insisted her documentation must be fake, and had threatened to detain her until she had been able to Kip her counsellor to send over a quick confirmation. She hadn't particularly blamed the customs guy for being suspicious, since it was probably the first time he'd ever encountered a "time-breach baby" like herself, but he'd been fairly nasty about it, so she didn't feel she owed him an apologetic attitude along with her explanation. Since then, she'd kept a spare virtual key handy with supporting documentation whenever she traveled abroad, just in case.

Mom and Ian almost never traveled outside the U.S., not since they'd gone to Paris for their honeymoon and said it felt like they were a tourist attraction unto themselves. At least at home most people had at least met a time survivor, and transplants were all over the country; abroad, it was apparently much rarer to the point of freakishness. Which made sense, since for so long survivors had been denied international travel. Plus, Ian was a recognizable figure, if not quite a real celebrity. After appearing on *A Moment in Time*, he had been contacted by an agent who saw an opportunity for a Kip channel combining his idea about classic music and retrospectives of famous people from before the Time Event. It had been kicked off immediately and was already a couple of seasons in at the time of their trip, and although his audience was limited (his followers were mainly historians, anthropologists, and time survivors themselves) it was also quite loyal. Now, thirteen years later, it was still his main gig and a fairly lucrative one, though he often said that the best thing to come out of that interview wasn't the idea for the show, but had been meeting his future family.

Anna Marie had never questioned in the slightest that Ian was family. Her real father had been a traveler, but they'd overshot his time, so the only things she knew about him came from stories and pictures, and that was enough to satisfy her curiosity. It wasn't true to say she missed him; and that was another way that she didn't fit into the boxes they wanted survivors to fall into – everything was marketed to them as having nostalgia, and she lacked that, since it was for a time and for people that she had never known at all.

But Ian had fit into their lives from the start. He had loved Buster, who reminded him of his childhood dog, and he was both fun and funny to have around. He had taken a lot of joy in creating the Kip channel, and running ideas past her and her mother, and even though she didn't understand most of the jokes and references, Anna Marie had been happy to join him for an occasional segment when he was recording and needed what he called "a fresh perspective" (mainly asking her to guess what a movie was about based on the poster art, or what a person was famous for based on their picture). It had all been in good fun. He was such an energetic, excitable person that people found his enthusiasm contagious, on or off the Kip.

For the wedding, he and Mom had created an invite that said "*When will then be now?... Soon.*", which was apparently very funny because it had become an iKnow overnight in the travelers' community Kip, and people still occasionally brought up 'Ian & Rachael's save the date' even after all these years. She had been a junior bridesmaid, with Aunt Kelly as the maid of honor, just a small party in the backyard of the bigger house they'd moved into, with Ian's Kip studio in the basement. She'd stayed with her friend DJ while they were honeymooning in Paris, and it had been a fun week. DJ's brother had taken them to a fancy restaurant and then on a special tour of Lake City via mobiscooter one day, and they'd been allowed to count it as school time because it was "educational". And when Mom and Ian had returned, they had brought her a beautifully sparkly platinum pendant of the Eiffel Tower as a souvenir, though she rarely wore it now because she was afraid the material would attract thieves out in public. Platinum-powered electrocells were a hot commodity, and even a small piece like hers would be enough material to build a lot of chips.

Speaking of which, she'd better get off the phone and get her auto-cam settings in place for the jump. She said goodbye to her mom, and promised lots of pictures would be streaming shortly. They would be gliding around the full peak today, since weather conditions were ideal, returning to the hololodge for dinner and then the hop down to their base camp the next morning. The views should be spectacular, with almost 100% visibility. Just two more days here in New Kathmandu, and then overnight in Tokyo before the longhop back to the States, where she planned to stay with friends for a few days on the coast before heading home. It had been a great trip, and she wasn't quite ready for it to end yet.

Once she returned home, there were some big choices to be made. On one hand, she could just move out west, or east, and get herself a random little job and be completely anonymous for a while. Her degree was a general applied sciences one, and she wasn't tied to any field specifically, nor did she have any particular interests that would send her down a specific path – the world was her oyster, and if she chose to leave the past behind, no one would try to stop her, certainly not Mom and Ian.

On the other hand, she had an internship already lined up with the newly completed Museum of Time on the outskirts of New Toledo. The orientation wasn't for another three weeks and the first opening date not for another month after that, so she had the rest of the summer to settle into the idea. It was an interesting role, a combination of leading holotours and talking to the public, and doing research behind the scenes. She'd applied because it seemed like middle ground, and that was where she was comfortable. It was appealing to think that she would not be fully immersed in either teaching or research, but still getting to mingle with tourists and students in an official capacity, and talking about a subject that was of course near to her heart. Having grown up around her mother, who had been on the ground floor of policy change, and Ian, whose whole career revolved around pop culture of the past, she was probably more well versed to lead a time tour than most people her age. And boy, had she watched a lot of really bad shows and movies to be this well versed – absolutely primitive special effects, and content too, in some cases. Some hadn't even been transferred to InfinityDrive™ yet, so she even knew how to use televisions and DVD players (Ian was a collector and had several working models).

At first, she didn't enjoy them – their plots and dialogue seemed so simplistic… but the way Ian had explained it, it was because she was seeing the original out of sequence, and all of the things she saw in today's culture were actually derivative. When she was about fourteen, he'd spent a whole episode on his Kip channel talking about it with her, with callers weighing in, talking to her like she was a real adult. It was one of her favorite memories, and one of his most popular episodes to date. She remembered how excited he had been to talk about one of his favorite childhood films.

"So, there was this really cool movie that came out when I was pretty young, still in grade school… and my mom wouldn't let me go see it in the theater because she thought the trailers looked too scary, but my uncle took me to see it anyway. And it was just so, so amazing. The directors had come with this new way to shoot a sequence as practical effect, not an animation or CGI (that's kind of like what you call an AiMod now) which always looked super fake, and it was just so unexpected, and mind-blowing to see on "the big screen" for the first time. The movie itself had such a weirdly distinct plotline, and a really stylized, graphic visual feel, minimal dialogue, and a lot of fighting, but again, in a stylized way, not bloody or scary like my mom had been worried about. It was just dark, and brooding, and beautifully shot. And I distinctly remember leaving the theater just feeling like that movie was the best thing I had ever seen, and all I wanted to do in my life was to kick ass and take names."

She had laughed, picturing goofy Ian kicking anyone's ass, and the Kips had gone crazy with other travelers, agreeing that they had loved that film, and historians throwing in random facts about it and it's cast to show off their knowledge.

"Anyway, the technique they had used at the time was ground-breaking, they had developed it, but within a few months every advertiser and television show was copying it. And for a while it was just overused, and then eventually just became a normal effect, something that could be achieved ten different ways. But still, every time I see that movie, I feel like it still holds up. And maybe that's just because to me, it was the first, and to someone like you, who is seeing it out of context, when it's 100-plus years old and not *avant garde*, it probably doesn't even seem like anything special, or even notable. And to me, that sums up how it feels to be a time traveler; there are things that to us, they're still incredible and astounding, like the idea of time travel itself... but to others it's just an everyday, accepted thing, and you've seen it and heard it a thousand times. But the original still deserves to be appreciated for what it is. So, we can't return to the past. But we can at least appreciate it for being the foundation of what came afterwards."

Of course, next family movie night they had watched it (on Ian's antique player and not a remastered VR version, to get the real effect) and she had tried to see it with fresh eyes and pretend she hadn't seen anything like it before, and she had decided that Ian was right. It was ok that it was old, and that some of the effects were choppy to her modern-day eyes, and the plotline too obvious from her point of view. She could appreciate it for what it was – a classic. She couldn't always get friends her own age to enjoy classic cinema, but family night movies were something special.

So, all of that knowledge she had about a past she'd never actually experienced herself would go to waste if she didn't do something with it, like work at the Museum of Time. But she was a little bit afraid that if she went down that path, she was going to like it... and that then she'd never really escape that wormhole after all. It would keep its loose grip on her life, and she would let it.

When she was feeling down and looking for someone to blame, she sometimes thought of the time stream as something that had wanted to suck her and everyone around her down into its depths... but mostly she had more optimism than that. Usually, she thought of it more as a lazy river... something that had caught them up, whirled them gently around, and had deposited them somewhere at random along the banks, but without any real sense of urgency or purpose. She also tried to always remind herself that she was lucky, because unlike most children from Toledo, she had reemerged *with* her mother, and that gave her a gift most time orphans would have killed for. No, the wormhole wasn't the enemy. It had just acted according to its nature, and it was just a mathematical construct, not something with any will of its own.

Even after all this time, a lot of people blamed the inventor, but she couldn't bring herself to do that either. It seemed unlikely that he was the evil mad scientist some people made him out to be. What advantage would it have given him to drag them all through time with him on purpose? He certainly wasn't benefitting from it himself, since he was still stuck in it.

Privately, she thought it was most likely to have been an accident, like that one silly kids' movie Mom liked where the characters became the size of ants. Sure, the inventor in that film had been trying to build a shrinking machine so ultimately it was his fault, but it didn't even work until an unlikely series of events put things in motion. If anything, neglecting to add a secondary, motion-activated kill switch and a lack of safety protocols were his biggest crime. She imagined the inventor of the time machine would prove to be someone like that; just someone who got lucky and as a result, very unlucky. She wasn't expecting an evil genius – more likely some very flummoxed physics teacher with a half-baked science fair project gone wrong would come stumbling out of the wormhole in a few years wondering what the hell had happened.

She felt like most people her age and younger had a more forgiving view of the inventor. It was older people that resented him, and that was likely because they found the science itself more intimidating, and therefore found the time machine itself more sinister. One thing that time orphans all experienced was the educational gap between themselves and survivors that were their parents' age. Having grown up in the present, both the live and virtual school curriculum covered the basics of relativity even in the early grades, and there was an emphasis on math and sciences that was apparently much more rigorous than schools of the past. Technology that was commonplace today was much more advanced than before the Time Event (that was to be expected) but adults emerging from the wormhole found the adjustment a lot harder than children and teens. It was, unfortunately, one of the reasons that there was a stigma around being a survivor that made Anna Marie and other young people underplay their status whenever possible when they traveled internationally, and if people asked where they were from, it was common to just say Detroit or Chicago to deflect awkward questions.

Looking around now, at the very top of the world and surrounded by sky and sun and snow, she just couldn't muster any bitterness towards the inventor, the time stream, or anything at all. If she'd been born in her own time, she definitely wouldn't be having this experience (Everest had been inaccessible to 99% of the world back then), or any of the experiences she'd had in her life. There was no point wishing anything had been different, because then everything would have been different. She might not be one thing or another, and she might always have to be compartmentalizing her life between the past and present, but honestly, right now the "now" was pretty damn good.

CHAPTER 72

Alpha Team Five – 95 years, 2 months, 30 days after the Event. Time populous: 12,775

Today the team was reworking a stretch of highway with a historically high death toll to its reputation, though of course most of those came from the early years. They were stringing the latest style of anti-gravity nets; models that had the potential to reduce reentry accidents by an additional 90% in field tests. The survival rates these days were amazingly high, even for reentries on roadways, something the early Alpha teams would never have believed possible. The Beta teams that had originally been primarily tasked with medical triage, transport, and collection of human remains had been whittled down to just a few small squads as a result. The Delta teams of civil engineers now held the most personnel of any branch.

At last count, there were still approximately 13,000 remaining citizens still lost in time. But that number was rapidly dwindling, and although the projected entry sites were still dispersed widely throughout the downtown area and suburbs, there were whole sections of the city that had been deemed as clear. For example, almost every business and office building that had been closed at the time the anomaly had occurred had been confirmed as complete in the past five years, and many of them had already been demolished to make way for new construction.

So too there were a growing number of residences with all occupants accounted for (survivors and casualties to reentry), many of which had also been removed to make way for new builds. The Delta teams had really paved a lot of ground in creating New Toledo on the bones of the old one, making progress section by section. The portion of the city that had been damaged in the infamous siege had been completely cleared and rebuilt with a new, stately harbor to be used for both air and waterway traffic.

In the early days after the Time Event, the sheer number of people missing and the lack of inputs about their whereabouts made any kind of tracking impossible. Now, nearing the end of the finite number of people still missing, combined with the collective inputs of hundreds of thousands of other travelers and the U.N.'s new sophisticated modeling system that could pinpoint the exact whereabouts of their reentry points, nearly 85% of the remaining 13,000 missing had projected reentry points identified that could be specially tagged and monitored.

"We're ready to test 'er out, folks. Everyone clear!" Lieutenant Fulton gave the signal, and Private Vladek launched the test dummy into the nets from the hoverskip above. True to the promised form, the dummy stayed twelve inches from the ground, stretching the anti-gravity net in a slow-motion arc that allowed it to cushion the falling object rather than merely bouncing off of it.

These models were a far cry from the ones first developed in the labs, but even those had been successful in the field when used in abandoned swimming pools. Several travelers that had emerged in residential pools had found themselves in a sludge of rainwater and fallen leaves, and that hadn't been much of a concern... until one hard winter when an unlucky time traveler who had been in mid-dive off the springboard broke his leg landing on solid ice, and the next year another reentry was found frozen solid. The decision had been made to empty all outdoor pools for safety, and the Delta squads had another task to add to their list of maintenance in the city (a seasonal task, since rainwater kept filling them back in), but with the invention of the GravNets™, one installation kept both rain and returning swimmers near the surface with a semi-transparent shield. The nets were only good for low-speeds, so the ones developed for traffic conditions had taken longer to engineer. The ones they were testing today were state-of-the-art; they needed to choose another launch angle to gather more speed, but the initial result looked good.

Tech Specialist Bartholomew noted the readings and gave them all the thumbs up to retrieve and reset their dummy. One of the nice things about the new nets was that you didn't need to take them down to enter their field, as long as you had your sensor on your person. You could stroll right in to help the survivor, while the net kept them comfortable and immobile while any physical damages were assessed. Vladek backed the hoverskip up a few hundred meters and they launched again, this time from a speed that would simulate real crash conditions. Again, the nets held.

"Well, ladies and gents, I think we can call this one a success! Only about eighty more yards to string and we can call it a day."

"Lieutenant, you think there's a chance we'll get a lot more in this sector before time runs out?"

"Beats me, Bartie. I think they just want this zone set up so they can run more tests. I don't see any flag saying they expect travelers here."

These nets were a prime example of how Toledo had basically morphed into a laboratory for field measurement testing. The earliest iterations of this tech had been literal nets that were motion activated only when an object (or person) moving at a specific range of speed was detected, and while that had some success here in the unpopulated Time Zone, it was worthless for regular road conditions and safety precautions out in the wide world. The later models worked in conjunction with sensors within the latest autovehicles, allowing them to move through the force fields unmolested until a crash was detected, or something in motion outside of a vehicle (in theory, a person being ejected from a vehicle) without a sensor tripped the launch.

Although some of the early field tests had been shaky, Abu Dhabi had volunteered to test it in real city conditions, and had paid for the outfitting of the anti-gravity nets in all of their city streets within a ten-mile radius. Combined with strict requirements for new vehicles to include the necessary sensor tech, and even stricter instructions for antique vehicles without hover options to travel under the speed that would trigger alerts within the city limits, initial findings had shown that safety was improved, with fewer crash fatalities and a lower rate of injury over a five-year period. Retrofitting was now underway with improved models, combined with expansion of the original testing area in the region. It could end up being a revelation in the field of autocar safety.

Fulton was actually pretty excited about this latest round of tech, because he was also an investor. Alphas and other employees weren't allowed to use their inside knowledge gained at Orien-Sadler for investments of course, but he'd actually inherited stocks long ago from the company that had only bought out the anti-grav tech in recent years. Since he'd been in possession of them way before that merger had taken place, with some minor housekeeping paperwork with human resources he'd been cleared to profit from them, so long as he didn't buy more. He kept it under wraps around his team, but from the looks of these readings, he'd be selling things off by year end and thinking about an early retirement.

No, he might daydream about it, but he'd be sticking it out here in the field to the end. He wouldn't mind the extra security in his bank account, but he loved Alpha work. Out here, you didn't have to be a technology genius, or a wizard with gadgets, or a doctor, or a soldier. You could just be a jack of all trades.

Alphas weren't quite as pared down as the Betas had become, but that day was coming. The unlikely potential threat of another attack on the city always remained, and there was talk that a military presence would remain in the city as it was repopulated, both for the peace of mind of the new residents and to monitor any unusual activity. But Fulton's guess was that would return to using a normal police force like any other city soon enough. New Toledo would likely revert back to being a moderate, mid-sized, Midwestern city, and soldiers like him would need to find a new gig. He would miss it, when it was gone.

CHAPTER 73

Official press release from Orien-Sadler – 99 years after the Event. Time populous: 2,591

Today, one year before the theorized closing of the time stream, we recognize the significant contributions of all our staff, past and present. Through cooperation at an unprecedented scale of scientists, researchers, experts in numerous fields, government and their leaders, and citizens like you, we have met the challenge of the wormhole, and are proud to say that we have persevered after all these years.

The Time Event that fateful May 15th revealed the mysteries of relativity to us, but the past 99 years since have revealed more about ourselves. One year from now, we hope to celebrate the final chapter of the Event and put it firmly in our past.

As the residents of New Toledo have begun settling into their new homes within the restored areas of the Time Zone, excitement for the future has been building worldwide. Well-wishes from all across the globe have come pouring in since the official ribbon cutting for the first residential neighborhood reopened, welcoming the travelers back home for the first time in 99 years.

For the next year, Orien-Sadler will closely monitor the remaining returns of all time travelers, while our counterparts from the International Time Committee will have oversight at the location where we believe the inventor will emerge. Upon his arrival, experts will attempt to gain understanding of his motives and methods, documenting answers to the many questions the world has.

Today, we cherish the memories of the thousands we have lost, with our genuine wish that we could have done more to save them; and we celebrate the lives of those who survived, with our sincerest hope that they found happiness and peace in some way.

It is our honor to have been of service.

CHAPTER 74

Johnathan Davidson's home – 100 years, 0 months, 0 days after the Event. Time populous: 1

The U.N. peacekeeping force had the exterior of the building completely locked down, and the Alpha teams had been assigned to guard the surrounding area in a five-block radius. The Panel of Experts and their elite security guards were the only ones allowed inside the building itself.

According to official records, every suspicious device found in Toledo that could potentially be a time machine had long ago been removed to the offsite containment centers and was there, pending destruction. The U.N. General Assembly had finally agreed that their demolition date would be set after the inventor appeared, confirmed which one was the real machine, and was persuaded to give up the secrets to how it worked... so that any precautions that might be needed in the deactivation could be duly noted.

The Panel was going to start questioning the inventor the moment he reemerged, of course. That had always been the plan, and the world was waiting with baited breath for the results.

What the rest of the world did not realize was that the Time Committee had privately decided, when the machine had first been found, that the risk of removing it from the site was just too great. It could very well be that opening a wormhole was only possible at this exact pinpoint location on the planet, combined with the machine itself and its settings. Moving it could alter the parameters and destroy that delicate conjunction of circumstances needed for it to work. And perhaps after 100 years it would no longer work anyway; anything from a stray particle of dust to the very air temperature could alter the conditions enough for it to never work again. But they weren't moving (much less destroying) anything until they found out its secrets. Right now, at the site, freshly reemerged and without time to think up lies, was the best chance at getting to the bottom of things with Mr. Johnathan Davidson.

The rest of the world would be satisfied with the capture of the inventor, who would be smuggled off to a secure location to answer more detailed questions at their leisure, and get filled in on the impact of his little experiment. He would be at the mercy of public opinion, and the committee could decide what his fate would be down the road. If he cooperated today, that was. If not, the public would just have to be content with the recovery of his body. Pity that the stress of reentry was too great.

Almost it was time, and they were all silently counting down, willing themselves not to blink and miss it. And suddenly, he was there, hand still outstretched on the button.

EPILOGUE
Johnathan Davidson

"FREEZE, MR. DAVIDSON. DO NOT MOVE. TAKE YOUR HAND OFF OF THE MACHINE."

Johnathan blinked in the sudden glare of lights, peering into the darkness behind them. He couldn't make out all the details, but there were at least a dozen armed people staring him down. His mind began to race.

Oh shit. I think maybe it worked. What in the hell happened? Those are definitely weapons, and they are pointed at yours truly.

Maybe I blew something up? No, there's not so much as a scorch mark on the coffee table.

Maybe I made someone important disappear by mistake? Why else are the police in my living room trying to arrest me? How did they even know where to find me? Maybe it didn't bend time, but space? Did I scramble the whole world up or something?

Maybe it worked wrong, and these guys are from the future? Did I pull them into the past? If that's the case, they seem pretty angry about it. SHIT. I'm going to get shot. But wait, how would they know my name if they just arrived from the future? Think-think-think, dammit.

Maybe I –

"Mr. Davidson. We expect your complete compliance, and we will not ask you again. Retract your hand from that button and move away from the device IMMEDIATELY. Put your hands on your head. This building is completely surrounded. There is no way out of this."

Well…

I can think of one way.